Call Me, Maybe

Stephie Chapman was born in England in the mid 1980s, which makes her thirty-something (but if you ask, she'll tell you she's 27). Now, she lives on the South coast of the UK, has a day job to keep her holiday budget topped up, and two kids and a husband to keep an eye on.

Also by Stephie Chapman

Call Me, Maybe
Swipe Right

Call Me, Maybe

Stephie
Chapman

hera

First published in the United Kingdom in 2019 by Hera

This edition published in the United Kingdom in 2023 by

Hera Books
Unit 9 (Canelo), 5th Floor
Cargo Works, 1-2 Hatfields
London SE1 9PG
United Kingdom

A CIP catalogue record for this book is available from the British Library.

Print ISBN 978 1 78863 854 8
Ebook ISBN 978 1 912973 30 9

This book is a work of fiction. Names, characters, businesses, organizations, places and events are either the product of the author's imagination or are used fictitiously. Any resemblance to actual persons, living or dead, events or locales is entirely coincidental.

Look for more great books at www.herabooks.com

Printed and bound in Great Britain by Clays Ltd, Elcograf S.p.A.

1

This book is for anyone who has ever been deeply besotted with a boy in a band.

And also for all the boys who are in bands. Keep on keeping on, fellas.

Prologue

A car pulls up on the drive, the hum of the engine stops and Adam glances out of the window.

'They're home,' he says, and sits back against the wall again. It's neutral. Like they could have just been gone a half hour. Like they could have been out running errands. Except they haven't. They've been on vacation. Ten days in Hawaii and we didn't get to go with them. We had to stay home with Grandma Ada.

Neither of us move. We don't look at each other, or even make any attempt to switch off the TV. We just sit there, our eyes glued to MTV. We've spent a lot of time up here, doing that, whilst Mom and Dad have been away. Grandma Ada is not good at enforcing the rules Mom set when they left. Soon enough there are footsteps on the stairs, absorbed by thick, spongy carpet, and then Dad pops his head around the door. A tan version of himself. His forehead is shiny. His shirt has flowers on it and I realize how much I've missed them. Ten days is a long time when you're twelve. He comes over and sits between us on Adam's bed.

'Whatcha watching, kiddos?'

'MTV,' Adam says. Dad puts his arm around my neck and ruffles my hair.

'Missed you guys,' he says.

'Missed you, too, Dad,' I say.

'Have you been good for Grandma?'

'Duh,' Adam says, rolling his eyes. Dad laughs.

'I bet you've given her hell,' he chuckles.

'Well, Travis said *asshole* at the dinner table and she made him take a time out,' I say. I whisper the word 'asshole', because I don't want to get in trouble. Not so soon after they've got home.

'You're a snitch, Jesse, you know that?' Adam says. He throws a pillow at me.

'Who was the asshole?' Dad asks. He wedges the pillow between his back and the wall and leans against it.

'Grandpa Nev,' Adam says, sniggering.

'Oh my god, not *Grandpa Nev*,' Dad says, and now we're all laughing. Dad doesn't like Grandpa Nev. Grandma Ada doesn't really like Dad. It's like a circle. Everyone knows about it, but no one ever says anything.

'Well, I guess I should go and find your brothers.' Dad stands up and walks towards the door. 'We brought you back something from Hawaii,' he says. 'Come down in a few minutes, okay? Your mom's missed you heaps.'

We traipse downstairs when our show has ended. Mom is curled up on the couch. She's hugging Brandon and she's stuck her nose in his hair, but she rushes over when she sees us and envelopes us both in her arms and kisses the tops of our heads. She can only just reach when she stands on her tiptoes. We are tall and gangly.

'My two eldest babies,' she coos. 'Let me look at you!'

She holds us back at arm's length and grabs us by our chins. 'Handsome,' she declares. '*So* handsome.' Adam rolls his eyes again. He does that a lot. 'Jesse, honey, I think Travis and Dad are out in the yard. Can you please go and tell them it's time to do the gifts? I can't wait a moment longer.'

They're shooting hoops at the back of the house. The ball bounces off the wall and down to the end of the yard and Travis runs after it as I open the back door.

'Hey, sport,' Dad says. 'Want to play?'

'Mom sent me out to get you. She wants us all inside now.'

Travis hurls the basketball at me. 'No fair, we only just started.'

'We can play again in a while. Maybe when Mom's making dinner. We have something for you from Hawaii, though, and I'm pretty sure you're gonna love it.'

Back inside, all four of us crowd onto the couch whilst Mom and Dad dig through their bags. They pull out boxes, slightly narrower at one end than the other. Dad hands us one each.

'Go ahead and open 'em up,' Mom says. She nods her head, encouragingly.

Inside are what look like miniature guitars, but they have four strings instead of six.

'What is it?' Brandon asks. He looks confused.

'It's a ukulele,' Dad replies. He takes them off us, one by one, and tunes them up. I had no idea he knew how to do this. He has an old electric guitar but I've never seen him play it. The strings are a little rusty and one of the pickups has fallen off, and anyway, he sold the amp.

'Lots of people play them in Hawaii,' Mom says. 'The man in the store made it look so easy. Oh, we also got you chord books.'

She doles them out, too, and I flick to the first page and copy the image to make a C major chord. It sounds nice. Cheerful. I play it a few times and then move on to the next one. A minor. I move my finger up to the G string, press down on the second fret and strum. All the notes ring out. It's not as happy as C major, but I like it just as much. There's something about playing it that makes me feel good. I like the way I can hear all the different and distinct notes and how they sound all together. I'm not really sure what I'm doing. I just play all the notes one at a time, up and down the neck. Figuring out a scale, one string after the other.

'Well,' Mom says. She wipes her hands over her pants. 'Looks like these are a roaring success. Who's hungry? I'll make grilled cheese.'

3

Dad stretches out on the floor. He puts his arms behind his head.

'Hey Trav,' he says. 'You still want to shoot some hoops?'

He looks up from his chord book and plucks at one of the strings on his ukulele.

'Nah, I'm good thanks Dad.'

–

We usually spend Thanksgiving at our grandparents' house the other side of Omaha, but Grandma Ada called and told Mom their oven is on the fritz. So this year we're having it here. Dad made a comment about Grandpa Nev just not wanting to host anymore, but Mom batted his arm and told him that was nonsense.

Now the house smells of turkey and cranberry sauce and sweet potatoes baked with marshmallows. We're all in the garage, practicing something on our ukuleles we're going to play before we eat. Now it's winter, it's freezing in there but it's the only place in the house we've been able to go where we know Mom won't hear us. She's mad on Duran Duran, and we're going to play 'Ordinary World' for her because it's her favorite. Every time she hears it she sings along. Sometimes she hums it when she's cleaning. Sometimes she jokes that the only reason she married Dad is because Simon Le Bon was spoken for.

'One more time before your cousins arrive,' Dad says, but right on cue, the doorbell rings. Inside, I'm beginning to feel a bit nervous. Playing that song in front of Adam and Travis and Brandon and Dad is easy; they don't care if I mess up. But I don't want to screw up in front of the rest of my family, and especially not Mom. I want it to be perfect for her, because it's *for* her.

At two o'clock, we're called into the dining room to eat. The table's been decorated and Mom's put out the fancy napkins. When everyone's seated, Dad clears his throat.

4

'Before we start,' he says, 'the boys have something to perform.'

Everyone looks at us and Mom clasps her hands together under her chin. Dad brings our ukuleles in from the hallway and we line up by the wall. This is it. My mouth has dried up, and all I want to do is take a drink. 'You ready?' Dad says, looking at me. I nod. He counts us in.

And then I start playing and I forget everything else. I forget that everyone is staring at me playing the beginning part of 'Ordinary World' by Duran Duran. I forget that no one knew we could do this until right this second. All I think about is how my fingers are gliding around the neck of my ukulele, pressing on the strings at various frets and how easy and natural it feels to me. In my head I can see where everything is meant to go. I can hear how everything is meant to sound.

Mom gasps. She's realized what I'm playing and I think, if the look on her face is any indication, that she loves it, and that makes *me* love it, too. I love that our version of that song is recognizable and how happy we've made her. I love how Travis and Brandon's harmonies sound with Adam's lead vocals. I love how I didn't mess up, not even once. Not even a single note. But most of all, I love the happy rush I'm feeling right now.

'That was just beautiful,' she sighs, when we're finished, and it's almost a whisper. 'My favorite song!' She's all choked up. She dabs her eyes.

'Can we dish up now?' Grandpa Nev asks, gruffly. 'What's an old man gotta do to get a meal round here?'

'Dad! Rude!' Mom snaps.

–

It's Christmas Day and Dad has lit the fire already. Usually he tells us to put extra layers on and suck it up, but today he built up a fire right after we ate breakfast, no questions asked. So either he doesn't care, or he sold a lot of cars last month. The lights on the Christmas tree twinkle and I stare at them until my eyes glass over. Mom's menorah is still in the window with the candles all burnt down. She does this every year. Lights the candles for Chanukah but that's really the only way she celebrates being Jewish at all, and she never remembers to put it away again when it's over.

Now she wanders into the living room with a basket of muffins, and sets them down close to the fire.

'Where's Dad?' Travis asks. He's asking this not because he particularly cares where our father is, but because he knows we're not allowed to open gifts until we're all together after breakfast.

'In the garage,' Mom says. Travis makes a move towards the interconnecting door but Mom stops him and now we're all intrigued. He looks from the door to her and back to the door again. Mom looks nervous. She knows if we all go, she won't be able to stop us. There's one of her and four of us. 'Can everyone just settle down?' she says. 'He'll be right out. Eat a muffin.' We do as we're told.

Besides, she's right. Soon enough Dad emerges. He's got his jacket and his hat on and he looks pleased with himself. He and Mom share a look.

'So, Santa came last night,' he says. Adam rolls his eyes, but he doesn't say anything. It's for Brandon's benefit. 'But your gifts were a little too large to fit down the chimney.'

Mom squeezes Brandon's shoulders.

'You guys,' he says. 'I'm eight. I'm not stupid.'

'Right. Well. Come on through,' Dad says. He gestures for us to follow him into the garage. It's freezing in there, makes the rest of the house feel like a sauna. He switches on the light and I can't believe what I'm seeing. There's a drum kit. There's a keyboard. There's a guitar and a bass. There are tags with our names on.

'So, we thought that since you got on so well with your ukuleles, that you might like to try something a little more challenging,' Dad says.

I take the bass out of its stand. It's so heavy. There are four shiny chrome tuning pegs and the thickest metal strings I ever saw on anything. It's bright red. And huge. And beautiful. I love it. The neck is so long. It makes my little ukulele seem like a toy. I've seen people play bass on the TV and I like the way it sounds on records. I don't know how to play it but I can't wait to plug it in and have a go. Mom's helping Brandon with his keyboard, and Travis is already trying to figure out a rhythm on the drumkit. Dad walks over to where Adam and I are standing.

'You like them?' he asks. But he knows. He can tell that we do. He rubs his hands together and blows on his palms. It's *that* cold in here.

'Dad, this is *the* most amazing thing ever. Thank you guys so much.' I put my new bass back in the stand and hug him.

'You're welcome kiddo,' he says. 'Now you can start a band.'

Chapter One

Cassie

London, April 2012

There's a knock at my front door. The hollow rat-a-tat echoes around the hallway.

'That'll be dinner,' I say, jumping up off the floorboards. 'Free prawn crackers. Bonus!' Down the corridor, Rachel's clanging about in the kitchen, gathering together cutlery and plates, and back in the lounge I unpack the aluminium cartons and peel off the cardboard lids one by one.

'After dinner I want to get your thoughts on table centrepieces,' Rachel says, nodding towards a pile of wedding magazines she's brought over with her. She picks up a fork and scrapes a pile of noodles onto her plate. 'I'd talk to George, but he's got stupid amounts of marking at the moment, and to be honest, Cass, I don't think he really gives a shit.'

I put on a serious face and salute her. 'Maid of honour, reporting for duty,' I say. She looks at me slyly.

'Are you bringing anyone?'

'To your wedding? You know I'm not,' I say, crunching on a prawn cracker.

'Because you can, you know. I've budgeted for you to have a plus one.'

'Aw that's kind. We can talk about my imaginary date later if you like.'

'There's time for you to make sure you bring someone non-imaginary. I've been thinking—'

'Oh, there it is,' I say. Rachel ignores me.

'Charlotte from work's just started seeing someone.'

'Bravo for Charlotte.'

'I'll show you how they met.'

Rachel grabs my laptop and types for a bit, then she spins the computer around on the floor and points at the screen. There's triumph in her eyes.

'*Date My Mate dot com,*' I say. 'No thank you.'

'You get a friend to write your profile.'

'Hard pass.'

'Oh, come on. You've been out of circulation for ages now. Anyway, I've already written yours.' She pulls a notebook out of her bag and hands it over. 'Did it on the train on the way here.'

'Out of circulation. You make me sound like a manky old penny. I hope no one saw you write this,' I say, skim-reading. '*Meet Cassie. Almost thirty, five feet seven, slim, eyes like lagoons, face of an angel, tits like the* Venus de Milo... Tits like the *Venus de Milo*? I don't think so.'

'You do have great tits though.'

'Rachel! Think of the sort of replies I'll get if you put *that* in there.'

'It'll be fine. Carry on.'

'*Cassie loves thoughtful dates, decent wine and being swept off her feet. She works in retail (Head Office – fun but sensible), has two odd but well-meaning housemates, and a mild dust allergy. She's keen on creative types (but not if that creativity is with the truth) and bonus points if you can play an instrument. Any will do. Probably. Maybe not the kazoo or bagpipes. Tories and marrieds need not apply...* I don't know what to say.'

Rachel grabs my computer back and logs into the site.

'I've actually already signed you up, on account of Charlotte's good fortune. She had a ton of matches, apparently.'

'No one is going to admit to having none,' I mutter. But it's pointless to argue. Rachel's like a dog with a bone, and I watch as she types in my bio, including the line about my boobs. She links my Facebook account so the photos pull through, and looks pleased with herself.

'Keep me informed,' she says, picking up the chow mein.

We turn our attention back to the TV. *All Whitney* on Box Hits.

'Too sad,' Rachel says, forlornly. She reaches for the remote. 'All she wanted was to dance with somebody who loved her. She didn't want to die in the bath.'

'Yeah. Still shocking,' I agree. 'It's nice to reminisce though, and that is a great song.'

But she flicks away all the same, only stopping on each channel long enough to register what's playing and make a snap decision about it, until we reach Now 90s. We sit and watch the Backstreet Boys dance around chairs, Take That sing in the pouring rain wearing very dubious coats, and NSYNC in matching outfits, dancing an energetic, highly choreographed routine. A teenage Justin Timberlake is lying on a bed, and his hair reminds me of dried ramen noodles. I thought differently when the song was in the charts. I still remember all the words.

'Do you ever wonder if they'll show Franko on this channel?' Rachel asks, her mouth still full of food. She waves her fork in the direction of the TV.

'I shouldn't think so,' I say. 'They were hardly in the same league as this lot, were they?'

Adam, Jesse, Travis and Brandon Franklin, AKA Franko, were our absolute favourite nineties boyband. We idolised them. Spent endless days listening to their albums on repeat, over and over, unpicking the songs until we knew every lyric and every chord inside out. We travelled to signings and every gig we possibly could, and we *always* tried to get backstage. It had worked once. The security guard shiftily nodded his head down the corridor leading backstage, and moved slightly so we could pass. Looking back now, the whole thing seems ludicrous. We found them milling around behind the stage and hung out after the concert while all the other fans stood outside, waiting to catch a glimpse. We flashed fake IDs at the bar, drank Archers and lemonade, and generally felt pretty smug about the whole thing.

'I wonder what they're doing now,' Rachel says slowly. There's a glint in her eye. She's got an idea.

'Who knows? Married off with kids probably,' I shrug. I shovel a forkful of cashew chicken in my mouth and think about that as I chew.

She sets down her wine glass and grabs my laptop. 'Let's find out. To Google!' she announces, and I have to admit, I *am* kind of curious and definitely more interested than I thought I'd be as she systematically types their names into the search engine. But the results are thin on the ground and we don't find much, just links to videos on YouTube, none of which have many hits, a sparsely written Wikipedia page, and a few links to a message board with an 'error 404' redirect. The image search results aren't much better; mostly screenshots from music videos and digital versions of posters I used to have stuck on my bedroom walls. There isn't much there that we didn't already know, and apart from Brandon, who seems to be a Mark Ronson-esque producer, it's as if they've collectively disappeared off the face of the Earth. And that's perplexing. People don't just disappear. Not in 2012 when information is so readily available if you know where to look, and not when the people you're searching for have a past.

Because there was a past. Franko had one fairly successful album, creatively titled *Franko*, and one definitely not successful follow up. The difficult second album. Ironically titled *Now or Never* (most reviewers said never). And when that was so harshly panned, they just stopped. We never heard from them again. Almost like they gave up. Music career over before they were even twenty, without so much as a press release from the record label, or an official announcement on frankomusic.com. It was crap. Even now, over a decade on, I still think they were great, and even though I know I'm definitely in the minority, I love *Now or Never* best of all. It's got a different sound to *Franko*. It's more grown up; edgy and gritty, a transition from pop to rock. There are no sugary love ballads on *Now or Never*. Adam screams out angsty lyrics and the bass lines are heavy and clever.

Dissatisfied with Google, but apparently on a roll, Rachel signs into Facebook, and I take our plates back out to the kitchen, picking at a piece of leftover bamboo shoot as I go.

'Cass,' she calls through from the lounge. 'You'll never guess who I've just found! Get back here. Bring the wine.'

She thrusts the screen at me as I enter the room. 'Look at this. I knew we'd find something eventually. Tell me that's not Jesse Franklin.'

It's hard to tell from such a tiny picture but it could be. Dark hair, a straight nose. Pretty, expressive eyes. Bit of stubble. Rachel's favourite had always been Travis, and for a little while, Adam, but I saw nobody but Jesse. My whole world revolved around him. He was tall, with the kind of skin that tans really well at the first hint of sun, and had those big brown eyes with flecks of green. He always wore his hair messy, as if someone had just ruffled it, and jeans slung so low that quite a lot of underwear was usually visible. He was quiet, too, and aloof. Almost as if he didn't really want to be there. Like it was all just a bit too much effort, and he'd really rather be anywhere else.

You knew where you were with the rest of them, but Jesse was mysterious. Jesse was a closed book. At signings, you were lucky if you got more than a quick acknowledgement from him, and if he actually looked you in the eye you felt like you might be in there. I lived for it, that eye contact, and the butterflies I got when I saw him.

'It certainly looks like him,' I say, peering at the screen, suddenly curious. In this instant I don't know how looking him up like this hasn't ever occurred to me before.

'Of course it's him,' she says, pointing at the job title under his name. *Freelance Musician*. 'There can't be two of them! Why would anyone pretend to be a pop star who was only mildly famous years before Facebook was even a twinkle in Mark Zuckerberg's eye?'

She has a point. *We* loved Franko, but they were hardly A list. Originally from Nebraska, they relocated to California to pursue the dream of being in a band when Adam was fifteen. Their debut album dropped in 1998, and it was then that Rachel and I had caught the bug. We were smitten.

She clicks through but the profile is frustratingly private and she's quickly bored. 'That's that then,' she says, closing the webpage and the screen. 'He was the only one I found, so let's get on to wedding planning.'

The magazines come out and so does another bottle of wine. We use different coloured Sharpies to circle things Rachel likes, and she marks pages with sticky tabs. She wants fish bowls for her table centrepieces, filled with scented, floating candles and those glass pebbles that look like flattened marbles.

–

During the week that follows my emails ping a lot. Turns out Rachel might have been on to something with this Date My Mate malarkey, and I'm excited the first time I log back into my profile. A bright pink number five flashes up from the corner of the screen indicating just how many eligible bachelors have been charmed by Rachel's depictions of me. My first match is Nick, thirty-four, from Balham.

I'd like to get my hands on your Venus de Milo norks.

No thank you, Nick. I delete his message without replying, and remove that line from the profile. The next one is Henry, twenty-eight, from Bromley. Henry hasn't linked his Facebook account, which is unsettling, but he has sent an additional photo with just a simple caption, 'U like wot U see?'

I'm already sceptical from the text speak but I click through anyway, and am confronted with a chubby hand with disgusting bitten-down finger nails gripping a fat but short penis, its mushroom-like head red and glistening under an alarmingly tight foreskin, nestled within a thick mass of greasy-looking pubes. No, Henry, I categorically *don't* like what I see. I can't help it. I retch. My housemate Sara looks up from the blanket she's crocheting.

'You okay?'

'Absolutely,' I choke.

You might think the only way would be up from Henry's gruesome offering, but you'd be wrong, and my other three matches are no better. It's a steady flatline. Makes me wonder just how low a bar Charlotte-from-Rachel's-work has set. I suspect so low she had to dig for it.

Grumpy, I stomp up to bed, and my thoughts turn to Jesse Franklin. Not for the first time since we found him, I allow him to seep into my head again, to bed down on the edges of my subconscious. Because now I know where I can find him, he won't leave me alone. Rachel might be content with what we unearthed, but I'm not, and I search for him again. I know it might be considered creepy, internet-stalking my teenage crush like this, but I shove that feeling back down where it came from because it's not as if he will ever know. It's okay to do this as long as he never *knows*, and he never will: you can't see who's searching for you on Facebook.

All it takes is a few seconds and I've found him again, *Jesse Franklin, Freelance Musician*, as handsome as he ever was. I know I should leave it, click away and forget about it, but I don't. I can't.

The crush was so intense that I was convinced it was love. Actual, fierce, slap-you-in-the-face, punch-you-in-the-gut, you-are-the-one true love. Never quite complete love though, because when you love a boy in a band, it's unrequited. Your thoughts are consumed entirely by him, but he doesn't even know you exist, and deep down, whether you can admit it to yourself or not, you know this. To him you are one of thousands, whilst to you he is everything.

But I'd felt it the first time we'd met. Him seventeen, me fifteen. On a freezing cold morning in February outside a TV studio. I'd tried hard to get him to notice me. I'd willed him to feel what I did. Even just a fraction would be enough. I flirted and batted my eyelashes. I let him listen to music through my walkman, sharing my headphones, and when Rachel snapped photos of us, I'd pressed myself against him and breathed him in until I was dizzy. I'd closed my eyes and sent him telepathic messages, and, just for those brief seconds, allowed myself to pretend that to him, I wasn't just another fan. That somehow, out of all the Franko-obsessed teenage girls in the world, he'd see that I was different.

And I knew when he eventually did, he'd take my hand and we'd be off. I never questioned that my parents might not be cool with their teenage daughter skipping town on the whim of an adolescent musician. In my head there'd be a tearful farewell before I left Amersham forever in a Toyota Previa with tinted windows. It'd be such a big deal that there'd be crowds of people in the street. All my school friends would hang around, looking on, commenting to the press about how they sat next to me in double science. I'd be whisked off to Heathrow to fly away on a private jet, champagne popped and flowing, even though nobody who featured in this particular daydream was old enough to drink it and access to a private jet was unlikely.

We'd live in a Beverly Hills mansion, or a Malibu beach house. There'd be paparazzi from which we'd have to shield our quirkily named children. I'd live the rock-star wife dream, pining for his safe return after months on the road. There'd be Grammy awards lined up on shelves in our bathrooms and I'd reinvent myself as a fashion designer. It was all planned out.

But in reality when *Now or Never* failed to chart they never came back to the UK. Our excited journeys to concerts or meet and greets stopped. There were no more TV appearances to record and no more hotels to wait outside. We were devastated, as if nothing in the entire world could make up for the gaping hole the four of them left behind. But gradually I stopped thinking so much about Jesse Franklin and he stopped appearing in my dreams at night. Posters were removed from my walls, and carefully rolled up and stored. Albums weren't listened to as much as they once were, and dust collected on the cases in my CD rack. I concentrated on school, went to university, and realised that when I wasn't pining after boys in bands, there were some right in front of me who I liked just as much, if not more, and best of all, some of them liked me back. No telepathy required.

And now, here I am. Living in a house share in Shepherd's Bush, West London, with Jon, who works in IT support at UCL, and tall, willowy Sara, who manages an independent art supplies shop close to Central Saint Martins, gets through more incense than a Catholic priest and likes facial piercings. They're nice people, and even though the three of us make quite the motley crew, we're all relatively fond of each other and by now we're well used to each other's habits. Occasionally, for instance, Sara will bring back a man (usually with a giant beard) she's met somewhere and there'll be small talk over tofu scramble the next morning whilst she giggles at him and I cradle a mug of coffee and Jon comments on the music she put on to muffle the sounds of them doing it. Likewise, Sara and I know that just before seven o'clock every morning, Jon vacuums his bedroom, and can't ever let any of his food touch. He never partakes in the tofu scramble.

Obviously, one day I'll want to re-evaluate things, but right now life's good. There might not be a rock star knocking on my front door with a giant diamond for my finger, but I'm pouring a lot of effort into my career, and as Phil Collins once sang, you can't hurry love. So I'll just have to wait.

I feel like finding Jesse on the internet has stripped him of his fame and rock god status. If it's even really him, because even though he doesn't seem like a prime candidate for identity theft, you don't often find the personal profiles of celebs. I lie and ponder over what he might be doing at this exact moment. Where precisely he is in the world. Does he have a partner? Kids? He'd be thirty-one now, so it's all distinctly probable. And it's whilst I wonder what sort of things we'd say to each other if we were ever to meet again, I give in to the herculean urge to take a chance on finding out. I can't help myself. I'm powerless to stop it. A box pops up on the screen of my laptop. It glares at me through the darkness.

Friend Request Sent

Instantly, there are two separate and distinct emotions. First, a sense of bubbly excitement, one that makes a shiver run down the length of my spine. It makes me feel as if there is a weight inside my stomach. It makes my palms a little bit sticky. Then it morphs and the second thing I feel is a sense of panic. What if he's horrible? What if he sends me a message demanding an explanation of just who I am and why I'm asking to be friends in the first place? What if it ruins everything I ever thought about him? The thought is excruciating, and now the back of my neck feels warm. I want to hide under my duvet and squeeze my eyes tightly shut. For a split second, I want to take it all back. I want to cancel the request. I could do that. It's an option. And yet, I don't.

Finally, my logical side takes over, and it tells me in a stern, yet soothing voice to stop overthinking it. *Don't panic, Cassie*, it's saying. *People add other people as friends on Facebook all the time.* I have exactly nothing to lose here. I'll either get accepted (hugely unlikely) or ignored (probably). Jesse Franklin will likely never give it any thought. He probably gets this all the time.

Chapter Two

From: Date My Mate
To: Cassie Banks
Subject: Message Received on Date My Mate... Could It Be Fate?

Hi CassieB83,
You've received new messages on Date My Mate.
Click here or log in now to read your messages and find out if it could be fate!
Good luck!
The Date My Mate Admin Team

Name: Tom
Age: 35
Location: Stoke Newington

Hi babe, spit or swallow?

Name: Mike
Age: 29
Location: Watford

Hey beautiful. Shall we swap numbers?

Name: Ronan
Age: 23
Location: Ealing

New in town, looking for a hook-up. How would sex with you work?

Name: Andy
Age: 34
Location: Richmond

How about some fun in the back seat of my car (Audi) in Richmond Park? Surrounded by deer and people.

Name: Fred
Age: 31
Location: Clapham Common

Just wanted to say hi. I'm pretty new at this, so sorry if this is lame/crap/a rubbish message.

I'm Fred, I work at a tech startup in Shoreditch, but I promise I'm not one of those dreadful man-bunned hipsters. Live in Clapham with my housemate Tyler and my cat, Martin. It's a proper lad's place, to be honest.

Anyway, it was Tyler who set up my profile. Still trying to work out if he's done me a favour or not. Like I said, this is new territory for me.

Sorry if you were expecting a picture of my penis.

Bye!

Fred.

p.s. I think you're very pretty.

To: FredTed49
From: CassieB83

Hi Fred,

Thanks for your message. I didn't think it was crap but I'm also fairly new at this so what do I know? It's hard to say if Tyler's done you a favour or not. Guess that remains to be seen.

I wasn't expecting a picture of your penis and truthfully, I'm relieved you didn't send one. I wouldn't have replied if you had. Actually this is the first time I've ever responded to anyone.

Thanks also for the nice compliment. You're not so bad yourself :) And don't you have to play the ukulele to be classed as a hipster?

I live in Shepherd's Bush with a couple of housemates, and I work at Beauchamp and Taylor head office in merchandising.

Thanks for not being a total creep!

Cassie

Chapter Three

Jesse

Two weeks ago someone called Cassie Banks sent me a friend request on Facebook, and this was odd for two reasons.

Firstly, I don't know anyone called Cassie Banks. *This* Cassie lives in the UK, and I've not been there for a long time. Maybe she moved there? Maybe she's someone from Nebraska I went to school with? I think back to all the people I've met at various studios and gigs and sessions over the years, but come up with nothing. The name isn't at all familiar. I can't place her. Each time I try, I draw a blank.

Secondly, I keep myself as low key as possible on the internet and I always have. Or so I thought, and the reason is glaringly obvious. I worked so hard to put Franko behind me, to get on with things after it ended. Family aside, everyone I am connected with on social media is someone I met after that part of my life ended.

In hindsight, now that sufficient time has passed, I know there are kids out there who'd give anything for the life we had, and in the beginning, when everything was shiny and new, it was a riot. But trust me, when you have a manager like Dad, who pretended that state laws for working minors weren't a thing, and didn't believe in time off, and you're constantly a little bit jet lagged because you're never anywhere long enough to acclimate, and half the time you're not even sure what day it is, it soon stops being the vacation you thought it might be. Neil Young says it's better to burn out than to fade away, but in my experience burning out is much, much worse. At least if you fade away, you're not so goddamn exhausted.

It occurred to me that Cassie would have to have thought she knew who she was searching for. She thinks she knows who I am, and that can only be because of Franko, which is a little unsettling after so long. If I had liked being that visible, then it's fair to say my life would have turned out differently. Perhaps I wouldn't have hated being in Franko so much. Maybe it would have been more bearable because I'd have accepted that those were the breaks. Perhaps if I'd have done what was expected of me, and sucked it up I'd be rocking sell-out stadium tours now. Who knows?

Still, it's reasonable to assume that since I'm not the only Jesse Franklin in the world, she may have got the wrong one. She won't have been looking for me. Why would she? No one has for a long time. No big deal. I left that friend request without responding, and didn't think about it again.

Today though, one of Travis' friends added me, and Cassie was still there. She's changed her profile picture and now, instead of a headshot, she's leaning on the shoulder of a brunette woman, and they are both smiling into the camera. Cassie is wearing sunglasses, and you can see that her arm is outstretched to take the photo in the reflection in the lenses. She has a wide, pretty smile, big silver hoop earrings in her ears, and blonde hair, pulled back off her face. She's wearing a necklace with a pendant in the shape of the letter C, and a black t-shirt. There's no point in denying it, she's definitely nice to look at, and I'm all kinds of intrigued.

The coffee machine in the kitchen beeps at me, and interrupts my browsing. I set the laptop down on the couch, and grab a cup to take outside, flicking on the stereo on the way out. It's a habit. Richard, my neighbor, has done the same. He doesn't look pleased that he can hear my music through the back doors, but then he rarely looks pleased about anything. Richard is a bit of an asshole. He spends half his time in Chicago, and half his time here, and he stands on his upstairs balcony and has shouty conversations on his cell phone, often culminating in him cutting the call and cursing loudly. I suspect his blood pressure could do with being monitored.

'Hey man.' I raise my hand in a half-assed wave over the wall.

'Hello,' he says. There's a slight pause, like he's trying to remember my name and can't.

'Nice day, huh?'

'Very pleasant,' he says. 'Are you working at home today?'

'Sure am,' I reply, glancing across at him, chipper as anything. He purses his lips. He doesn't like it when I work from home. He won't come out and say it, but occasionally he'll hint that the noise from my amp disturbs him. Well, too bad, bro. I don't know what he does exactly, but the noise he makes screaming at people in various offices around the world sometimes disturbs me, too, so I guess we're even. And at least my noise is melodic.

'I see,' he says, gathering up the papers he was reading through and deliberately tapping them into a neat stack on the edge of his table.

'Bye, Richard,' I call out, as he slams his back door closed behind him.

When I go back inside, the computer catches my eye again. Cassie Banks' new profile picture is still static on the screen. You can retract friend requests, and she hasn't done that. Best Coast have put me in a good mood. I let my curiosity win out. *Who are you, Cassie from England, and what do you want from me?* This time I click to respond, and she and I are now connected. Just like that, on a Tuesday morning.

Chapter Four

Cassie

Jesse Franklin has accepted your Friend Request

I stare at the message until it fades out. Surely not? *Surely. Not?* But there's a tick indicating our friendship and obviously I'm now going to snoop, and if he's at all internet-savvy he'll be doing the same. Now we're pals it's like I've found the entrance to Narnia. There's the usual stuff people post; a couple of links to news stories, a few sporadic updates. Photos of his basses, photos he's been tagged in, and, oh my days, he's still completely lovely. The years have *definitely* been kind to Jesse Franklin. I go to the profile photo and enlarge it. It's definitely him. I'd recognise him anywhere. He is looking away from the camera, and all in all still *quite the dish*.

Racking my stalker level up by yet another notch, I systematically go through *all* his photos. There are some of Jesse with Travis, or Jesse with Brandon, but none of Jesse with Adam, and this intrigues me. There's a story there, I can feel it. Something has happened. The only photos of them all together are a couple taken at Christmas or Thanksgiving. Always in the same dining room, with wooden panelling on the walls below a dado rail and a gold coloured sixties-style wall clock that looks like the sun. Jesse and Adam are never sitting near each other.

Next I find a couple of Brandon with his family; a pretty wife with a button nose and green eyes and a rosy toddler called Nancy who looks like her mum. It's interesting, seeing photos of Brandon all grown up with a family. He would have been fourteen the last time I saw him. There's a photo of Jesse holding Nancy as a newborn. She is swaddled in a blanket and her dark eyes stare up at him, wide and unblinking, and he's looking back at the camera, holding this tiny infant like she's the most precious thing in the world, and smiling. It tugs at my heartstrings. I'm pretty certain that inside me, my ovaries are going into overdrive.

I carry on clicking through the photos, careful not to like any of them, and scrolling down his time line, and I even go to his friend list to see if I can find anyone else, but it's set to private, and we have no mutual friends, so it's blank. I'm half expecting him to message me, but he doesn't. And when I see he's offline again, I close the page.

The rest of the week passes in much the same way as normal. Mum calls and talks about my aunt's sprained ankle for far longer than is necessary. At work, the creative team sign off on an initial colour palette for next year's Autumn/Winter kitchenware range. It's all reds and purples and mustard yellow and teal, and I spend the week researching how similar colours have sold in previous years. Sam, my kitchenware buyer counterpart, is excited, and his face lights up like the Blackpool illuminations when we discuss it. He's spotted some gorgeous melamine in just the right shade of grapey purple.

On Friday evening I meet Rachel at The Dog and Duck; a small, but conveniently located pub about halfway between our offices.

'I'm glad you wanted to meet,' she says. 'I have some wedding stuff I need help with.'

'Okay, but first… I have something to tell you.'

'About Date My Mate?' she asks, hopefully. 'How's that going? Any matches?'

'Yeah, a few, but—'

'And? Any dates?'

'Nope. I've seen everything I need to and it's a no from me so far.'

'I think you're being too picky, Cassie.'

'Really? I think perhaps Charlotte isn't picky enough. No thanks to your tits comment, which I've removed, by the way, all I've had are offers of a shag and dick pics. And not even pretty ones. Although, I got one message from someone potentially passable but then he went quiet.'

'Can a dick really be pretty?'

'Jack's was,' I shrug.

'Yes, well Jack was a cheating ratbag. If a nice-looking cock was the best thing he had going for him then that says a lot. Anyway, don't give up just yet. And I need to ask that you never mention this around George. That cool?'

'Why?' I laugh.

'Because he is not so secretly hoping for a union between you and Marcus, and I'll never hear the end of it if he thinks I'm sabotaging it.'

I wrinkle up my nose. 'Gross. Marcus is a pig.'

Marcus is George's rugby playing, Ralph-Lauren-polo-shirt-wearing, champagne-swilling, grammar-school-educated best friend and I find him repellant. His claim to fame is going to the same school as a Tory backbencher. George can wish upon as many stars as he likes, but it's never going to happen.

'Hmm, yes,' she says, diplomatically. 'I tend to agree. But I obviously can't say that to George.'

'Oh no,' I say. 'He thinks it's all going to happen at the wedding doesn't he?'

Rachel's shoulders slump, and I don't think it's because I've busted her fiancé's matchmaking plans.

'The wedding I've been left to plan entirely on my own, you mean? Can you help me?'

'Yes, but first, I have to tell you—'

'Oh Christ, yeah, sorry. I interrupted. What did you want to tell me?'

I'm sipping my beer, trying to be nonchalant. 'I did a thing.'

'Uh oh, sounds ominous. What kind of thing?'

'Do you remember that evening we looked up Franko on the internet?'

'Yeah,' she says, shaking her head and looking bewildered.

'Well, that was my thing.' And then I find it hard to get the words out. 'I couldn't stop thinking about Jesse after you left.'

Rachel rolls her eyes and suddenly I'm hugely embarrassed.

'Here we go again,' she says.

'Yeah. Anyway, I went back for another look, and got a bit curious. And added him as a friend. On Facebook.'

'Oh, Cass,' she says, giggling. 'You absolute *loser*.'

I stare at her for a few seconds whilst she giggles into her glass. This is not the reaction I was hoping for. It's a bit of a slap in the face, if I'm being honest.

'Aah, I can just imagine it! A lost love rekindled.' She clasps her hands together and sighs and stares, dreamily, into space.

'Maybe,' I say, shrugging. 'It could be. He added me back.'

Suddenly she's not laughing any more. Suddenly shit's got real.

'You what?' she says.

'Took him a couple of weeks, but yep,' I say, smugly.

'What the fuck? Have you spoken to him? You have the app on your phone, right? Cassie, you need to show me *immediately*.'

'I haven't spoken to him.'

'Then how do you know it's really him?'

'*You* said so, Rachel. You said, *why would anyone pretend to be him?* And anyway, there are photos.'

'Yeah, when it was just a little picture and a job description. What do *I* know? You have to initiate contact. You'll know immediately if it's him or not.'

'Hmm. Not sure. What would I say?'

I've given it a lot of thought, but it always ends up the same way. The things that spring to mind are mortifying. I'd probably panic and spout off about how I used to want to marry him.

'What's the matter with you? Start with *hi*. He's probably expecting you to say something. Get your phone out. I want to see.'

We snoop again, heads huddled together, anonymous in the corner of the pub, but I don't scroll back as far as I did on Tuesday night.

'Yeah, you crack on, but I feel like he's so normal it's boring,' she says.

'Probably,' I say, but I'm unconvinced. 'What was it you wanted help with?'

'Sample menus,' she says, without missing a beat.

I buy another round and try to prise more information out of her about why George isn't helping more with their wedding, but she rolls her eyes.

'He wanted beer pong at the reception,' she shrugs. 'I think Marcus suggested that to be honest.'

'Not very you,' I say, diplomatically. 'Anyway, it's not up to Marcus.'

'Exactly,' she says. 'But it's not just that. He hasn't sorted his suit and I'm annoyed about that, too. Is that silly? It's the marriage I want. Not just the wedding. It shouldn't matter what he wears, right?'

'I guess it's easier for blokes,' I say.

People come and go. We share a few packets of crisps and some peanuts. Our 'one for the road' turns into 'two for the road', and by the time we leave, we are at that stumbly stage of drunk where everything is funny. Rachel's wedding and George's lack of suit is suddenly funny. The fact that I am now Facebook friends with a pop star I used to fancy is hilarious. We lurch down Oxford Street, stopping to coo at clothes and shoes in the shop windows. Eventually we are at the tube station. She's going north towards Islington, I'm heading west.

On the train, I listen to *Now or Never*. It's nice. I'm in my own little Franko bubble and no one else knows about it. I bet I'm the only person in London listening to this album at this moment. Possibly even the only person in England. I'm right back in my bedroom in Amersham in 1999, sprawled on my bed with my headphones on and a Coke float on my nightstand. All the words to all the songs come back to me, and I'm sixteen again. Lost in it. Happy.

By the time I'm back in Shepherd's Bush I'm still three sheets to the wind and have developed a serious case of the munchies which I satisfy at a chicken shop on the green. Now the air feels thick, the way it does before it rains, and the sky is covered in a blanket of smoggy, orange clouds. My heels clip along the pavement in time to the music still in my ears, and by the time I get home I'm full of salty chips and deep fried chicken and conscious of every little noise I make. The key in the lock, the creek of the front door. Water filling a pint glass. My shoes on the stairs. Running the tap in the bathroom. I can't sleep. The chicken's sort of repeating on me and when I'm still wide awake at two, listening to rain pattering on the window and feeling faintly sick, I give up and reach for my laptop. Maybe I'll see if Date My Mate has gifted me any more potential suitors.

But before I do, I nip over to Facebook. It's a force of habit, the first thing I ever do when going online. I don't even think about it. Rachel's tagged me in a photo of our drinks. She's scattered peanuts around the bottom of the glass and captioned it *Wedding planning and ALL the gossip with my BFF.*

And the message icon's lit up. I click it open. Jesse Franklin. Good grief, were his ears burning or what? There's a little green circle next to his name. My eyes snap open. My food lurches inside me.

Hi there

I stare at the message for a minute or two before I think about replying.

> Hello.

I watch the screen, transfixed. The house is so quiet that I can hear my own heartbeat, and it's so dark that the illuminated screen looks like the light at the end of a tunnel.

> You already said that.

> I did?

> You did.

I *did*. Bloody Rachel, the mischievous cow. I knew she'd looked like she was trying to hide something when I came back from the loo. I scroll to the top of the chat window.

> 'Sup, hot stuff ;-)

Oh, no.

> How are you?

> I'm OK thanks. Can't sleep though, even though it's raining and that usually gets me right off! So that's why I'm up at 2am. And I got the munchies on the way home and sprung for some chicken I'm regretting now, like a complete numpty. How are you? By the way I didn't write that. At the beginning. It was my (now ex) best friend.

Oh my god, what's wrong with me? Talk about verbal diarrhoea. That bit about the rain was poorly phrased to say the least. And numpty? Of all the words in the English language, I choose 'numpty', proving once and for all, that I am one.

> 2am huh... you really are in England then.

It's not a question, and he doesn't answer mine. I'm just relieved he doesn't ask why Rachel hijacked my phone.

> Yep. Where did you think I was? The moon?

> Venus, actually. I'm not sure I know anyone from England these days. Are you sure you were looking for me?

> Yes, if you're the Jesse Franklin who used to play bass in Franko.

As soon as I send the message, I'm worried. What if he really didn't want to be found? But then why accept my friend request at all? I stare at the chat window waiting for him to reply, but he doesn't for ages and I begin to panic. Then:

> How did you find me?

> I just typed your name into the search box, and then recognised you from your photo.

> I see. Is this something you do often?

Excruciating. This is excruciating. I'm cringing. I'm mortified. I don't know what he thinks of me, but I'm certain it involves the phrases 'nut job' and 'internet stalker.' I need to keep this as lighthearted as possible.

> No. Never actually. You're the first (congratulations).

> Ha. But why me?

> Well I was quite keen on you back in 98. Just tell me to bog off if it's a problem. I promise I won't be offended.

Please don't tell me to bog off. *Please don't tell me to bog off.* I won't be offended, but I'll definitely be gutted.

> But how do you know it's really me? How do you know you're not getting catfished?

> Well, I guess I don't. Though your reactions suggest it is ;-) It is you, isn't it?

> Yep.

As replies go, you can't get much more direct, or, I think, much less interested than that. This is going just about as well as I'd imagined it would. Why did I ever think this was a good idea? My fingers hover over the keyboard and they are definitely trembling a little.

> Great. That's good to know. I'm pleased to hear it. Nice to meet you. I'll leave you alone now if you like.

I don't like this one bit. I don't know how to talk to him, so perhaps this is for the best. I'm fully expecting him to agree that my leaving him alone is a good idea, but he doesn't and I'm surprised.

> Hold up, after all that trouble you went to find me, you don't even want me to prove it...? I could send you a picture if you like?

Oh my god. Be cool, Cassie.

> If you like, yeah. That'd be nice, thanks. Only if you feel like it.

> LOL right...

It all goes quiet, and with each passing second I feel more and more ridiculous. And what if this is actually quite dodgy and he's trying to reel me in under false pretences? What if the picture he sends is nothing more than a scan from *Teen Beat* circa 1999 and doesn't prove anything? What will I do then? But on the flip, what if it does prove once and for all that I am sitting in bed, laptop glaring up at me through the darkness, talking to none other than my teenage crush?

The chat window lights up again and suddenly I'm so nervous I can hardly stand it and I look at the screen through squinty eyes. The photo is unmistakably Jesse Franklin, sitting on a dark blue sofa, in front of a bright white wall, and shelves stacked with *stuff*. Books, a plant, a lamp, piles of CDs. Sunshine streams in from his left. He's holding up a notebook in one hand, and pointing to it with the other, and *Jesus*, his hands are beautiful. He's smiling into the camera and one eyebrow is slightly raised. My stomach flips. I deeply fancy him all over again. I enlarge the image and read the bit of paper. *Hello Cassie Banks, from Jesse Franklin.*

I stare at the photo for a second or two. I'm slightly slack-jawed. Genuinely, I can't believe it.

> Now you go.

> Huh?

> It's your turn. Fair's fair. How do I know I'M not getting catfished? You could be anyone.

I reach for my light, and scan my room for some paper. All I can find is the back of an envelope that once contained a bank statement. I reach for a pen and scrawl, *Hi Jesse Franklin, from Cassie Banks*, and I'm immediately ashamed of my chicken scratch handwriting. His is much nicer than mine. But not that curly American-style cursive handwriting you always see in movies. Just nice, considered, neatly printed letters. I position my computer at the end of my bed and switch on the camera. I lie on my front, pile my hair over to one side and try to look cute. If I'm doing this, I'm going all in. I tip my head, and flash what I hope is a winning smile as I take the photo, clutching my scrawled on envelope. My computer makes a noise like the aperture on a lens closing and opening and I like the result, all come-to-bed eyes and swooshy hair. No double chin either. Not bad. I definitely know how to work my angles at two in the morning. Off it goes. And then I wait.

> Well, hello there Cassie Banks.

Bit flirty. My my, how quickly the tide turns. Who cares, I'm going with it.

> You already said that ;-)

I feel like I can ease up a bit now we've both checked each other out. If we were in a bar, I'd be flicking my hair and batting my lashes and getting him to buy me a drink.

> I did… so what's keeping you up so late?

> You are!

Does that sound a bit creepy? Could that be misconstrued?

> Well, I mean, NOW you are. But in all honesty,
> it's more likely I just had a bit too much to drink.

> Oh really? Cassie the party girl, huh?

> Megalols! Not really, just went out for civilised drinks with my best friend.

Silence for a while, and then:

> Sounds fun. But hey, I have to get going. Going for my own civilized drinks. But maybe we'll chat another time.

Ah, shit! No, don't go. Stay and talk to me all night. Please? I'd put money on us never talking again after tonight given the way this has gone, what with my horrible choice of words and general weirdness. Megalols? I'm too old for that. I deserve a slap.

> OK. I'd like that. Enjoy your evening out!

> Thanks. Well, bye then, Cassie.

The green circle turns to grey and he's gone. I like the way he went to the effort of typing out my name. Not many people would bother. I imagine him saying it and decide it definitely has a nice ring to it in an American accent. Kind of drawly with the accentuated A. I close down my computer and curl up under my duvet, trying to digest what has just happened. I can still feel the warmth where my computer was, and I can't quite believe it. Inside I'm all fluttery and silly, and one thing's for sure, even if that didn't go quite the way I'd hoped, my mammoth crush on Jesse Franklin is back.

36

Chapter Five

Jesse

Travis calls shortly after I've traded photos with Cassie.

'Duuude,' he hollers. He's in a bar. He's doing that shouty talking people do when they can't hear you very well. 'I'm in Los Alamitos with Seth. Come on down!'

I'm eighty-five percent down for hanging out; it is, after all, Friday night, but fifteen percent of me would be more than happy to stick around here and see whether I'll get any more glamour shots.

'You've been let out for the evening then?' I say, pushing the computer away. It's not a secret that Holly keeps him on a tight leash.

'Yeah, you're real funny, you know that? Invitation withdrawn. Bye.'

'I'm kidding,' I say, suddenly feeling like a beer. 'Don't be like that. Where exactly are you in Los Alamitos? I'll be there in half an hour.'

'That long?'

'Twenty minutes then. I'm just in the middle of something, but I'll wrap it up. I have an early start tomorrow so it's not going to be a late one, though, okay?'

'Well aren't you a bundle of fun?' he laughs, and reels off the name of the bar they're at, and I tell Cassie I have to go, lock up the house, and grab my car keys.

On the drive I consider how out of all the Jesse Franklins there are in the world, I was the one she was looking for, and how that makes me feel. A little uneasy, honestly. I worked so hard to put it all behind me after what happened on that day in Berlin, and it's been so long since Franko has been mentioned that I'd been lulled into a false sense of security that it would never happen again. I don't want to talk about it, and especially not with a random British woman from the internet, however pretty she is, and yet, I stuck around, traded photos, didn't unfriend and block immediately. Didn't unfriend and block at all.

And that photo. Jesus. Mine was a zero-effort snap from the camera on my laptop, but hers… well. She was trying, she was really trying. Lying on her bed with her hair flipped over and that eye smile thing like something off *America's Next Top Model*. And she's hot, too. Definitely the exotic European from the profile pictures. She knew exactly what she was sending. And it worked. Well played, hot British Cassie, well played. I saved that photo. Drag and drop.

I park my car on a side street and head inside. It's a sports bar. The three of us have been here before. It's loud and boisterous when there's a game on the giant screens, but today there isn't, and the whole place has more of a meat market feel to it. I bet Seth picked it.

'Hey, you gonna try and pick someone up tonight?' he asks. 'We gotta live vicariously through you now, dude.'

Called it.

'Uh… no? Why?'

'Just looking out for you, man. It's been how long since Nicole ran for the hills?'

'Just about five months actually, and thank you for bringing that up.'

'Eeesh,' Seth winces. 'Your balls must be blue as fuck, bro. 'Bout time you got back in the saddle.' He mimes sex with someone from behind. Travis laughs. A group of women standing close by look disgusted and shuffle away from us. Seth's an unintentional cock-blocker.

'Alright. Yep,' I say. 'Not tonight though. I have shit to do early tomorrow.'

'You thought about going online?' Travis says and for the briefest of moments I almost say something about the earlier part of my evening. But Seth would be Seth about it, and Travis would want to see the photo, and showing him would be a dick move. So I leave it.

'I don't need to go on the internet to meet someone, thanks. I'm good,' I say instead. And anyway, it's not a lie.

The joshing between the three of us continues into the evening. Holly keeps texting Travis, which no one is surprised about, and which he ignores until she starts to call, and whilst he's speaking to her, I get a text from Brandon:

> I've just put your name forward for a project, nothing too exciting and it's little more than a favor to someone. I'll know more at the beginning of July. You down? Feel like coming up to visit around then? Your niece has been asking for you.

A trip north would be nice, and I could certainly do with a change of scenery for a while after driving in and out of LA for days on end, so I text back right away:

> Well, if I've been summoned by Nancy I'd better clear my schedule. What's the job? I actually have a free week at the beginning of July, would that work? Love to Lainey and of course little N!

> Fourth of July week then! Right on! I'll tell you more when you're here. Little N will be stoked! Party time!

'Get off your phones, you antisocial pieces of shit,' Seth grumbles.

'Sorry,' I say, putting it back in the pocket of my jacket and pointing to his now empty beer bottle. 'You want another one?'

He nods and I head off towards the bar.

'Get some wings, too, man,' he calls after me. 'I haven't eaten anything proper tonight. Cindy served me up fucking *salad*. It tasted of sadness.'

Back home, much later in the evening, I open up my laptop again and look at that photo Cassie sent me. It's dim and cozy-looking in her room, and the picture is grainy, but behind her is a stack of books, a glass of water, an alarm clock on a nightstand, and photographs taped to the wall. Heaps of pillows, too. More than one person could ever need, assuming there isn't anybody else sleeping next to her in that bed on nights other than this one. She's wound string lights around her bed frame, and the bedding is white or cream, but it's hard to tell on a photo that isn't white balanced.

She seems nice and she's definitely gorgeous, but I'm still undecided about her. It's something about her finding me all these years on. I don't know if it's kind of cool, or just a bit creepy.

I'm not stupid enough to think this hasn't happened before. I know people will have put my name into search engines in the past, and like Cassie, it will have been me they wanted to find. That's just part of being in the public eye, but I wasn't so readily accessible back in ninety-eight, and I'm not sure I really want to be now, and what's happened here is the reason I try to steer clear of it all. I could cut her off in an instant, and yet, I don't.

Instead, I sift through her photos again. I *am* curious about why she doesn't have anything better to do than stalk me on the internet. There are pictures of her hanging out with people, and she'd said she'd been out tonight, so she's clearly a sociable being. The brunette in her profile picture features heavily. Her name, I learn, is Rachel. Wonder if she's the ex friend who allegedly sent that first message. There's another, Marie, who crops up often, and another, Lauren. Marie and Rachel have the same last name and look vaguely similar. Cassie and Rachel have been to Paris, and Amsterdam, and to a festival in Spain, where they both wore straw hats and necklaces made from glow sticks. They've been friends since they were kids. There's a whole album devoted to New Years' Eves through the years, as far back as the early nineties, and I think it's cool to have a progression of photos taken on the same day every year like that. The photos are grainy. Their parents are in some of the earlier ones, but that stops at the year 2000. They're by the river in London. The tips of both of their noses are red and they're bundled up. Cassie's wearing a green scarf and for a second there's a flicker of... I'm not sure. Something vaguely familiar perhaps, or maybe it's just the color. As soon as I try and place it, the feeling's gone. I don't try and recall it. It was probably nothing.

There's a stocky guy with short curly hair in the latest one. Looks like your typical frat boy. Boyfriend? He has his arm around her shoulders and looks very pleased about it, but she less so. Her entire posture in those photos is completely different from all the others. She's more rigid, less comfortable-looking. She's twisting her body away from him. Her smile doesn't seem quite as natural. It definitely doesn't reach her eyes. He's tagged: Marcus Lewis. He's not her boyfriend, though he definitely wants to be. Or maybe he just wants to fuck her. I open up the picture she sent me again and compare the two. Her eyes are definitely different in my one. Warmer. More receptive. It's interesting.

The clock on my laptop catches my eye. I have to be up in six hours. So much for getting an early night. Twelve twenty-seven a.m. here means it's eight twenty-seven a.m. in London, right? I wonder if she's awake. Whatever.

Chapter Six

Cassie

I can't bring myself to read back over my chat with Jesse until Sunday evening, and when I do, I cringe right into the centre of the Earth. I'd wonder what I was thinking, except it's abundantly clear that I was not. And that photo. Eesh! Seemed such a good idea at the time as well, making my eyes all big and my mouth all pouty. But in the cold, sober light of day, I don't look hot and nubile, I just look like I haven't taken off my make-up properly. So you can imagine my surprise, and, okay yes, sheer unbridled joy, when I get home from work on Monday to a message. Clear as day.

> Hey!

He's not online but I send a reply and walk away from it because I will not be the sort of girl who waits around for a man. I haven't told anyone. The only person who'd care would be Rachel and for now, something is stopping me from mentioning it. She'd want to take all the credit, and to see the messages and then she'd have an opinion I might not like. She'd critique my performance and I've done quite enough of that already, thanks.

I can't imagine Jon or Sara would know who Franko were, much less Franko's bass player. So I say nothing during dinner, or whilst we watch TV, and when Jon asks why I keep scampering off upstairs (because checking sporadically throughout the evening is *definitely fine*) I tell him I'm in a heated bidding war on eBay for a designer handbag and watch as his eyes glaze over.

Eventually, during an ad break, it's there. Another message, and a greyed out circle. We're playing a game of message tag and I'm it.

> How's it going, party girl?

> Not too bad, thanks. You?

A quick Google tells me it's almost three p.m. in California. What's he up to? Seems an odd time to be free. Maybe he can just hang around online all day if he feels like it. Maybe Franko made such an obscene amount of money he doesn't have to work ever again, the jammy swine.

As I head out of my room, I hear that familiar ping of a message received and I stop at the door and look back at my laptop. That's the rest of my evening spoken for, then. Suddenly I've lost interest in the TV. I get ready for bed before going back to it. Don't want to look *too* keen, after all.

> All good here.

This is already going better than last time. This time he's initiated it. He *wants* to talk to me. God knows why.

> I feel like I should apologise for the other night.

> What do you mean?

43

Erm. My horrible drunk chat/inappropriate photo. I'm sort of amazed you wanted to talk to me again.

I liked the photo, not gonna lie.

Oh my god!

Ha. Well. Hooray!

So no apology necessary. Really. We're all good.

Did you hear that, world? We're *all good*!

Cool. OK! So, what do you do these days that means you can sit on the internet in the middle of the day? If you don't mind me asking.

I'm a session musician.

Still bass?

Still bass :) Bass forever.

Snazzy! What does that involve?

A lot of time in studios. A few gigs now and then. It keeps me out of trouble.

Sounds like fun. How did you get into that?

Seemed like the obvious thing to do. It has its moments. I couldn't really see myself stuck in an office or something. What about you?

I am stuck in an office or something. Five days a week.

Oh, wow! Sorry!

Don't be. It's not for everyone. I like it though.

What do you do in your office?

I work in the head office for a chain of department stores as a merchandiser in kitchenware.

I don't know what that is.

Basically I make sure there's enough stock, in the right stores at the right time at the correct price etc etc. I work with buyers and deal with suppliers. In a nutshell.

Sounds cool. Any I'd have heard of? Have you always done that?

Doubt it, unless you're secretly an expert in British retail brands. Beauchamp & Taylor. We don't have shops abroad. I suppose it would be the UK equivalent to Bloomingdales or maybe Nordstrom.
I got into it on a grad scheme. I thought I'd get into buying (on account of my love of shopping) but ended up in merchandising instead.

Gotcha.

Pretty sure I sound like a giant cliché with my love of shopping line. Still, I can't erase it now, better to just commit to it and carry on.

Are you doing any gigs at the moment?

No, I have some downtime right now. Which is pretty nice.

Are you all still musicians?

> Us all, as in me and my brothers? Of sorts;
> Brandon is producing, Adam DJs and Travis is
> still a drummer. He's actually recently married.

> Oh wow that's very lovely. You can·pass on my
> best wishes. If you like.

Is that weird?

> LOL. Thanks.

He definitely thinks so. Shit.

Suddenly I want to ask if he's spoken for. I didn't see anything to indicate a girlfriend on his profile but that doesn't mean jack. Mainly out of masochistic curiosity, because I'm terrified of the answer, but at the same time, I have to know if there's a chance he could be for me after all, because obviously that's where my mind's gone since all this started. And definitely since he told me he liked my photo.

I can barely look at the screen as he's typing. This is where he tells me he's happily married and has a herd of pretty children who play right outside the house every day and who catch a yellow bus to school. This is where I learn she's sitting right next to him. She's probably laughing at me for asking such banal questions and getting my hopes up, because she'd definitely know they were up. They probably had a stunningly beautiful beach wedding, with reportage photography later showcased on a trendy bridal website. Her dress would have almost certainly been floaty. He probably rolled up his trousers to his ankles and didn't wear shoes. I bet the Foo Fighters played in person at the reception and then Dave Grohl did a speech. Obviously, because if you have Dave Grohl at your wedding, you *definitely* get him to chink a spoon against his glass and talk for a bit. In fact, he probably got ordained to marry them. I can't bear it. It's all too sickeningly perfect and cool. He's still typing. What the hell kind of paragraph is he writing? I'm about to get the wedding story and I'm bracing for impact.

> LOL no, I'm not.

Yes! The image in my head pops like a bubble. Back in the game.

> Oh, I'm sorry to hear that.

A barefaced, shameless lie if ever there was one.

> It's fine. I'm sure when I find her, I'll know it. Are you? Since we're asking ;)

Not since I found a lipstick print on a wine glass in the kitchen of the flat that we shared in a shade of baby pink I haven't worn since I was fifteen. But he'd been so adamant it was mine that for a while I'd begun to doubt myself. He might have been a gaslighting prick, but it turned out he didn't have an answer about the earring I later found under the pillow in our bedroom. It's fair to say that catching him out in the way that I had soured the relationship somewhat. I moved out the next day and slept in Rachel's spare room and the house share in Shepherd's Bush came along soon after. She still loathes him for being a cheating bastard to this day.

> No, I'm free as a bird :-S

I'm not resentful. I'm totally over it. Good luck to you, Jack, pal. I hope life's giving you everything you deserve. Crabs, for starters. With a side order of the clap.

> My friend has just signed me up to a dating website, as it happens. It's called Date My Mate. It's just about as hideous as it sounds.

> Sorry, but that's hilarious. You had any luck?

God. Am I really talking about this with him?

> No. Just dick pics.

> Unsolicited

I hasten to add.

> Ha! Well, good luck with your search for the D.

Argh! No. This is suddenly terrible. He's going to think I like the dick pics. That I actively seek out the type of man who sends grainy, hastily snapped photos of his junk as a means to getting laid. We're both quiet for a few minutes, and just when I'm beginning to think he'll sign off, like he did the last time we spoke, he asks me if I like living in London and I, relieved by the change in conversation, launch into a spiel about how much I *adore* it here. This city is the one *other* crush I never really got over. So much to see, so many opportunities to grab. Something new around almost every street corner. And always, *always* somewhere to get a decent cocktail.

> Did you like it when you came here?

> We were never around long enough to really enjoy it. It was always a day or two there, before we headed off again. But it looks fun. I'd like to see it again some day, especially now you've sold it to me so enthusiastically ;)

> You are in California, right?

> Yep, Orange County. Just south of LA.

Of course he is.

> And what's LA like? I've never been.

> Busy. Sprawling. Nice beaches. Some crazy-ass people though.

I flick to a new window and search Google for LA beaches. They *are* quite appealing. Surfy waves and endless stretches of golden sand dotted with lifeguard huts. Palm trees and pink sunsets and piers and the fairground at Santa Monica. There are definitely worse places to live. I glance outside my window through the crack in my curtains. A couple are arguing with a cab driver out in the street. A fox knocks over a bin and scuttles away with a chicken carcass, and I rest my case.

> Sounds lovely. But if I lived in the OC, I'm not
> sure I'd be sitting online when there is a beach to
> lie on. Just saying.

> Ha, well, I can go down the beach whenever.
> Plus it means I get to sit and talk to you :)

This is nothing like how he was at all those signings. It's as if he's given me the eye contact we all craved and I am here for it. And talk we do, until my eyes feel heavy and I'm scared to look at the time because I know it isn't many hours until I have to get up. There's a team meeting in the morning, and it would definitely behove me to be compos mentis for that. Begrudgingly, I decide it's probably time to call it a night.

> Alright. Well, it's been fun. Until next time?

> For sure. Sweet dreams.

> You too… for much much later on ;-)

Sweet dreams! How cute! As if I could ever have anything but, after this. I keep telling myself not to read too much into it, not to overthink it, but I'm shit at taking my own advice.

In the morning I can hardly concentrate. My mind wanders. I dream up ways to get him to notice me when I should be thinking about stock uplift in all our stores in time for the Diamond Jubilee, and have to wing it a little when my boss, Mimi, asks for sales reports. I'm pretty sure she knows I'm not with it today, but Sam rescues the situation by inviting us all to the street party he's throwing.

'A party for the Queen, by a pair of queens! It's going to be fabulous.' He wiggles in his seat. 'You have to come: the dress code is red, white and blue-tiful. Bring cake and champers.'

We all nod along and then my mind's gone again. Maybe I'll just put up a witty status and see if he likes it. I'm in such a predicament. On one hand, I am a grown woman and ought to know better than to get mixed up in all this again. On the other, I'm talking to Jesse Franklin on Facebook. And he liked my slutty picture.

This cannot be healthy. I need to get a grip. At lunchtime I take myself off for a walk around the flagship store, underneath our offices, and give myself a stern internal pep talk at the make-up counters. I am acting like a crazy person and I know it, mooning around like a lovesick teenager. It's the middle of the night in California. The chances are Jesse is sleeping. He doesn't care about my witty status update. *Oooh, that's a nice eyeshadow. Pearly.* And even if he is awake there's absolutely no way he's sitting around waiting for me. *And I definitely need a new lipstick. Be rude not to with my staff discount.* I need to see Rachel. If there is one person who will be able to sort me out, it's her.

I don't like to admit it, but the truth of it is that I'm a bit worried she'll want in on it all. After all, she was just as into Franko as I was. Who's to say she won't fancy a chat too? I mean, she did start mine for me. But then, she's far too preoccupied with her wedding to revisit old crushes. She's got George, and they own a flat in Crouch End. I've got Jon and Sara and expensive rent in W12. She'll let me have this, I'm sure of it.

Free tonight? Quick drink? Chat? X

Sure. Usual haunt? x

She's already there when I arrive, and I sit myself down opposite her and take a long sip of the drink she's bought me.

'Hello to you, too,' she says, curtly, after I set the glass down.

'Sorry. How's things? Thanks for the drink.'

'No problem,' she says. 'Hey, have you had a chance to look over those menus yet?'

'Argh. 'Fraid not. Been super busy.'

'Oh,' she says. 'Okay. Do you think you can look at them soon? I really just need another opinion on whether tarte Tatin is going to work better than strawberry shortcake.'

'Okay, tarte Tatin. It's more autumnal than the strawberries. And you won't run the risk of them being woody.'

'Thanks.' She smiles at me, but it's weak. 'What did you want to chat about?' she asks, composing herself.

'Nothing,' I say, chickening out. 'Just wanted to have a gin with you.'

'Rubbish. I'm here ready to be offloaded on. So… offload.' She holds out her hands and wiggles her fingers. Closes her eyes and laughs. 'Come on, I'm passing up an M&S Dine in for Two with George for this.'

'Okay,' I say. She raises an eyebrow. 'There's been an update. I spoke to him.'

'You are welcome.'

'Yeah, please don't do that again.'

'I was going to type out the lyrics to that Carly Rae-whatever-her-name-is song that was number one a few weeks ago… Jetson? I almost gave him your number and told him to call you, maybe.'

'Jepsen. And thank you for *not* doing that.'

'Next time. Anyway, was I right? Is he boring?'

'God, no.'

'You've gone red. What happened?'

'Well, it was awkward at first, but the second time it was actually pretty great.'

'It was awkward at first, but then it was pretty great,' she repeats, slowly. 'Cassie, this is like when you lost your virginity to what's his name at uni. Harry. Did you actually just get your tits out on cam?' She smirks, and tears open the bag of Kettle Chips she's bought, flattening out the bag so the crisps are in a mound between us.

'I mean, they weren't *totally* out,' I say, taking a couple. Rachel coughs.

'So they were out a bit? Nipple out? Or just a lot of cleavage out?'

'Cleavage out.'

'Only you, Cass.'

'He said he liked it.'

'Of course he *liked it*. He's a man who fancies women. Chances are boobs will be one of his enthusiasms.'

'*I* definitely fancy *him* again. I feel like I did when we were sixteen and met them.'

She sips her drink, and thinks for a bit.

'Do you reckon you feel like this because you've been single for a while, and now you're getting a little bit of attention, or do you think you feel like this because of who you're getting the attention from?'

I shrug. 'Probably a bit of both. I mean, it's been ages, hasn't it? And I haven't really been making any effort to date. So maybe more the fact that it's him than the fact I'm suddenly getting attention, because I could go on dates if I wanted to. Does that make sense?'

The way she sighs makes me think she's a bit irritated with me, probably about those menus.

'That's why I signed you up to Date My Mate. So that you might meet somebody. Okay, I'm just going to say it. Don't read too much into this. He's very far away, and he's probably just... killing a bit of time, and I daresay this is very flattering for him. I'm sorry, you look a bit sad. I feel like I've burst your bubble. Maybe I'm being a bit cynical.'

'Maybe you are,' I say. 'Maybe this is me meeting someone. What's wrong with it? It could happen. Why couldn't it happen?'

'It's just not very likely.' She wrings her hands and crunches down on some more crisps. 'Is it? Be realistic, you don't really know anything about him.'

She's right, of course she is, saying all the things I know in my heart when I really think about it, but don't want to admit.

'Well. Okay, fine,' I say, and shut up. I don't want either of us to say anything we might regret.

'Any joy with anyone a bit closer to home?'

'Still no,' I say, sullenly.

She presses her lips together. 'Are you sure it's definitely him?'

'Oh, it's him alright. He sent me a picture which absolutely proved it. He has very nice hands.'

'Well, I'm going to need to see these messages, and the picture. We're going to scrutinise the fuck out of this, nice hands and all.'

But her words about my lack of realism puncture me and hook themselves into my subconscious, and even though Jesse and I start talking almost every day, I resolve to try to leave past crushes where they are, and just see it for what it is. That would be the grown up and sensible attitude to take. Except I lose my resolve whenever he's online, and those good intentions fall by the wayside, and it turns out I definitely *am* the sort of girl who waits around for a man. I stay up late just so I can feel the buzz of seeing that little green circle next to his name and hear that message notification sound, provoking an almost Pavlovian response in me. What does it matter? There's always coffee, and afternoon naps at the weekend.

I start to worry about things outside of my control. What I'd do if Facebook got shut down, or if something happened and I just never heard from him again. Would it be easier this time around because I'm twenty-nine now, and have bills to pay and a job to hold down, and therefore no choice other than to pick myself up and get on with things?

Or would it be harder? Would it reopen the cavity that was left when the band broke up and they stopped coming to England? Because I'm back to exactly where I was when I was sixteen; talking to him in my head and wondering what he'd think of me. And it's gone further than it ever did before, because this time I'm getting something back. I'm getting responses and I feel as if I'm being let in, if only a little bit.

And I like how it feels; exciting and exhilarating. I stop checking Date My Mate and everything seems brighter, more positive. There's a skip in my step and I'm sure it's down to him. So it must be okay to feel like this because how can it possibly be wrong?

Chapter Seven

Jesse

Brandon got the go ahead for whatever his project is, so I visit as planned, at the beginning of July. Laurel Heights, San Francisco, via the Disney Store. Nancy is now the delighted owner of a sparkly Merida purse, a packet of Brave-themed crayons, and a silver plastic tiara. She insists on showing me all her Disney toys, one by one, in minute detail, and instructs me to put the movie on. Nancy is the sassiest two-year-old I've ever met. She puts on her new tiara and parades around the room, before insisting I wear one, too.

'You spoil her,' Lainey says, leaning against the door. 'Nice tiara.'

'Of course. She's a princess.'

'I'm a princess,' Nancy agrees, nodding at her mom.

'Looks to me like you both are. Hey, it's almost time for dinner, come wash your hands before we eat,' Lainey says. She holds out her hand for Nancy to take, but Nancy hangs back and looks reluctant. She hasn't finished showing me all her Disney stuff.

'I wanna sit next to you,' she says, looking at me.

'Sure you can, sweetie,' I tell her, '*if* you go with your mom and wash your hands.'

Later in the evening, Lainey is settling Nancy, and Brandon and I are sitting up in his office. Clouds billow across the sky, visible through the skylight. His desk is messy. There are piles of papers, stacks of hard drives, printed off emails, random bits of kit and equipment. A blown-up photograph from his and Lainey's wedding, taken in a vineyard, hangs on the wall. They're standing amongst the grapevines, in front of a gnarly old oak tree. The sun shines through the branches and they're holding hands and kissing and for a few seconds, as I'm looking at it, I think that it must be nice to have that with someone. He's going through this job he wants me to work on.

'You're going to laugh. It's a tiny job and I took it on as a favor.'

'Go on.'

'It's for a couple of commercial jingles for radio. They want heavy on the slap. Actually, the client sent me this.' He pulls up a commercial for Nike with Michael Jordan slam dunking a basketball in slow motion. It's very 'of a time'. That time being the nineteen-eighties. I can't help but snigger. Brandon generally works with well-known recording artists.

'How exactly did this end up with you? Surely not through your agent?'

'No, through someone I met at a dinner. I *may* have been a bit liquored up. I was asked to pull together some musicians and obviously I thought of you. They have everything composed, you'd just have to show up, run through, and record. Up for it?'

'Yeah, sure.'

'It'll be very easy money for you.'

'You don't need to convince me. When is it?'

'Next Tuesday. The tenth. You can expense your flights. It's in New York.'

I flinch. New York is where Nicole moved to and the last time I saw her was… well it wasn't the best night of my life.

It was New Year's Eve, and we'd planned to watch the fireworks by the *Queen Mary*. We ate at the Vietnamese restaurant around the corner from her apartment. The same place we went on our first date, and lots of times after that, so it had sort of become *ours*. And after, we decided to blow off the fireworks and go back to her apartment instead. She opened the door, dropped her purse on the side table and kicked off her shoes. She poured us both a drink, which neither one of us finished before she took my hand and pulled me towards her bedroom, all in exactly the way she had on dozens of occasions over the fifteen months we'd been seeing each other.

But this time something different happened.

'So, I need to tell you something,' she said, slightly nervously, straight after we were finished having sex. 'I'm leaving.'

She looked across at me and her hair was coming loose from her ponytail. I reached over and ran my finger over her nipple and watched as it pebbled into a little pink peak.

'You can't leave,' I said. 'This is your apartment.'

'No, Jesse,' she said. 'I mean, I'm leaving town.'

'What? When?'

'Wednesday.' She wrinkled her nose, almost like she was apologizing for it.

'Huh? Nicole, it's Saturday evening.'

'Yeah, I know,' she paused and shifted. 'I got a new job. I start the following Monday. It's just a contract, but—'

'Where are you going?'

'The UN, so… New York.'

'Wow. How long's the contract? Are you coming back?'

'Uh. I don't know. I wasn't planning to.'

'Wait… okay. So, possibly a stupid question, but, what does that mean for us?'

She fidgeted, looked at the ceiling, took my hand and dropped it again, tried to look normal, but Nicole's poker face was shocking.

'Well. I mean, we're going to be in different time zones—'

'Oh, what the fuck, Nicole? Are you kidding?' I moved and she rolled away from me.

'I just think… I'm going to be so busy, especially at the start. I guess you can come visit, but I feel like that's going to just delay the inevitable.'

'Delay the inevitable,' I repeated, slowly, forming the words in my mouth and allowing the gravity of them to sink in as I said them. Each one felt heavy and sticky. Like talking through a mouthful of taffy. I reached to the floor for my clothes and started to pull them on.

'What are you doing? Are you leaving?'

'Are you serious? Have you or have you not just dumped me? What did you expect me to do? Stay over? Of course I'm leaving.'

I looked back at her and watched her chew her lip. Outside the fireworks were just starting down by the ship. People were ringing in 2012, full of hopes and dreams and resolutions, and as far as I could tell, I'd just been dumped. During sex. After picking up the entire check at the restaurant. Worst New Year ever.

'You don't have to go, Jesse. I don't want you to go. We should talk about this.'

'Yeah, I don't think so,' I said, dressed by then, and taking advantage of the fact that she wasn't. I could be out of her front door before she'd even put her robe on. I could have rounded the corner before she'd even left her apartment, and she'd never argue with me in the street. Besides, I didn't want to talk about it. I just wanted to get home. 'You literally could not have been clearer.'

'Please don't be like this.' She sat up, clutching her sheets up over her chest. She swung her legs over the side of her bed and I took that as my cue to leave.

'Happy new year, Nicole,' I said, slamming the front door behind me as I left.

–

Brandon seems to sense my discomfort at the thought of going to New York.

'Maybe you could see where the land lies?' he says, gently. 'I mean, it's been a few months and you haven't mentioned anyone else...'

No sooner are the words out of his mouth than Cassie's profile picture pops into my head. Wavy hair and Wayfarers, and how in the snapshot she sent me the first time we talked she's all mussed hair and intense eyes and bare legs.

Suddenly I want the comfort of our everything and nothing conversations, but it's four in the morning in London and she won't be awake yet. I reach into the pocket of my hoodie and clamp my hand around my phone. I'll just send her a message. She'll get it when she wakes up. Then she'll reply and we'll go from there.

'So, I'll put you down, then?' Brandon says, and it pulls my attention back to what he's saying.

'Err, yeah, definitely. Wednesday. Thanks.'

'Tuesday,' he corrects. 'July tenth. Things alright? You seem a little distracted.'

'I'm fine.' I let go of my phone. That message can wait. I don't want to admit that I might be crushing on Cassie from England because that's just an exercise in pointlessness. But at the same time it was her I thought about just now. 'It's just been a really busy couple of weeks,' I say.

'Good thing you're up here for a few days then. I don't know how you still deal with LA.'

'I like LA. For one, it's great for work. And I'm not really in LA proper am I?'

'True enough. You seen Mom and Dad lately?'

He always asks me this when I visit, and the short answer is no, even though they only live a half hour drive away. We're not close and it's been that way since Franko broke up in 1999. Mom stops by sometimes, and she always brings food and fusses around and tries to do my laundry and looks a bit sad about the way things turned out. But Dad is never with her, and aside from family events, we haven't spent any time together in years.

'Nope.'

'We saw Adam recently. He's good. I'm sure you could crash with him in New York if you needed to.'

I roll my eyes. 'I'm sure I couldn't. Dude, come on.'

If the relationship with my parents is strained, then the one with my elder brother is practically non-existent, and has been since that day in Berlin. He was serious when he screamed at me that we were done, and when we do see each other it's mainly so Mom doesn't get upset. She tries to brush everything that happened under the carpet, and no one talks about it, but I know my leaving Berlin the way that I did caused a huge rift that may never be healed, and ergo, it wouldn't have even occurred to me to call him when I'm in New York. There's something fundamentally irreparable there.

Brandon nods slowly. 'Trav okay?'

'Seems to be.'

'Feel like getting a drink?' he says, standing up. The chair rocks up and down and rolls back a little.

'Sure.'

—

Lainey and I are sitting in the yard the following morning, drinking coffee and making loose plans for the week, mainly revolving around keeping Nancy amused and where we can see the best fireworks on Wednesday.

'I just get so sleepy,' Lainey's saying. She pats her little baby bump. 'It's tiring making one of these.'

'I don't doubt it,' I say.

'It doesn't help,' she continues, 'that your brother spends all his time in his office lately. I asked him to go to the grocery store the other day and he refused!'

'Douche,' I say, deadpan.

'Right? I hated on him for the rest of the day. Like, hello! Are you growing a foot? No? I didn't think so. Get me a snack, already!'

She takes another sip of her drink.

'Well, let me know if you want me to take Nancy out for you,' I say. 'Or, you know, get you a snack already.'

Lainey's expression changes and she looks incredulous. 'You don't have to. That's not the reason Brandon asked if you wanted to visit. At *all*.'

'Well, I mean she's a nice kid.' We both look over at her. Nancy is playing with a baby doll. She's sat it up in the grass and is crouching next to it, pouring an imaginary cup of tea into a plastic teacup which she then holds to the doll's mouth. The sun has lightened her hair and tight ringlets fall from a ponytail. 'Plus, I wouldn't want to obstruct your foot-growing schedule. And she likes me. How hard can it be?'

'She adores you. Don't tell Travis but you're absolutely her favorite. She was super excited when we told her you were visiting.'

'It's 'cause I bring her Disney crap isn't it?'

Lainey laughs. 'No! You're good with her. Patient. When are you going to get married and have your own?' The tone is jokey but I think there's some underlying concern there.

'I don't know,' I shrug. 'There's a vital component missing these days, in case you hadn't noticed.'

Lainey purses her lips.

'Don't worry about it, Lainey, I don't.'

'It was a shame about Nicole.'

'Yeah well, shit happens.'

She wrinkles up her nose and looks like she's about to say something when my phone rings, and I'm relieved. Saved by the bell, quite literally. The number is withheld.

'Hold that thought,' I say, not meaning it. She nods but I think she gets the gist that the conversation is done. 'Jesse Franklin,' I say into the phone.

'Hi. My name is Mick Paulson,' says the guy on the other end. I don't know anyone called Mick Paulson. He sounds like a gangster from a Guy Richie movie. What's with the British looking for me lately? 'I'm the tour manager for Kitten Tricks.'

Who?

'Kitten Tricks. Right,' I say.

'I'm looking for a bass player. Are you available?'

'Uh. I don't know, what kind of work is it? And for when?'

'It's short notice,' Mick says. 'And I'm sorry for that, but it's this Thursday and Saturday night. The last two dates of their European tour.'

'You *do* know I'm in California, right?'

'I do mate, yeah, and because it's such a tight turnaround, rates are negotiable, and obviously there's per diem as well. And I'm aware it's a holiday for you this week but we're in a bit of a spot to be honest, so basically, name your price. Our guy's had an emergency and had to pull out. Anyway, your name cropped up, hence the call. Are you clear for international?'

'Depends. Where are we talking?'

'London.'

Well, *shit*. Things suddenly just got interesting.

'I'm there,' I say without hesitating. The words may have come out quicker than a blink but the thought process was clearly defined: one, it's a long way to go for a couple of gigs, but two, the money will absolutely be worth the jet lag. And three, *Cassie* lives in London.

'What?' he asks.

'I'll do it. Can you send me the setlist, the itinerary, and a contract?' I ask.

Mick audibly exhales down the line. 'Well, that was easier than I thought it might be. Consider it done. And thanks, mate.'

Lainey's pretending not to listen, angling her face up towards the sky and scraping her fingers through her hair, but I'm fairly sure she is. As soon as we've finalized the details and ended the call she asks me where I'm off to.

'London,' I tell her. 'On Wednesday night.'

'Oh Jesse! You're going to miss the Fourth! And what about the jingles?'

'I'll be back on Sunday. It'll be fine.'

'You'll be exhausted.'

'It's too good an opportunity to pass up. They're going to pay me a *lot*. Plus, I can sleep on the plane.'

Lainey raises her eyebrows. 'Well, that's all good then,' she says.

'It does mean I've got to go back today. I'll have to get everything in order. And I'll have some songs to learn.'

'Figures. Nancy's going to be bummed.'

'I'm sorry. I'll bring her back something nice from England. Is there a British Disney princess?'

'Sleeping Beauty.'

—

Kitten Tricks are an all-singing, all-dancing girl group. Almost certainly manufactured. Probably put together on a talent show. Four of them. Young, and pretty in a chocolate box sort of way. Trendy. Big eyes and hair and bigger voices. I download the songs from the set list Mick sends over before I leave San Francisco, and listen to them all the way home. Their sound, predictably, is catchy, rhythmic, girl-power pop and the bass lines are funky with nice fills and slap tones thrown in. Even so, nineteen songs to learn in as little time as I have, plus travel, is a tall order, so it's fortunate they all sound similar.

When I wake up the morning after getting back from San Francisco, the thought I had as soon as I decided I was going to London re-emerges and it plays on my mind all day. I'm going to ask Cassie if she wants to meet. But when it comes to it I'm sort of lost for words and I type my message over and over until I'm happy with it, and wait until I know she won't be online to send it because this doesn't feel like the easy conversations we've been having. This isn't chitchat about our days and the things we're doing, or whether pineapple truly belongs on pizza, or what sitcom spin off is the best. This is levelling up, and it ends up kind of nonchalant, which isn't how I really feel about it at all.

So… remember that time a couple of months ago when you said I should make time to visit London? Well, I've landed a last minute gig there this Thursday and Saturday and I have the night off in between. So I know it's really short notice, but do you feel like hanging out? Maybe you could show me around?

As soon as it's gone the nerves hit, and I instantly wonder what she's going to make of it. It's not lost on me that it's as if the tables have been turned. She contacted me in the beginning, and yet *I'm* the one who's gone out of the way to set something up. I'm the one who jumped at the chance to go to London and I'm not entirely convinced it wasn't at least partly because I know she's there. Nope, none of that is lost on me at all.

Chapter Eight

Cassie

Holy Moses! I don't believe it. Do I want to hang out? What kind of question is that? Is the Pope a Catholic? Do bears defecate in tree populous areas? *Of course* I want to hang out.

> Way to shock a girl on a dull Tuesday afternoon. Yes, hanging out sounds like fun. What do you feel like doing? And when do you get here? And how has this come about so quickly? Is that enough questions for now??

Rhetorical question; that's *definitely* enough for now. I send it and quickly close down the window, because now I'm terrified of that little green circle. Then I sit back in my chair and stretch my legs out under my desk. Our office is open plan. Rows of giant white desks stretch the entire length of the room. Each desk houses four workstations, and there's a fictitious clear desk policy, which in theory means no one is supposed to have photos of their other halves or their kids and pets taped to their monitors, but in reality isn't the case at all, and I know that Mimi stashes custard creams and an impressive array of pharmaceuticals in her desk drawer, and Sam has a boyfriend called Tarka with impeccable dress sense and that they're cat dads to a silver tabby called Miles.

I'm acutely aware that a timescale of such minuscule proportions doesn't leave me long to calm down and get my shit together. But when I try to arrange to meet up with Rachel she tells me she's busy with wedding stuff all week, so I have to go it alone. I spend the rest of the day doing what anyone in my situation would. I sack off work, take an extra long lunch break, and hit the shops instead. Mimi's out of the office for the day, and Sam won't snitch.

At home, I look at all the things I've bought and have a little panic, and not just at the estimated size of this month's credit card bill, but also because of the reason I bought it all in the first place. I got a new pair of super skinny black jeans that make my bum look *phenomenal*, a few tops, and a bodycon dress for if I am feeling brave on Friday and lay off carbs for the rest of the week. Trendy, but not try-hard, apart from the dress, which definitely has an agenda all of its own.

Later on, in bed, I lie with my covers pulled up to my chin and read Jesse's follow up message.

I'll explain everything once I'm there. But in a nutshell, the bassist pulled out of the last two shows (some family emergency) so I got hired. Kerching $$$! I've had to rush home from San Francisco to sort everything out and learn the songs, and I'll be leaving here on Wednesday night. I'll be in touch properly when I arrive and let's just see what happens. Is that OK? Are those answers satisfactory? :)

I tap out of the app and put my phone on my nightstand. I couldn't type anything coherent or sensible right now if I tried. It would be nonsense. He'd instantly know that deep down I'm not a cool girl, and I can't have that. I'm not though, I can't stop grinning. The Cheshire Cat has nothing on me. I can't stop squeezing my hands into fists.

The rest of the week is agony. I turn into one of those girls who sits and refreshes her messages far more than necessary. But the only thing that arrives is another message from Fred from Date My Mate, and my interest in that waned weeks ago.

> **To:** CassieB83
> **From:** FredTed49
>
> Hi again Cassie,
> It's Fred from Clapham. Sorry for the radio silence since our first message all that time ago. Things have been a bit weird to be honest. Martin went missing for a while. And then Tyler's sister tried it on with me. And I didn't know what to do. Turns out there's no right way to handle that. Tyler went mental.
> You've probably met someone who is quicker off the mark than I am by now.
> Anyway, hope you're having a nice week. Sorry again for not replying sooner.
> Fred

> **To:** FredTed49
> **From:** CassieB83
>
> Fred! You're alive.
> That was a loaded message if ever one was received. How is Martin?! That's definitely a predicament with Tyler's sister. I'm not surprised he went mental if you shagged her. Is that not part of Boy Code?! Aren't sisters off limits?
> I'm still very single. But, full disclosure; I am meant to be having a drink with someone (who I did not meet on DMM) on Friday. I'd say wish me luck, but it would probably be better for you if it all went to shit.
> So, I'll just say, talk to you on the flip!
> Cassie

To: CassieB83
From: FredTed49

I didn't shag Tyler's sister, and that's why he went mad, which I thought was weird to be honest. Asked why she wasn't good enough for me. You can't win with some people. Anyway, good luck, Cassie. Knock him dead.
Not literally. Maybe literally? Too much?
Fred

Definitely a bit much, Fred.

Chapter Nine

Jesse

The plane touches down in London just after midday on Thursday, and Cassie seems to be up for meeting. At least, I think she is. She asked a bunch of questions in reply to my message and then went quiet, but I've had no time to dwell on it; I took a taxi straight to the hotel, checked in and dumped my bags, before going on to the venue. The driver clocked the flight cases and talked all the way there. His daughter, he told me, was going to go mad when she heard about him driving me to the gig.

'Is she a fan then?' I asked.

'Oh yeah. Mega. She'll be there tonight. Loves them, and that boy band. You know the one? Five of them. Girly-looking fellas. All about seventeen. Too young really. The fame, it can go to their heads, can't it? They'll be spat out by the industry in no time flat.'

I have no idea which boy band he means, but I nod at him through the glass partition and he catches my eye in the rearview mirror. *You're preaching to the choir there*, I think.

'And then what?' he continues. 'They'll be cutting keys in Soho by the time they're twenty-five. They need time to be normal teenagers. Let kids be kids, I say. Plenty of time for all that.'

'There definitely is,' I agree. 'Still, I hope she enjoys tonight.'

You can never see much of the audience when you're on stage because of the lights. It's just a mass of darkness interspersed with pinpricks of light from people's phones, but Kitten Tricks are definitely popular. I wasn't sure what to expect but they are slick and polished with their jokes and engagement with the audience and their spot-on vocals.

An assistant is hanging around backstage and she ushers us all together for a photo. We're all tired and sweaty, and she'd have been better off taking the photo before the gig.

'It's going on Twitter,' she says, chirpily. 'The fans will love it.' She shows us the tweet.

Thanks to our amazing band. We couldn't do it without you guys! #KittenTricksLDN.

In the photo, Ryan, the drummer, is spinning his drum sticks like batons. Within seconds it's been retweeted and replied to over and over.

'I quite fancy a beer,' he says, once we're packed up and ready to go. 'Anyone feel like going to the pub?'

I'm exhausted but still buzzing from the show, and it can't hurt to network a bit so fuck it, I'm going.

We go to a pub he knows around the corner. It's dark and quiet and we sit at the back, huddled over our drinks.

'Long way for you to come for two gigs,' he says.

'Ah, yeah. Well, Mick said my name came up, though, I have no idea how.'

'Mick knows everyone,' he shrugs. 'Have you worked for the label before?'

'Subsidiaries of, yeah. I get a lot of sessions from Trajectory back in LA.'

'It's probably that then. He was relieved you could make it. You sticking around after Saturday?'

'Not this time, it's a bit of a flying visit. I'm in the studio on Tuesday.'

'Session musician life. I hear you. What are you doing tomorrow? Sleeping off the jet lag?'

'Ha. Well, I won't be setting an alarm, that's for sure. Though, I'm supposed to be meeting someone at some point. But, I don't know...'

'*Supposed* to be?'

'Yeah, she seemed pretty down, but that was at the beginning of the week and,' I check my phone for anything from Cassie. 'Nope, nothing. So... Maybe not.'

'Oh I see, mate. You're talking about *meeting* someone. In the Biblical sense. I like your style.'

'Well, I probably wouldn't put it that way,' I say, but I'm not really sure if I believe myself. I think I definitely *would* put it that way, if the opportunity presented itself.

Ryan picks up his pint glass and swirls it, and the beer sloshes around inside. 'I'm sure it'll happen. Women love a musician. Even a bass player.'

'Says the *drummer*!' We both smirk. We've heard the jokes before.

'Touché, mate. All I'm saying is, I bet she shows up and I bet she won't look like a sack of shit.'

I don't think Cassie could look like a sack of shit if she tried.

Back in my room I lie awake for ages, exhausted but unable to fall asleep because of the jet lag and the niggling feeling that Cassie's gone cold on me. It's gone two a.m. when I decide to send her a final message.

> Hey you. One show down, it was great to be back on stage, such a cool vibe. So, like I said, I have tomorrow night free. I'm staying at the Bellborough. Do you know it? It's probably easiest to meet there, is that OK? I haven't heard back from you so I get it if you want to take a rain check and that's cool, too – no worries!

If she doesn't reply to this… well then there's really nothing I can do. It'd be nice to meet the woman I've been chatting to for the last couple of months, since the opportunity landed so serendipitously into my lap, and I definitely hope she is up for hanging out, especially after what Ryan said.

–

It's lunchtime when I wake up. Hardly surprising after my exhausting day yesterday, and besides, I'm still running on Pacific time. Thank fuck I remembered to hang that 'do not disturb' sign on the door. I order room service and eat it in bed as I catch up on emails and invoices with the TV on in the background. I don't like to admit it, even to myself, but I'm sort of afraid to check Facebook; the last thing I want is the ego-bruising indifference of a greyed out message icon.

But eventually, I'm all caught up. I've procrastinated over life admin for long enough. There are no more unread messages in my inbox. My accounts are up to date. My calendar is now organized into tidy blocks of color depending on the type of work, and it all looks kind of neat, but I really can't put off checking Facebook any longer and the relief I feel when I see she's responded is so momentarily overwhelming that it gives me a rush.

> I'll be there at 7ish. You gonna be somewhere or shall I tell the concierge when I arrive? And if so, is there some kind of rock star alias I need to know about? ;-)

How cute and how funny. I don't think we even did that with Franko. Also, *she's coming here at seven*, which is only five hours from now. So I guess we're really doing this. But why wouldn't we be doing this? Why does it feel like a big deal? Why am I so nervous? Because it's unfamiliar and I'm out of my comfort zone? That must be it. So I downplay what was already pretty mediocre fame in reply and tell her I'll catch her later.

I may be maintaining my cool over the internet but inside I am full of worries that mainly revolve around what will happen if I am a huge let-down to her. What if, after everything, we have nothing to talk about face to face? What if she stays for one drink and then makes her excuses and leaves?

Other worries creep in, too, and they are just as irrational. What if she just doesn't show? Or she's not at all who she says she is? What if after all this, she's little more than a bored housewife with a penchant for the nostalgic? What will I do if despite that photo, she's somehow managed to construct some elaborate online persona and she's not the hot girl with the blonde wavy hair who used to like Franko at all? What if, after everything I joked about in the beginning about how *she* should be careful about getting catfished, *I* am the one who's been misled? Disappointment wouldn't even begin to cover it.

Because I've come to realize that I've relied on this set up between the two of us far more than I have been able to admit until now. I've needed the random conversations about TV shows and pizza toppings and our jobs and our families and friends. I've had a burst of... something... on those occasions when those chats have taken a turn and gotten a little suggestive, and I can't explain it, but it feels a whole lot like dopamine. And it's as if everything lined up perfectly, even the Franko thing sort of made it easier. If I'd had to explain it all I don't think I'd have been in the right frame of mind to bother, because at some point, it would have come up. After all, you can't keep my sort of past a secret. You can't hang a platinum disc on the wall and expect people to ignore it.

Suddenly, my room feels claustrophobic and stifling and I need to get some air, which means getting out of here because the windows don't open. I need another coffee and a distraction. I need to find a Disney Store. I need to immerse myself in Disney princess gifts for Nancy, and right now I need to not think about this evening.

Chapter Ten

Cassie

I'm so relieved when I wake up to his message that I'm almost hysterical. He's right though. I've spent the last thirty-six hours in a state of panic over not hearing from *him* again and all the time *I* hadn't even replied in the first place. Whoops! The Bellborough. Close to the river in Borough and definitely *not* a Holiday Inn. A rain check? I think not.

And now, first things first: a day to night outfit that's sexy as hell, but that I can still pull off at work without raising suspicion. The dress is probably out, but those jeans will work. With a black cami, and a cute summer jacket over the top. I fish out a fairly saucy and definitely sheer underwear set from my drawer and put it all on. It's a nice result. Shoes: flats for work, chunky-heeled sandals for later. Make-up: rosy pink cheeks for the day, heavy black eyeliner and illuminating highlighter for the evening. Accessories: midi ring, necklace, and oversized hoop earrings. I scrunch my hair and paint my nails. I check myself out in the mirror and I'm pleased with who's batting her eyelashes back at me. *I* definitely would not kick me out of bed.

I try again with Rachel as I get off the tube at Oxford Circus:

> Rach! I know you're busy but it's genuinely imperative that I see you really quickly after work today. Will explain later and the drinks are on me.

I push open the door to Starbucks, and that, at least, feels normal.

All morning I try to press on with my work, really, I do, but I can't concentrate and people are noticing. Sam tells me I'm away with the fairies, and when Rachel replies, I jump a mile.

> OK, I'll meet you after work but it will need to be a quick one. Is everything OK? Rx

> I only have time for a quick one. I am meeting someone!

> OOHH! Date My Mate? Mine's a G&T x

By midday I'm on my third coffee, and now, whenever I think about this evening I get a rush down the entire length of my spine that isn't just a caffeine high. Every vertebra tingles. I'm picturing it all in my head: the evening, and all the possible outcomes, bad outcomes as well as good because I feel like a little bit of realism is required. I imagine how disappointed I'll be if, after all this time and all this build up, we have nothing to talk about and it doesn't go well. How excited I'll be if it does. How nervous I'll be if it *really* does. How much effort I've poured into today, so it'd better bloody go well. And I think about how I know there's a reason I picked out that bra and those knickers and it's not so much about that secret confidence boost you get from wearing decent underwear, and almost entirely down to the fact that I want him to see them.

I refresh my messages all through my lunch break, sitting at my desk, attempting, and failing to eat a salad. Nothing. I'm a fizzy bundle of fraught, pent-up energy. Who the hell do I ask for at the hotel? Probably just him, but I need to be sure.

Mimi peers around the side of her iMac opposite me, and eyes me suspiciously.

'You're jumpy today,' she says. 'Everything alright?'

'Yes. Sorry. Yes. I'm meeting someone for a drink after work. Just feeling a little nervous.'

She doles out a raised eyebrow and a knowing look. 'Why are you nervous? Is it a date?'

'No. It's just a drink with a friend, who I haven't seen... in forever.'

Technically it's not a lie.

'A male friend?'

'He is male, yes.'

'A platonic male friend?'

'...Yes.'

'You hesitated. So that's a clear no.'

Mimi has a nose for bullshit, and I can't keep a straight face. My nostrils are flaring.

'It really is just a drink.' I say, looking back at my screen and randomly clicking my mouse so she thinks I'm working, and not checking my social media accounts.

'I believe you, Cass. Thousands wouldn't.'

'Ah, well, I'm glad *you* do, Mimi.'

She laughs. 'Well, I hope you have a good time on your platonic date that isn't a date.'

Four forty-five rolls around at last and I check Facebook one last time, letting out an audible sigh of relief as I click open my messages, styling it out as a wheezy cough. Sam looks over and then pretends he hasn't. He catches Mimi's eye across the desks and smirks.

> Hahaha! I wasn't that famous, kid. Real name all the way. Room 508, and yeah, have someone call up. Catch you later!

78

'Okay,' Mimi announces, standing up. 'I know we all have better places than this to be, so I'm off for the weekend. You can go, too. Enjoy your evening. I'd get one inside you pronto.'

'Excuse me?'

'A drink, Cassie. She means a *drink*.' Sam laughs. 'Gosh, your mind!' He looks up at Mimi. 'I reckon she's on a promise,' he says.

'She's not even denying it,' Mimi agrees.

'Details on Monday, bitch,' Sam says.

I hurriedly cut down the quieter back roads behind Oxford Street to meet Rachel and sip nervously at a white wine spritzer whilst I wait for her to arrive. If she doesn't get here soon, I'll drink her gin, too. Finally, she pushes the door open and I'm unable to contain myself. I throw myself at her, pulling at her arm and shaking it until she yanks it away.

'I have a date that isn't a date. In less than two hours. He's here and I'm meeting him, and I'm actually terrified.'

She rubs her wrist and looks around the pub.

'I know it's been a while but calm down. Who are you meeting? What's his name? What does he look like? He's not a dick pic man is he? You shouldn't meet a man who sends you pictures of his penis before you've had sex. That's advice for life, right there.'

'Jesse!' I squeal. 'I'm meeting Jesse. No one off that stupid website, and obviously I haven't seen his penis.'

She holds up her hand and cuts me off. She's still confused, but she's getting there. Piecing the information together like a puzzle.

'What? You're meeting *Jesse*? As in *Jesse Franklin* Jesse?'

'Yes!' I say. It comes out like the hiss of a radiator being bled.

'I'm so confused. Why do I only just know about this? You've got to stop keeping stuff from me, Cass. I thought all that had fizzled out. You haven't mentioned him in a while.'

'I did try to meet up with you on Tuesday. You were busy. And no, *of course* it hasn't fizzled out.'

As if I'd let it fizzle out. 'Anyway, I didn't think you approved.'

'Christ. You make me sound like some kind of maiden aunt. I just told you not to get your hopes up but clearly you shouldn't listen to me. Anyway, I'd have moved a phone call with Eloise the wedding planner for this. We could have had time to prepare. Though judging by your outfit, you've already done a fair bit of that.'

'He's doing some shows here,' I shrug, like this is a normal state of affairs. 'It's all very last minute. He asked the other day if I wanted to hang out.'

Rachel snorts and rolls her eyes. 'Oh, come on,' she says. 'He's clearly trying to hit on you. He's in town for a few days and he's trying his luck.'

'Hmm. I'm not sure it's like that. It's probably just because he knows I live here and it's nice to meet people you know, isn't it?'

The way her eyebrows slant suggests she thinks I am being dim.

'I don't think so. And neither do you, really. Also,' she continues, 'he's a bassist, so he's going to know exactly what he's doing with his hands. And what's more, you've thought about that, too, which is why you've gone to so much effort. I see you. And I see your sex bra. Are you wearing the matching knickers?'

Foiled. One hundred percent. She knows me too well.

'Possibly,' I say.

'There you have it then.' She picks up her glass and takes a long drink. 'Can't you see how obvious this is? One kind-of famous pop star from the nineteen-nineties gets tracked down and befriended by a fan who still cares enough to get in contact, and who then jumps at the chance to meet up with him when he's *conveniently* in town. I bet he's got this entire rock star-groupie fantasy playing out in his head.'

'Nooo,' I protest. 'We've had very wholesome chats… mostly. It's probably not like that.' But I know that's exactly what it looks like, and maybe that's because it's exactly how it is. And maybe all this pretending I haven't seen it is pointless because after all, I got the Veet out this morning, and put on my sex knickers, and you don't wear see-through knickers unless you want somebody to see through them.

'Mostly?'

'Yeah. Well, you know what it's like when there's wine involved.'

'Jesus, if this wasn't so exciting I'd be annoyed that you've kept it from me.'

'I just… wanted to keep it for me, Rach, that's all. It wasn't anything calculated.'

'Lord, can you imagine if you'd known about this happening when we were sixteen? Like, if we'd been able to look into the future and seen that somehow, someday, you'd be chatting up Jesse Franklin over the internet and then he'd travel all this way to shag you.'

'That's not what's happened here,' I protest, but she shakes her head slowly and stares off into space and I have to admit she's right; back then I'd have just about died over this.

'Now, how is that Dutch courage working out for you?' she asks.

I nod. It's working out just fine.

Before I know it, six thirty has rolled around and I am definitely beginning to feel the effects of the wine. I've been to the loo twice and both times I have pouted in the mirror, scrunched my hair, and readjusted my bra. I am gorgeous, really, I am. My bum is magnificent in these jeans. My boobs are exceptional in this bra. The Venus de Milo would be well jel. Rachel and I walk arm in arm back to the tube station.

'Call me the minute you get home,' she demands, 'I want details. Unless it's really *really* late, in which case, call me tomorrow morning!'

'I will,' I promise. 'Be prepared for the mother of all debriefs.'

'I think you really ought to be the one preparing for a debrief.' She kisses my cheek. 'God, you're so jammy. You're going out on a date with a hot rock star and I get to go home to George.'

'I'm not even sorry,' I tell her.

She shoos me off through the barriers. 'Off with you. Have a great time. Don't get pregnant. Make him put something on the end of it. Text me updates if you can, but *only* if it's not obvious. So maybe when he's paying for drinks or has nipped off to buy condoms from a machine in the gents.'

The journey to the hotel feels like it's going to last forever. My heart pounds the entire time, and I begin to feel sicker and sicker with each passing station. By the time I've changed trains and we eventually arrive at Southwark I can barely cope. Outside, the evening is balmy. Traffic is backed up along the road; cars and taxis and buses full of people who look like they'd rather be anywhere else. A cyclist who looks so happy to be out riding in the sun reminds me of the way dogs poke their heads out of car windows.

I don't blame him for looking so pleased, because summer in London is the best. Long, hazy evenings, finally giving way to heady darkness, illuminating city lights that make the place seem almost magical. I walk up the road towards the Thames, and then the hotel is on the next block on my left; glass-fronted, with an enormous chandelier and a gold velvet chaise longue in the lobby. There are a couple of people milling about, but on the whole it's fairly empty and I can't decide if that's a good thing (little chance of being interrupted), or not (bar staff who listen to conversations, and then smirk like you're now staff room gossip fodder when you catch them). I look at my watch – five minutes to seven. Perfect. I push open the door and my heels click-clack noisily over the shiny floor all the way to the front desk. The concierge looks up and smiles and suddenly I feel remarkably self-conscious.

'I'm here to meet—' I stop abruptly, momentarily annoyed with myself. I've planned every single moment of how I'm going to be this evening, apart from, apparently, this one. What is he to me? I clear my throat and carry on, 'my friend.'

'And is your friend a guest with us?' She cocks her head to one side and stares.

'He is,' I say. I stare back. *Look, lady*, I want to say, *this isn't some kind of* Pretty Woman *scenario*. Girls meet boys at hotels all the time, don't they? I mean, *I* haven't before today, but that doesn't mean anything.

'Okay, I'm going to need a name and a room number.'

'It's Jesse Franklin,' I say, and saying his name to the person who is about to connect us makes him more real than ever. 'Room 508.'

Chapter Eleven

Jesse

The phone in my room rings just before seven, and I mute the TV before I answer it.

'I have a lady at the front desk. Says you're expecting her. Her name's Cassie.'

'Awesome. Yes. Can you tell her I'll be right down.'

'Of course.'

'Hey, if she waits in the bar can she charge a drink to my room?'

'That's not a problem.'

'Great, thank you.'

The line cuts and this is it. I kick my bag under the desk, shut down my laptop, lock my passport in the room safe and give myself a final once-over before leaving.

There are exactly three people sitting in the bar; an older couple, and a woman who is unmistakably Hot British Cassie. I scan the room quickly, just to make sure no one is lurking, because apparently my insane concerns from earlier haven't quite dissipated. In any case, there she is, the cute blonde from Facebook, and suddenly she's not just a few photos and some typed out messages anymore, she's tangible and very, very real. She's perched on a bar stool with a glass of white wine on the bar next to her. She's zipping up her purse and after she places it, carefully, on a hook under the bar, she looks up slowly and stares at me. For a second or two she just *stares* at me, and then she blinks a couple of times and her face breaks into a smile, wide and pretty. She fidgets in her seat as I weave through the empty tables towards her.

'Cassie?' I ask, even though I know it's her. She's smiling with her eyes again, gray-blue, and clear, framed tonight with heavy make-up.

'Jesse,' she says, and she's smiling at me so wide that the corners of her eyes are slightly crinkled. 'Hi.'

Chapter Twelve

Cassie

Oh god, he's only absolutely flipping gorgeous isn't he? Hotter even than in the photos, and I'm the emoji with the hearts for eyes. He's taller than I remember, too, with quite long, Pantene-shiny dark hair and a strong stubble game. He's wearing a faded blue and white checked shirt, with the sleeves pushed halfway up his forearms, a white t-shirt, and charcoal grey skinny jeans with low top Converse, and I like it more than I thought possible. All of it, right down to the knotted bracelets on his wrists and the grubby laces on his shoes. Suddenly my mouth feels like it's stuffed with cotton wool and I can't shake the feeling that something in the world has shifted fundamentally; as if sitting here at this bar, on this evening, is the very first moment of something life-altering and enormous. Suddenly time doesn't feel quite so linear.

'Cassie?' he says. His voice is deep and American and drawly. Him saying my name is the single most amazing thing I've ever heard. His eyes are brown with green flecks in them.

'Jesse,' I say, and I know I'm beaming. 'Hi.'

He stands in front of me for a few seconds, and we just look at each other as time slows right down and the whole room sort of mutes. And then, as if he remembers what to do next, he leans in and slings his arm around my shoulders in a quick hug and I swear I can feel a crackle of electricity surging through me. I am tingling everywhere he's touched me. Sound cranks back up again. Time returns to normal. I pat his back and as we pull away from each other I run my hands down his arms.

86

'You made it,' he says, pulling up another bar stool and waving the bartender over and ordering himself a beer. We are sitting so close our knees touch. Black denim against grey. Neither of us move away.

'I did,' I say. 'So did you. How mad is this?' But also, I want to add, how *rad* is this?

He runs a hand through his hair and rests it on the back of his neck whilst he looks around the bar, and that little movement does something to me. I crumple a little. In fact, I crumple a lot. I have turned to mush. Inside, I am wet, mulchy papier-mâché, and I have to work hard to keep it together and not whimper. I sip my wine and force myself to look away.

'Yeah, crazy, huh? When I heard the other guy dropped out I figured why not? I could do with the vacation.'

Playing two gigs and here for less than a week. Some vacay.

His drink arrives and we clink our glasses and both take long sips. How is us being here having a drink together like this even remotely possible?

'So, how was your gig?' I ask. 'Who were the band? You never told me.'

'Some girl band who call themselves Kitten Tricks,' he says.

I laugh. I can't help it. Kitten Tricks. They're huge here but it's like he's never heard of them. It's funny.

'I'm sorry,' I say. 'I shouldn't laugh, but they're only the hottest girl band here right now.'

'Yeah, it was a sell-out show, so I gathered they weren't exactly unheard of. But they are back home. I mean, after I got the call my sister-in-law and I had to do some research. And I haven't done anything on that scale for years. It was cool, though, you know?'

Not having ever played so much as a recorder on stage, I don't actually, but I nod like I do and he carries on, 'I've done sessions for so long, it made a nice change.'

'I'll bet,' I say. He gazes at me intently and I begin to feel a little self-conscious.

'You're staring at me,' I say, pushing my hair out of my face.

'I was trying to figure out if I recognize you, other than from off the internet. Since… well, you know, the Franko thing.'

'And do you?'

He shakes his head. 'No. I don't think so.'

'Because, technically,' I hold up my index finger to reiterate the point. '*Technically* this is not the first time we've met.'

Sweet days, Cassie, what the bloody hell are you doing? He knows I liked Franko, but coming across as a mega-fan who never grew up is definitely not cool. Rachel would shake me if she saw this. I'd be hauled off to the ladies for stern words.

He laughs. 'I did wonder, hence trying to place you.'

'I mean, I didn't expect that you would be able to. It was years ago. Thirteen, maybe fourteen. And you must have met loads of girls every day. What with being famous and everything.'

God, first hint of a moment's silence and I'm running my mouth like there's a gun to my temple. I'd be a shit spy.

He looks into his glass, and I think I see his cheeks colour a little.

'Ha, well, there were a few, that's true enough.'

But none of them are sitting here now, I think, smugly. *Sucks to be them*.

'I did get backstage once though.'

'You did? No shit! How did you manage that?'

He really doesn't remember. Not even a little bit. We'd had a chat and I'd sat next to him and turned my body towards him and Travis took a photo. It was so important to me, and he doesn't remember at all. A hairline crack appears in my stupid, irrational heart.

'Erm, I don't think the security guard gave much of a shit. He just let us through. Probably his last day.' I shrug in what I hope is a cute and whimsical sort of way and sip more of my wine. Jesse laughs.

'And did it live up to your expectations?'

I giggle, 'It made my life. Up to that point at least. So, do you get recognised a lot?'

He ponders this for a moment. Wrinkles up his nose. Wraps his hand around his glass, disturbing the condensation.

'Literally never. It actually hasn't happened in years. I mean, outside the industry. And even then, bands starting out now don't have a clue about Franko… But I like it that way. I like being able to come and go and not have to worry about disguising myself or watching for cameras when I need to run errands. I like normality, always did.'

'Oh, yeah that makes sense,' I agree.

'I have to tell you, it made me laugh when you asked about me using a different name to check in here,' he continues, chuckling.

'Well, what do I know about all that?' I ask, slightly embarrassed. Now that we're here, it seems so obvious. I'm laughing, but I know I'm blushing a little. He brushes his index finger down my forearm, absentmindedly, as if touching me that way is a normal interaction between the two of us. As if it happens all the time. I stare at the trail of goosebumps on my skin and wonder if he's noticed.

'I'm just kidding, Cassie,' he smiles.

'So, I have a little confession to make,' I say.

'Oh yeah?' He looks a bit worried about what I might be about to say.

'I didn't realise until this morning that I hadn't replied to you about this.'

'Wait, what?'

'Yeah, sorry about that,' I say. 'I couldn't think of anything coherent to say when I got your message about coming here, so I thought I'd sleep on it, and then I guess I'd forgotten I hadn't replied.'

'I kinda thought you'd decided not to,' he says.

'Oh, God, no! No way!'

'Well, I'm glad about that. I feel like this trip is immeasurably better for it.' And then, before I can reply, or process what he's just said, he adds, 'hey, are you hungry?'

'Maybe. What are you thinking?'

'I'm going to do nothing to challenge the American stereo-type here, but I could really, and I mean *really*, murder a burger.' He grins at me again. It's glorious. Heartbreaking. And somehow breaks any remaining ice there might have been. Melts it away. A burger. Probably with fries. Nothing fancy or starry about a burger at all. Hell, I could probably go for a burger. He picks up a sticky, dogeared menu from the bar and scans down it. 'Do you want to stay here, or...'

I look around. There's still only us and that one other couple. 'We should definitely go somewhere else,' I say, getting a flash of inspiration. 'In fact, it's your lucky day. I know exactly where to go, and it's just over the river from here. Fattest burgers ever, with pretty much whatever you like stuffed in there. Even mozzarella sticks. We should probably go soon if we want a table though.'

'Sounds awesome. We'll go right after we're done with these,' he says, nodding at our drinks.

The air is cooler when we leave. We walk slowly across the bridge to the north bank of the river, dodging a taxi as we cross the road, and cut down an alley which opens out into a wider road lined with restaurants and quirky independent shops. It's pretty. Festoon lights hang from trees, illuminating the street, and little groups of people are dotted outside pubs, their drinks in hand. I've taken us on foot partly because London is perfect at this time of year, and I want to show it off, but mainly because of the way it feels to be with him. We walk closely, and sometimes his rolled up shirt sleeve brushes against my arm. Sometimes the way we look at each other, and the things we say to each other, are flirty. Sometimes, when we touch, our reactions are slightly awkward, and I don't want to forget a second of it.

At the far end of the street is the restaurant and he holds the door open for me. *How nice*, I think. *How chivalrous. How nicely brought up. Mum would love him.* We're seated by a window looking out on to the street. The place is dimly lit with framed vintage posters hanging on exposed brick walls, and mismatched tables and chairs. Tiffany lamps hang low from the ceiling giving off a cosy glow. They serve remarkably strong frozen margaritas from a slush ice machine. I'm on my second before the food arrives, alternating between that and water because the edges of everything are becoming a little frilly.

'Is this not the most insane burger ever?' I say, between bites, amazed I'm able to eat anything at all. A splodge of burger sauce dribbles down my finger and I wipe it off on a napkin, and stuff a chip in my mouth. Mum would be horrified.

'Definitely. Way better than dinner last night. This burger...' he holds it up for me to see. Melted cheese oozes out between the meat and the bun. A slice of pickle threatens to fall out on to his plate. '...is incredible. Everything here is incredible.'

'*Every*thing, hmm?' I say, without even attempting to stop myself. He looks at me and then away again. He blinks and the way his eyelashes close and open again remind me of butterfly wings. When he looks back the hairs on my neck stand up and I can't think of any other time that someone has had this effect on me. 'What was dinner last night?' I ask, and my voice is hoarse.

'Room service at two in the morning,' he says, and we don't break eye contact. In my peripheral vision I see him move his free hand a fraction towards mine, but he stops himself and for a second I wonder if he'd meant to take it. I want him to. I wouldn't pull it away.

'Can I get you guys anything else?' The voice is chirpy and cheerful. Our waitress is beaming down at us with an electronic tablet in her hand. *Girl! Read the room. Can't you see I'm trying to make this deeply beautiful man fall in love with me? Can't you tell I'm wooing him with burgers and eyelash flutters? Are you aware you ruined A Moment?*

'Not for me,' I say, pulling another napkin out of the chrome holder and dabbing my mouth. Jesse shakes his head. Now things are quieter between us, like our momentum is slowing. Like neither of us knows what to say next. I watch a group of people drinking beer outside a pub across the road.

'Hey, it's such a nice evening,' he says, when we've finished. 'Do you feel like taking a walk?'

'Love to,' I reply.

We head back the way we came, but turn right at the bridge and veer off along the Thames embankment for a while, past an Olympics-themed shindig on a party boat. Across the water, the lights of the Oxo Tower and the South Bank light up the skyline. Further down the river, the London Eye trundles slowly around, the pods lit up bright blue.

'So,' I say, nudging his arm as we stroll along, 'how's London working out for you so far? Glad you came? Think you might come back?'

He stops suddenly, leaving me walking ahead, but grabs hold of my arm, and I pivot around on my heels until I'm facing him. My huge handbag swings into his legs. He steadies me, and we are close now. So close. My heart is in my mouth; it's beating in my ears. I can hear my own blood. And I can't look at him in case he can see exactly how suddenly scared I am.

'Cassie,' he says. It's almost a whisper, and he looks a little nervous, too. Now my entire body feels woozy, as if someone is pulling at a thread of me and I'm unravelling from the inside out. Because I know exactly what's coming. I've played it out hundreds of times in my head at various points in my life. Countless times when I was a teenager, obviously, but over the last few weeks as well. It's as if I'm living out my very own romcom, what with the river, and the lights, and the slightly nervous way we are around each other. It's all completely perfect, and I lean back against the embankment wall, gripping it so hard I am sure my knuckles have turned white. He tucks my hair behind my ear and I am done for.

I close my eyes and he presses his lips against mine. I loop my arms around his neck and he exhales against my cheek as the kiss deepens, and all I can think of is that I am being kissed by Jesse Franklin. Jesse Franklin has his tongue in my mouth and his hands on my waist. I have Jesse Franklin's hair twisted around my fingers. I can feel the curve of his neck under my hand. If sixteen-year-old me could see this, she'd go bananas.

He pulls away and runs a hand through his hair, looking nervously past me, out on to the river.

'I… I just… I'm—'

'About time,' I say, cutting him off. 'I've been waiting for you to do that all evening.' He looks visibly relieved. 'I mean, I've wanted to kiss you all evening too, but I don't think I'd have been able to stand it if you'd told me to piss off.'

'I wouldn't have told you to piss off,' he grins.

'Good to know,' I laugh and look down at the pavement between us. He takes one of my hands, and I watch as our fingers interlock.

'Come back with me. To the hotel. Right now,' he says and I gulp. Bloody hell, Rachel was right on the money. 'I just figured, you know, we're having a good time,' he pauses and studies my reaction. 'Nothing has to happen if you don't want it to. We can just… hang out. I don't know.'

Oh, please. What a line. Yes he *does* know. We *both* know. If I go back to that hotel with him, we are definitely going to have sex, and I am one hundred percent down for that. 'Sure. Why not? Let's do this.'

Jesse's expression changes again, and his eyes flick over me in a way they haven't before, but I can tell just from that cursory glance that he wants me very badly, and it's very, very arousing. And I also know, from the reaction I've just had, that he is going to absolutely ruin me for anybody else.

I reach my arms around his neck again and we kiss some more and this time it's positively drenched with anticipation. This time it's not tentative at all. This time his hands slide down from around my waist over my bum and back up my sides, pulling up my top until it's almost at my bra. *Dude*, I think, *we are in the middle of the street. There is traffic, and there are people, and this ain't no peep show.*

'Oi oi!' an oiky lad yells from the window of a Transit van stopped at traffic lights. 'Get a room!'

With my arms still around Jesse's neck, I flip my middle finger up in his general direction, and then there is laughter and wolf-whistling as they move off. Time to take this somewhere less public.

'Hotel?' he says, his mouth still on mine, and I nod. 'Jesus Christ, *yes*,' I breathe.

Chapter Thirteen

Cassie

The entire walk back to the hotel is hurried and humming with nervous energy and a *lot* of sexual tension. By the time we get through the lobby and into the lift you could cut the air with a knife. He jabs at the buttons for the fifth floor and the doors close painfully slowly, and as I lean back on the hand rail I decide there's no one in the world I have ever wanted more in my life. We have a cliché lift kiss, and he holds my wrists up above my head and my ring clinks against the mirror.

Outside the hotel room door, he reaches into the pocket of his jeans and pulls out a keycard. The tiny light on the door flashes green and as it clicks open he takes my hand again and pulls me inside. As soon as it slams shut all the sound from outside mutes and it's like a vacuum. And my nerves have gone as well, broken up and scattered to fragments of nothing because something about the way we are around each other just seems to fit. I drop my handbag and kick off my shoes and now he's standing by the edge of the bed, and I go to him. Pushing him down on to it, I climb on to his lap, our faces inches apart.

'Hi,' I whisper. I push his shirt down his shoulders and he pulls it off and throws it to the floor behind me.

'Hi.' He lifts my top over my head and I shake out my hair and he stares at the flimsy black netting of my bra, and if I could high-five this morning Cassie for a choice so obviously well made, I would. Now his hands are all over me and he's kissing my neck, just under my ear, and along my collarbone, and dragging my bra strap over my shoulder and down my arm.

And then he flips me on to the bed and we're making out like teenagers, and I like the weight of him on me, like the way his skin smells and the hardness of his body against the softness of mine after we've grappled with his t-shirt and pulled it off. Like how our limbs are tangled up and our faces are mashed together and the contrast of his dark hair against the crisp white bedding. I reach down and unbutton my jeans and wriggle a little in what I hope is an encouraging way and suddenly he's off me and the coolness from the air conditioning hits my skin again. He's pulling them off me now, agonisingly slowly, and all I can do is stare. They land in the ever-growing pile of our discarded clothes on the floor and just when I think he's going to remove his own and fuck me all the way into next week, he kneels down on the floor and pulls me down the bed until my legs hang over the edge.

'So,' he says. 'These panties.'

'What about them?'

'Are they, like, sentimental?'

'No.'

'Could you replace them if you wanted to?'

'Er, yeah, probably,' I say, beginning to wonder if he's got some sort of kinky knickers fetish. But he yanks them off me instead and I distinctly hear the fabric rip at the seam. Good grief. Blown together. 'Oh,' I say. 'I don't have any others. With me. I mean, I have others. But just not here. Felt like bringing some might have been a tad presumptuous.'

Shut up, Cassie, shut up, shut up. Shut. Up.

'Did you?' he asks. He doesn't believe me. I can tell by his glinty, smirky eyes.

'Maybe,' I say, giggling. 'Is that your signature move?'

'Nope,' he says, shaking his head. He balls them up and tosses them behind him and I lie there, staring up at the ceiling now, because I didn't foresee *this* level of intimacy, and yet, there he is, my teenage crush, bass player from the band I loved fourteen years prior, inching up my thighs, getting closer and closer to

96

my very naked vagina and I *think* that might just make me a bit of a groupie. Right on!

In any case, he shows me what I suspect might be his signature move and it's not long before I'm a spent woman, trembling and laughing with my breath still hitching and my hands over my face.

'You're fucking ace,' I laugh, and he grins at me because he *knows*. He sits on the edge of the bed, back to me, rummaging in a duffel bag, finding a condom, and I notice two things. One, he's got rid of his jeans and his pants. When did he do that? And how didn't I see? Was I too busy seeing stars and biting my fist, or is he actually Houdini? They're tight jeans, as well, I noticed that at the bar downstairs. He looked good in them. I liked the shape of his thighs in them. How they clung to him. It was very, very lovely. And two, he has a constellation of moles scattered across his back. Like they've been thrown there, haphazardly. I want to trace my fingers over them. Join them up with imaginary lines. Kiss every single one of them. He turns back towards me, and the moment has passed.

He scoots up the bed towards me and we get under the covers, and face each other and kiss again, except this time there's a whole lot more touching, and my bra is removed and flung across the room, and he rolls on to his back.

'Can we switch off the light?' I ask, and I don't really know why. He has seen every single inch of me without clothes on, but something makes me want us to do this in the dark.

'Uh huh.' He nods, reaches back and hits the switch and now it's dark in here and all I can make out are the lines of his features and the shape of him illuminated by the glow of the moonlight. And finally, this thing that I never truly thought would happen, does, and it's perfect.

Afterwards, I pull the duvet right up over my face to my eyes, and I watch as he disappears off to the bathroom. There's the sound of a tap being turned on, and then off again, and the metallic shudder of a pedal bin. And when he returns there's an awkward couple of seconds where I make a big show of not looking.

'Well,' I say, 'that was an unexpected turn of events.'

'I guess it was.'

I scoot over and turn on to my side as he climbs in next to me. 'But, unexpected in a good way, right?'

'Of course. The best way.'

He turns on to his side and slings an arm across my hip, pulling me a little bit closer.

'You're beautiful, Cassie,' he says, looking right into my eyes. 'You know that?' And I think, if they tested my oxytocin level right at this second, it'd be off the chart.

I trace my index finger from his chin all the way down his chest to his stomach and make circles there with my fingertips. He wrinkles up his nose and I pull my hand away.

'Sorry,' I say.

'You don't have to stop,' he says. 'I'm just ticklish, is all.'

I replace my hand. Make infinity signs. 'Are you really? That's fun to know.'

'I probably shouldn't have told you that.'

'I think I'd have figured it out, eventually.'

I shift closer still and kiss him again, softer this time, less insistent and frantic, though inevitably it becomes that way and leads to more and soon he pushes his thigh between mine, and leans over me.

'I think you're probably going to need another one of those,' I say, nodding towards the little pile of silver packets on the nightstand. It doesn't escape me that there are quite a lot of them. Pre-empted? Was it *really* an unexpected turn of events?

'Uh huh, yep, I think so,' he says. And this time the vibe is different, and we look at each other the entire time, through the silvery darkness. And my fingernails dig into the flesh on his back when I come. And he pushes my hips right down into the mattress when he does. And he kisses the part where my shoulder turns into my neck and I stroke back his sweaty hair and in my heart I know I'm completely in love with him.

'So probably not *that* unexpected, then?' I whisper, after a few minutes.

'What do you mean?'

'Well, you seem to have rocked up, excuse the pun, pretty well prepared for this.' I pat his back and gesture between us and around the room. 'Did you actually just think I was a sure thing?'

He sits up and studies me and I don't know what he's thinking.

'Literally not at *all*.' He raises an eyebrow. 'But, would it have been better if I hadn't?' I shake my head. 'And we'd have had the awkwardness of finding a late night pharmacy and… picking something up.'

'Pretty sure I saw a vending machine down the corridor,' I say, giggling.

'Well either way, that's okay then,' he says. I stretch myself out and then curl back into him and close my eyes and as I'm falling asleep I try to memorise all of this; imprint it on my brain so I can hold on to it forever.

Chapter Fourteen

Jesse

There's a red standby light on the TV and I've been staring at it since I woke up. I don't know for how long exactly, but long enough for it to be the only thing I can see in here now. On the nightstand, my phone lights up and I reach over for it. But it's just an email, and not an important one.

Four thirty-two a.m. Next to me, Cassie stirs and moves. The slight frizziness of her hair giving way to the outline of her neck and her shoulders. The shape of her underneath the sheets. Curled up, facing the window. The calmest she's been since I sat down opposite her in the bar downstairs and even in sleep she shifts and fidgets. I like it, though, the fidgeting. It didn't feel nervous, more enthusiastic and energetic. And I like the way she gesticulates and gets really animated when she talks, and how, when she's recounting something funny, she puts her hand over her mouth and laughs as she's talking and her eyes light up and the corners crease into folds.

Now she shifts on to her back and turns her head a little to the side. She brushes her arm against mine and reaches for my hand, like she's checking I'm still here. She's not really asleep after all. Not deeply, anyway. She did this a lot throughout the evening, kept brushing her arm against mine as we walked along, and I'd assumed it was accidental, until it became apparent that it was almost certainly deliberate. And as we hurried back here, she squeezed my hand as we waited for the lights to change.

There are other things I like about her, too. That ass in those pants, for example. Oh my god, and out of them. *Especially* out of them. I'm only human. Those pants are now in a heap on the floor by the bed, next to her top. And also the contrast of her skin against her black, lacy, somewhat see-through underwear. That was absolutely *not* every-day underwear. I've seen my fair share of women's underwear in my life and I know sex panties when I see them. These were they. *Were* being the operative word. I'm not even sorry.

Which brings me back to the red standby light on the TV. And how I'm lying here, thinking about all the things I've learned about her tonight and forcing myself to remember the one thing I already knew before all this happened: that she was a Franko fan all those years ago.

Which means she could so easily have been one of those girls Dad kept us away from. Fans were off limits, tarred as untrustworthy girls who wanted something from us. And when Adam was caught making out with one, the ban was extended, arbitrarily, to include pretty much all girls. It's a wonder any of us ever managed to develop normally functioning attachments to anyone.

I make myself think about that and consider it carefully because I want to work out if it makes any kind of difference at all to me. I always knew that about her and yet I still went out of my way to make all *this* happen, when usually I'd give anyone and anything Franko related a wide berth. Before, I would never have dreamed of hooking up with someone who was in any way tangled up in that part of my life. So on that basis alone I don't think it does.

I am acutely aware, though, that this room is like a sort of bubble, entirely devoid of any kind of reality for either of us, and in a few hours the bubble is going to pop and give way to real life again. She'll go back to her everyday, and I'll get on a plane. So I guess the only way to really tell is to see whether I'll *still* feel like this or not after she's gone.

Cassie turns over. She half opens her eyes and kisses me again, but she's sleepy and it doesn't go anywhere. Within less than a minute she's fallen back to sleep. My eyes begin to feel heavy.

–

There's a distinct absence of her the next time I wake up, an empty space where she was. A dip in the mattress. Her clothes are still on the floor, her shoes still kicked off by the bathroom door. I reach my hand across and the bed's still warm. I turn my head and she's by the window, peering out at the day with a sheet draped around her.

'Hey, you,' I say sleepily, watching her from under the covers. She turns around. Tightens the sheet in her fist.

'Hey *you*,' she says.

I flick my hair out of my face and pat the empty spot on the bed.

'Whatcha doin' up there?'

'About to head out to a toga party. Isn't it obvious?' She gestures at the swathes of fabric around her.

'Yeah? Forget the party and come back to me,' I say, my voice heavy with sleep. 'Leave the toga.'

–

'Hey, Cass,' I say, quietly, after we made the morning last as long as possible. She's running her thumb across my collarbone and I'm tracing my fingers up and down her spine. There are goose pimples on the top of her arms.

'Mmmhmm?' she says, leaning up on her elbows. There are specks of make-up in the corners of her eyes.

'So… I'm going to have to get going in a bit.'

It's categorically *not* what she wanted to hear. Her eyes flicker around and she sits up and pulls the sheets over her.

'Oh, okay,' she says, like she's weighing the words up in her head.

'It's just… I have a rehearsal for tonight, and then a sound check and stuff… I'm sorry.'

'No, it's fine,' she says, but I don't believe her, because now she's looking down at her hands. This was not how I wanted things to be. I'd ditch everything to spend the day with her if I could. It'd be so easy, but it doesn't work like that. You're only as good as your last gig, and it's not cool to dick people around. 'I expect you'll be going home soon, won't you?' she says, quietly.

I shift a little, and she hugs her knees to her chest.

'My flight's tomorrow morning,' I confirm, almost apologetically. But she knew this was the deal. I was very explicit in telling her I only had the Friday evening free. 'I actually have a stupidly busy few weeks.' I don't know why I'm going into this level of detail. It sounds like I'm blowing her off, and I'm not. 'A load more sessions, one in New York next week, and then back to San Francisco…' I trail off.

'Sounds like you have a busy life,' she says and I watch her face for a few seconds to see if I can figure out what she's thinking, and now it's uncomfortable and not at all how I want to remember her when I think back on this.

'Yeah, often,' I say before leaning over and kissing her forehead, 'I'm going to go take a shower.'

When I come out she's sitting on the edge of the bed, dressed and ready to leave and I'm surprised.

'I took that as my cue to get moving,' she says, flashing a wholly unconvincing smile. 'I think I'll probably go in a bit. Leave you to it.'

'I didn't mean for you to rush off,' I say. I didn't. I have a few bits and pieces to get done but I'm not leaving for a little while, and whatever this is, is exactly what I wanted to avoid.

Now she's telling me she doesn't want me to be late and that she understands I have somewhere to be and all I can do is nod. She stands up and runs her hands over her thighs, wishes me well for tonight, and turns to leave.

What am I doing? If she walks out of here now I'm scared it might snuff out the spark. What if I let her go and she thinks I didn't do anything to try and stop her? What if she leaves this hotel room now and I never see her again?

'Can I call you later?' I say. 'Probably not today, but tomorrow, before I go.' The words are out before I even knew I was going to say them.

She looks surprised for a second, and then composes herself.

'Err, yes, if you like.' She writes a number on a pad of note paper, leaves it on the nightstand, and turns to go. 'So... bye,' she says, and she's got her hand on the door handle. This is beyond awkward.

'Look, Cassie, wait. Are you sure everything's okay? I feel like maybe it's not. I don't know?' And the last of her resilience crumbles. It's the first time she's shown any vulnerability at all. She's definitely more fragile than she makes out. She lets go of the door and shoves her hands into the pockets of her jeans, takes a breath, blinks really slowly and chews her bottom lip.

'Look, I get it if this was just a one night thing, and I know how crazy this is with the distance and how different our lives are. But if you're not going to call me, don't tell me that you will. Just... please don't mess me around, yeah?'

'I wasn't going to,' I say. 'I don't know how any of this is going to play out, but if there wasn't something there, then none of last night would have happened.'

I mean it, as well. I don't need to travel halfway around the world to get laid. If there hadn't been any chemistry, we'd have had that drink and maybe gone to dinner and that would have been that.

She smiles at me. It looks genuine, but I can't be completely sure. 'Okay.'

'So, I'll call you. I promise. I like you. This has just thrown me for a loop, and I didn't come here expecting that. Keep your phone with you tomorrow, and Cassie,' she looks up from the floor and into my eyes for the first time since we were having sex just half an hour earlier. Hers are gray-blue. Wide. Beautiful. I want to look into them every day. 'I'm sorry I can't spend more time with you now. Would that I could, but this is my job, and the biggest part of my life, you know?'

'I know that,' she says, nodding her head. 'I get it.'

I wrap my arms around her and we kiss one last time. A typical goodbye kiss. She presses her nose into my t-shirt and breathes deeply, and then she pulls away and starts along the corridor. She doesn't look back.

After she's gone, the room feels different somehow. Dimmer. Cooler. Duller. I might just get something to eat and then head to Hammersmith early because I'm not sure I really want to be in here.

Outside, Cassie crosses the street and stops. She fishes around in her purse for something – headphones – puts them in her ears and carries on walking. She doesn't look up. She's gone back to her real life, and when I turn away from the window I've gone back to mine. The bubble has popped.

Chapter Fifteen

Cassie

Instead of making a right out of the hotel and heading straight back down into the tube station, I turn back towards the river, cross the road and duck down the steps on the bridge to the South Bank. I walk past the Tate Modern and Shakespeare's Globe and the *Golden Hinde* replica, taking in lungfuls of fresh air, and cutting down a side street to get to Borough Market, where I weave through the crowds to find a cup of coffee. Drink in hand, I amble over the bridge and into the tube station at Bank.

And all the way home I replay the last fourteen or so hours over and over in my head, leaning against the glass partition by the train doors and analysing everything that happened in minute detail as the train rumbles west. *Not just* the glorious, glorious sex, but the little things as well. All the incidental touches and the way we continued conversations we'd started online. The anecdotes about what it was like being in Franko. How once, early on, Adam had snapped three guitar strings and it threw them all off. How it turned out all the stories were true, and the change was life-altering for a kid born and raised in the Midwest, but now he can't imagine living anywhere other than the OC. How genuinely interested he was when I told him how desperate I am to peer down into the Grand Canyon, and feel spray from Niagara Falls on my face, and visit Machu Picchu, and the pyramids at Giza, and see the carnival in Rio, and watch the northern lights dance across the sky. How, most weekends,

I like to take myself off, pick somewhere on the tube map, and have a mooch around a part of London I haven't been to, or would otherwise have no reason to visit.

And I remember how I felt just before he kissed me and I was just waiting for it to happen, and knowing that it would, with my head tilted back and my eyes closed and my fingers grabbing on to the embankment wall like I might collapse and fall if I let go of it.

Only an hour earlier he'd said that he *liked* me, and that he'd felt it, too. Those wild sparks and that palpable, reactive chemistry between us, obvious from the very beginning. Popping and igniting over and over, like a lit splint in a test tube of hydrogen.

So why am I not reassured by all that? There's something holding me back and I know what it is, too; leaving that hotel room. There was no easing back in slowly. I went from being with him, where everything was lovely and I had exactly what I wanted, to a mucky train heading back to Shepherd's Bush, and that's one hell of a comedown.

And there's a cynical part of me that doesn't know if I really believe he'll call. Perhaps now we are apart the reality of it all seems slightly less vibrant and magical than it did whilst we were snogging under the lights of the Oxo Tower. How easy would the trade-off be between saying what I wanted to hear and getting what he wanted? How simple to fly away and delete me from his life altogether. And if he does, there won't be anything I can do about it. I don't like the heavy feeling in my chest. I want to remember him telling me I'm beautiful, snuggled up and sleepy. *You're beautiful, Cassie, do you know that? I want you, Cassie. I like you, Cassie, and it's thrown me.*

By the time I get home, all my adrenaline has ebbed, and a hangover has set in. I grab a packet of crisps on my way upstairs, flop on my bed and make lists in my head of all the possible ways this can go whilst I eat. Just like I had yesterday at work, before we'd met. Before all this. I only manage half the crisps. Prawn cocktail was not a good choice. I feel a bit sick. At some point in the afternoon, I fall asleep.

My phone's vibrating in my handbag and it startles me awake. I have no idea what time it is, but it's light outside and I'm disoriented. I don't *think* it's Sunday, but I can't be sure. Suddenly I am wide awake, I tear my bag open and grab for the phone before it stops ringing. It's Rachel. My heart sinks.

'Where have you been?' she shrieks down the phone as I answer it. 'I was beginning to wonder if you'd be found washed up at the side of the Thames somewhere. Why didn't you text me? I've been pacing.'

'Well, you can stop pacing. I've been napping,' I tell her, pinching the bridge of my nose and glancing over at the clock on my radio. Four thirty-three. Wow, I've been asleep for hours. 'I'm fine. One hundred percent not drowned in the river. It's all good.'

There's a silence on the other end of the line.

'Well?' she says eventually, and, I think, somewhat tentatively. 'How was it? What's he like?'

I scoot back on my bed, leaning against the wall.

'Do you mean in general? Or just what he's like in bed?'

'Fuck! Called it! Tell me everything. No, wait, the shagging. Argh, no, I need it in chronological order. But get to the good bits fast.'

So I start at the beginning, but she doesn't care about what we talked about at the bar, or what we ate for dinner, or that two slushy margaritas is almost certainly one too many after two large glasses of wine and I'm sort of hanging today. She definitely wants to hear about when things got saucy and she hurries me along. We go over and over giant sections of my night, combing through details, like watching a favourite part of a movie on VCR, or listening to a cassette on repeat. Rewinding and analysing again and again, like we used to do with their songs. Pulling apart the riverside kiss and exactly why he had a jumbo pack of condoms in his bag, as if people just carry that many around with them on the regular, and how everything that happened inside that hotel room was Very Much a Good Thing.

And then we get to this morning, and I begin to feel like I'd been a little petulant. Like I'd been a bit of a baby about the whole thing. It's not like I didn't know he had a gig today. He'd always been upfront about it.

'Well. Isn't all that exactly what you wanted?' she asks. 'Didn't I tell you that would happen? I don't know what the problem is.'

'The problem is, I just can't see how this can end well for me, realistically.'

'Maybe it will, and maybe it won't. For now, though, I think you should just go with it.'

'What if he doesn't call me though?'

'Pessimist. Stop it. I didn't get the impression you got an arsehole vibe from him,' she says. 'But if he doesn't, you'll always have the memory of his face between your thighs.'

My pulse races again and I let out an involuntary squeak.

'Sooo, are we still on for tomorrow?' she asks, slowly, in case I've forgotten, 'Covent Garden. Brunch. Wedding shoe shopping.'

'Of course.'

'Mimosas?'

'I might just stick to coffee. Not sure I want a drink again any time soon.'

'Have a can of Coke. Put some vodka in it, that'll see you right.'

'God. No. Hideous,' I groan.

'Get Jon to make you a cheese toastie.'

I contemplate this. Carbs and fat and salt sound brilliant. 'Not a terrible idea.'

'I'll see you tomorrow.'

She hangs up and I rub my eyes and search my nightstand for paracetamol.

'Jon,' I yell from my bedroom door. There's a vice inside my head and it's squeezing my brain. I wince. 'Are you in?'

—

Sunday morning is dull, the bright blue skies of the previous week are shrouded in a blanket of white cloud. Friday night feels further away now, and the things that happened unreachable and almost dreamlike. There are no notifications on my phone but I turn up the volume anyway, and check that the vibrate function is still working. It's not leaving my side today, and it comes into the bathroom with me as I shower, and downstairs whilst I make coffee. I keep pressing the home button as I'm getting ready, worried that my hair dryer might drown out the ringtone. I hold it in my hand all the way to the station, but it stays silent.

I think, deep inside, I knew I'd miss the call. How else could it have gone? I step out of the busy tube station at Holborn, and reach in my bag for my phone. I wave it around in the air and curse at it as it takes ages to pick up any signal. I am just about to give up and toss it back in my bag when the jolty vibration of a notification makes the phone buzz. One new voice message. Nooo! As I shakily dial into my voicemail I hope against hope it was Rachel, but Rachel would have sent a text.

'*You have one new message,*' the posh, robotic voicemail lady says, and then he's talking. It's disjointed and he sounds a bit nervous, like it's thrown him that I haven't answered the phone.

'Hey Cassie, this is Jesse. Calling you like I promised. I'm at the airport, and...' there's a pause. 'Wow, really thought this would be easier... So, Friday was nice, huh? Didn't really feel like a one night thing. And I don't want it to be. I meant what I said about liking you, and I've been thinking a lot about that.' Another pause. 'Sooo... oh man, I so wish you'd answered your phone. I hope that you really were okay when you left. I just kind of bummed around for a bit and wished that we could have hung out for longer. It felt kind of weird in there after you'd gone.' He sighs down the phone. '*Any*way. I hope you're having a nice day, whatever it is you're doing. Tell me about it later, okay? Oh! They're calling my flight. I'm gonna have to wrap this up now. I'll talk to you when I get home. 'Kay. Bye.'

The message ends with voicemail lady advising me to listen again (press one) save the message (press two) or delete the message (press three) and I realise I am standing in the middle of the street in Holborn, with my phone pressed to my ear, and not giving a single fuck that I am getting jostled and bumped and tutted at by people. Right at this second I don't care about anything. I replay the message again as I cross the road, and again as I walk down towards the coffee shop where Rachel and I are meeting. Inside, I sit down and order – one latte with an extra shot, one cappuccino – and I listen to it some more whilst I wait, only stopping when the drinks arrive.

'So, I take it that was lover boy on the phone,' Rachel announces. She sits down opposite me and makes me jump. 'I was watching you for a moment from outside. Didn't want to interrupt,' she explains, pointing towards the window. 'You looked flirty, what with your hair-scrunching and the way you were leaning on your hand. How is he? Alright?'

'I wasn't on the phone,' I say. 'In fact, I missed the call. He called whilst I was on the tube, didn't he? But listen to this.' I pass her the phone and study her face as she plays my voicemail. She makes tiny movements with her eyebrows and her lips, and when it's finished, she slides the phone back across the table towards me.

'Bloody hell.'

'I know!' I breathe.

'He's... well, he seems quite taken with you, doesn't he?'

I nod and take a sip of my coffee.

'You must be a dynamo in the sack. What are you going to do now you have all this unfinished business?'

I shrug, 'I'll send him a message when I get home.'

'Is that it?'

'What else can I do? It's not as if he lives down the road, or even in the same country. He's flying back to California right this second. That's over five thousand miles away.'

'Meh, you should have gone to Heathrow.' She spoons the froth from her cappuccino into her mouth, and I think, *rats! I should have gone to Heathrow.* 'Anyway, I'm going to go right ahead and assume you're pretty keen on him too?'

I sigh, and lay my head down on my arm. 'Like you wouldn't believe.'

'Oh God,' she says. 'I *would* believe it. It's like ninety-eight all over again.'

'I couldn't stop staring. Actually, full on *staring*. I had to keep making myself stop because I think he noticed. And I felt so odd, but in a good way. Nervous but also really calm. Like it was…' I stop talking. I don't want to say it because it sounds a bit pathetic.

'Like it was…?' Rachel prompts.

'Like it was mapped out. Meant to be. Whatever,' I say, studying the grain of the wood on the tabletop. My eyes flick up to hers for her reaction, and to her credit, she doesn't laugh, or react negatively at all. She just looks back at me and chews her lip, and I feel compelled to carry on. 'But the whole way there I didn't really let myself think it might be reciprocated, in case it wasn't. I kept telling myself it would be a drink and maybe some dinner and that would be that, just in case that's all it was for him.'

'Cassie!' Rachel laughs, but there's a lick of exasperation there. 'None of what either of you did was subtle.'

I shift in my seat and play with the plastic wrapper from the biscuit that came with my drink. 'I meant the bit after the evening. What he said when I was leaving, and especially that message. I wasn't expecting that.'

'And yet, there it is. Look, he just likes you. It's both as simple and as complex as that. And can you stop putting him on some pedestal he doesn't even want to be on, please? You're overthinking this because he was a minor celebrity once upon a time and it sounds like he would absolutely hate that.'

'Okay, okay,' I say.

'Anyway, he said he was going to call you, so why wouldn't he? If he was just up for a one night stand with some bird off the internet there would have been no reason at all to ask for your number.' She slurps her coffee. 'It's not like you could easily have gone after him. Do you even know where he lives?'

'Somewhere near Los Angeles,' I say. 'Orange County.' I look at her and even though she's reassuring me, I feel a bit like I'm being told off. She puts her hand over mine and her engagement ring catches the light and reflections from the diamond dance across the table.

'If it's meant to happen, it will,' she says. 'So let it. You might want to downplay the Franko thing a little though. Obsessed fan doesn't exactly scream sexy.'

I look at her over the milky dregs of my coffee. 'And therein lies the reason I'm finding it hard to keep him off that pedestal. Because I know that if he wasn't Jesse from Franko, we'd never have even met. If he hadn't been in our favourite band, there is no way our paths would ever have crossed. Not when we were teenagers and certainly not now. And it's difficult to separate that and how it all just hit me when he walked into that bar...'

I stop talking. My head is muddled. Rachel can tell.

'You don't know that. You couldn't know that. If it's written in the stars you'd have found each other somehow. Anyway, tell me he's smoother in real life than on the phone,' she says, looking at me with doe eyes.

'Oh yeah, much, *much* smoother. He's very, very charming in real life. Held doors open and paid for dinner and everything.'

'Didn't you say he tried to cop a feel in the street and ripped your knickers to bits? Such a gentleman.'

'All in the throes of passion. If George has never fucked you with reckless abandon well then, more fool him.'

Rachel smirks. 'You're never deleting that message, are you?'

'Nope.'

'Can we talk wedding stuff now? George is being useless.' She looks tired suddenly. My head cranks into gear.

'Of course. Let's go. What's he not done?'

'Anything. He hasn't done *anything*. I finally badgered him into looking at the seating plan with me, but he got distracted after a few minutes and went off to mark exam scripts.'

She's tapping her foot against the table leg now, and it's making the whole thing tremble. In the space of thirty seconds she has morphed into a smaller, more fractious version of herself, and it worries me. Brides are meant to love wedding planning, but Rachel isn't loving this. 'It's three months away, Cassie. I have hardly crossed anything off my to-do list. Why is he being like this?'

'What a bloke,' I say, sniffing. 'Tell him if he doesn't muck in, he might find himself without an invite.' Rachel looks anguished, and I take her hand. 'Try not to worry. We'll cross off a chunk today. We'll find the shoes. And have you got your undies sorted? We can look for something that's going to knock his socks off if you like.'

'You're a godsend,' she says. 'Are you saying that because you need to replace your torn up knickers?'

I shake my head. Today isn't about me. 'Latimer Abbey isn't going to know what's hit it,' I tell her, reassuringly.

'That's the plan,' she says.

Chapter Sixteen

Jesse

The notification symbol is lit up on Facebook when I switch my phone back on at LAX, and I could jump in the air right now.

> Hey… I got your voicemail ;) I was on the tube. Sorry! Typical! I went out with Rachel to do wedding stuff. We talked about you…

> OK, so I was going to wait until you replied but that could be hours.

> I'm sorry if I seemed off when I left. I didn't mean to, but I didn't want it to end and I think you knew that. I like you too, and I also think you know that. So where does this leave things?

> Wow that was heavy. How was your flight?

After an eleven hour flight, it's precisely what I wanted to see, and I breeze through passport control and out to my car like nothing in the world can get me down. I feel like I know exactly how Tom Cruise lost his shit on Oprah's couch. Pretty sure I called the immigration officer 'buddy' after he welcomed me back into the country, and not even the hefty parking fee or the traffic on the freeway kills my buzz. I just sit there with my shades on and the windows down, enjoying the sun and this feeling of whatever it is that's all up in my insides. *Not even* Richard berating a group of teenagers on the beach from his balcony, or the lack of anything to eat in the house dampens my spirits. I order a pizza. The kid delivering it gets a twenty dollar tip.

I feel like a middle schooler all over again, passing notes between desks in class. *Do you like me? Circle one. Yes. No. Maybe.*

> Hey! The flight was fine but long and I have to go to NYC for a session tomorrow, and then straight on to San Francisco.

> Bloody hell, you weren't joking about being busy!

> Really wasn't. Did you think that I was?

> Noooo! Course not. I so want to see you again. I'm not sure how that's going to work though.

> I want that too. We'll figure something out, don't worry.

–

The week is peripatetic to say the least, and I'm back in San Francisco after my whistlestop session in New York. So far I've taken Nancy to see the sea lions down at Fisherman's Wharf, and I've watched a lot of Disney movies whilst wearing princess accessories. Today, Brandon is home and we're running errands. It's the first time I've properly spent with him since I arrived.

'So,' he says. He's coaxing Nancy down a slide at a play park three blocks away from their house. She looks reluctant. There's a line of small children forming behind her. 'How was London?'

'London was good, yeah.'

'Fast turnaround, though, did you find out why the other guy quit? Come on Nancy, you got this, baby.'

'No, and I didn't ask.' I hold my hand out for Nancy and she sits down and takes it. I pull her down the slide and she lands on her feet in the sand at the bottom.

'Back in the stroller for you,' Brandon says, scooping her up. 'It's time to go.' He straps her in and we head towards Starbucks. 'Did you do much whilst you were there?'

'I, err... no, not really.' It's hesitant. He stops and looks incredulously at me. I can't blame him really, I have a shit-eating grin all over my face.

'You, *err, no not really*? What does that mean?'

'It means I did the gigs, and not much else. I wasn't there long, I had to get back for your jingles, remember?'

'Sure. How did that go?'

'Yeah. Easy. They don't call me Jesse "One Take" Franklin for nothing.'

Brandon laughs. 'I didn't know anyone called you that at all. But anyway, back to London, you just stayed in your hotel room the entire time?'

'Of course not... I hung out. I went for a drink with the drummer. He seemed like a nice guy. His name was Ryan. Had a kid about the same age as Nancy. Oh, and I bought that Sleeping Beauty dress. Why all the sudden interest?'

'No reason in particular,' he counters. 'Just like to hear what you're up to. Why so defensive?'

'I'm not being defensive,' I say, quickly. Definitely too quickly. Almost, you might say, a little defensively.

'Yes. You are.'

'Alright, whatever you say,' I say, pushing my hands deep into my pockets. I can feel him watching me as we walk along. He stops as we turn onto California Street, pulls his baseball cap lower on his head and adjusts his shades.

'What's up, little bro? Worried someone is going to recognize you?' I'm kidding, but an album he produced *did* just go multi-platinum and it's definitely got him noticed. These days, Brandon is undoubtedly the most successful of all of us.

'Please,' he scoffs, shaking his head.

We grab a couple of coffees and the bits Lainey needed before heading back towards the house.

'So, all in, London was uneventful then?' he asks. *Jesus, let it go*, I think.

'Sure was,' I say lightly. There's that stupid grin again.

'Do we believe him, Nancy?' he says, leaning over the back of her stroller and ruffling her hair. 'No, we do not.'

'Do not,' she repeats. She squints up at us, and laughs. 'No, we do not.'

Later the same evening Lainey and I are chilling in the den. We're relaxing on their giant, L-shaped couch, with the TV on, but I'm not really watching it. Cassie is online, even though it's stupidly early in the morning for her. Is this how things are going to be now? She's changed her profile picture again, and this new one is a black and white shot of half of her face with her eyes all made up.

'Did you see that bit?' Lainey says, referring to something on the TV.

'Nah,' I say, not even looking up. I'm busy typing instead.

Hey you

There you are! How was New York?

Swift. I was back on the plane the same evening. I'm now visiting family I bailed on last week.

Was it worth the bailing though?

Absolutely.

Lainey leans over and tries to see my screen but I angle it away and try and style it out as if I'm shifting position.

'What are you doing?' she asks. 'Who are you talking to?'

How long are you in San Fran for?

Just til the weekend. Back to it after. What about you?

Erm... not sure if you remember but I'm not in San Francisco :-D

Haha! I knew that. I meant, how are things going? How's your job etc? Is it raining? Hang out with the Queen recently? Mary Poppins?

No rain this week, but there's still time. Things are good. I'm just working as normal. I've got a dress fitting for the wedding on Saturday. The Queen says hello. She popped by for a cup of tea yesterday evening as it happens. All very civilised. Mary couldn't make it.

'I'm not talking to anyone. I'm just looking at stuff on the internet. Amps mainly.'

I'm not looking at amps at all. I'm looking at *flights*. Someone's going to have to board a plane if we're to see each other again, so I'm scoping out the possibility of Cassie coming out here.

'Okay... It's just you keep smiling. Who knew amps could spark so much joy?'

'I keep smiling? Is that a bad thing? Should I not?'

'To *yourself*,' she laughs. 'Don't think I haven't noticed. You're doing it now!'

'I wouldn't dream of it. I know you see everything, Lainey-Lou. You're like the all-seeing eye of this family. If there's business to be known, you'll know it.'

'Exactly, so you might as well tell me yours now and get it over with.'

'Honestly, I don't know what you're talking about.'

'Sure you do.'

'No. I don't,' I say. She's right though, I can't keep a straight face for trying. She leans back on the cushions and sips her drink, eyeing me suspiciously, but she doesn't try and look at my screen again.

'I *will* figure you out, Jesse Franklin. You mark my words.'

'Consider them marked,' I say.

Bummer! So when did you say this wedding was again?

13th October. Why?

Cool. Just wondered. BRB getting eyeballed by Lainey.

'Hey,' I say, closing the screen of the computer. 'I need to buy something online. Credit card's in my room.'

'Alright.' Lainey looks incredulous. She doesn't believe me. I don't care. 'There are some chips in the cupboard next to the microwave, can you bring them in here before you go off to do whatever's so important on your computer?'

'Sure thing, Lainey,' I say.

Upstairs, I make my purchase using information I've gleaned from our conversations, mainly about the wedding dates and her full name for the ticket. Cassandra. I probably wouldn't have guessed that. It's impulsive and not really like me at all, especially not to check beforehand. But then, I've never been in this situation before, so maybe it is *exactly* like me and I just didn't know it before?

Hey can I call you on Sunday?

Of course! You can call me any time.

Will about midday my time be OK?

Yeah perfect. I promise I'll pick up.

–

We're having dinner on my last evening in San Francisco. I'm getting a late flight home in a while.

'It's been lovely to see you and spend some proper time,' Lainey says.

'Well, thanks for putting up with me, as always,' I say.

'It's hardly putting up with you,' she says. 'We love having you visit.' She passes over a bowl of mashed potatoes and I spoon some onto my plate. Brandon opens a bottle of wine and Lainey fills her glass with water instead. She pops a green bean into her mouth and chews. Nancy sticks her fingers in her potatoes and digs around.

'What are you looking for in there?' I ask her. 'Treasure?'

Lainey scoops some food on Nancy's fork and shovels it into her mouth.

'It's better if you use your fork, honey,' she says. 'You might find your treasure faster.'

We carry on eating, and there's a little chat, but not much. Brandon inhales his food and Lainey chastizes him for it. Nancy absolutely cannot be bothered with cutlery. I like being here. They make a nice family.

'You gonna tell us what happened in London then?' Brandon asks, as we're finishing up. I roll my eyes.

'Nothing happened in London. Why do you keep asking?'

Lainey takes his hand over the table and squeezes. 'Neither of us believe you, sweetie,' she says.

'You've been uncharacteristically chirpy,' Brandon continues. 'It's cool, but it doesn't seem like you.'

'Right? And he keeps grinning to himself. Did you notice that?'

'I definitely did. As soon as you mention the trip to London.'

'And he's had his nose in his laptop or his phone every single evening. Something's up, for sure.'

'Alright, enough. Firstly, it doesn't seem like me? What does *that* mean? Secondly, once again, nothing happened in London. It was just the buzz of playing live on that scale again, is all.'

This seems to shut them both down, and I am relieved. It's not that I don't want to tell anyone about Cassie. It's just that until I know for sure I am going to see her again, I'd rather keep things quiet. Lainey and Brandon look at each other for a few seconds before replying.

'It's not a bad thing,' Lainey says, quietly. 'It's just nice to see you happy. Whatever is making you that way.'

'Well, thanks,' I say.

We finish dinner and then I have to haul ass to SFO. And this time, as I leave LAX and get on to the 405, I wonder if the next time I do this Cassie will be in the car with me.

Chapter Seventeen

Cassie

On Saturday, I catch the bus over to Chiswick for a dress-fitting with Rachel, her sister Marie, and our uni pal Lauren. The shop's just off the high street and is basically Mecca for brides: racks and racks of bridal gowns, from bouncy meringues to sleek and fitted. Some with a lot of lace. Some plain and elegant. Every kind of accessory; ruched satin garters, sparkly tiaras and veils in all lengths. Jewellery and corsages. Shoes with decorative sparkles or flowers in ivory satin. High heels and kitten heels and flats. It's really quite the eye-opener. A one-stop shop for the bride who refuses to be easily overwhelmed. I had thought it perfect for Rachel, but after our coffee last week, I'm not sure she's as unflappable as she'd like to think.

We're rallied around, the fabric of our half finished dresses marked with tailor's chalk, pinned and measured. The fit and length have been adjusted as necessary, and I have to hand it to her, Rachel has done well for us. These dresses were a good choice: Shantung silk in teal with a Bardot neckline, a fitted bodice and a full, knee length skirt with layers of cream tulle petticoats peeking out from the under the hemline.

She's talking, animatedly, about her plans for us on the day. 'Dark, heavy eye make-up,' she's saying. 'But a nude lip. And we're going to sweep up their hair and pin in loads of little pearls.' She pushes up the sleeves of her cardigan and chews on a fingernail as if contemplating it.

The assistant sighs. She *really* loves her job.

'The perfect bridesmaids for the perfect bride,' she coos, and her accent is so affected with hyperbolic enthusiasm that I almost laugh. Rachel beams.

'I think the bouquets will really complement the dresses,' she continues, and I wonder if she's feeling more in control today because this is her domain. No one would expect George to have anything to do with bridesmaid dresses.

'Do tell,' Enthusiastic Assistant gushes.

'Purple freesias. With cream roses and sprigs of gypsophila,' Rachel says, still calm, because again, flowers are very much her thing, and the assistant nods as if this was absolutely the obvious choice.

'Oh, *gorgeous*,' she says. 'I almost wish I could be there.'

Marie shoots me a look, and I've known her long enough to know she can't wait to leave.

After our fitting, we go for tapas and wine.

'You all looked beautiful,' Rachel announces. She cuts a slice off a slab of tortilla. 'I got a bit emosh. Thank you, again, for agreeing to be my bridesmaids.'

'Get it all out now,' Lauren laughs. 'You don't want to ruin your eye make-up over us on your wedding day.'

'She won't,' Marie says, dryly. 'Can you pass me the squid?'

'I'm getting a bit nervous,' Rachel says, ignoring her. 'There's still so much to do and so little time to get it all done.'

'It's going to be amazing,' I tell her, patting her hand. 'And don't worry, we're all here to help with whatever you need.'

I'm wondering if she's going to admit she's feeling over-whelmed and ask for help so we can all chip in. But she doesn't say anything more, and I figure she won't want to let that mask slip too much. Her face changes again, and that tiny flicker of vulnerability is snuffed out.

'Ah, she's alright, aren't you, Rach?' Lauren says. 'She's not worrying.'

'I'm fine,' Rachel lies. 'Just pre-wedding jitters. We're all good. I have my wingwomen. It's more the build up, anyway, not the *day* so much. I couldn't imagine marrying anybody else, you know?'

'Not really,' Lauren says, flatly. 'None of us are even close to all this.' She looks at Marie and me in turn, like she wants some validation, and we both shake our heads.

'It's true what they say, when you find the one, you just know,' Rachel continues, dreamily. Then she looks at me pointedly. 'Isn't that right, Cass?'

Marie and Lauren turn to me and stare, expectantly, waiting for details I am nervous about sharing yet. It could all so easily fizzle out and I don't want to ever have to explain that.

'You got a new boyfriend?' Lauren asks.

'No, stop it.' I say. I'm embarrassed. And it's not even true, even if I do want it to be.

'Details, please,' Marie demands.

'*You*, especially, are going to love this, Maz,' Rachel giggles. I shake my head again. Skewer a square of potato on to my fork and use it to mop up the tomato sauce it came in.

'It's really not that big a deal, and it's sort of complicated anyway. *And* it's not even really a thing, so…'

'Oh it *so is* a big deal,' Rachel scoffs. 'She's met the love of her life, and it's definitely a thing. Do you remember, Marie? The *love* of her *life*!'

'What?' Lauren says, and I feel for her, because she didn't know us when we were sixteen, so she won't have a clue what it means to the rest of us. Rachel ploughs on.

'If I said the name Jesse Franklin to you, what would you think?'

'I'd wonder why you were bringing up the surly one in that boyband you liked once upon a time.'

Rachel stares at her sister, widens her eyes. Marie looks confused. 'Wait, *what*?'

'Exactly,' Rachel whispers, and I can feel my face flushing.

'Can someone please fill me in?' Lauren asks. 'Should I know who this chap is?'

Rachel carries on.

'Lauren, do you remember that band, Franko? Four of them. Brothers. Famous for five minutes back in ninety-eightish.'

'Not at all,' she says. 'I remember Hanson though.'

Marie is smirking. 'Don't feel bad, Lauren. Nobody remembers Franko.'

'Last Friday night Cassie went on a date with Jesse Franklin, who was the bass player in that band. When we were sixteen, she adored him. Worshipped the ground he walked on. I mean, really, she was completely in love.'

'You were, too, Rachel,' I interrupt. 'It wasn't just me. You loved Travis.'

'Yes, but this isn't about me,' she says.

'This sounds exciting,' Lauren giggles.

'Okay, we went out for dinner, and then… I stayed over with him, and he left me a voicemail before he left, and that's that.'

'Bloody hell,' Marie says. 'I've not thought about them in years. How did that happen?'

'He had some gigs here.' Rachel makes air quotes, which I'm not too sure about.

'Well, he did.'

'Yeah, but all I'm saying is that's a long way to go for two nights' work,' she says, dismissively.

'No,' Marie says. 'I mean, how did you get to meet him? You can't have just randomly bumped into him. I don't believe in coincidences like that.'

'Alright, a while ago, Rach and I looked them up on the internet.'

'Bit weird, but okay,' Marie says, and now she's beginning to irritate me.

'And then Jesse and I just got talking. And we talked quite a lot. As in, almost every day—'

'What did you talk about?' she interrupts again.

'Normal stuff,' I say. 'His job, my job, what we have been up to. Stuff I like, stuff he likes. You know. Regular things that people talk about.'

'I'm confused,' Lauren interjects. 'I think you missed some bits out. How did it go from that to you meeting up with him, and then you *having sex* with him? And more to the point, exactly how did you start talking in the first place?'

There are no flies on Lauren.

'It's probably fairly obvious how we ended up sleeping together,' I say. 'The same way people do all the time. As for how it all started, erm, I *may* have added him on Facebook, and he *may* have accepted that request.' I say this bit quickly and quietly, because I've basically just admitted that I shamelessly stalked him and tried my luck because he is Jesse Franklin. 'Then, he came to London for a couple of gigs, and asked if I wanted to hang out. So we did, and then… all… that… happened.' My face is burning and my mouth is drying out. I knock back some more wine. 'Bit warm in here, no?' I can feel them all staring at me.

'No,' Marie says. 'You're hot because you're all red. Also, that is a pretty bizarre story.'

'Well,' I say. 'It didn't seem at all bizarre last Friday night. Seemed pretty bloody marvellous actually.'

Marie holds up her palms. 'Consider me hushed,' she says. 'It's all very cute. I'm sure you'll end up living happily ever after. I'm sure you'll have herds of bass-playing children and all your dreams will come true. And I'm absolutely *convinced* Rachel doesn't wish this was happening to her and that little drummer boy she liked.'

'Hmm,' I say, and then to shut it down, 'top-up, anyone?'

'So, has George told you where he's taking you on honeymoon yet?' Lauren asks, helping me out by deflecting the attention back to Rachel. I am relieved.

'No! He's being completely evasive about it all,' she says, shaking her head. 'Won't talk about it at all.'

'Let's hope he's arranged it,' Marie says, and Rachel turns pale.

A little bit after eight on Sunday night my phone buzzes into life. I watch as his name flashes up on the screen. *Jesse Franklin*. Suddenly I'm nervous and excited all at once. I clear my throat and slide my finger across the screen to answer the call.

'Hi,' I say, and I hope I sound sultry and a little bit sexy. Like Emily Blunt or Thandie Newton.

'Hey.' My god, he definitely does. That accent. Lucky I'm sitting down. 'You good?'

'Really am,' I say, and I can't hide the smile in my voice. 'When did you get home and what did you get up to in San Francisco?'

'Yesterday evening,' he says. 'I was helping Lainey out, mainly, so I took my niece out a few times. We went to see the sea lions and I took her for a burger and to the park. Kid stuff, you know?'

Jesus, my ovaries. He's actually the best. Deeply gorgeous, talented and successful, *and* good with children. Fertilise me, please?

'Well, that's just lovely,' I say.

'Ah, I dunno. She's a nice kid. Fun to hang out with. She keeps it simple. Plus I felt bad.'

'What for?'

'I was visiting them for July Fourth when I got the call about Kitten Tricks and I kinda broke her heart a bit by not being there for the fireworks.'

'Sounds like you made up for it, though.'

'It's nice to talk to you, Cass,' he says, changing the subject suddenly, and he sounds a little less confident and self-assured than when he was talking about taking his niece to the park. It's almost as if he's a little bit nervous to tell me that.

'It's nice to talk to you, too.' I feel giddy again, like the first time we hugged in the bar, and the moment I knew we were going to kiss, and when he told me I was beautiful. *I want to talk to you all the time*, I think. I want you to talk to me about things you did in your days and about the things you did in your past and the things you wish for in the future. I want to be the first and last person you speak to every single day. I want phone calls to be the exception, not the rule. *I want to see you again. When can I see you again?*

'So, what were your weekend plans?' he asks.

'Just mooched today. But I had a dress fitting for the wedding yesterday.'

'Uh huh, so are you excited? Do you know much about it?'

'Yeah, it's going to be in a picturesque little church back near to where we grew up. Then the reception is at this old abbey a few miles away. Pretty standard. Photos. Dinner. Speeches. Dancing. Money behind the bar. Handsy best man. That sort of thing.'

'Pretty standard,' he laughs. 'That's a nice thing to say about your best friend's wedding.'

'Ah, stop it. I didn't mean it like that. It'll be gorgeous. They're very, very much in love.'

'How do you feel about the handsy best man though?'

'Eh, he's harmless. Bit gauche. He'll probably try to cop off with Lauren.' I don't want to tell him that he might well try to cop off with me too, and worse still, that the groom thinks it's a good idea.

'Is she another bridesmaid?'

'Yeah, there are three of us.'

'Awesome. October thirteenth, right?'

'Right. Good memory.'

'Ha. Well. It sort of segues nicely into what I wanted to talk to you about,' he says, and again, that cautiousness is back. Again, he sounds nervous, and I'm beginning to think he didn't ring up just for chit-chat.

'Oh yeah?' I say, and my voice is wobbly.

'Uh huh. So, I know we left it pretty up in the air about… what happens next. You know, with how things were last weekend.'

'We did,' I agree.

'On account of me having to get back. And I told you that I had some super busy weeks coming up.'

'You did. Is that still true?'

He laughs. 'Yeah. But I was thinking on the way back from New York that maybe it doesn't have to be.'

'What are you getting at?' I say.

'You like adventures, right?'

'I love adventures. Remember? Machu Picchu, the Grand Canyon. Spray on my face at Niagara, et cetera.'

'Good. I was hoping you'd say that. Check your email,' he says.

'How did you get my email address?'

'I did some detective work. And by that I mean it's there for everyone to see on your Facebook profile.'

I boot up my laptop and sign in.

'There's nothing there,' I say, crestfallen. 'What is it?'

'I only just sent it. Like, whilst we've been talking. Maybe refresh?'

And then, there it is. In my inbox. An email from him, which feels like a sort of dated yet still amazingly cool step up. And before I even click on the message I gasp, because it's *hugely* exciting. So exciting in fact, that I can't quite trust that what I'm seeing is true. I blink a couple of times, try and reset the image in my head, but it's still there, and there's silence on the other end of the phone whilst he's waiting for my response.

From: Jesse Franklin
Subject: FWD: Virgin Atlantic e-Ticket Confirmation

'How about California?' he says.

God, he's smooth.

'Is this what I think it is?' I whisper.

'You'll come then?'

'You just try and stop me,' I say, laughing. 'What are we going to do?'

'Whatever you like,' he says, and now he's laughing, too, and this shared joy crackling over invisible airwaves spanning half the planet is delightful. 'It's your vacation.'

I scroll down, hardly daring to believe what I'm seeing, and yet there it is, in black and white. Heathrow to LAX, August twenty-ninth – exactly six weeks away.

'Oh my god,' I say. 'How did you…? How is this…? I actually don't know what to say. This is *crazy*. In a good way. This is the most brilliant thing ever. This is… God, thank you.'

'So you're going to be okay getting the time off work?'

'I shouldn't think it will be an issue. But you have to let me pay you back for this.'

'No way, it's not a big deal.'

'Err, it's a return flight to California. It's definitely a big deal.'

'I'm not taking your money. Really, I'm not. I *wanted* to do this for you.'

'Amazing. This is amazing. *You're* amazing,' I tell him, without even thinking about it. 'No one has ever done anything this cool for me.'

'I don't believe that, but okay,' he says.

—

Rachel! I'm going to California!

WHAT? When?

August 29th! For 2 weeks!

Christ! That's quite a massive deal! How exciting. I bet you're beside yourself aren't you?

I'm nervous and excited and OMG I don't know what to do with myself.

I'll tell you what to do with yourself. Get on the pill.

I open up my emails again and stare at my travel details for a while and it all feels like some sort of crazy dream. I don't quite know what planetary alignment has occurred for all of this to happen, for me to end up in a situation where my teenage dreams seem to be coming true, and for Rachel to dole out *that* sort of advice, as if it would ever be a possibility. But I can't let myself analyse it too much because if I do, I start feeling so wired that I might never ever sleep again. I have to force myself to go with it because if I give in to the nerves, and the rapidly accelerating pulses of adrenaline, it all begins to feel enormous. I can't let myself admit that I don't know how I'd ever get over it if it all falls apart.

Chapter Eighteen

To: CassieB83
From: FredTed49

Cassie, pretty Cassie, where for art thou Cassie?
I think your drink probably went alright, didn't it?
Fred

To: FredTed49
From: CassieB83

Hi Fred,
Yes it did go rather well, thanks. A lady never tells, so we'll leave it at that.
But I feel like I should probably tell you that he's invited me to go and stay with him in America for a couple of weeks, so with that in mind, I probably won't be trying to meet up with anyone from on here.
I hope your search is going well.
Cass

To: CassieB83
From: FredTed49

I'm pleased for you, really. Gutted I missed the boat, but pleased for you all the same.
Maybe I'll give Tyler's sister a call...
Fred

She might be The One, Fred.

Chapter Nineteen

Jesse

Travis stops by and we eat burritos in front of a Judd Apatow movie we've both seen before, and he talks all the way through it.

'Brandon called on Sunday night,' he says.

'Yeah?'

'Talked a lot about you, as it goes.'

'Well I *did* just visit. I don't know, he was weird.'

Travis laughs. 'My dude, he said the same about you. He said you seem happier than you have in a while.'

'Oh.'

'Are you?'

'Quite possibly.'

'Said he saw you just before you went to London and when you got back you seemed different.'

'And what did you say?'

'Nothing, but now that I'm here, I think he might have a point.'

I look over at him sitting on the couch and I don't know why I'm hiding it from him. Travis is the person I'm closest to in the entire world. 'Alright,' I say, slowly. 'I *may* have met someone in London.'

'Yeah? Right on, man. You fuck her?'

Straight to the point, as ever.

'It wasn't like that.'

'So you didn't? Missed a trick there.'

'No… that definitely happened. But…' I trail off.

'But?'

'I don't know,' I shrug. 'I just like her. A lot.'

'Does this mystery woman have a name?'

'Her name is Cassie.'

'Where'd you meet her?'

'In a bar,' I say, and leave it as vague as that. I'm not telling him I met her on the internet, especially after I shut down his idea to do pretty much exactly that when we went to the bar in Los Alamitos, and I'm definitely never going to tell him she liked Franko. I'm not telling anyone she liked Franko. I'm certain there'd be questions and comments and preconceived ideas and I'm not down for that.

'She hot?'

'Yep. Gorgeous. It's more than that though, there's this energy about her. I feel like it sucked me in a bit.'

He puts his hand on my shoulder. 'Jesse, that was just her mouth.'

'My *god*, Travis, what is the matter with you? Eat your burrito.'

'I'm sorry,' he laughs. 'That was too easy.'

'You're an ass.'

'Do you have a photo?' he says. I pick my phone up from the table and show him her Facebook.

'Connected on social media already,' he says and I stifle a laugh because he doesn't know the half of it. 'I bet that made for some nice pillow talk. Yeah, good going. I'd give her a solid seven and a half, with a bonus point for being British. Anyway, is it true?'

'Is what true?'

'What they say about British girls.'

'I don't know what they say about British girls.'

Travis sips his drink and puts it down on the table. 'Kind of nasty.' He smirks again.

'Travis, what the fuck, man? You've been spending too much time with Seth. I'm not talking about this with you.'

'Does she sound like she's from London?' he asks, mimicking the line in *Forgetting Sarah Marshall*. It's funny. We both laugh. Travis coughs up a pinto bean and I nudge his beer towards him.

'Of course she does. That's where she's from.'

'I mean, I don't know if you know this, but that's pretty far away. I didn't think long distance was your thing. You gonna chalk it up to a fun weekend and get on with shit? Or are you going to be spending time in England now? The fact you've already added her on Facebook would suggest the latter. Anyway, looks like I owe Lainey twenty bucks.'

'Wait, you guys made a bet?'

'Just a little one. Relax.'

'What about?'

'She thought you'd hooked up with someone. Said she caught you being all secretive on Facebook chat and that you fed her some bullshit about looking at amps, like you don't have enough of those. You need to get a better cover story, dude, she's not stupid.'

'First of all, eugh, why have you guys not got anything better to talk about than this? And also, you bet *against* it? You know me better than anyone and you bet *against* it?'

'Uh huh,' he says, taking the last bite. 'That's *the reason* I bet against it.'

'I… I don't know what to say.'

Travis finishes his mouthful and swallows. 'Then don't say anything. Just let it happen,' he says, scrunching up the foil packaging into a tight ball and throwing it towards the kitchen. It lands in the sink. 'In one!' he says, and leans back on the couch. 'Watch the movie, Jesse.'

–

A couple of nights after, Holly calls, and this seems odd because she's never been the type to call me for a chat, and things have been a little strained since Nicole and I broke up. Guess that'll happen when your brother's wife made friends with your now ex-girlfriend. I'm about to tell her Travis isn't here, but she starts the conversation on a whole different note.

'So,' she says, coolly. 'New York was too far, but London somehow isn't? Jesse, do you even know geography?'

'Excuse me?'

'Travis mentioned you'd met someone in London.'

'Yeah, so?'

'And that you're seeing her again?'

'What's your point?' I sigh. 'Am I not allowed to move on? I wouldn't say this is entirely your business.'

'I just think the way your relationship with Nicole ended was shitty, is all.'

'Did you tell her that, too? Because as I recall, she said carrying on would just delay the inevitable. Are you just calling to bitch me out about something that happened between two people that aren't you, or did you want something else?'

'I still maintain you could have tried a little harder, Jesse. Made her feel like she was worth a little more than just walking out on.'

'Holly. You have a completely skewed account of what happened that night. And again, not your business.'

'I mean, not that it matters now, I guess,' she continues, ignoring me. 'She'll have enough to deal with soon anyway. I'm sure she'll be glad to hear you've moved on.'

'What does *that* mean?'

'You know,' she laughs, sing-song.

'Not really, but okay.'

'You really don't know?'

'I'm not playing, Holly. Tell me or don't. Whatever.'

'Erm,' she says, and the change in her voice is audible.

'Holly?' I say, and there's a creeping feeling of unease. 'What's going on?'

'Jesse,' she says, doubtfully, 'Nicole is having a baby. Really soon.'

'Excuse me?'

I can't have heard that correctly, surely.

'Wait, you really didn't know? I thought you were shitting me. I thought she'd have told you.'

'No. Why would she have told me?'

'Because by really soon, I mean in a couple of months. And because she didn't leave that long ago.'

I can't respond. I'm trying to absorb the news whilst at the same time figure out a timeframe. I've never needed math so much in my life. Nicole's having a baby in a *couple of months*. She moved out of state seven months ago. A human pregnancy is nine months. Is that nine *whole* months? Or when you *reach* the ninth month? I might not be an expert in obstetrics but some very basic arithmetic would suggest there is a chance our business is very much unfinished.

'Jesse?' she says again, her voice tinny and trebly, on the other end.

'Do you have any more information than that?' I ask.

'No,' she admits.

'I gotta go,' I choke, and end the call.

And now I feel lightheaded and sick and I definitely need to sit down. This can *not* be happening. Nicole wouldn't keep news like that from me, would she?

I didn't see her after I left her apartment on New Year's Eve. I didn't answer my phone when it rang as I was driving home, or when she called the next day, and I didn't respond to any of the text messages she sent. But on Monday I found an old oversized Ramones t-shirt she sometimes wore to sleep in in a drawer, and I noticed there was a toothbrush and a box of tampons, and a couple of hair elastics, and a purple disposable razor in the bathroom. And downstairs, a magazine she'd been reading the week before, a book she'd left once, and some diet soda in the refrigerator. Little traces of Nicole all over the place. Things she might want back if she was going. And I guess a part of me still hoped she'd changed her mind, at least about us. So I made a call.

'Hey,' she'd said, answering on the second ring.

'How's it going?' I'd asked.

'I'm sorry about Saturday night,' she'd said, at exactly the same time.

'Hmm, yeah, that kinda sucked. That's actually why I'm calling.'

'Right.'

'I have some of your things here. I didn't know if you wanted to come and collect them.'

'Ahh, you can toss it all.'

'Really? There's some decent stuff there. Your t-shirt, that book.'

'Yeah… I know. But it's okay.'

'I can bring them to you if it's easier?'

'Jesse,' she'd said, and sighed.

'Right.'

'I really am sorry.'

'Are you? Okay.'

'Look, opportunities like this don't come around often. I can't just stay here transcribing fucking court cases in Spanish forever. Don't make me choose between you and my career.'

'I wasn't asking you to choose. You said it was a contract.'

'Yeah, but…'

'You know, now I feel like this isn't just about your fancy new job.'

She sighed again and made a sort of humming noise, and I knew. It wasn't just about the job at all.

'You're so… closed off,' she said, finally.

'Sorry?'

'I just feel like…'

'Like what?'

'Like I never properly knew you, you know?'

'I've never been dishonest with you, Nicole.'

'But you have never really truly been open with me either. There's stuff you never want to talk about. That you always skirt around. I always felt... *peripheral*.'

'I'm not really sure about that.'

'Why? It's true. Stuff about your family. I mean, don't you think it's weird that we were together over a year and I didn't even get to meet your brother?'

That word, *were*. So final, so past tense, such a kick whilst I was down.

'I mean, that's just sort of the way—'

'It is, yeah, you always say that. But you never go into why.'

And I felt myself close up, so I guess she was right, in a way, but I didn't want to revisit what happened when Franko ended, especially not during an uncomfortable telephone conversation with someone who wasn't going to stick around either way.

'Why are you only bringing this up now?'

'I guess I was hoping things would change.'

'Are you seriously telling me that in fifteen months you didn't think I opened up to you at all?'

'I mean—'

'Because that's bullshit, Nicole, and you know it.'

'Look, I don't want to hurt you but—'

'Oh, do me a favor. Never follow those words with a *but*.'

She heaved out another sigh.

'Look, the job is like, ninety per cent of this, but I can't be with someone so closed up, and so I'm walking away. And you shouldn't try to change my mind. When someone finishes with you, please just accept it.'

There was absolutely no point in continuing this.

'Are you flying? Or driving?'

'Flying,' she'd said. 'My car's off to a lot tomorrow.'

'Want me to take you to LAX?' I asked.

'Uh, I think it's probably easier if we don't do that.'

'… Right.'

'Holly's going to take me,' she explained.

'Wow, okay.'

'Don't be like that Jesse, she's a good friend.'

And apparently she was. She took Nicole to the airport and kept her secrets, and now, seven months later, she's using them against me, drip-feeding just enough information to unsettle me and leave me back-footed and only in possession of half the facts.

I know I have to contact Nicole, but it takes me a while to build up to it and I'm afraid of her response, and what having all that information will mean, and when I eventually call, it rings and rings but she doesn't answer and I can't bring myself to leave a voicemail, but she texts instead.

> Hi Jesse. This is unexpected and yet sort of not.

> Hey Nic, yeah. I heard your news. Not really sure how to ask this…

> Oh wow, seriously?

> Well, yeah. I mean, you can understand, right? Given when you left. If that's the situation then obviously we need to have a discussion.

I sit and watch the screen on my phone. She types for a bit. Stops. Starts again. Stops. Then the screen times out and I don't get another message at all. And I don't know what to do with myself or how to get rid of the foggy cloud of panic and dread that's settled around me. I could try to prise more information out of Holly, but I think she'd love that now she knows she was the bearer of unwelcome news. She'd get drunk on the power and wouldn't let me forget about it. I could speak to Travis, but I don't know how much he knows. I'm pretty sure she didn't stay in touch with Seth and Cindy, so that's a bust, and if she didn't, and I brought it up, Cindy would deliver a lecture on responsibilities and the importance of loving and stable homes, and Seth would undoubtedly make loud and inappropriate jokes in bars.

> Nic. Please can you reply. I've met someone. I don't want to fuck that up. So I just really need to know.

Not delivered

Well, fuck.

Chapter Twenty

Cassie

'Los Angeles! Bit swish!' Mimi says, when I clear my holiday with her. 'Who are you going with? Rachel? Last debauched girls' trip before she becomes Mrs... whatever his name is?'

'Nope, going on my own,' I say. 'But I'm staying with someone when I get there.' I widen my eyes and am deliberately cryptic because I hope she'll ask more questions. Now *this* has happened, I feel like we're deeply involved and I want to shout it from the rooftops.

We must be. You don't invite someone to stay with you from the other side of the world if you only have mediocre, lukewarm feelings for them, do you? And that night was anything but lukewarm and mediocre.

But she's busy and doesn't ask any more questions. Killjoy.

'Email the dates to HR,' she says. 'And please copy me in.'

At lunch time I eat at my desk whilst writing a list of everything I need to do before I go away.

1) Get a wax.

Natch. Better make that appointment now. Everyone knows good waxers get booked up fast.

2) Buy new underwear.

There's no way my usual, every day knickers are going to cut it out there. Absolutely not. It's got to be cute Brazilian knickers at the very minimum.

3) Get on the pill.

I underline point three and realise that all three items on my list relate back, in some way, to my vagina. Which I think probably says a lot about my priorities and my intentions.

Later on, I email Marie and Lauren and by the end of the day, a rough plan for Rachel's hen night is in place. Striking the balance between a night of drinking and finding something Rachel will enjoy is trickier than we had anticipated, but eventually we settle on a plan. Lauren puts herself in charge of sourcing lewd accessories, Marie is in charge of invitations, and I opt for dealing with bookings and anything else that crops up. Come five o'clock, I'm satisfied with my day's work. I've booked some painful hair removal. I've made an appointment with my doctor. I'm ahead of the game with my bridesmaid duties. The house is empty when I get home. Jon is out at his monthly movie club night, and Sara's gone to stay with friends in Somerset.

—

> I booked time off work today. I am so excited I think I might actually explode!

> Please don't explode. I, for one, would be bummed out about that.

> Oh, you!

> It's 2am here now. That means it's 10am there, right? I just got home. I did a triple session today. 3 separate jobs in one day. I'm exhausted. Anyway I'm going to sleep now. Can't. Function. Anymore.

It was… it's not anymore. I'm at work now. My colleague keeps trying to peer over at what I'm typing. If I'd signed on half an hour earlier I might have caught you. I've been Googling California today, on work time, obvs.

Have you got any ideas about what you want to do whilst you're here? I'm gonna call you later… 10pm your time going to be too late?

I have plenty of ideas, none of which I am divulging over the internet ;-) 10pm is fine.

–

Morning! Before I left for work this morning, Jon moaned that I'd kept him awake. *sigh* it's about time something did. I've lived with him for 2 years and I've never known him to go to bed after 9pm.

Jon sounds like he's fun at parties.

He's OK on the whole. Quirky. Can't deal with people. Definitely all about his job, and his routines. Pretty sure he's on the spectrum. I said I'd keep it down from now on because I felt bad. I'm seeing Rachel tonight anyway.

Rachel and George live in the eaves of a three-storey town-house. I love visiting their flat. It's small, but perfectly formed. She has nice taste, and it's the kind of place I'd like to live in if I ever grow up and buy property. There are varnished floorboards in her living room, a fancy Persian rug, a squashy sofa, and shelves made from pieces of driftwood. There are church candles arranged inside a cast iron fireplace, and piles of the sort of books people place artfully on coffee tables, and a record player in the corner because George has a thing about collecting old vinyl. Some, he says, are quite valuable. Rachel is convinced that if there was a fire, he'd save his record collection before he'd save her. Once, he didn't speak to her for days after they'd fallen out and she'd threatened to toss them out of the lounge window. Now, every time I see the records, arranged neatly on the shelf, I imagine them flying out across Crouch End, like frisbees, or liquorice roll up sweets.

George is out, and we eat dinner sitting at the little foldaway table in their kitchen. She complains that it's tiny, but I tell her that having a small kitchen has its benefits; not having to get up to get more wine from the fridge, for instance, which I then demonstrate perfectly. Or being able to throw your cutlery directly into the sink. I don't test that theory. She wouldn't like it. After we've finished eating, we take our wine into the living room and she asks more about my trip. She seems excited for me, but there is also something not quite right. She's good at composing herself but when you've known someone since you were four, you know when they are hiding something.

'What's that look for, Rach?'

'What look? There's no look.'

'There's absolutely a look. Do you think I shouldn't go? I'm definitely going. I'm getting on the pill and everything.'

'It's not that,' she sighs. 'I want you to go and be happy. It's just that it's all happening quite fast, and it's quite a significant amount of time to spend with someone without a break. What if you get there and you don't like each other?'

'What if I get there and we do?' I counter. 'And anyway, you were the one who told me off for worrying about whether he'd call me or not. You were the one who told me to let it happen. What am I doing if not exactly that?'

She takes a deep breath in, holds it for a few seconds and blows it out through her nose.

'You're right,' she says. 'I'm sorry. I am excited for you, of course I am. I just don't want you to fly all that way to be disappointed, that's all. Not after what Jack did. I want you to keep a part of yourself back just for you, until you're sure.'

I look around her living room. She has a nice life with George. All their stuff, here in this flat, it melts together so you can't tell where her stuff ends and his begins. Now it's just *their* stuff. Their sofa and their rug and their contemporary art prints on the wall, and their names, jointly, on the mortgage. It must be nice, I think, to have that with someone. Not the *stuff*, but just knowing you're not on your own anymore. That you have someone always on your side. I was just beginning to think I'd got that with Jack, but finding that earring was like pulling the pin out of a grenade, and the aftermath of him blowing us up left me hollow and small for months.

And now I'm getting ahead of myself and wondering if my shot at this happens to be on the other side of the world, and that's why I am so excited about going to California.

I want to tell her all this but I don't know if she'd really understand. Or she'd tell me to stop reading too much into it, because after all, Jesse and I have only really properly met once as adults, and how can you even begin to think about being with someone when you've only spent fifteen hours with them?

'I'm not going to be disappointed,' I say. 'I just know I'm not.'

'Okay,' she says. She tucks her feet under her. 'So here's an idea. Invite him to the wedding.'

'Pardon?'

'Yep. Invite him. When you're visiting. It's quite a big deal being invited to a wedding as a plus one, especially if you need to travel that far for it. That will give you an indication of how invested in this he is. If he says yes, then love with reckless abandon. If he's not so into it, then guard your precious heart.'

She's right. It is a big deal. It would make a bit of a statement. He'd be in the photos, his name written on the card. *Lots of love, Cassie and Jesse.* He'd be woven into memories of that day forever. My parents will be there, too, and there'd be no getting around that. I'd have no option other than to introduce him to them. Dad would bumble through and make well-meaning but embarrassing comments about how I used to have posters of him on my bedroom walls. There'd be questions about what exactly happened, and awkward jokes about how sad I was when the band broke up. Mum would cluck around. She'd dine out on me bringing a once minor celebrity as my plus one for *weeks*, and it would almost certainly deflect her not so subtle comments about the state of my love life, at least for a while. *When are you going to meet a man, Cassie? I was married with a toddler at your age. It's all very well being focused on your career, but what about a family? Look at Rachel's life, Cassie. Look at where she's achieving and you're not.*

And if Jesse was there, George's bizarre and wildly inappropriate plan to set me up with handsy Marcus would be foiled, and I wouldn't have to subtly smack his hand off my arse during the dancing.

'Is this like some sort of test?' I say. 'Because I don't want to invite him if that's the case.'

'No,' she says slowly. I don't know if I believe her.

'But you'll hold it against me if he says no. And he might have a valid reason to, it'll only be a few weeks until the big day at that point.'

'No, I won't. I want him to say yes. I want you to be happy and to love with reckless abandon.'

'Okay. Thank you. I'll ask him.'

'One thing, though.'

'Anything.'

'Please don't stop being excellent. I don't mind if George takes more of a back seat as long as I have you helping me.'

I know what she's really saying. *Don't lose your focus on me, Cassie, if he comes to my wedding.*

'I promise,' I say.

'You're all lit up,' she says, smiling. 'It's nice.' She pours us both another glass of wine, and I decide I'm staying in her spare room tonight.

–

Have/hope you're having/had fun
Say hi to your friend.

I stayed in her spare room last night. Didn't feel like traipsing all the way home on the bus.

You don't have a car?

No. I live in London remember?

So?

So not everyone has a car here. We just jump on the tube.

Everybody has a car here. I bet things are crazy in London right about now, right?

For the Olympics? Yeah it's heaving. The HR team at work are going to watch the athletics. Not so much fun to be had in our dept though.

How did they get to go and you didn't?

They won Team of the Year but my manager reckons it was rigged! Mainly because one of the HR ladies is shagging someone in senior management. They like to think they're discreet but they're not. Everyone knows.

Chapter Twenty-One

Cassie

There's an away day at work. It's held in a conference centre in Earl's Court in a venue with grey carpet tiles that haven't seen a hoover this side of the millennium and strip lighting on the ceiling. There are team building workshops, one of which involves blindfolds, falling backwards, and a lot of trust. I don't like it. I've been paired with Polly, the merch assistant, a crotchety little finance graduate with a taste for poorly fitting trouser suits and calf-length grey skirts. Sam's thought she's abhorrent ever since she missed him off the tea run and offered an unsolicited opinion on gifts for pets at Christmas.

'Don't get me started,' he'd said to me after. 'I just find her despicable.'

We sit through a dreadful talk given by someone in a shiny suit and horrible loafers who earnestly tells us all that assuming things makes an 'ass' out of 'u' and 'me,' and he scribbles it on to a flip chart to reiterate his point. He draws a smiley face next to it which I think is to show us that he's a lighthearted sort of fellow, but actually he's woeful, and I reckon he probably drives a Saab. Sam grabs the fleshy bit just above my knee and squeezes under the table. He takes his phone out of his pocket, types, and angles the screen so I can see.

I'm biting my cheeks.

Me too. Awful.

Can you believe we have to stay for lunch?

WHAT? I was hoping we could escape to a pub?!?

I look up at him but he shakes his head, sadly.

Not a chance, doe eyes, Paula is on the prowl! She knows if they let us leave we won't come back.

'I don't see why we couldn't all have gone to watch the athletics,' he sulks to Mimi as we're queuing for the buffet. 'That would have been far better for team morale than listening to this prat.'

'Because there's supposed to be an element of professional development,' she says, and then lowers her voice. 'It's a box-ticking exercise. I completely agree that it's a pile of old shite, though.'

After a lunch of egg and cress sandwiches with curled up corners, stale crisps and dry melon, we are forced into an endless game of charades. It's mandatory. Paula, the head of buying for Beauchamp and Taylor, doesn't let anyone off the hook. She's got a glass bowl full of folded up bits of paper with movie or song titles on. She thinks it will be fun, but it's not. It's terrifying. When it's my turn, I am lumbered with *Back to the Future*. How am I meant to act out *Back to the Future*? I tap my back. Everyone gets it. I hold up two fingers. Everyone gets it. I flail around. No one gets it and I feel myself losing the will to live. How is no one getting this from *back* and *to*? Who are these pop culture ignoramuses I am forced to work with? They'd all be shit at a pub quiz. I try to act out a flux capacitor and Sam takes photos on his phone. In the end I flip him off and flounce back to my seat.

'*Back To The Future?*' he asks.

'You're a bellend,' I hiss.

'You love me. I'm your work husband.'

'I might work divorce you.'

Later on, he uploads his photos to Facebook. I look like I'm doing the robot in a couple. He tags me in them. Jesse likes all the photos. I am mortified.

> Nice pics. Definitely more entertaining than track and field even if it is the Olympics.

> Oh God. Don't. I am cringing.

> Are they your best moves? Am I going to see them when you're here?

> Behave yourself. Or you'll see nothing. Nada.

> You don't mean that.

> You're right. I don't.

> In other news. Not too long now! It's like counting down to the summer holidays when you're a kid in school. I used to make a chart and mark off each day. Did you ever do that?

Well, we were home schooled from when I was 14, so we could concentrate on the music. So I don't really remember counting down the days to the summer vacation. We didn't stick to a school year as such.

Ah yeah that makes sense. Who taught you?

My mom. She's a teacher so she kind of knew what she was doing. Kind of. It was pretty lax at times. I think we'd have been better off with a tutor, but having someone else in control wouldn't have worked for Dad. At all.

He does this occasionally, drops little hints about his life but never quite enough for me to really connect it all up. But the more he does, the more I am absolutely convinced a lot of shit hit the fan with Franko, and I'm dying to know about it.

Have you told anyone about me? Or are people going to be really confused to find a random English woman hanging out in your house?

I may have mentioned you to a couple of people...

Ooooh! Who?

And what did you say? Have you told anyone I used to listen to your music back in the day?

Trav knows you're coming. So do Brandon and Lainey. So here's the thing. I haven't actually told anyone you liked Franko. To be honest it was just simpler. I think it would dredge up a lot of stuff that's better left in the past. So that's really just between us at the moment. Is that OK?

Yeah that's fine. What did you say about how we met though?

Just in a bar. I kept it vague.

Works for me. It's sort of true in a tenuous sort of way. I won't be bringing my old Franko t-shirt then ;-)

OMG, please don't bring that. That would be so, so weird.

I'm just kidding! My mother threw it out when I went to university.

I often forget that about you.

That I am educated? Bit rude…

Haha no… the Franko thing.

Well I often forget that you were a dreamboat pop star in a past life as well. Will you tell me how it all went the way of the pear?

Maybe. Probably. I'm sure it'll come up at some point.

Only if you feel like it though. I'm not going to bug you for info.

Thanks Cass.

Chapter Twenty-Two

Cassie

On August twenty-ninth, I'm startled awake. The house is quiet and it worries me. I'm positive I've slept through the alarm on my phone, *and* when the radio comes on automatically for an hour, *and* the every day noises Sara and Jon make clattering around, getting ready for work – boiling the kettle and making toast, and Jon's bizarre and somewhat antisocial seven a.m. hoovering habit. They've left the house and gone for the day, I'm sure of it.

I squint at my phone. Six fifteen. Good *grief*, I'm on edge. Can't wait for a nice calming gin on the plane. The house is quiet because no one is up. My alarms won't go off for another fifteen minutes. The plane definitely has not left without me. I lie in my bed for a few minutes, mentally going through everything I'm taking until I hear Jon scuttle down the hall to the bathroom, and Sara pad downstairs. Passport, check. Clothes and shoes for almost every eventuality, check. A lot of expectation and hope and the potential for the most broken of hearts, check, check, check.

Downstairs, my bags are stacked up by the front door and I join Sara in the kitchen for a coffee.

'Today's the day then,' she says. She pushes down the cafetière plunger and I pull out a chair. 'You'd better get dressed before you go.' She pours us both a cup and laughs at her own joke.

'Aha, yeah, good shout,' I say, humouring her.

She looks earnestly at me. 'So what do you think it will be like?' she asks. Her eyes are wide and catlike. Her kimono-style robe is pulled tightly around her, right up to her neck. She adjusts her septum ring.

'What do I think what will be like?'

'You know,' she says, widening her eyes and nodding her head. 'Going to California, staying with a man you hardly know...'

'Pretty sure it's going to be fine,' I say. 'And it's not like we're strangers. We've seen each other's bits, so how bad can it be?'

'You like him a lot, don't you?' she says.

'Very, very much so.' I sip my coffee and she rests her chin on her fist.

'I wish I was gutsy enough to do that,' she says. But it's never really occurred to me that flying out to stay with Jesse is gutsy, it's just what you do when you like someone, isn't it? You make yourself available and you see them whenever you can. Maybe things are just on a bigger scale when there's five thousand miles between you. Maybe it just seems brave because I have to leave the country. 'I hope it all works out for you,' she smiles. 'I think Jon's out of the bathroom. Any second now,' she says, and we both know what's coming. Directly above us, he turns on the hoover. The sound moves rhythmically across the room. Sara and I simultaneously look at the clock. It's five minutes to seven.

'There it is. For goodness' sake,' she mutters. 'God knows what the neighbours think. I'm going to sneak into his room and turn up the volume on his clock radio. Then we'll see how much he likes loud noises early in the morning.'

'Mean,' I say. She laughs.

'You'd better get on. I'm on a late shift today, so you can use the bathroom now.'

An hour later, I'm ready to leave. I've dressed in a pair of summery, ankle-grazer trousers and a grey v-neck t-shirt. There's a fresh one in my hand luggage, along with some make-up because there's no way I'm walking through the arrivals hall at an airport looking like I've just spent a day on a plane. No way at all.

Sara's lighting some incense in the lounge as I'm heading out and she stops as I poke my head around the door.

'Have a great time,' she says. 'Don't expect Jon wished you bon voyage before he left, did he?'

'Course not,' I say. She rolls her eyes, but we both know it wouldn't have occurred to him. He probably won't even notice I'm gone. There's a smokey, slightly sickly scent wafting out of the room now. It's claggy. She has nicer smelling sticks than this, and anyway, eight a.m. is a funny time to be burning incense. What's Jesse going to think of Sara and Jon when he comes here? Will we hide away up in my room, listening to Jon's hoovering and getting wafts of Sara's incense? Will we all sit around the table and eat dinner, the way we do sometimes at weekends? Will Jon be happy with someone who isn't listed on our tenancy agreement staying all that time? Will I even want to share him at all? Maybe we should stay in a hotel. Or find one of those serviced apartments to play house in for a week. I'll have to gauge it when I'm there.

I think about all this as I wheel my suitcase down the road towards the station, with my colourful tote bag slung clumsily over my shoulder. And how with every passing minute I'm getting closer and closer to seeing him again. The journey to Heathrow passes in a daze, the planes get bigger and lower and louder, and my heart races at every stop. I *can't wait* to see him again.

Sitting in departures, I indulge in a little people-watching with an extortionately priced almond croissant and a watery cup of tea, and I wonder if anyone here is doing the same thing as I am. Crossing an ocean to start something with someone. Seeing if it has the spark of potential you so desperately hope for. Swallowing down the excitement and the nerves and anticipating what's going to happen when finally, after hours of travelling, you pick up your bags, get a stamp in your passport, and head out to be picked up.

I'm daydreaming now, about the moment when I walk through and he's there. About him wrapping his arms tight around me. About looking up into those lovely eyes and kissing him and knowing that for the next fourteen days, at least, he's mine. My tea's gone cold. I check and double check my boarding pass, and I can't stop fiddling with sugar wrappers, drinks stirrers, the receipt from my order. Anything to keep my hands busy. I text Rachel for a bit of support;

> At Heathrow. Bricking it a little x

And she texts back,

> Go get him, tiger x

Finally, there's a gate for my flight and I make my way down corridors and along travelators, and I sit and watch the plane I am about to get on. Baggage-handlers toss cases into its belly, to-ing and fro-ing in their little vehicles until all the luggage is loaded. A lorry loads in all the in-flight meals and smartly dressed cabin crew huddle until they are allowed on board.

I'm seated next to a friendly American lady on her way home, who tells me about her vacation in London and how it had been her dream to stand outside Buckingham Palace and see the changing of the guard. She pulls out her phone to show me the photos. I want to tell her about Jesse, but she doesn't ask why I'm going to LA, and I can't slot it in there. Just before departure, I fire off a final message.

> On the plane, and we're about to take off. See you soon x

And then the reality of it all hits me. It really *is* a big deal. Now I'm here, buckled into my seat, and we're pushing back on the tarmac, moving slowly towards the runway and the sky, it does feel pretty ballsy. The cabin crew run through the emergency procedures, fastening and unfastening seatbelts and pointing out the exits, but I'm not really concentrating. We're racing down the runway now. The engines are roaring. The entire plane judders and shakes as it soars high up into the sky. The land below us gets ever smaller and smaller as we climb. The sky above us bluer and bluer. My ears pop with the change in pressure, and tiny ice crystals form on the windows.

Eleven hours later, after two movies, almost an entire novel, two meals, and a restless kip, I've flown across the Atlantic, over mountains, lakes and plains and we're descending into LAX. I've managed pretty well to suppress my nerves but each time the plane bounces further down in the air, my heart is in my throat and my stomach feels like it's housing an entire kaleidoscope of butterflies. And finally, we land. I stare out of the window as the plane taxies towards the terminal. It's so different to London. Clear blue skies and mountains. An air traffic control tower and the iconic Theme Building. I'm in Los Angeles, and it can't be long now until I see Jesse again. The bubbly excitement is back. He could be here right now. He could already be waiting.

I catch sight of myself in a pane of glass as we're herded off the plane. I'm dishevelled. Robert Smith has nothing on me. My ponytail looks like a bird has taken up residence in it, and my eyeliner is smudged. I pass through immigration as quickly as I can and they ask me questions about my trip. Who I'm visiting. Where I'm staying. The things I'm going to do.

'He your boyfriend?' the immigration agent asks, looking over my ESTA form, and I'm surprised. Seems a little personal.

'I… er… maybe?'

'You want him to be?' he says, not missing a beat. I blush.

My passport is swiped and stamped, my fingerprints are taken.

'Welcome to the United States,' he barks, apparently satisfied. 'Next!'

I grab my passport and hurry to the ladies' room, lock myself in the cubicle and sit down on the toilet. I'm so nervous I'm shaking. I change my t-shirt and shake my hair loose. I reapply my eye make-up in the mirror. Push my toothbrush around my mouth to get shot of any lingering remnants of aeroplane food. Pout at myself in the mirror and spritz a little perfume on to my neck. I'm still not looking my best, but at least I no longer resemble a member of The Cure.

I push my Wayfarers into my hair, take a deep breath, and head out to arrivals.

Chapter Twenty-Three

Cassie

I don't see him at first. In fact, I'm a little confused. Arrivals appears to be little more than a wide corridor between baggage reclaim and the exit, not really like at other airports I've been to, and not really what I was expecting. People are dotted around, leaning against walls, crouching on the floor, looking at their phones, and there are a couple of people with placards, but not nearly as many as you see at Heathrow. And as I squint around I think this is not the romantic airport scene of my imagination. This is not like the beautiful beginning of *Love Actually*, and for a second or two I wonder if I'm even in the right place, but the only other doors lead outside.

And then he calls my name from the left and I turn towards the sound and beam, literally beam, when I see him. My heart is fluttering. He looks relaxed and chilled and happy to see me, and just absolutely gorgeous. A pair of Aviators are folded over the neck of his t-shirt, and the first thing I think is that it's cute that we match with our Ray-Bans. And he's *so* much better than I remember and I hurry over, close the gap between us, slide my free hand over his shoulder and hook it around his neck. He smells delicious, of suncream and aftershave.

'Hey, you,' I coo. Just like that, the nerves have melted away, but the butterflies haven't. He wraps his arms around me and pulls me close.

'Hey, *you*.'

We kiss. I drop my case. It clunks to the floor and a woman with mousy brown hair and a visor whines at me. The handle caught her foot, but I don't care.

'Just you wait til I get you home,' he says, eyes glinty. We both know what's happening when he gets me home. *Jesus*, I hope the traffic is light. He picks up my bag and takes my hand. 'Let's go.'

I follow him out into the bright California sunshine to where he's parked, and as we walk I look down at our linked-together hands and I like the way they look. Like they fit perfectly, as if they aren't meant to be held by anyone else.

'Were you waiting long?' I ask, as I slide into the front passenger seat of his car. A silver Honda, probably not top of the line, but definitely not at all shabby. He flicks on the air conditioning.

'Nah. Twenty minutes max. I was tracking your flight.' He shoots me a sideways glance as he reverses out of the space and tucks some of his hair behind his ear, and that movement, as small and normal as it is, is lovely. I want to remember it forever.

'That's very sensible,' I say. He laughs, and pats my knee.

'You're so very British,' he says. Then he presses a button on the steering wheel and the car fills up with the end of a Don Henley song. He taps out the beat on the steering wheel and I try hard to be inconspicuous with my staring.

'Ahh the classics never die, right?' he says, when it has finished.

He gets straight onto the highway and we head south. The road curves around and the cluster of LA skyscrapers whips in and out of view. The roads are wide and flat. The signs point to places I've heard of. Long Beach. Huntington Beach. Anaheim. Santa Ana. And it occurs to me that even though I submitted his address on my ESTA form, I don't know much about where it is. Seal Beach, California. A town in Orange County. South of LA. I forced myself not to look it up. I want to see his place with brand new eyes.

Half an hour later we pull into a side street and he stops in front of an off-white rendered house with painted trims. The trims have definitely seen better days and could do with another coat of paint, but still, it's charming and I like it.

'We're here,' he says, switching off the engine. He hits another button on the dashboard and the boot clunks open. 'Home sweet home.' We retrieve my bag and I look up at the house whilst he fumbles around for a front door key. So this is where he lives. It's not what I'd imagined, but now the things I have imagined have disappeared, instantly overwritten by reality and never to be recalled again. There's a mesh-panelled screen door and a long, wide window to the left of it with white Venetian blinds, and a plant with big, shiny, waxy leaves directly under. It's all so, so normal. Definitely not the Beverly Hills mansion of my teenage daydreams; there are no pillars, no driveway with a fountain in the middle. No driveway at all, in fact. He's parked on the street, which is little more than a glorified alleyway. There isn't even really any pavement. The doors open right up on to the road. He's got the key in the lock now. He's going inside and I'm following. It's nice and cool in here, and I take a look around as my eyes adjust to being inside. It's all open plan. There's a kitchen to my left with brushed chrome appliances and glossy white cupboards, a coffee machine, one of those fridges with a water dispenser that also makes ice and a sink under that window with the blinds. There are a few bits and pieces on the sides but not all that much. A breakfast bar separates the kitchen from the rest of the space and there's a stack of paperwork and unopened post on it.

Further in there's the navy blue sofa he was sitting on when he first sent me that photo, and it's big and squashy-looking. A cream throw is chucked, jauntily, over the back of it and an enormous TV hangs on the wall opposite, its cables hanging down towards the socket. A low, oval, sixties-style coffee table is positioned on a stripy rug. He's hung two basses on the wall to the left of the TV and they're the first things I've really seen that give any insight at all into what he does. But as soon as I've clocked them, I begin to notice other things; a big black amp pushed against the wall underneath, a flight case leaning up against the breakfast bar, a box of cables on the shelves behind the sofa. And there, hung on the wall, is a framed platinum disc and inlay booklet from *Franko*.

'This is pretty cool,' I say, walking over to it. There are sales details and the release date under the disc. 'Five hundred *thousand* sales in Germany. Jesus.'

I don't know if that's a lot in the grand scheme of things. To me, five hundred thousand of anything seems pretty vast.

'Hmm, that old thing,' he says, dismissively. 'I guess.'

'No, it really is,' I say gently, but I don't press it because I'm getting that same vibe that there's more to the demise of Franko than he's let on. He's looking out the back doors now, fiddling with one of the bracelets on his wrist, and I follow his gaze from across the room. Outside is a narrow decking area, and beyond that is a sand dune, and he really wasn't kidding when he said he could go out to the beach whenever he liked because it's right there, outside the house.

'Christ on a bike!' I exclaim. 'You never told me the beach was right there. Is that the actual Pacific Ocean out there?'

'You never asked,' he says, shrugging, but he's smiling at me, and any discomfort surrounding that platinum disc has evaporated. 'And yes, that is the *actual* Pacific Ocean.'

'Look, I get that this is normal for you, but I live in a Victorian terraced house in West London. It's full of cracks and it's spidery in autumn, and there's textured wallpaper every-where. What's more, I have to get on a train to get to a decent beach, and you have it right here. So… allow me a little amazement.'

'Alright, I'm sorry,' he laughs. 'We can go out there later. There's a pier a little way up the beach, it's nice to walk along. But right now,' he holds out a hand for me, 'come on, I'll show you the rest of the place.'

We go up the stairs and back on ourselves. 'Bathroom,' he says, pointing to a closed door. 'Spare room,' he nods towards another door, this one open just a crack, and then we're at the end of the hallway and there's only one room left to go into. 'And this is—'

'Yep, mmhmm,' I say. It doesn't really need any explanation, because now he's got me home and I don't need to wait any longer. He puts my case on the floor, takes my face in his hands and we're kissing again. We're kicking off shoes and grappling at clothes and our hands are everywhere, because this is apparently how things start with us. We fall on to his bed, and it's big and comfy. And for a split second I wonder how many other times this has happened in here between him and someone else. Did they tug at each other's clothes the frenzied way we are now? Were his hands all over her in this room the way they are now all over me? I know I'm being crazy but I don't want to think about that. So I push him backwards and make a giant theatrical show of positioning myself between his legs and pulling down his pants and letting my hair fall over my face as I dip my head. Sixteen-year-old me would be in total awe of twenty-nine-year-old me. Hell, twenty-nine-year-old me is pretty impressed. It's been a long time since I did this and I'm a little out of practice. Still, I must be doing alright because when I look up at him he is watching everything I'm doing, and I think, if the look on his face is anything to go by, that he's enjoying it.

'Don't look at me,' I say, suddenly feeling scrutinised.

'Why not? This is *so* hot.'

'I'm shy.'

He starts to laugh. 'Cassie, you're so *not* shy.'

'Right now I'm a bit shy,' I say, but I'm smirking and I can't help it.

'Alright,' he says. 'I won't look.' He closes his eyes, and I carry on for a bit. And then he starts shifting a little, 'Oookay, Cass, you have to stop now.'

'Aww, you had enough?'

'Um, definitely not, but all this is going to be over way too soon otherwise.'

I know, buddy, I think. *I can taste it.* I crawl up the bed towards him, lie on my side and lean my head on my arm. We're looking at each other now. I'm studying him intently, committing everything to memory. Etching it on to my brain. Noticing things that I didn't before. Like, how his bottom teeth are just a little bit crooked, and how one eye has more green in it than the other. How they're still the same eyes I looked into when I was sixteen, and I felt all this then, too, but nowhere as intensely as right now. He runs his fingers across my shoulder and down my arm and his fingertips have a hardness to them. He rolls over and opens the drawer of the nightstand.

'So, you might be interested to know that I'm on the pill,' I say, casually. Staring up at the ceiling, drumming my fingertips together. Immediately he stops. Looks back at me. Quirks an eyebrow.

'Oh yeah? That is super interesting to know. I'm *very* interested in that piece of information.'

'Yeah, I thought you might be,' I say. He slams the drawer closed and moves on top of me and we start to kiss again and don't stop as I reach back and grab hold of one of the slats on the headboard of his bed and the tendons in my wrist flex.

Afterwards, the day catches up with me and I can't keep my eyes open. I'm trying, really I am, but my body thinks it's early in the a.m. and I've got that post-shag endorphin rush happening.

'Why don't you take a nap?' Jesse says. He's stroking my hair, and that's not helping with the lethargy. It feels nice though, and I don't want him to stop.

'I feel like I should just power on through.'

'Just a little one to take the edge off. I'll wake you up in an hour or so. We'll get some dinner. Then we'll go down to the beach.'

'Okay.' I'm yawning again. 'Stay with me a while?'

'Sure.'

He's warm. He smells good. He puts his arm around me. I close my eyes to blink but I can't open them again.

He isn't there when I wake up, but it's still light outside and the clock on the nightstand reads 18:23. For a few seconds the unfamiliarity of it all throws me, and I look around the room properly for the first time. There's a window above me, panoramic, with the same white wooden blinds as in the kitchen. A chest of drawers sits to my right, on top of which is a stack of books, a laptop, an iPhone docking station and Bose speakers. In front of me are built-in wardrobes with mirrored doors. There's a door to the left and I get out of bed and push it open and it's another bathroom. I pull on my clothes, and lock myself in, because obviously now I'm going to snoop and I can't have him catching me. There are towels in the cupboard under the sink. Toothpaste and mouthwash, and only one toothbrush in the cabinet above it. A packet of Tylenol, another of Advil, shaving stuff, soap. In the shower is shampoo and body wash and I open them both and sniff. The body wash is one of the brands marketed towards men. Ferny and sort of earthy, and now it will forever remind me of him. I'm satisfied. There are zero traces of girl in this bathroom. I pat some cool water on my face and muss my hair before going back downstairs. He's sitting outside with a bottle of beer, tapping away at something on his phone. He looks up when I slide the door open.

'Hey. I was just thinking about coming to get you.'

'Was I asleep for ages then? I didn't know what time it was after we… you know.'

'No, I just figured you were probably a bit worn out.'

I snort. 'Modest,' I say.

'From the *flight*,' he laughs. 'Do you want something to drink?'

'Yeah. Thanks.' I pull the sleeves of the cardi I fished out of my bag over my knuckles and pull out a chair and he makes a move to go inside. The air is warm but still has that fresh beachy smell to it. People are walking their dogs along the path between the back of the house and the sand and beyond it I can hear the ocean. I'm going to climb that dune later on. And stand at the top and look out to sea. Breathe in the air and secretly contemplate the fact that if Rachel and I hadn't Facebook-stalked Jesse back in April, I wouldn't be here in California right now. I'm going to look at the view and think about how funny life is. He's back now. He hands me a bottle and I pull my legs up on the chair.

'Are you hungry?' he says. 'Shall we get some dinner?'

'I could eat,' I say.

'Do you feel like going out?'

'Hmmm… Yeah?' I don't really want to and he can tell. My energy levels are taking a nosedive. Tonight what I really want is to relax with easy food, take a paddle in the sea, and then hit the hay.

'Would takeout be better?'

'God, yes. Much. Takeout sounds pretty perfect actually.'

We eat off our laps whilst watching TV, and it's like we're living out the random conversations we had on Facebook before any of this started, about the things we like to eat and what we watch on telly. I don't know if he remembers, and I don't say anything about it. It's comfortable, though, sitting here with him, eating soba noodles and drinking beer. It feels good. Sometimes I glance up at the platinum disc on the wall, though, and when I do, I'm reminded of exactly who I'm here with, and all the things that have happened between us, and how none of it would have done if he wasn't who he is, despite what Rachel said about things being written in the stars. He's holding my hand now, and my heart is hammering in my chest. *I'm so besotted with you*, I think. *So, completely, unequivocally and hopelessly besotted.*

Afterwards, we take a walk along the shoreline. We climb over the sand dune up towards the pier and we look back at the houses with their lights on, and out across the dark sea towards the oil platform off the coast. And further up towards Long Beach. On the way back, I take my sandals off and let the water wash over my feet and my ankles. Not for long though; it's freezing.

'I like being here,' I say. I've hooked my thumb through the belt loop of his shorts and he has his arm slung loosely around my shoulders.

'Good,' he says. 'I like you being here, too.'

'What are we doing tomorrow?'

'Whatever you feel like doing. How's the jet lag?'

'Not too bad thanks,' I say. 'Why? Are you planning on shagging me senseless again when we get back to your house?'

'What do you reckon?' he says.

Chapter Twenty-Four

Cassie

It's Thursday, my first morning in California, and I wake up to a cup of coffee being placed on the nightstand and the feeling of weight on the edge of the bed.

'Morning,' he says. 'Wake up, Cass.'

I rub my eyes and try to look cute, stretching out and sighing, and hope I wasn't snoring or sleeping with my mouth open or dribbling. He's dressed in a slightly stretched out t-shirt and sweatpant shorts and he looks like he's been out already. 'Hey. What time is it?'

'Nine-fifteen.' He notices me eyeing up his clothes. 'I've been out. Went for a run.'

'I had no idea that's something you do.'

'I feel like there's a lot of things you don't know I do,' he says.

I sit up and blow on my coffee. 'Probably. What's the plan for today then?'

'We can stay here, or take a drive, or go to LA, or—'

'Take me to the Hollywood sign,' I say, interrupting. He laughs.

'Of *course* that's what you want to do.'

'*Obviously* that's what I want to do.'

'Okay. We'll go to Griffith Park. We can go to the observatory as well. It's super cool, and I haven't been there for years.'

'Can you see the sign, though? The sign is important.'

'Yeah, you get a great view from there. It'll look small, though.'

'That's fine. It's for photos. Zoom lens.'

He takes a long sip of coffee and laughs and rolls his eyes.

'What? What's that for?'

'Just, the first thing you want to see is the Hollywood sign. I don't know. It's cute.'

'Whatever,' I laugh, picking up a pillow and lobbing it at him. He dodges. It lands on the floor. He picks it up and chucks it back.

'So,' he says. 'Do we have some time to kill before we do the tourist thing?'

'You tell me,' I say.

'I think we do.' He takes the cup from my hands and puts it back on the nightstand. He does the same with his and pulls off his t-shirt. God, yes, I fancy him so much. I have an incredible urge to bite his shoulder, but I don't. I lean forward and drop a kiss on it instead. He's slightly salty. A little bit clammy. Dude definitely worked up a sweat on that run. He's about to work up another. 'Feel like taking a shower with me after this?' he says. He's all glinty eyes and smirk.

'Insatiable,' I say. 'You're absolutely insatiable. Aren't you?'

'Mmhmm. Yep,' he says.

–

After a late breakfast, we get in the car and head for Griffith Park. The observatory's at the top of a winding road and before we even get there I can see that the view out across the city is beautiful. We make for the right hand side of the building, and he doesn't even laugh when I get altogether too excited about the white letters perched on the hill. We take photos of ourselves with the sign in the background. Someone offers to take one for us. In one I've stood up on my tiptoes and I'm kissing his cheek, so hard that his stubble prickles my lips.

Sunlight reflects off his Aviators. My hair is untamed and a little wild. Looking at it makes me feel fizzy.

Inside, we look through the solar telescope. We wander around the exhibits and watch the Tesla coil demonstration. Outside again, this time at the back of the building, we stare at the view across Downtown LA for a long time.

'This place is beautiful,' I say and I lace our fingers together. 'The view is amazing. Thank you for bringing me here.'

He doesn't say anything back. He just leans down and kisses the top of my head in response.

Later on, back in Seal Beach, we stop at a diner for drinks, and take them a little way up the pier. The beach is busy. People sunbathe on the sand. On the flatter part behind us, a group of people have set up a game of volleyball and swat the ball over the net at each other. It looks strenuous in the heat. People paddle and swim in the ocean. Gulls skulk around, scavenging for scraps of food. Through the tiny gaps in the wood, I watch the sea slosh against the legs of the pier. The blistering sun beats down on my neck and I untie my hair to keep from getting burnt.

'So how are you liking California so far?' Jesse asks.

'Well, twenty-four hours in and so far, so good,' I tell him. 'You're lucky to live here.'

'It certainly has more going for it than Omaha,' he says.

'You're not tempted to go back then?'

'God, no. It'd be weird now, I've lived in California for so long, Nebraska wouldn't feel like home anymore.'

'Do you have any family back there?'

'My Grandma Ada lives there. Mom wanted her to move out here when my Grandpa Nev died, but she wouldn't have it. Other than that, there's my aunt and uncle and a couple of cousins, as far as I know... they might have moved. All other immediate family live in California. Oh, except for Adam. He's in New York.'

'Do you see much of them?'

'Trav, yes. He's not far away. Brandon and Lainey, when I can, and Adam...' he trails off.

'Adam?' I press.

'We don't really talk.' He wrinkles up his nose and squints out to sea. I know I need to tread carefully here; to straddle that line between curiosity and nosiness.

'Oh?' I say.

He looks at me, like he's debating whether or not he wants to talk.

'Do you want to know what happened?' he says, eventually, and it's like he can read my mind.

'Only if you want to share it,' I say, but of course I want to know.

He takes a deep breath in and releases it slowly before talking. 'Franko ended because I quit,' he says, simply.

What? This is brand new information. He doesn't wait for me to say anything, and neither does he look at me.

'I loved it when we first started, you know? It was *seriously* awesome. We moved here. They yanked us out of school. We lived in a big house in a nice part of LA, a world away from where we grew up in Omaha. We came here having never seen the ocean before, and the first day we arrived, they brought us to the beach, and I have this vivid memory of the first time I ever stood in the ocean. Anyway, we got to spend every day making music, and doing shows, and meeting people. The record label threw money and promotion behind us. We got passports. We got to travel. What kid wouldn't love that, right?'

He takes a sip of his drink and pushes back his hair. 'But then, slowly, Dad turned into this crazy megalomaniac. By the time we made the second album, he'd... well, he'd completely switched from how he was in Omaha. He was just a normal guy when we were little kids.' He shifts to face me a bit more to explain. 'He was our manager, so in control of *everything*. Like, we had to run every single little thing past him. He got to decide what we did, and when we were allowed breaks – which

177

was never, by the way – and how we sounded. He totally pushed us to make *Now or Never* the album that it was, and it turned out he didn't know quite as much as he thought he did. Because obviously that album bombed. And I don't think it's where we'd have gone if we'd been left to our own devices a bit more.'

'Yeah, I remember it didn't do too well. I loved it, though.'

'Thanks,' he says, and squeezes my knee. 'It pushed us all creatively, and I don't regret that, because I learnt *so* much making it. But anyway, there we were, in a hotel in Berlin, having breakfast, and he came storming in with this magazine we were reviewed in. And it really wasn't a good review. And he slammed it down on the table and just lost it.'

'Shit. In front of everyone?'

'Yeah. Nice, huh?'

'Was your mum there? What did she do?'

'Absolutely nothing. She just sat there. I remember watching her stare into her cup of tea, and so wanting her to say something to him. Or make him stop, or do anything to diffuse it, but she didn't. And this kind of thing had been going on for ages. Like, years, and it was the last straw because to be *that* young, and to have everything you've poured yourself into for months be shot down? Well, what you need is kindness, not public humiliation. So, I got up, walked out, packed up my shit and left. And that was that. I was only nineteen.'

'As simple as that?'

'God, no, there was nothing simple about it. Dad cut me off immediately. I got nothing for a long time. None of the royalties I was due... But that wasn't really anything new either.'

'What do you mean?'

'Well,' he says, ruefully. 'Let's just say, we didn't see a lot of the money we were making, even when we were doing well.'

'No!'

'Yeah. Our parents always had full financial control on account of us being minors. We got allowances, but it was definitely nothing like what it should have been. Dad said it was to keep us grounded and like regular kids, but really he just kept it.'

'Wow. What a dick. Sorry.'

'Don't be. It's true. He's a grade A asshole.'

'So what did you do when you got back?' The questions are coming thick and fast now.

'I just got on with shit. I was staying… with someone, and we got an apartment and I just starting doing what I do now.'

He was staying with someone. A girl? Must be. There was a clear and distinct hesitation when he told me. Suddenly I'm not sure I want to know much more, but at the same time, I want to know everything about him.

'Were your family cross?'

'Uh, yeah. Travis was okay. Disappointed, but he knew things weren't great. Brandon was gutted and Mom was apparently upset, but I didn't see her, or Brandon actually, for months, so I don't know if that's true or if Dad just used it as a guilt tactic.' He shrugs. 'Adam was super mad, though. I don't know if he's ever really gotten over it. He thought I ended his career. The day I left, we sort of got into a fight over it.'

'What, like, an actual tussle?'

'Yeah. He shoved me against a wall and called me a stupid fucking asshole. So I retaliated and Travis ended up intervening. It was just frustration and anger and pent-up hormones, really, but we'd never fought like that before, so… definitely not my finest moment.'

'And your dad?'

'Dad was just afraid he'd have to go back to being a car salesman. Not that selling cars is a bad profession, but he always was one to dream big. He didn't have to though, because he bought a house in Anaheim, and Mom went back to teaching.'

'So he nicked all your royalties, bought a house, and then what?' I sound incredulous.

Jesse laughs. 'He took "early retirement",' he says, making air quotes. 'I don't know what he does. Genuinely, no idea. I mean, I guess he must do *something*, but I don't know what. Can't imagine those royalty checks are supporting them these days.' He sinks back in the seat and rests his legs on the side of the pier, crossing them at his ankles.

'Maybe he sells cars in secret?' I say, nudging his arm.

'Maybe he does.'

'So you don't see them then?'

'Not really,' he shakes his head. 'Thanksgiving, Christmas. Last time I saw them together was when Nancy turned two. Mom sometimes drops by. Dad never does. And if I go over there, it's small talk, nothing particularly meaningful. We wouldn't, for instance, go to a bar or anything like that. There is no father–son bonding time.'

'That doesn't really sound like he's put the past behind him,' I say.

Jesse snorts. 'You think?'

'And are you okay with that?'

'It is what it is,' he says, shrugging.

I can't imagine it. Really, I can't. I shake my cup and the remaining ice rattles around. Mainly I just think it's all a bit sad. I don't know how I'd feel if I was so obviously used as cash cow by my parents, but my hunch is, not good. And then to have to deal with all that rejection on top of it. Walking away from everything familiar like that can't have been easy either; getting on a plane and having to start over when you've barely finished being a kid, without any real transition into adulthood. I sit there and polish the lenses of my sunglasses, and try to imagine my own parents behaving like that, but I can't fathom it. They're a funny pair, definitely stuck in their ways, and there have been times when I've done things they would rather I hadn't. Mum might have pursed her lips and made a comment and Dad might have shaken his head and looked disappointed. But they'd never have cut me off because of it. They'd never cut me off for anything.

'Anyway,' he says, shrugging. 'Now you know. What about you? Any weird skeletons in your family closet?'

'Not at all,' I shrug. 'My aunt had it off with a vicar once. They had an affair for a bit, but that's it. We're very ordinary.'

I'm not downplaying it. We are. Dad's an accountant. Mum's a housewife. I grew up in a nineteen-thirties semi in Amersham. They still live there. The house is too big for just the two of them, but they'll never move. Mum's garden is far too well established for that. Jesse laughs harder than my comment deserves.

'Ordinary is nice though, right? You know where you are with ordinary. Not that you're ordinary.'

'Good save,' I say, twisting myself towards him. I lean my head on my hand and watch him slurp up the remaining tea in his cup.

'Do you get on with your parents?' he asks.

'Yeah, well enough.'

'See them often?'

'Not as much as I probably should,' I admit, feeling guilty that the last time I went back to visit was weeks ago. 'I wouldn't say we are massively close.'

'Have you told them that you're out here?' he asks.

'They know I'm in California, but they don't know I'm with you,' I say, shifting on my bum.

'You didn't tell them?'

'Not yet.' I shake my head. 'There'd be a lot of questions. I mean, can you imagine that conversation? Mum, Dad, just FYI, I'm going to spend two weeks with the bass player from that band I used to like when I was a teenager.'

'Well, if you put it like that then, sure, of course there'd be questions.'

'Do you think I should have told them?'

'Of course. That's just common sense, right? What if I turned out to be some kind of murderous asshole who was luring you to your death?' He pauses and looks me right in the eye, 'I'm not, by the way.'

I laugh. 'You know, call me naive, but I just didn't get psycho killer vibes from you.' I nudge his arm, 'I *will* tell them. Don't worry.'

He nudges me back. 'I'm not worried. Shall we get going?'

'Sure.' I haul myself up, throw my cup in the bin. 'Hey,' I say. 'The observatory was brilliant.'

'Ah, but did the *sign* live up to expectations?'

'The sign was pretty cool, too.'

–

'Cassie,' he whispers, much later on, just as I am falling asleep.

'Mmhmm?'

'All that stuff I told you earlier, about my dad and about the money thing.'

'Yeah.'

'I haven't told anyone that before. Ever.'

'Really?'

'Really.'

'How come?'

'I just haven't felt like I wanted to before today. Someone once told me I was closed up. So I'm really trying not to be.'

I reach behind and pat his arm, sleepily.

'I'm pleased you felt like you could tell me.'

'You've made it easy though,' he continues. 'Even before you came out here and we were just talking on the internet I wanted to tell you stuff. I don't know, it's probably stupid.'

I roll over so we are facing each other. My eyes have adjusted and his look glassy in the darkness.

'It's not stupid. But I don't understand why you'd keep it to yourself. It's nothing to be ashamed of. Sounds like things were pretty shitty for you, to be honest.'

'Usually I just try not to think too much about it. If I went into detail, people would have questions. So I just said we were dropped. Seems like that's easier to swallow. Anyway, no one's asked for years.'

'But there must be *some* people outside your family who knew? People you dated? No?'

'No one outside my family knows the *full* extent of it, other than you,' he repeats. 'And I think Adam – and probably Brandon – would have a different take on it. Adam's similar to Dad, so... and Brandon was too young to know, really. Plus, he was kind of babied a little. Especially by Mom.'

'I think that probably happens quite a lot with the youngest. Rachel's younger sister Marie is a bit like that.'

He yawns. 'I think it's because I don't feel as if there's an agenda with you.'

He's wrong about that. There's absolutely an agenda. I want him to fall completely in love with me, the way I am with him. I want us to laugh at that stupid giant distance and make it work. I want the babies Marie joked about when we went for tapas. But I just can't seem to say any of it yet. I can't even hint at it. I lose my nerve every time.

He carries on. 'And when we hung out in London, there was not one single time when you seemed like you wanted something from me. We just seemed to have a really great time.'

'Like we are now?' I ask.

'Like we are now.'

'Well, for what it's worth, when I added you on Facebook, I didn't do it expecting all this to happen.'

'Right? It's been surprising.'

I can feel my eyes getting heavy. It's been a full-on day, tiring both physically and mentally. I think probably for both of us.

'Do you feel lighter for telling me?' I ask.

'I think so.'

I push my arm under his pillow, scoop him closer to me, kiss his forehead and stroke back his hair the way he did mine yesterday when I was napping.

'Good,' I whisper. 'Maybe you're a little less closed up for it.'

Chapter Twenty-Five

Jesse

It's the second morning Cassie's been here and we're sitting in the kitchen, eating breakfast and deciding how to spend the day.

'Okay, so we can tick off the Hollywood sign and Griffith Observatory. What do you feel like seeing today?'

She wraps her hand around her mug and taps her fingernails against it.

'I want you to take me somewhere *you* love to go,' she says. 'Show me the things you love about living here.'

'Hmm,' I say, picking up a piece of toast from the pile we are sharing and biting off the corner. 'So many options.'

'Mmhmm.'

'Okay, well there's an awesome music store over in Hollywood. I like to hang out in there sometimes and just sift through old records.'

'Perfecto,' she says, taking a bite of toast and rubbing the crumbs between her fingers.

'Are you sure you won't be bored? We can do something else.'

She smiles and shakes her head whilst chewing.

'Okay, good.'

We continue working our way through the mountain of toast and when we're done she jumps off the stool, and starts to clear everything away.

'I'll do that,' I say.

'It's done now,' she says, stacking the dishwasher and closing the door. 'No biggie.' She shrugs and it's cute.

'Hey, Cass, you got something on your face.'

'Where?' she asks, rubbing her fingers over her mouth. 'Peanut butter?'

'No. Just here,' I say, tapping the corner of her bottom lip and kissing her.

'Oh, ha ha,' she says. 'I'm going to sort my face out and then shall we go?'

'Yeah. No rush though. We have all day... Hey,' I call up the stairs, after her. 'So if I ever visit you will you show me all the places you love in London?'

She leans over the banister. 'Of course. We won't get through all of it in one go, though. You might have to come back.'

—

Amoeba isn't particularly busy. There are a few people milling around; a couple of tourists, some scene kids with brightly colored hair and heavy eye make-up, and a grungy-looking dude wearing a muddy green sweater and headphones around his neck. He's trying to sell some old cassette tapes at the trade counter but isn't getting too far.

'But, they're vintage,' he argues.

'Sir, they're not in the greatest of condition. And cassettes aren't in high demand. Also, this is a mixtape. We can't sell that.'

'How do you know it's not a compilation?'

'Because you've written out the track listing on a generic inlay card.'

Cassie giggles and nudges my arm. 'Are you hearing this? I'll take his mixtape,' she whispers. 'Who doesn't love a mixtape?'

'I kind of want to know what's on it. I mean, he thinks it's good enough to sell.'

'Definitely some Nirvana,' she says. 'And Soundgarden. What do you reckon?'

'I'd bet the world on both of those,' I say. 'See also anything that came out of Seattle circa the early nineties with a whole lotta distortion.'

We watch the exchange over the top of one of the racks of CDs. He wants more than the store are willing to give him. In the end he stacks up his tapes and sweeps them back into his bag. Dramatic motherfucker.

'Now we'll never know,' Cassie says.

'Did you ever make mixtapes?'

'Yeah, Rachel and I used to make them when we were teenagers. Did you?'

'Still do. Not tapes though, but sort of similar. For my car mainly. It's kind of a thing... that I do. Sometimes. When I want to remember something. Or a feeling, or, like, a specific time. I dunno, maybe it's dumb.'

'It's not dumb. Can we listen to one on the way home? Or are they just for you?'

'We can listen.' We carry on up the aisles, stopping here and there, poking around.

'This place is very cool.'

'I thought you'd like it. They have live music in here some-times, too.'

'I feel like I've stepped into some kind of *Empire Records* experience or something.'

'Ha, yeah it definitely has that vibe to it,' I say, opening my record bag and rummaging around inside for a notebook.

'What's that?'

'A shopping list of sorts. Rare stuff, though they don't often have any of it. Still, I live in hope.'

She looks over the list. 'I have never heard of any of those bands.'

Honestly, I'm not surprised. None of it's mainstream and she definitely seems like a mainstream kind of girl.

'No? Well, these guys,' I say, pointing to one of the bands on my list, 'are especially great. In fact, if we find this, be prepared to hear it a *lot* whilst you're here. *In fact*, even if we don't, I have other albums of theirs. So you can't leave here without listening to them.'

'Okay,' she laughs, and it occurs to me that I know next to nothing about her music taste, aside that she knows almost all the lyrics to *Boys of Summer* and she once told me on chat that she quite liked Maroon 5.

'Sooo, name me some bands you're into, but ones that I was never a part of.'

She looks contemplative for a few seconds. 'I feel like you're going to judge me for my obvious commercial radio style taste in music. Basically, I tend to like what's popular at the time.'

'I knew it.'

'Alright, music snob,' she says, and it's jokey but there's a touch of defensiveness there, too. 'How did you know it? That's a bit stereotypical; I could be into some obscure Siberian drumming collective for all you know.'

'Are you? Because, I mean, that'd be pretty cool, and I daresay Trav would be especially interested to hear about it.'

'No. But that's beside the point.'

'It's just… a vibe I got from you.'

She's staring at me blankly. I don't think she's impressed.

'It's not a bad thing,' I shrug.

'I know it isn't. There are bands I've liked for years too, but unless I really want to listen to them, I just put on the radio.'

'Right, but isn't it then always just almost in your subconscious? Like it's just background noise. If you listen to what's popular at the time, as soon as it's not anymore, don't you just forget about it?'

'Sometimes. Sometimes not. Sometimes I'll really like a song and then not hear it for months, and when I do, it's incredible. It takes me right back. Like magic.'

'Okay, that I *totally* get.' That's the reason I make the playlists. Entirely for that feeling she just described.

She leans in and slides her arm around me, so I don't think she's really mad.

'I don't know,' I continue. 'Mainstream pop music just feels so disposable.'

'Oh, does it really? Jesse, don't you make your living from mainstream pop music?'

'Touché. Yeah, okay. Good point.'

'So what else have you got in your notebook?' she asks.

'Random things. Just, you know, scribbles, lists…' I flick through it to show her. 'Tab. Notes I've made in various sessions. Et cetera, et cetera.'

'Tab?'

'Yeah, it's a very basic way of writing out what you're playing.'

She looks at the page with the tab scribbled on it.

'Looks complicated,' she says.

'It's not really. To be honest I don't use it much because it's kind of restrictive and there's almost always more than one way to play a bassline, but it's good if I need to remember something quickly. The numbers represent where you fret, and the lines represent each string. Remind me at home. I'll show you.'

'I'd like that. Are there any songs in there? Do you do that?'

'Nah. Not really my forte. I haven't written anything since… well probably since Franko. And to be honest I wasn't even all that into writing lyrics even then. I've never been very good at the words. I cared more about making it sound cool rather than what Adam was singing, you know?'

'Mmhmm,' she says.

We stay at Amoeba for another hour or so. They don't have any of the records on my list and it's just about lunchtime when we're back in the car.

'So, these playlists of yours.'

'In the glove compartment. You choose.'

She rummages around for a few seconds, finds the CD wallet and holds it up.

'In here?' she says.

'Yep.'

'CDs? I thought you meant on your phone or an iPod or what have you.'

'There's a reason!' I laugh, starting the engine. 'It's because they are specific to something. Like, a feeling or a memory. If I commit a bunch of songs to disc, I can't easily change them, so, when I listen to it, it's like the memory stays true to the actual event.'

She flicks through the wallet. She can't tell much from the discs and the titles won't mean anything to her. Some are numbered; some just have a word scrawled on with a Sharpie.

'Gosh, this is like an insight into your mind. This one okay?' She picks one out and waves it in my direction.

'Sure, whatever you like,' I say, not really looking at it. She slots it into the disc drive.

But the minute the song starts to play I wish I *had* looked at it. Because instantly I recognize the beat. And the synthy chords. And the sexy little riff. And the sort of bizarre lyrics about baking bread and the night train. Oh my god, *no*, Cassie's picked out a playlist I made for Nicole. One we put on when we were *together*.

I stare straight ahead and concentrate on the road, but I can sense Cassie's looking at me. It's so awkward. It's such a fuck song. Has she figured that out yet? She has ears, she must have done. And if so, she's got to be wondering why I have this song on a CD in my car. She's got to be wondering who else I've listened to it with. She's got to be wondering, at this very second, what I wanted to remember and what feelings I wanted to recapture when I'm listening to it, and if that's happening now.

'So this is a song and a half,' she says, eventually.

'Hmm. I guess,' I say. I'm trying to be nonchalant. It's not working. Never have I been so desperate for an outro. Because now I'm thinking about Nicole. Her dimples, and her auburn hair. Nicole peeling off her clothes, and how now she's about to have a baby, and I still don't know if… *Jesus*. I don't want to look back on this day and remember that I thought about this. Actually, I don't want to think about this at all. I don't want my memories of her to combine and jar with the ones I'll have of today. I want them to be clear and distinct. I want to throw the disc out of the window; to see it shatter on the asphalt, or get crunched under someone else's wheels. 'Aw crap, you know what?' I say. 'I just remembered this CD skips.'

She's still looking at me. 'Ugh, that is the worst,' she says, eventually and flatly, stopping it and ejecting. I don't think she's buying it. She puts it back in the wallet without looking for a scratch or a smudge or anything on the disc, and I'm relieved because that isn't even remotely true. Nicole's having a kid that could be mine, and that CD plays just fine.

I am expecting her to pick another but she re-tunes the radio instead and settles back into her seat. She opens the window and leans her arm out of the car. She re-adjusts her sunglasses and her hair flies around her face. 'Call Me Maybe' by Carly Rae Jepsen is playing. Of course it is; it's all that's ever played at the moment, and despite what I said earlier on about mainstream pop it's catchy and I like it. I start to sing along and almost immediately Cassie giggles.

'What's funny? My singing?'

'No, that's actually very nice. But remember how Rachel sent my first message to you?'

'Sure.'

'Well, when I confronted her about that she admitted she was actually going to send the lyrics to this song.'

'Yeah? Was she going to type your number and be like, "call me"?'

'Maybe,' she shrugs.

'I see what you did there,' I say, laughing, and Nicole fades out of my head. For now.

Chapter Twenty-Six

Cassie

By the time we get to the restaurant, Jesse's weird reaction to the CD has ebbed, and as I put it back in the case I made a mental note not to pick it again because something felt unresolved. He perked right up when I switched on the radio and we sang along to pop music all the way here. It was goofy and cute and couply. *We're* so couply, and I like how that feels. When I leave here, will I be able to call us that? Does he even see me like that? Could he? The distance might prove to be too much. He might just see us as friends with benefits. Although I doubt he'd need to cross the Atlantic to get a shag. But that plane ticket felt like a bit of an investment. You don't invite someone you're just interested in having sex with halfway across the world to stay for two weeks. You don't open up to them the way he did to me yesterday. You don't take them to your favourite places and tell them your secrets. We're more than that, I know we are. I'm sure of it.

We park up and head inside. It's heaving. The queue is almost out the door. There's sawdust on the floor and service is quick and efficient.

'So, it's a sandwich, dipped in meat juices?' I ask, feeling slightly dubious about the whole thing as we wait in line to order.

'That's right,' he says, earnestly. 'Don't look so incredulous. You'll like it, you can't not. This place is legendary.' He looks distinctly excited about it.

'Doesn't it go all soggy?'

'I mean, the sandwich isn't saturated. Just nicely *moist*, for lack of a better word. Look, there are thousands of places to eat in LA; do you think the line would be this long if they weren't good? Be prepared for an education.'

We're shuffling towards the front now, and I'm completely confused.

'Alright. Can you order for me, though? I don't know what to get.'

'Of course,' he says.

We carry our food over to a table, and he's right; it's a good sandwich. In fact, it's a *great* sandwich. I feel silly for doubting him.

'On these grounds alone,' I say. 'I don't want to go home.'

He stops eating, and wipes his mouth with a napkin before speaking.

'What other grounds might there be?' he asks.

'I dunno. Nothing,' I say, and pick at my jus-soaked roll. I'm annoyed with myself. I can't bring myself to look at him. I don't know why I can't seem to tell him how I feel about him. He told me he liked me the morning after we first met, and I didn't say anything back until he was a safe distance away. He's shown me, too. In all sorts of ways, big and small, like buying my flight out here and everything he said on the pier, and I've happily taken it all, grabbed it with both hands and basked in it. And yet, here we are, having a nice lunch and I've made a comment more loaded than a TGI Friday's potato skin that I can't even seem to expand on. He must know, though. As if a sandwich could affect someone that much. 'Coleslaw's nice, huh?' I say, stiffly.

'Sure is,' he agrees. He finishes up his food and dusts off his hands. The time to say something has gone.

In the evening, we go for a walk on the beach again, and I hope it will become something that we do every night. Jesse's quiet, though. He's been a little bit less like himself since lunch-time. Just quieter. Distracted, perhaps. I don't like to think that it has something to do with what I did or didn't say, or that bloody CD. We amble up over the dune and along the sand.

'How would you feel about Trav stopping by at some point?' he says.

'Tonight?' I look at my watch. It's getting on a bit. I'm flagging.

'Not tonight, but at some point whilst you're here? He's been calling…'

'Is this a curiosity thing?' I ask. 'Because it is for me.' Jesse laughs.

'Probably. He's called me a few times, asking if I'm intending to keep you to myself the entire time.'

I squeeze his hand. 'Are you?'

'As much as I would love to, I think he believes I made you up.'

'Been that long, has it?'

'No,' he says, slowly. 'It's more that you're from the UK and ergo, all kinds of exotic. And I haven't been with anyone British before.'

The comment makes my mind race. Maybe that *is* where we are. Has he just implied we're together? As in *together* together. Not just geographically or physically at this moment in time, but in a proper relationship sort of way. I want to ask him about it but something, again, stops me.

'Well, we can't have him thinking I'm a figment of your imagination,' I say instead.

'He'll probably just bring some drinks over and want to chill out. Maybe we'll have some dinner. If you're sure it won't be weird, or too much.'

'It will be fine. Probably, the hardest part will be remembering your cover story about how we met. What happened again? Our eyes met across the bar, and you thought I was the most beautiful creature you'd ever clapped eyes on. And as soon as we touched there was all this incredible electricity. Time slowed down, and, throughout the evening you couldn't help yourself. You just fell more and more in love with me.'

193

I'm saying all this because it's true, at least, for me.

'Yeah, something like that,' he says pushing his hair back. But now he won't look at me, and there's a slight tinge of awkwardness between us.

'Okay, well, seems like we're on the same page then,' I say, too cheerfully. There's silence for a minute or two. 'You alright?' I ask, eventually.

'Uh huh,' he says. He's looking down at the sand now, flipping a shell over and over with the toe of his shoe.

'Okay.'

More silence. I squeeze his hand. The waves lap against the shore and slap against the pier, and there's music coming from one of the houses behind us.

'Are you really, though?' I'm worried I've been too flippant. This isn't the time now for me to try and be the cool girl, or jokey, breezy Cass who doesn't take anything seriously and uses humour to cover up her emotions. He hesitates for a bit.

'Let me ask you something,' he says. 'Why do you think I bought you that plane ticket out here?'

I'm a little taken aback, to be honest, and not really sure of my answer. He doesn't wait for it, anyway. 'Because I liked you. That night in London... I did, I *liked* you. And I told you before that it came as a shock because I wasn't expecting to, as much as that, anyway. So I just wanted to take a chance and see where it would go. And I know we talked about it yesterday, but all that stuff about Franko is hard for me. So it really is easier to just keep it vague.'

A cool breeze blows around my bare arms. I rub them vigorously and wish I'd had the sense to grab a cardi before we left. I'll never make a California girl, that's for sure.

'Okay,' I say. 'I won't say anything.'

But now I'm feeling dejected and a little small. Like I want to stop time, rewind the last half a day and start it again. This time I'd say something different at the restaurant. I'd steel my nerve and tell him that even though it's only two days in, I don't want my trip to end. I'd tell him I don't want to leave because it leaves an air of uncertainty. I'd tell him the truth; that I'll miss him when I don't get to see him every day. That my real life doesn't seem so appealing anymore, and I'd rather be a part of his, and that's a conflict in itself, because I love my life back home. I look out to sea, at the faint strip of land on the horizon. What's after that? Nothing for miles and miles. Just ocean.

'Now I feel as if *you're* upset about something,' he says, and fleetingly, I think we're both a bit silly.

'I'm not, really. Maybe all this has just caught up with me. And I feel like you might be a bit off with me. I'm sorry.'

'No,' he says. 'I was just trying to explain.' He's turned to face me now. He wraps his arms around my shoulders and I breathe him in. He's the only thing I know in America. I'm so desperate for things to stay nice between us.

'I wish I was better at this,' I admit. I'm floundering. I finally settle my arms around his waist, slide my hands underneath his t-shirt, rub my thumbs over his skin.

'You're fine at this,' he says. 'But seriously, I can just tell Trav to leave it.'

'I don't want you to do that,' I say, looking up at him. I really don't. I want it to be simple and easy when we see each other, because there isn't anything really simple or easy about long distance.

'Let's go home,' he says, breaking away and I like the way he refers to his home as if it's mine, too.

But something occurs to me on the walk back up the beach. I hadn't given it any conscious thought since before we met, but it's an idea so well formed in my head that I wonder if it's been floating there all along and has only just bubbled up to the surface. Or maybe I didn't allow myself to think about it in case somehow it broke the spell. Because the thing is, none of it makes sense: us meeting in London, and my being here now, when his locked-down Facebook profile and the way he's so adamant about being anonymous suggests he didn't want to be found. So when I *did* find him, why did he let me in at all? You don't just wake up one day and decide to be open with strangers on the internet, do you?

It's later on when we are lying in bed that I broach it because unlike my big feelings, now that I've thought it, I can't not say it.

'So, I have a question.' I'm lying on my side with my arm underneath my head. 'Why did you add me back? On Facebook.'

He looks over at me from his phone. 'Really?' he says. 'You're asking that?'

'I really am,' I coo.

'Honestly? At first I wondered if you'd got the right person.'

'Yeah, I remember you saying. But it didn't occur to you that I could have been a Franko fan?'

'Not really, no. No one has ever done that before.'

'Really? Not even anyone from Germany? You were massive there.' I am genuinely surprised and I can't hide it. He sniggers.

'Not even anyone from Germany.'

'Okay,' I roll over on to my front and bend my knees so my feet make a tent of bed sheets. 'So knowing what I know now about how private you like to be, why did you keep talking to me once you knew I liked your band and definitely did mean to find you? Why did you choose to open up to *me*? How come we ever chatted again after the first time? I mean, it went so horribly, I convinced myself that was it.'

'You thought it went horribly?'

'You *didn't* think it went horribly?'

'Not really. I got a nice picture of you out of it. I still have it on my laptop.'

'It was awkward, what with you asking me if I did a lot of online stalking, and the *s'up hot stuff* message Rachel sent. I was mortified.'

He smirks. 'It was because you were so far away and it didn't feel real. You were just someone on another computer halfway across the world, and I figured I could just stop it whenever I felt like it. Like, if you encroached too far into my life, or it stopped feeling good I could just cut you out of it with a couple of clicks.' He's looking at the ceiling and drumming his fingertips on his chest.

'Wow,' I say. 'Brutal.'

'But,' he says, quickly, 'the point is that I didn't. The point is that I *couldn't*.'

'But *you* were the one who made it real. *You* came to London for those gigs. You didn't have to meet me. You didn't have to even tell me. How would I have known? If anything, it was you who encroached on *my* life. You made this happen. You were the catalyst. You crossed over into my reality far more than I could have ever crossed over into yours.'

'I mean, you have to admit the whole Kitten Tricks thing was pretty serendipitous…'

'What if I'd said no?'

'Then I'd have done the shows and come back and… I don't know. Carried on as normal, I guess. Anyway, are you complaining? Would you rather I hadn't wanted to hang out with you?'

Answer the question, I think. 'Course not. Don't be silly,' I say. 'You can be so evasive, you know that?'

He looks at me for a few seconds.

'Curiosity, more than anything, I guess. I was having a quiet day and you came online and I figured I'd say hi and then you'd realize you didn't mean me at all and that would be that. And it's like I told you the other night; you didn't seem like you wanted anything from me. It was when you said you'd leave me alone. That's when I wanted to carry on talking to you. I found you intriguing. I don't find many people intriguing.'

Is this what reluctant fame does to a person? Makes them mistrusting and a little bit cynical and shut off? I'd hate it, too, I think. Hate people knowing my business. Hate the expectation to be a role model. Hate growing up in public the way he had to. I'd be one of those famous people who loses the plot and ends up getting arrested for something ludicrous. My mugshot would be all over the tabloids, sallow and sorry. Mum would talk about rehab and Dad would be grave about the entire thing.

'Anyway, going back to your question,' he says, 'I think you should just go with it.'

I don't say anything. I just nod. He reaches over and flicks off the light and moonlight casts a white glow against the wall. He snakes his arm around my waist and I still can't quite get over the fact that all this is happening. I feel as if it is all just some kind of wildly realistic dream and that tomorrow morning I might wake up in my bed in Shepherd's Bush. I don't want that, and in fact, the longer I am here the less I ever want to wake up in my bed in Shepherd's Bush ever again.

Chapter Twenty-Seven

From: Marie Michaels

To: Cassie Banks, Lauren Rivers, Mandy Michaels +6 more

Subject: Hen do

Hello hens,

First of all, thank you all so much for getting back to me. Cassie, Lauren and I are so excited to give Rachel the send-off she absolutely deserves.

Here's the plan: We'll meet at her flat at 4pm on the day (Sat 6th October) for some fizz, general chilling/girl time/getting ready. Then we're going for a meal at her favourite restaurant. They've been amazing and have put together a special Italian wedding menu. Sort of like a tasting menu. I went to try it when we booked and it's excellent. After this, we're heading over to Vauxhall for a night at the ROLLER DISCO! Rachel was obsessed with roller skating when she was younger. She always said she was going to audition for *Starlight Express* when she grew up. She never got round to that, but she'll love this instead.

So, please bring:

1) some fizz for the afternoon.

2) something nice to wear for the meal. But also,

3) the most roller skatery outfit you can cobble together for the disco. We will be providing neon accessories and leg warmers, but otherwise, go as kitsch and cute as possible. The meal is £55 per head, plus drinks, and that's all booked. Cass is sorting out the roller disco, so she'll be in touch about that.

See you soon,
Marie

From: Marie Michaels
To: Cassie Banks, Lauren Rivers, Mandy Michaels.
Subject: Fwd: Hen do

Hi all,

Cass, can you book the roller disco please? Everyone who is coming is on my other email, so you'll have numbers/contacts.

I've also copied in our cousin Mandy, because she's kindly offered to do make-up for us all.

Lauren – Just checking you have all the accessories.

Hope you're having a good time in the US banging that pop star of yours like a drum?

Marie x

From: Lauren Rivers
To: Cassie Banks, Marie Michaels, Mandy Michaels, +6 more
Subject: Re: Hen do

Hi ladies,

I have decorations for the table at the restaurant, and heaps of vulgar penis-themed accessories, including straws. Bit realistic. Definitely gross. Also chocolate dicks with mint fondant inside. Think filthy After Eights.

I've also got neon snap necklaces, leg warmers, confetti, loads. Can't wait to meet you all.

Lauren xx

From: Mandy Michaels
To: Cassie Banks, Lauren Rivers, Marie Michaels +6 more
Subject: Re: Re: Hen do

Happy to do a make-up sesh before we go out and defo before we go skating.

But more to the point, Cassie is shagging a pop star? Anyone good? Details please?!

Mandy Michaels
Professional makeup artist

From: Cassie Banks
To: Mandy Michaels, Lauren Rivers, Marie Michaels +6 more
Subject: Re: Re: Re: Hen do

He's not a pop star anymore. His name is Jesse and he used to be in a band called Franko.
Cass x

From: Mandy Michaels
To: Cassie Banks, Lauren Rivers, Marie Michaels, +6 more
Subject: OH MY GOD

I just Googled him. Cass, are you shagging a 19-year-old? Does he still have those highlights? I know someone who can fix that for him. You total cougar though. Respect!
Mx

Mandy Michaels
Professional makeup artist

From: Cassie Banks
To: Mandy Michaels, Lauren Rivers, Marie Michaels, +6 more
Subject: Re: OH MY GOD
1 attachment: CJ14.jpg

No Mandy, he's not 19 anymore. Those are old photos you're looking at. Here's a recent one. Come. To. Mama.
Cass x

From: Marie Michaels
To: Cassie Banks
Subject: Roller Disco?

Have you booked this yet?

From: Cassie Banks
To: Marie Michaels
Subject: Re: Roller Disco?

It's all in hand Marie. Also I am on holiday.

Chapter Twenty-Eight

Cassie

On Saturday morning, we take a drive down the coast for brunch: strawberry French toast and coffee and fresh orange juice, eaten outside in the sunshine, overlooking the sea. I love the calm of the waves below. The white crests peak and disperse. The morning sun reflects off the water.

'There are whales out there somewhere,' Jesse tells me. He waves his fork towards the water, and I stifle a laugh.

'No shit,' I giggle. 'The ocean *is* where they tend to hang out, no?'

'No, I mean close by. You can get on a boat and go whale watching. It's a thing.'

'Can we do that?' I ask. I want to see whales.

'Sure. I think you probably have to make an advance booking though, so it might not be today.'

'Have you been before?'

'Nah,' he says, shaking his head.

'Not your thing?'

'It's not that. It's just one of those things you vaguely think might be fun but never actually get around to doing.'

'Well then we definitely must go,' I say. I like the idea that he's never done it before. Now, whatever happens between us, every time he thinks of whales, he'll remember we went whale watching together. In some small way, I'll be imprinted on a synapse in his brain forever. 'Next week?'

'For sure,' he says. He seems more himself today, and I'm relieved.

'Do you want a bite of this?' I say, cutting off a corner of my French toast. 'It tastes of America.'

'It tastes of America?' he laughs. 'What does *that* mean?'

'I think it's the cream and the syrup. To a British person, this is America summed up in a mouthful.' I push my plate towards him.

'That'll be the Cool Whip,' he says, chewing.

'You mean Cool *Hwhip*,' I say, mock Stewie Griffin.

'You're eating hair!' he says, continuing the line from *Family Guy*. We laugh. We're hilarious. We can make off the cuff jokes about things we've never once talked about and both get them. If that's not a sign from the universe that we're meant to be, then I don't know what is.

'You know, back home,' I say, pulling my plate back and loading up another forkful, 'we call this eggy bread.'

Jesse screws up his face. 'Well *that's* disgusting,' he says.

'Why?' I laugh. 'That's basically what it is.'

'Because… *eggy* bread. No. Ew. Crazy Brits.'

'Wait, what? It's bread dipped in milk and eggs and fried. It's *literally* eggy bread. My mum used to serve it with ketchup.'

'No, Cassie, she didn't.' He's shaking his head.

'She absolutely did. Kid breakfast.'

He balls up his fist and presses it against his mouth. 'Sacrilege,' he says. 'French toast should *always* be eaten sweet.'

'Good job it was actually eggy bread then. Don't knock it 'til you've tried it,' I say.

'Think I'll take your word for it,' he says. 'You want another coffee?'

–

We're back home via the grocery store early in the afternoon, and I put on my bikini, grab a beach towel and my sun cream.

'I'm going to lie on the beach and work on my tan,' I say. 'Come, too?'

'Yeah, will you get in the water?'

'I daresay.'

But it feels freezing in the heat and I can only take it up to my knees. Instead, I go back for my book and sit on the sand. Jesse definitely thinks I am a wimp. He got straight in without even a flinch, and I watch him swim about from behind the pages of my novel, taking full advantage of my sunglasses to hide the true extent of my perving. His hair is sticking to his face, and sometimes he pushes it back. I like the way he moves in the water. I want to get in, but I'm not sure I can handle the temperature. I lie back and close my eyes.

He's back a few minutes later, standing over me and dripping all over the place. Cold splashes land in perfect droplets on my legs and my stomach and my shoulders. His skin is glistening. Sopping board shorts and sand cling to his legs. Hot *damn*.

'You're coming in,' he says, as if I have no say in the matter.

'I do want to but the thing is, I'll actually freeze.'

'You actually won't. Look, if that little kid can do it,' he points to a tiny child in a pink wetsuit. She's trotting in and out of the waves, white blonde hair stuck to her chubby face. She scoops a handful of sand, turns, and throws it into the water. Her mother claps. 'Then so can you.'

So I try again, and this time I inch in slowly until a wave sloshes over me. Frigid water laps at my hips. I turn to leave again but this time Jesse's having none of it.

'Come on. Come for a swim. It's... refreshing.'

'It's baltic,' I say.

'I'll make it worth your while.'

'I mean, I'm pretty sure you'll make it worth my while whether I get in the sea or not... so... not much of an incentive.'

'You just have to take the plunge, Cassie.' He picks me up and wades further in, as if carrying ten stone of wriggling female in cold water is no big deal. He's definitely stronger than I gave him credit for.

'Je-*sus*,' I howl, clutching him. The water's higher now, up to my chest. My nipples are like bullets. He must be able to feel them. He drops me in with a splash and I'm shocked at how cold it is. My lungs feel like they are being sucked into themselves as I surface, eyes wide and blinking salt water off my eyelashes. It's not deep, I'm barely in up to my armpits.

'Your face!' he laughs, swimming out a little deeper. 'Swim now, it's the only way to warm up.' I follow him out and he's right. It *is* refreshing and I *do* warm up. After a minute or two of frantic breast stroke, I am calm and serene in the ocean. It's not so cold when only your head is poking out of the water. I am like Ariel and he's my Prince Eric. I swim over to him.

'See, it's alright isn't it? Once you're in,' he says.

'Definitely not terrible at all,' I say, but even so, I'm looking forward to lying back on the sand and feeling the sun warm my skin.

'You're hot in that swimsuit,' he says, copping a bit of a feel under the water. Saucy man. Eric never said that about Ariel's seashells. We're deeper now, the waves are carrying us up and down.

'You're not so bad yourself,' I say. Then we start something that really should have been saved for somewhere a little less public. Something that definitely does not happen in *The Little Mermaid*. For a couple of minutes we are all touchy-feely hands and gaspy breaths. My bikini top gets pulled down, and he's *definitely* into my bullet nips. I really hope it's not too obvious that we're having sex in the sea, but then also, I sort of like the risk of getting caught.

'We should go back now,' he says. 'Finish this somewhere more comfortable.'

'Yeah, Jesse. *God*, this is a family beach,' I snigger.

'And these tricks are definitely *not* for kids,' he says.

It's later in the evening, and we're chilling out and listening to music in the lounge. We were outside most of the day, and not only does my skin have that glowy warm, slightly tight feel to it you get after a little too much sun, but I also have hot day lethargy. I'm flicking through my magazine, not really paying any attention to what I'm reading.

'Hey, can I borrow your laptop for a bit?' I need to sort the hen night if I don't want any more chaser emails from Marie, and besides, now's as good a time as any to do it.

'Of course.' He nods to the computer. I flip the screen up and it boots into life. 'There's no password.'

I tap away for a few minutes, make the reservation, and throw in some ludicrously priced optional extras: Prosecco in an ice bucket. VIP entry so we don't have to wait in line. A free cocktail voucher, on account of it being a hen do. 'Whatcha doin' on there?' Jesse asks.

'I'm booking a night out at a roller disco for Rachel's hen do,' I say.

'A roller disco?'

'Yeah, you know, a club where you wear roller skates and dance around. Cheesy music, shit drinks, bruised arses.'

'I know what one is, I just didn't know you could skate.'

'Well, it's not usually the first thing I say to people,' I say.

'I'm going to want to see pictures.'

'Oh god.' I laugh. 'I'll probably look ridiculous.'

'You'll probably look like you're having fun.' He brushes his finger between my toes and it tickles. 'Sand,' he explains. 'Anyway, what was? The first thing you said. To me.'

'In the hotel bar?'

'Yep.'

What a bizarre thing to ask. Does he not remember? Or is he just testing me?

'I think it was, Jesse, hi, or something.'

'Right, but what about after that?'

'Erm…' I make it look like I'm trying to remember. But of course I remember. I might have been busy falling in love but I absolutely remember every single thing we said to each other that night. I replay it in my head often.

'You said, "you made it," and I said, "so did you. How mad is this?"'

'Did you think it was mad?'

'As a March hare. Didn't you?'

'Completely nuts. Do you *still* think that?'

'No. This is fun. I'm having fun with you,' I say. I want to say more. I want to tell him everything, all these big, terrifying feelings I'm having and how I'm barely holding it together, but I don't, and besides, this is a step up from the jibbering idiot in Philippe's, bigging up the coleslaw and not being able to look him in the eye. Baby steps. He bends over and kisses my knee.

'You about done on there?' he says.

'Yep.' I close the webpage and put the laptop back on the table.

'Do you feel like going out somewhere?'

'Oooh where?'

'We could go for a drive. Head out somewhere there isn't so much light pollution. Do some stargazing.'

Lord, if that's not the most romantic thing anyone has ever suggested to me.

'Oh my god, yes.'

'Okay, cool. There's a spot down in Laguna. Maybe on the way back we can go get a drink somewhere.'

I sneakily look over at him as he drives. And I think that for someone who claims to be a closed book he definitely finds it easier to talk about his feelings than I do. And maybe I should steel my nerve a little more. Throw caution to the wind, even close my eyes if I need to, and just tell him how I feel about him. Just tell him everything. I could do it whilst we're counting stars. Hell, I could do it right now. My fingers curl around the hem of my skirt in anticipation. I start to form a sentence in my head.

'Music?' Jesse asks. He switches on the car stereo. I swallow my words back down.

'Lovely,' I say, instead.

Chapter Twenty-Nine

Jesse

'So when do I get to meet your girlfriend?' Travis asks, when I eventually answer the call I've been avoiding since Cassie arrived a week ago. 'Can we call her that yet?'

'I don't know. It's complicated. She's going back to England next week.' I don't like the thought of it.

'So is that the end of that?'

'I'm not intending it to be. You're welcome here whenever. You know that.'

'Yeah… but… I'm not just going to come over unannounced when you're on your two-week date with Cassie from London. Which I'm going to assume is going well, if your radio silence and obvious call screening is anything to go by?'

'Okay, well how are you fixed for this evening? And yes, your assumption is correct.'

'Yeah?'

'Yeah. You'll like her. You can't *not* like her. She's amazing.'

'I mean, I distinctly remember you saying that about Nicole, and look how fast you managed to switch that particular light off when she wasn't going to be local anymore.'

'Low blow, Travis. And I don't know what you've been told about that, but I feel like it's very different to the version I lived through, you know?'

'Well, either way, you *did* say after she'd gone that it was probably for the best with the distance and all.'

Oh, fuck that.

'She dumped me, dude. I thought things were fine. But apparently they weren't. And I know I said that, but people say shit when they're mad.'

'Relax, Jesse. Why are you so tetchy?'

'I'm not tetchy,' I say quickly. It's a lie. Thinking about Nicole makes me all kinds of tetchy, and I want to change the subject.

'Hmm.'

'What's that for?'

'Nothing,' he says. 'Anyway. Yes to later on. I'll bring some beer. Does she drink beer?'

'She does.'

Cassie rounds the corner of the landing and bounces down the steps.

'Hey, I have to go. Come by at seven, okay?'

I end the call and she leans over the back of the couch and links her arms around my neck. She rubs her cheek against mine, but I haven't shaved for a couple of days and there's a scratching sound.

'What are we doing today?'

'Well, Trav's coming over this evening. But for now I thought we could maybe go to Venice? It's pretty nice. There are canals and usually something to see on the boardwalk, and obviously another beach, if you're not completely bored of beaches?'

'I'm never bored of beaches,' she says, and kisses my cheek.

'Hey, actually, can you ride a bike?' I ask.

'Of course, why? Can't you?'

'Feel like riding from Venice down to Santa Monica?'

'Yes. Let's go.' She pats my shoulders. 'Up you get.'

–

'If you could live in any of these, which one would it be?' We're strolling by the canal and she stops to look around. She's leaning against the white bridge and behind her, a couple of row boats float in the still water. We're not far from the bustle of the beach and the boardwalk but it's quiet here. I look around at the houses, some newly renovated with painted fascias, sitting right alongside older, quaint bungalows.

'I think that one,' I say, nodding over to a larger house with floor to ceiling windows and a high, dark green, wood fence around it. 'I bet it has a pool.'

'And brushed chrome kitchen worktops. For that industrial chic look.'

'And a huge table in the dining room.'

'With those trendy Eames chairs around it. And a double-sided fireplace in the middle of the lounge that you switch on with a remote,' she says, and giggles. 'Like you see in movies.'

'And it's got a bathroom for every bedroom. Plus a half bath downstairs.'

'Err, definitely. I'd expect nothing less. And in the master bedroom, the bed is right in the middle of the room. *And* there's a walk-in wardrobe.'

'And heated floors for when it gets cold in winter.'

'I bet it doesn't really get cold here in winter,' she says, looking around.

'Maybe sixty-five?'

She Googles the conversion on her phone and scoffs. 'That's not cold! That's like summer in England.'

'God, really? Fuck that temperate shit.'

'You get used to it,' she says, and then pauses. 'So, actually, about England… I've been meaning to ask you something.'

She looks down at the water again, and there's a nervousness about her now. She's gripping on to the bridge.

'Yeah?'

'Yeah. About Rachel's wedding.'

'Okay…?'

'Right, so the thing is, I don't have a date.'

'I thought there was a handsy best man?'

As soon as I say it, I wish I hadn't. I don't want to think about that frat boy putting his hands on her. Or even trying to.

'Aha. Yes, well he'll be there… but, I was wondering if,' she catches my eye but only for a second before looking away again. 'If maybe you would like to come. With me. As my date.'

I'm sort of taken aback, but compose myself quickly.

'Uh… remind me of when it is?'

'Thirteenth of October. Look, don't worry. It's a big deal, and you're probably busy, and it's a long way to come and you'll only know me, and…'

She stops and exhales as she watches me check my calendar on my phone. The week's free. At this point there's nothing stopping me from going. It does feel like a big deal, though. But *too much* of one? Rachel obviously knows about Franko, and no doubt, after Cassie goes home, she'll know about how it all ended as well. But it's been thirteen years since all that, and besides, everyone's focus will be on the bride and groom.

I could tally everything up in my head. Figure out pros and cons. Pit reasons to decline against reasons to accept, but really, the outcome remains the same. Saying no means I don't know when I'll see her again and saying yes means that I do. She's still watching me, wide-eyed, still nervous. Travis telling me to let it happen comes to the fore again.

'I'd really like that, Cass,' I say.

Chapter Thirty

Cassie

We didn't stay in Venice late; Travis is coming over to quell his curiosity about me, and that freeway gets busy in rush hour. Jesse doesn't know if he's bringing Holly but he reckons it's very unlikely. As he says her name he makes a face, but when I ask about it, he just shrugs it off, and now Travis isn't the only one with curiosity. I hope he *does* bring her.

I don't say anything to Jesse, but I'm nervous. I'm sure that's normal. Who wouldn't be? I want to know what he's like now, and whether he's still how I remember him in Franko, excitable and chatty and funny, or whether that was a kind of façade. I want to see the dynamic between them, and I want him to like me. I realise, as I'm rinsing a glass under the tap, that I'm desperate to win his approval.

The screen door rattles just after seven. Jesse's upstairs, and I've perched myself on the corner of the sofa, and I grab at the first thing I see, a magazine about guitars and amps and stuff that looks technical. Seconds later Travis saunters in, carrying a white plastic bag. There's no one with him, so I guess Holly isn't coming. It's too late for me to find anything else to peruse, so I flick to the middle and peer over the top of the pages towards the front door. He hasn't changed much either. What's with these Peter Pan types? He's about the same height as Jesse, perhaps an inch or so taller, but his frame is slightly more wiry. He has the same straight nose and skin tone, a small silver hoop punched through one of his ear lobes and his hair is much shorter than Jesse's; cropped at the sides and messy on top. He's wearing a white linen shirt and faded black skinny jeans with rips in the knees. I can't wait to tell Rachel. I'd like to think she'd be swooning all over again, but truthfully, I'm not sure he's still her type. I couldn't picture her with him after seeing her with sensible George. Travis still doesn't look sensible.

'Yo, Jesse,' he calls through the house. He doesn't look my way at first. He puts the bag down with a clink on the side, pulls out a few bottles of beer and makes his way to the fridge. After he's stocked it up, he looks out towards the back doors, and it's only then that he clocks me.

'Jesus fucking Christ,' he says, stepping back. 'You're so quiet.'

'I'm sorry,' I say, chucking the magazine back on the table and standing up, but he's smiling and it isn't awkward. 'I'm not really all that quiet.'

'So you must be British Cassie,' he says.

'Argh, what gave me away? Was it the accent?'

He laughs and it instantly puts me at ease. Now I don't know why I was ever nervous at all.

'Heard a lot about you,' he says, raising an eyebrow.

'Oh yeah?'

'All good things,' he says.

'Phew!' I say. 'Though it might be a bit weird if he'd been slagging me off to you whilst I'd been here.'

'Slagging you off,' he says, slowly, mimicking my voice. 'That's a fun expression. I'm going to use that. Anyway, where's the boy? It's time to get this party started.'

'He just nipped upstairs,' I say.

'Okay. Well,' he waves a bottle opener at me. 'Shall we? He'll catch up.'

'It'd be rude not to.'

'Right on, British Cassie,' he says, grabbing some drinks. We head outside. 'So, California treating you well?'

'*Very* well. I like it here a lot.'

'Bit different to London, huh?'

'Hardly the same at all,' I say. We both look out towards the sea. 'Jesse tells me you're recently married?'

Travis nods.

'Congratulations.'

'Thanks.' He pauses for a few seconds and shifts in his seat. 'Holly already had other plans, otherwise she'd be here, too.'

I nod slowly, take a sip of my beer. It fizzes and foams up the bottle neck, stinging my top lip slightly. I think back to what Jesse has said and wonder briefly if Travis was making an excuse for her absence. There was something in the way he shifted in his seat and looked away. Now I'm even more curious about her.

The sound of footsteps on the stairs makes us both turn to look back inside and Jesse emerges. He's changed his t-shirt. He spins on his heels when he spies our beers, and grabs one for himself from the kitchen, and he squints a little as he steps outside. Travis stands up and they hug, clapping each other on the back affectionately as they do. It's brotherly. Fleetingly, I wish I had a sibling to hug like that.

'So how have you been, bro? It's been, what? At least a week?' Travis asks as Jesse pulls up a chair. He sits between us and rests his hand on my knee.

'Good, good, yeah,' he says. 'I've been busy with this one.'

We grin at each other. Travis definitely notices.

'Well, that's very nice,' he says. He catches my eye and I wonder what he's thinking. Is he making his mind up about me? Deciding whether he likes me or not? Figuring out whether I'm good enough for his brother or just a summer romance that will invariably fizzle out. 'What have y'all been up to?'

'I feel like I should let Cassie fill you in on that,' Jesse says. He looks encouragingly at me. I open my mouth and I don't stop talking, I *can't* stop talking, for ages. I talk about it all; Griffith Park and Amoeba and Philippe's, selling them to Travis as if he's never been there. Except I'd put everything I own on him having been to all three. He's lapping it up though, joining in, asking if I noticed specific little things at the observatory, asking how I liked the sandwich, telling me, like Jesse did, that it's a bit of an LA food landmark. We're getting on well. I'm making a good impression, I'm sure of it, which I'm happier about than I'd care to admit. I know they're close, and those first impressions count.

During a lull in conversation, Jesse pushes back his chair and stands up. He moves behind me and places his hands on my shoulders, and I look up at him. His hair is falling in front of his face. I reach up and tuck some back behind his ear.

'Feel like eating now?' he asks.

'Definitely. Let me help you bring stuff out,' I offer, but he shakes his head, and squeezes my shoulders, and heads inside. I look over to Travis, but suddenly his expression is blank. He looks behind him, back into the house before he speaks.

'Be careful with him,' he says, quietly. I lean forward, pretty sure this isn't a conversation Jesse is supposed to hear.

'Pardon?'

'That sounded more ominous than I meant, but the way things ended with Nicole hit him harder than he admits to. And he didn't want to go long distance with her,' he continues. 'So the fact you're here is a really big deal.'

'Travis,' I say. 'I don't know who Nicole is.'

He shakes his head and rolls his eyes. 'For real? He's not said anything?'

'Nope.' I look past him. In the kitchen, Jesse's pulling stuff out of the fridge. Suddenly my mouth is dry and I feel sweaty.

'Where to start. Jesus, okay. Jesse and Nicole were together for a year or so. Maybe a little bit longer. And then one day, out of the blue she tells him she's got this new job doing something she knew she was going to love. Sounds cool, right? Here's the kicker, it was in New York. She told him she was going on New Year's Eve, and he was not invited.'

'Wow. That's...' I realise I don't know anything about this woman's relationship with Travis, so I probably shouldn't start mouthing off about her. 'Wow,' I repeat.

'Right? And then she says it's not just because of the job, and accused him of being shut off. Which, I guess, if I had to defend anything I'd probably agree with to an extent. But only because of the way shit ended with Franko... wait, you know about this, right? Franko?'

'Yeah, little bits,' I say.

'Okay, interesting that you know about that but not... anyway.' He shakes his head, as if clearing his thoughts. 'So we all knew he'd been sucking it up for ages. Since right after the first album. Dad started putting a ton of pressure on us and he found it hard to cope. He never felt heard, like, he'd try and confide in our mom, and she'd make these empty promises. I think she tried but, well, Dad's a bit of a character, and the whole thing was his dream from the very beginning. And in the end it all just got too much. So Jesse quit, and that ended the band. Dad wanted to find someone else but Mom put her foot down, said no. Anyway, since then he's not been one to open up easily. He's just super afraid of getting hurt again I think.'

'Oh my god. He's not said anything. About the girlfriend, I mean.'

'Hmm well, keep this on the down low then. I'm sure that conversation is coming.'

'I don't want to make things tricky for him. I just want to make him happy.'

'No, I get that,' he says, quickly. 'But I think, with Nic especially, the relationship was almost at the point where he was thinking things were going places. If she'd just stuck around...'

The comment stings though I don't think he means for it to. My stomach twists. He looks out to sea again. He's unreadable. It's like he's covered in a protective layer of lead and I'm an x-ray machine. It's frustrating. I look down at my half empty bottle of beer and try to peel off the label with my nails. It tears in shreds, which I ball up and stuff between the slats of the table.

Jesse's coming back out now, and it's fair to say he's struggling a little.

'Let me get that,' I say. 'I'd have helped, you know? At any point.'

'It's cool,' he says, but I take a bowl of nachos and the salsa and Travis grabs the new beers. When I look now, I see an extra layer of him. A thin film of vulnerability. And all I want to do is keep him safe, and protect him from everything that isn't wonderful in the world.

—

Before Travis goes home, we take our nightly walk up the beach with a final drink. 'One for the road,' he says, but he's driving so his one for the road is a bottle of tamarind flavour soda, and ours are measures of bourbon in glass tumblers. We walk along the sand, cool under my bare feet now, and Jesse keeps me tucked in close to him the whole time.

'So, I'm going to get Brandon and Lainey down here at the weekend,' Travis says. 'I feel like this needs marking.' He waves his hand about in circles in our general direction.

'She's not some sort of *exhibit*, Trav,' Jesse says. 'You can't just invite people over to look at her.'

'You know Lainey,' he says, rolling his eyes. 'She'll want in on this. Conversation's already been had, dude. She's bringing lasagna.'

Jesse sighs.

'Don't be like that,' Travis continues. 'People care how you're doing. You being *this* happy is nice to see.'

'I don't know, Trav. What if we had plans?'

'Well, change 'em,' he says, shrugging.

'We don't have plans, and it's fine,' I say, cutting in.

'So then, Saturday,' Travis says, and he's beaming. His phone rings, and he answers it and wanders a little way ahead of us.

'We don't have to see everyone on Saturday,' Jesse says.

'Yeah we do,' I say.

He kisses my forehead.

'It's nice here,' I say. I'm looking out at the sunset, at the salmon-pink sky and the sun rays shining down on the sea. The beach is calming. The way the sea sucks at the sand. It's constant. Whatever happens, it never stops. I want to be here to see it more than just this week, but the future all seems so uncertain, especially after what Travis said, and I can't think about it for too long. Until today we hadn't talked about what happens after I leave. I wouldn't expect to under normal circumstances, not this early on, but this isn't a normal circumstance. Whilst our situation is as it is, we'll only have snippets of time together. We don't have the luxury of seeing how things pan out. Every phone call, every visit, will need to be meticulously planned.

'It sure has its moments,' Jesse says, squinting up at the sky. 'Right about this time every night.'

Travis has finished his phone call now. He's bounding back towards us but he looks a little apologetic.

'Guys, I have to run,' he says. 'You stay here, enjoy this. I'll let myself out. This has been beautiful, truly.' He finishes up the last of his soda and envelopes me in a hug. 'Nice to meet you, British Cassie,' he says.

'You, too,' I say.

'Until Saturday.' And then he's gone, scrambling back up towards the peak of the dune.

'Why do you think he left like that?' I say when he's disappeared from view.

'Holly,' Jesse says, and shrugs.

It's a little darker now but we don't make any moves to go back inside. We sit and I set my glass down in the sand at my feet, twisting it in a little. It makes a satisfying squeaky grinding sound as grain rubs against glass. We stare out to sea for a while, and then I lean my head on his shoulder. He moves in, rubs circles on my back, and I can smell clean clothes and that ferny shower gel.

'I think he likes you,' he says, eventually.

'And what about you?' I say, still staring out to sea, fuelled by the alcohol. 'Do *you* like me?'

He's silent for a bit. Only a few seconds, and now my heart is in my throat. There are butterflies in my stomach, hammering to get out. He twists some of my hair around his fingers, and finally, he speaks.

'I... haven't felt like this about anyone in years. You make me want to go out and do things I haven't felt like bothering with before. When I'm with you, everything is bright and clear and colorful. This week has been the best week I've had in, well, I can't remember how long. But a long time. A really, really long time.' He pauses and takes a deep breath and his shoulder rises and falls under my head. The exhalation breath sounds a bit shaky. Then he continues; 'Isn't it obvious, Cassie? I absolutely adore you.'

–

Rach! Couple of things. I put on my big girl pants and invited him to the wedding and it's a YES! I was very terrified, and now I'm just very excited, OMG what is my mother going to say? Then, your boy Travis came over (not sure he'd still be your bag to be honest). Do you remember him having an earring? I don't, but he does now. Anyway, he told me all this stuff, secret squirrel style, about some ex called Nicole who Jesse was apparently serious with, and then she just upped and left for NY. But this was the first I'd heard about her and now I can't stop thinking about it! I'm like, so totally buggin'! Then he said Jesse isn't keen on long distance, and let's face it, you can't get more long distance than California to London. What would you do? After Travis went home, Jesse and I were sitting on the beach watching the sun go down, and he said he ADORES me. And that is actual verbatim. This is good yeah?

Aww bless your heart! Fortune favours the brave, this all sounds very lovely! What else did you find out about this ex? Any traces of her knocking around? How recent are we talking? She can't have been that important if he hasn't said anything… especially if she just upped sticks and moved. Travis definitely did not have an earring back in the day and to be frank, he sounds like a troublemaker now. Try not to worry about it, especially if he's telling you that sort of stuff on beaches at sunset. It's very good news, but I suspect you didn't need me to tell you that. I'll tell your mum to buy a hat, shall I? George had a girlfriend once, called Ariana. I always thought she sounded really exotic and I was convinced for ages he'd go back to her. But she's an ex for a reason, and that reason was her weird obsession with porcelain statues of pigs in racy poses. Nicole's old news. Don't sweat it x

Chapter Thirty-One

Jesse

The morning after Travis came by feels comfortable. More so than before. We sit outside, flicking through magazines and checking our phones and eating, as if it's a morning rhythm the two of us have kept forever. Gulls hover in the air, people walk their dogs, and amble up and down the pier. Richard's house is shut up, so it's peaceful, too.

As we're finishing up, the elderly couple who live down the street are walking along the path. They've been here as long as I have, possibly even decades longer, and I've noticed them walk past most days, but I don't know them particularly. This time they stop at the back of the house and lean against the wall.

'Hey there,' the man says, and waves.

'Hiya, good morning,' Cassie replies. She smiles warmly at them and pulls the t-shirt she's wearing down her thighs as far as it will stretch. It doesn't stretch very far.

'Lovely day,' says his wife, and we both nod.

'I've seen you around,' he says, to me.

'Oh, well yeah, I live here, so—'

'Haven't seen you before, though, honey.'

Cassie shifts her chair closer to mine. 'You won't have. I'm just visiting.'

The old lady beams.

'What an accent!' she says.

The conversation continues for a few minutes. They've lived here since they got hitched in the late fifties and take a walk down this path every morning. He isn't keen on how busy the beach gets, but I'm not sure what he expects from a beach town in Southern California. She seems more tolerant of it all and tells us her favorite thing to do is go over to Catalina Island, and I make a mental note for us to do that because it would be fun and I've never been there either. After a while they say goodbye and carry on up the beach, and Cassie sips her drink.

'Well, *they* were adorable,' she says.

'I think he thought you were pretty adorable,' I tell her.

'Is that so?' she says, leaning over and kissing me. Orange juice and coffee. She pulls away and sighs. 'Let's get ready for the day.'

Much later on in the afternoon, we're tapping through scanned in photos on my laptop, studying them, intently, one by one. Looking back over snapshots of my life. I almost never look at these because of all the discomfort that surrounds how that part of it ended and I've certainly never shown them to anyone else. But she's enjoying it which seems to make it a little bit easier. And it's nice to look back at photos of Mom with us all around her. Snippets of normality in an adolescence that was anything but. One, I think, was taken on Mothers' Day. All four of us are hugging her. There's another where we should have been doing school work, but you can clearly see Travis playing on his Game Boy. Adam is looking at the camera, bored, and I'm chewing on the end of a pen.

'Do you ever miss this life?' she asks. It's an innocuous enough question but it, alongside all the photos of it all, makes me flinch. 'Would you ever go back?'

'Sometimes I miss the way it was in the beginning, but no, I don't think I'd go back.'

'Is that what stopped you joining another band?'

'Yeah, I think so, deep down. Because what if it's always like that? Then I'd have thrown it all away for nothing. I wrecked things with Adam, I can't revisit that.'

'Everyone always said you were the quiet one. I think people – your fans – knew something was up.'

'I don't think I was very good at hiding it. By the time it all went to shit I didn't care anymore. I was just constantly looking for a way out. But I don't want you to think it was all bad. It really wasn't, in the beginning. It was the dream.'

'We met once, you know? In the beginning,' she says. She hovers over a thumbnail image of me and clicks it open and grins. 'You looked like this.' I have chin-length hair with some stupid blond highlights a stylist had insisted on. I'm wearing an oversize basketball jersey – Lakers, obviously – baggy shorts and bright white hightop sneakers. Black rubber bracelets, tens of them, on my wrists. And a choker. A fucking *choker*! What was I thinking? I can't have dressed myself that day, surely.

'Yeah, you mentioned you got backstage once. Judas *Priest*, look at the state of me.' I click the photo closed and laugh nervously.

'No, it was before then,' she says. 'A different time. Just after "Come and Get it" was released.'

'Yeah? What happened?'

She puts the laptop down on the table and shifts. Takes my hand, crosses her legs.

'It was at a TV studio by the Thames. Early on a Saturday morning in February, and I had my Walkman with me. And you clocked my headphones when you signed the inlay card of my CD, and asked me what I was listening to, and instead of just telling you, I gave you one of my earbuds, and we listened for a bit. And it was cold. So cold, and I was wearing a—'

'Green scarf,' we both say simultaneously.

'You remember,' she whispers.

Something's clicked and I have a vague memory of this. Because that wasn't the norm and I was impressed that she wasn't listening to our album. Every now and then for weeks after, I'd think about it, just for a few seconds. A morning so cold you could see your breath, and all the colors looked muted, apart from her, wrapped up in a green scarf. Wide smile. Wavy blonde hair. Pretty eyes. Green scarf. The photo of a New Year's Eve on Facebook. She's wearing it. That scarf.

'Do you remember what we listened to?'

'Of course. The Cranberries,' she says. '"Linger", to be precise,' and it's weird, this shared memory we have from 1998. I had no recollection at all of her getting backstage, but this had stood out. And when her friend had wandered over, camera in hand, she'd moved in close and held on to a handful of my jacket tightly in her fist. After the photo, she just stood there, pressed against me and holding on for just a fraction longer than necessary. Her friend said it was time to go, and nodded towards Travis, and I gave her shoulder a quick squeeze through her coat. She'd looked back at me as she was pulled away, and again right after she'd snapped a photo, and one last time before it was time for us to head back inside, and I'd known because I was looking back at her. And now she's sitting on my couch, holding my hand, and I'm looking at her again. At the same wavy blonde hair, now pulled back off her face, and the same pretty blue-gray eyes.

'I asked your name but you wouldn't tell me,' I say.

'I said there was no point, you'd never remember it, and now we'll never know,' she laughs. 'But if I'd told you, you might have done, and decided not to get mixed up in all that again, and then we wouldn't be sitting here now.'

She looks up at the platinum disc on the wall and then glances around the room. 'I had such an enormous crush on you,' she whispers. 'Still do, really.'

'Do you think we need to talk about… what happens with us? After this week.'

'Well, you're coming to visit next month, no? You haven't had second thoughts, have you?'

'Of course not. What made you ask that?'

'I don't know.' Her eyes keep darting around, and I notice them flit towards the platinum disc again. That thing's like a hex. I'm going to put it in the spare room. 'Just something Travis mentioned,' she continues.

'Yeah? What exactly was that?' I ask, sitting back on the couch.

'Something about Nicole—'

'Nicole?' I interrupt, suddenly panicked. For clear and obvious reasons. I need to know exactly what he told her.

'Yeah. Nicole. Your girlfriend who moved to New York.'

'Yeah I know who she is. But how did you end up talking to Travis about this?'

She looks at me blankly.

'He just sort of told me. It wasn't unpleasant. I think he just looked at us and… his intentions were good.'

'Right, well, he shouldn't have said anything.'

'Well, what can I say? He did. Would you have told me if I hadn't asked?'

'Yeah, probably.'

'He said that, too.'

'Yeah?' I say, grouchily. 'Anything else?'

'Something about her upping sticks and you being sad. I don't know. It's your story. Why are you asking me to tell it?'

'Nicole made a big decision. And we never sat down and discussed any of it. She just came back from a trip and told me she'd been offered her dream job.'

'And then what?'

'She said she was going, and that was sort of that.'

'Would you have gone if she'd asked you? Travis said you don't do long distance.'

'Well, Travis doesn't know shit. She didn't want me to, and she ditched me. But I don't know, to be honest. It's a big ask.'

'Okay, but you realise at some point one of *us* might have to make that decision. Would it be a big ask then, too?'

'I mean, I guess I just thought—'

'That it would definitely be me?'

'Well… yeah.'

'Do you realise you've just done pretty much exactly the same thing?' she says, incredulously.

'What's that supposed to mean?'

'Well, you've laid it all out for me. Sold me this life *out here*. *I* can move, *I* can get a new job. *I* can make all the sacrifices whilst you just carry on as normal. All the expectation is on me.'

'Wow. That's not *at all* what I was getting at. I just said we never talked about any of it, and that was never on the cards in the first place. It's not really the same thing. And this is nice, isn't it?'

'This is lovely, but it's also a holiday and different to if I actually lived here and surely you know that? What would I do for a job? What would it be like when you're off doing whatever you do? You were so busy after London and there were times when we hardly spoke. How would it be if I lived here? I'm just trying to inject a little bit of realism into this, you know?'

'Well, it'd be different because you'd be here. I still come home every night. Usually.'

'And just say it didn't work out for... I dunno, reasons. And I had everything here. Would I get to stay or would I have to go back to England, and start over, tail between my legs. I wouldn't have anything to fall back on.'

'I don't know, Cassie. No one can possibly know all that.'

'My life is in London. Everything I know and everyone I love is in London. Can you not see how this is a huge ask of me? And something you just said you weren't sure you'd have been able to do for Nicole.'

'Okay, can you *not* bring her into this? Like I said, nothing about us is the same.'

She bristles and stands up.

'Okay, you know, I think I need to go for a walk for a bit.' She pushes the back door open and slips on her sandals. 'I'll be back later.'

What the fuck? This is *nuts*.

'Is that a no?' I call after her as she walks up the beach. And now I don't know if she's so into this after all. That the crush she mentioned earlier is just that, and nothing more than an

228

extension of fifteen-year-old her. She turns around and shakes her head.

'No.'

'So is that a yes then?'

'No! It's a *give me some time to think about uprooting my entire life for you.*'

I don't follow her. Why should I? Instead I try to behave normally, despite being entirely knocked for six, and destabilized, and sort of mad at Travis.

And I think about it whilst I stack crockery in the kitchen, and it plays on my mind whilst I throw on some laundry, and I don't know why she's comparing us to a previous relationship when the two are entirely different, or why she's picking at something she only has second hand, inaccurate information about. I get lost in some work for a bit; listen to a demo track I've been sent, synthy and incomplete, and start to figure out a bassline for it. But it's not at all challenging and it doesn't take long. Common time, key of C major. I invert some chords. I throw in a few passing notes and a bit of slap, and by the time I'm finished, it's late afternoon and she's still not back, and neither has she answered the text I sent her. Part of me wants to leave it, but she's a long way from home and I don't want things to be difficult between us, and anyway, perhaps her phone is off, or upstairs, and before I've talked myself out of it, I've locked up the house and I'm heading up the beach.

Chapter Thirty-Two

Cassie

Fuck! How did that go so badly wrong? He was offering up everything I've been dreaming of on a plate and I… acted like a crazy bitch. The air is warm and heavy and still, and a haze coats the sky. The beach is calmer than I've seen it recently and sand collects in the seams of my shoes as I walk down to the shore. I head up towards the pier along the peak of the dune. People are milling around, looking out to sea, strolling along, talking. They're all just getting on with life. Could that be me? Could I fit in? Would it matter if I didn't? I'd only really have to fit in for him and we seem to do that just fine. I continue up the beach, past the playground, on to the pier, idly wondering what my life would be like out here, and I get almost to the very end and back again before I find an empty bench. It's definitely pleasant here, I could be happy, I think. Of course I'd be happy; I'd be here with Jesse, and there are bound to be jobs like mine.

But am I really ready to give up everything I know for him? Because really, there's a lot riding on this and my gut reaction back at the house was not that of someone who's about to throw caution to the wind and move across the world.

And that's surprised me. I always thought I would.

I cross and uncross my legs. Lean forwards and rest my elbows on my knees as I stare out at the horizon, the faint outline of Catalina, and the offshore oil rig, but my eyes always want to drift back across the sand to the row of houses. I've left him in one of them and I don't know what he's doing.

My parents could come and visit. Dad would love it, but Mum might be a little nervous. She likes her home comforts. She'd worry about driving on the right, and *me* driving on the right, but I think she'd love going to see the tourist attractions. Dad would be a big fan of this beach. I can imagine him walking along it in khaki shorts, wearing his sandals with socks, talking about the tides and befriending the locals. He'd buy a slice of pizza from the takeaway on the seafront when Mum wasn't looking. Rachel and George could come, too. We could drive north, drink a lot of wine in Napa Valley. We're good at that, Rachel and I. That's how all this started. I pull my phone out of my pocket.

> If I moved here, would you visit? Xx

I stare at it for a few minutes but she doesn't reply. It's late at night in London, so I can't blame her, really. I slide the phone back into my pocket.

There's not much point in dwelling on when things began to get a little snarky earlier, and anyway, it was sort of my fault. Maybe I shouldn't have brought up Nicole, but surely he can see the parallels.

The light changes as the sun moves across the sky, but I don't move. The beach is getting busier again, people are out for evening walks. I've lost track of time, and it's gone seven when I check the time again. Just a few more minutes and then I'll think about heading back. I'm getting hungry anyway, and I reckon Jesse probably is, too. I'll go back and we'll make dinner. We'll sit and eat it outside, and then I'll rest my legs up on his lap and we'll watch as the sky turns pink and purple and then fades to darkness. I don't want to admit that I might have been a bit of a diva, flouncing off in the way I did, and I definitely don't want to think that things between us might not be so nice.

I'm so caught up in my thoughts and my people-watching that I don't notice immediately when he sits down next to me and holds out a plastic cup.

'Is this the bench we sit on for chats?' he asks. 'You've been gone for ages. Here, peace offering.'

I look over and he smiles at me, but there is something nervous about it. I take the cup from him and take a sip. It's iced tea. Of course it's iced tea.

'Thank you,' I say.

'Are you okay? I missed you. You didn't answer your phone.'

Oh, shit. Three missed calls and a text. It must have switched to silent when I shoved it back in my pocket.

'I am. I'm also sorry. I shouldn't have brought up your ex. That was rude and I panicked.'

'It's fine,' he says, stretching out. 'And anyway, it's not like you were completely wrong. But here's the thing, Cassie.' He pauses. 'I want to be with you all the time. Not just little chunks here and there when it's convenient. But always. Every day.'

Awww. He's looking at me very earnestly. He really means it.

'I want that, too,' I say. And I put my drink down next to me and kiss his cheek and curl myself against him, clinging on tight and thinking how perfectly we fit next to each other. And I flash back to the conversation we had in Philippe's and what I said whilst my mouth was crammed full of food. It stopped us short then but it's never been truer than right now. I said I didn't want to go home. Made out that it was because of the sandwich, but we both knew it wasn't. There was no need to talk up the coleslaw in the nervous way I had. No need at all. But if I'd had the guts to tell him what he means to me then, maybe I'd have felt more able to voice all the other meaningful shit I've wanted to since I've been here. Maybe then he wouldn't have to coax out the things he wants to hear from me, because they'd be out there in the world. Fledgling declarations of love. Scattered into the air, carried on the wind, settled and present everywhere they were said. Laced into memories, the way his words are in mine.

'And I was wrong,' I say, steeling myself. If ever there was a time to tell him how I feel about him it's now, with the pretty, colourful sky and the situation we've made here. 'Not everyone I love is in London. You're here. And I'm hopelessly in love with you. Have been for ages, actually. I'm just *shit* at showing my feelings.'

He takes my hand and brushes hair out of my face.

'Aww Cass,' he says. 'I'm hopelessly in love with you, too,' and we kiss, and then he leans his forehead against mine.

'Take me home,' I say, nodding back towards the row of houses on the beach front.

'What do you want to do about food?'

I laugh. What a boy thing to say.

'Erm. Chinese? Pizza? I don't mind. Something we can order in that requires zero effort. Also,' I say, batting his arm, 'don't kill the moment, you absolute melon.'

–

Later, there's a pizza box between us and a movie on the laptop. *Thor*, because of course it is. But for once I've barely even noticed Chris Hemsworth.

'Yeah,' I say. 'Alright then.'

Jesse hits the space bar and the movie pauses.

'Huh? What do you mean, *yeah, alright then*?'

'Yeah, I'll come here. Alright then, I'll get a visa. One day, when it's right.'

'Really?' he asks, sitting up quickly. The computer falls off the side of the bed. 'Shit,' he mutters, reaching down for it.

'Really.'

'But I thought you said—'

'Ignore that. I was talking bollocks. But I need to know you won't get bored and finish with me. Meet someone closer, more convenient. Not five thousand miles away.'

'That would never happen.'

'And if they won't let me come here, because I feel like that's a possibility, I'll need to know you'll come to England.'

He opens his mouth to say something.

'Only as a secondary option,' I add, quickly, 'but I can't get invested in this, with you, if you won't budge for me. I wouldn't get over it. I meant what I said before, you know? About how much I liked you when I was younger.'

'Okay,' he says, and squeezes me tight. 'I guess it doesn't really matter where we are in the long run.'

'Fucking hell,' I squeak. 'Where's my phone? I have to tell Rachel.'

Chapter Thirty-Three

Cassie

All Saturday morning I can't sit still. I drink a lot of coffee. I change my clothes a lot. Jesse's family come today and I am nervous. I do and redo my hair. He says it doesn't matter what I wear, but to me it does. He says I'll be fine, and that they'll love me, but what if he's wrong? What if they hate me? I have, after all, swooped in and made life-changing plans with him, and as far as they're concerned, we only met in July.

In the end I settle for skinny jeans and a v-neck grey marl t-shirt. I'm casual. I'm cool. I can do this. At least, I think I can. I sweep my hair to the side and hold it in place with my sunglasses.

The house is tidy apart from the pile of mail stacked up on the kitchen side by the front door. It's been there since I arrived. Jesse hands me a bottle of Coke and I drink it even though I am shaking slightly from too much caffeine. What's a little more?

Just before midday, the doorbell rings and I jump out of my skin.

'Jesus, relax, Cassie,' Jesse says, nodding towards the front door and patting my thigh. 'It's only Travis.'

He doesn't wait for Jesse to open the door, instead he lets himself in the same way he had the last time he'd come round. But this time he's followed by a tall, slender woman, muttering something about waiting until people answer. She has that kind of pale, porcelain-like skin you have to really take care of, and doll-like features; big green eyes under flawless brows, and rosy pink lips. Her hair is black and shiny, and cut in a long blunt bob with a heavy fringe. She's wearing a maroon skater dress, a short denim jacket and black lace-up ankle boots with a chunky high heel. So this is Holly. Travis claps Jesse on the back and kisses my cheek. Holly hangs back and looks around the room until Travis retreats and guides her further in by her elbow.

'Some introductions!' he announces, rubbing his hands together. 'Cassie, this is my old lady, Holly. Holly, this is British Cassie.'

'It's really nice to meet you,' I say, flashing my friendliest smile. My accent sounds silly. Affected and stuffy compared to the laid back, west coast drawl I've been surrounded by. She flicks her eyes over me and shifts on her feet.

'You too,' she says.

I don't believe her, but I also don't know why she'd be off with me. I glance over at Jesse for any kind of help, and he moves next to me.

'Holly,' he says, stiffly, giving her a nod.

'Jesse,' she replies with the same stiffness. The atmosphere is suddenly a little tense. It's a vibe I never felt when Travis was here on his own the other night. All four of us flounder for a few seconds, then Holly grabs hold of Travis' arm, and her face softens.

'Baby,' she says. There's a childish tone to her voice. 'I'm super thirsty, can you go get me a drink?' She's batting her lashes at him and he instantly complies. Jesse and I step back simultaneously to let him through into the kitchen.

'What do you want?' he calls, over his shoulder, his head inside the fridge.

'Anything. I don't care,' she says, flippantly. She's looking at her nails and picking at a cuticle. I drop my hand and link my little finger with Jesse's. Travis returns with a bottle of mandarin soda, Jarritos, the same brand as the tamarind one he drank the other day, and Jesse lets go of my finger and moves his hand up to the small of my back, clutching at a handful of my t-shirt, stretching it slightly over my stomach.

'Does this mean I'm driving?' Holly asks petulantly, looking at the drink, her bottom lip pouty, her green eyes wide.

'Uh, no?' Travis says. 'You said you didn't care... it's only just midday.' Holly sighs dramatically.

'Shall we sit outside?' I say, overly brightly. I'm trying to diffuse the situation.

'Sure,' Holly says. Travis exhales, Jesse lets go of my top and leads the way. Mission accomplished, I think.

Except it's not really. Unless the mission was just to move the awkwardness outside. I can't put my finger on it exactly, but every time Holly says something, Jesse stiffens, so when he goes inside to get more drinks, I follow.

'What's up with that, then?' I ask, whilst he pokes around in the fridge.

'What's up with what?'

'As if you don't know. Holly. Why is there weirdness?'

'I don't know what you mean,' he says, shortly, grabbing the bottle opener from a drawer. And then he pushes me against the cupboards and kisses me. Slides his hand down over my bum. 'Those jeans, though,' he murmurs against my cheek.

'Yeah? What of them?' I giggle.

'They make me want to do bad things to you.'

'Best wait 'til everyone's gone home for *those* kinds of shenanigans.'

Outside there are footsteps, and the tinkly babble of a toddler talking. We both look out of the kitchen window. The red-haired woman I've seen on Jesse's Facebook is standing outside, holding a big dish of something covered in foil. She's wearing a bright maxi dress which skims over a very definite pregnancy. Brandon is behind her, and he's carrying the toddler on his shoulders.

'That's Lainey,' Jesse tells me, nodding towards the window. 'And Brandon is carrying Nancy.' Lainey rings the doorbell and the welcome is remarkably different.

'I've brought lasagna,' she announces. She plonks the dish down heavily on the side and throws her arms around Jesse,

237

squeezing him tightly and kissing both his cheeks. It's so warm and familial that I can't help but smile. She holds him at arm's length and says, 'Now, where's this English rose of yours? I'm just *dying* to meet her.'

I don't think I've ever been called an English rose before. I like Lainey already. Jesse gestures to where I'm still loitering by the fridge and I hold my hand up in a little wave and she embraces me in the same tight hug as she gave Jesse just moments earlier.

'Are you having a lovely time?' she asks, and I nod. 'Is he being good to you?' she looks back at Jesse slyly. I nod again.

'When he wants to be.'

'Oh my goodness,' she gushes. 'You sound just like you could be on *Downton Abbey*.' I laugh. I can't help it. I couldn't sound less like I could be on *Downton Abbey* if I tried.

'Lainey is a huge fan,' Brandon explains.

'Huge,' she repeats, 'I've seen them all. Have you seen them all?'

'I've caught a couple,' I say. Brandon releases Nancy who runs to her mother and eyes me suspiciously. I crouch down to her level.

'And you must be Nancy,' I say. She nods, slightly nervously. 'I've heard lots of lovely things about you. I've been told you're a little princess.'

'And she knows it,' Brandon says. I stand back up and he extends his hand for me to shake. 'It's good to meet you.' He's the youngest of all the Franklin brothers, and yet somehow, he seems like the eldest. I suppose that's what happens when you have a blossoming family, and by the looks of Lainey, that family is definitely blossoming.

'Did you invite Mom and Dad?' he asks. Jesse shakes his head.

'I didn't invite anyone. This was all Trav's doing, no?'

'Trav and perhaps Lainey,' Brandon smirks. Lainey elbows him in the ribs.

'Never mind,' she says. 'We'll see your folks before we head back.'

'Uncle Jesse?' Nancy asks, but the J sounds like a D. 'Can I have some different songs on?' He picks her up and hugs her, and the affection between them is obvious. She grabs his hair and pulls it over his face. He doesn't stop her. It's adorable.

'Sure, what's your favorite?'

'The one about brushing and brushing and brushing my hair.' She pulls at her own hair. Jesse looks confused.

'Uh. I don't think I have that, sweetie.' He's so lovely with her and it reinforces my decision. One day I'll move out here and he can get me pregnant and be adorable like this with *our* babies.

'She means the soundtrack to *Tangled*,' Lainey explains. 'We have it in the car. Brandon, can you grab it? And the DVD, too.'

Jesse puts the dish into the oven, and we head back outside. The conversation breaks off into little groups. The boys in one, the girls in another, and Lainey and I talk about my trip. She tells me to head north the next time I'm here. This is good. Distance be damned. She thinks I'll be back.

'If you like good wine, you'll love it,' she assures me. 'There are vineyards everywhere. It's beautiful. We got married in one. Oh, and you can stay with us.' She's bubbly, talkative. I look at her, sitting just down the table from her husband, and I immediately want to take her up on her offer. I want to see the vineyards, I want to visit their house and I want to be part of their lovely family. A warm, calm feeling washes over me and I sit back in my chair. She turns to Holly.

'And how are things with you? Married life treating you well?'

'It's fine,' she says. 'What about you? How was the trip down? Did you stop off at all?'

'Not too shabby,' says Lainey. 'We flew. I couldn't stand to be in the car for all that time. My ankles swell, you know?'

'How far along are you now?'

'Twenty-four weeks,' she says. 'Six months.'

'Oh right, a couple of months behind Nicole then,' she says, but she's not looking at Lainey when she says it, she's looking at me. And then her eyes bounce over to Jesse, and her eyebrows raise a fraction, and her lips curl up into a smirk. 'Right, Jesse?'

'Huh?' Lainey says. She shifts uncomfortably.

'Holly!' Travis says.

'Mommy?' Nancy says.

'Come on, Nancy.' Brandon scrapes back his chair and carries her inside.

'Wait, Nicole, as in…' I say. I point at Jesse and his face really says it all.

'Um… Yeah?' Holly says, and her tone definitely suggests I'm not quite the full shilling. But how was I supposed to know? Up until Travis came over, I had no idea this woman even existed.

'And you said she's further along than Lainey? Who, and I'm sure she won't mind me saying this, is really quite pregnant. Congratulations, by the way. Happy news.'

Holly sits back in her chair, and surveys the chaos she's created, and I'm beginning to get an inkling that I know exactly what the atmosphere between her and Jesse is about, but I still can't put my finger on why.

'Did you know she was having a baby, Jesse?' I say in an odd, slightly high-pitched voice. 'Because you didn't say.'

He looks at the table. He definitely knew. I turn to Holly. 'How pregnant is she?'

'I don't know exactly. Far, though,' Holly says. 'Really far. Pretty close to having it I'd say.'

'Holly,' Travis repeats. 'You shouldn't—'

'And when did you say she went to New York?' I interrupt, calmly. I'm working it all out and the answer I keep coming to makes me want to vomit.

'January,' he says quietly. There's fear in his eyes and it hits me like a punch in the gut, because he's done the exact same

240

maths in his head, too, and the one thing about maths is that it is consistent.

'And it's September now and she's *really far gone*. Did *you* know?' I ask, turning to Travis. 'When you were here the other day. Did you know? When you said *that conversation* was coming, is that what you meant?'

He nods but says nothing. Bet this is awkward for him after how well we got on. He side-eyes his brother, who's now looking like he'd like the world to open and swallow him whole.

'Please can someone tell me if this is just a really shitty joke? Like some kind of elaborate initiation, or something.'

But no one says anything, and I know it isn't. And the other thing no one is doing, is reassuring me that Nicole is holed up somewhere cosy on the east coast, with a nice boyfriend, who is definitely the father of the child she's about to give birth to.

'Right. Excuse me,' I say, and I push my chair back and go inside the house. Jesse stands up too, but I stare at him and he stops. 'Don't you even think about it,' I hiss.

Chapter Thirty-Four

Jesse

Travis glares at Holly. Holly stares at her nails. Lainey cradles her head in her hands, and for a few seconds nobody says anything. And then, 'That was a dick move, Holly,' Lainey mutters, and we all look at her. Lainey never has a bad word to say about anybody. 'An *asshole* move. And for what? Huh? And *you*,' she turns to me. 'Why are you still sitting here? You need to go to her.'

'But she said—'

'Oh my *god*,' she hisses, and throws her hands up in the air, as if it's obvious.

Upstairs, Cassie's sitting on the edge of the bed. She's wringing her hands and looking at the floor.

'How long have you known about this?' she asks, quietly. She doesn't look up. 'Truthfully.'

'Since July,' I admit. 'Since I got back from San Francisco.'

'And you didn't tell me, why? Why didn't you tell me, Jesse?'

'Because it didn't seem important.'

'It didn't seem important. Are you kidding me? Are you or are you not about to have a baby with your ex?'

'No,' I say, quickly. 'I'm not. It's not... And that's why it wasn't important.'

She looks up for the first time, and I take that as an invitation to step further into the room. 'How do you *know*? How can you be *sure*? Has she said that? Did she leave you for someone else?'

'I mean… no? But… I feel like she'd have been in contact before now if the baby was—'

'Don't you think there's a possibility she found out after she was settled in New York? Didn't want to leave the job she loved. Figured you didn't want to be with her anymore and decided to go it alone?'

'I…'

'And say down the line she realises it's tough being a single mum and actually, she wouldn't mind a bit of help, or at the very least a bit of child support, and she comes knocking.'

'She's not—'

'She's not what? Like that? She'd be entitled to it. Why wouldn't she be like that? What happens if she wants to make a life with you and your ready-made family?' She spits the words out bitterly.

'Cass,' I say, but I've got nothing. Because what she's saying makes perfect sense, and this is the first time I've really thought about the ramifications.

'And you never told me,' she says. 'And I think that might even be worse.' She doesn't even look mad. Just disappointed, and that definitely *is* worse.

'If I'd told you,' I say, sitting down next to her on the edge of the bed, 'it could have changed everything. And I was afraid you might not want to visit. If we'd had this conversation before you left England you might… and then I wouldn't ever see you again, and we wouldn't have this… and I didn't know how to tell you. How do you tell someone that, Cassie? With those dates. How do you stop them jumping to conclusions? Because I *know* okay, I know how this looks.'

'So, what, you were hoping it would all just go away? And never come out? Because, mate, I have news for you.'

'No.'

She rubs her fingertips in circles over her temples.

'Did you see her? When you came back from London and went straight to New York. Did you see her?'

'No,' I say. 'I told you, I didn't even know about this then.'

She nods her head slowly. 'I mean, either way this is a giant lie by omission. You had ample opportunity to tell me, and you didn't. It was weird enough hearing about her from Travis, but now hearing about *this* from Holly. It should have been you. It all should have been you. You have no idea how much of an idiot I feel,' she whispers. 'I thought…'

She rubs her hand across her face and her fingers settle over her mouth. Her eyes are shiny. She rests her elbows on her knees and runs her hands through her hair. 'When you love someone you tell them the *truth*. You don't allow them to be humiliated like that. How much can I mean to you if I wasn't important enough to know about this?'

'Cassie, I *love* you,' I say. 'You are important. You're *the most* important. I'm sorry. I fucked up. I should have told you.'

I go to put my arms around her but she shakes me off, stands up. Covers her face and chokes out a sob. 'It doesn't mean shit,' she says. 'Please can you just go?'

Downstairs I lean on the back of the breakfast bar and rake my fingers through my hair. Holly and Travis are nowhere to be seen, which is probably just as well. Brandon is sitting back outside with Nancy on his lap, and they're coloring a page of a book. He's keeping things as normal as possible for her. Lainey peers around the door.

'Is she okay?'

'What do you think?' I ask.

'I think maybe she needs some time.'

I just stare down at the top of the unit, because I don't know what to believe anymore. 'Where's Holly?' I ask.

'Travis thought it would be best if they went for a walk. She tried to explain after you went upstairs. I don't think she meant for all this.'

'Oh well I guess that makes it all okay, then,' I snap. Lainey purses her lips and stares at me. She's about to say something when there are bumps down the steps, and it takes a second or two to realize the thudding sounds aren't Cassie's feet, but her suitcase clunking down heavily behind her.

'Jesse,' she says, in a small, quiet voice, 'I think, given the circumstances, it's best if I go home.'

Her fingers are gripped so tightly around the handle of her case that her knuckles are white. Her eyes are big and round and watery. There's a black smear directly under one of them.

'Wait!' I say, panicked, and the magnitude of the situation hits me. 'No. I'm sorry about this.'

She stares at me and the look in her eyes is unsettling. The dimness of them stops me from saying any more.

'It's a bit too late for apologies,' she whispers.

'What do you mean?'

'I need some space from this. And you need to find out. You can't be with me if you've made a baby with her. It's not fair. On anyone, really.'

'Cassie, no. Don't do this. Please?'

She shakes her head.

'You can't build a life with someone when you can't fully trust them.'

'We don't know anything for certain, sweetie,' Lainey says, gently.

'We know for certain I've been taken for a complete mug. He's known about this for *months*. And I've come all the way out here, and the whole time there's been this giant *secret* that was kept from me. Do you have any idea how *not okay* this is?'

Lainey nods and looks sad. She definitely knows how not okay this is.

'Let me call her,' I say. I'm clutching at straws because my final message to her was never delivered, and I don't think it was because she was out of range.

She lets go of her bag and folds her arms and I take out my phone and dial. But it doesn't connect and all I get is a busy tone before it cuts off.

'What about Facebook?'

245

'She's not on it,' Lainey explains.

'So how is Holly the font of all knowledge?' Cassie asks.

'They're friends,' I shrug. 'I guess they've talked.'

Cassie shudders.

'Your sister-in-law is friends with your ex who might be having your baby. And she definitely loved telling me. Can you see why this is totally fucked? I have to go.'

'No! Stay tonight,' I beg. 'We'll talk. We can figure this out.'

People always see things more clearly after a night's sleep. Everyone will leave. We'll look carefully at all the different scenarios, and in the morning we'll wake up and see it with fresh eyes. In the morning, everything will be fine again. All she has to do is stay.

But she's shaking her head as she tucks her hair behind her ear.

'Me staying tonight is not going to change anything.'

'Please, Cass. Not now. Not like this. Please?'

She closes her eyes and a single tear rolls down her cheek. She wipes it away and shakes her head.

'It's done. I've called a taxi.' She looks at me and her eyes are hollow. Dulled and muted and sad. And now everything about her seems small and flat and nothing like the girl I've fallen so hard for. I pull her towards me and there's neither resistance nor reciprocation. She's limp and motionless and disengaged. I might as well be holding a rag doll. A car stops outside. 'Cab's here,' she mutters, and pulls away. I follow her outside.

A bored-looking driver slouches behind the wheel of the waiting car. He's chewing gum and he watches our exchange from his open window. He's pretending not to listen but he definitely is. Of course he is. We both know I'm defeated. He pops the trunk and she hauls in her case. She kisses me on the cheek, and reaches her arms around my neck, breathing into my shoulder, definitely trying to hold it together. Her fingers are in my hair, her fingertips caressing the back of my head, and for a second I blindly let myself hope she's about to change her mind, that she'll unload the car instead of getting inside it. That she's not about to do this. But she backs away and opens the door instead. I want so desperately to stop her, to just take her back inside the house, get rid of everyone else and figure it all out. But I can't do any of that. I can't even move as this all unfolds around me. I am rooted to the spot. Now the car door is shut and she's looking at her lap. The driver confirms her destination and she answers and nods. He hits the gas and it's all over.

Someone puts a hand tentatively on my shoulder, and I don't even have to look round to know it's Lainey.

'Come back inside,' she says gently, and when I don't move, she presses her palm against my back and guides me back towards the house.

Travis is inside now, too, and Holly. They're loitering by the door.

'Jesse,' Holly says. 'I need to say—'

'No. You don't *need to say anything*,' I interrupt, mad as fuck, spitting out the words through gritted teeth. 'This is all your fault.'

'I think she's trying to apologize,' Travis cuts in.

'And you probably shouldn't start, either,' I snap. 'You're not exactly a paragon of virtue here.'

'I'm sorry,' Holly says, hand over her mouth. Travis goes to her and puts his arm around her protectively. He gives me a look which tells me exactly whose side he's on here, and it's not mine.

'What do you want us to do?' Lainey asks, calmly.

'I just don't know, Lainey,' I say, and head back upstairs.

Chapter Thirty-Five

Jesse

Outside, there is muffled talking. The sound of chairs on decking. Plates and glasses being cleared away. Gulls. The back doors opening, and closing again, and then silence. Inside, my bedroom is a mess. The bed sheets are crumpled. There's no longer a make-up bag by the mirror. There's no longer a purple and white toothbrush on the shelf in the bathroom, or a bikini top hanging on the towel rail. There's no longer a bottle of citrusy perfume on the chest of drawers. The suitcase left in the corner of my room has gone and it's shadowy in here now, where the sun has moved across the sky, and an orangey glow is beginning to creep across the walls.

The talking has moved inside the house now. People are in the living room. Nancy's wandering around. She's steered out of the kitchen by Lainey.

'I'll take her to Anaheim for the night,' Brandon is saying, 'I'll call them and explain.'

'Okay, but maybe go out front to make that call,' Lainey says, and I know why she's said it. My room is at the back of the house and my window is open. Someone is scraping dishes and stacking the dishwasher, before switching it on. The rhythmic hum just about reaches up the stairs.

Later, there's a tentative tap at the door, and without waiting for me to answer, Lainey pushes the door open.

'It's dark in here,' she says.

'Uh huh.'

'Can I come in?'

'I think you already did.'

She walks over to me and sits on the edge of the bed. 'Wanna talk about it?' she asks.

'I don't know what there is to say.'

She scoots back and switches on the side light, smooths her hands over her baby bump, and crosses her ankles. 'Oh, come on, Jesse,' she says. 'That was... I don't even know what that was.'

'I should have told her. I didn't because I didn't think it was an issue.'

'When exactly did you find out?'

'July. Like, right after I got home from seeing you guys. I bought the flights for Cassie. I told Trav about her. Then, I get a call from Holly and she just dropped it in there. I didn't even hear it from Nicole.'

'But you spoke to her, right? Once you knew.'

'Yeah, and that, too, was a bust. Take a look.'

I scroll back to the texts on my phone and hand it over.

'My god, Jesse, that's not how you ask that question. How were you raised?' She hands it back to me and purses her lips.

'What do you mean?'

'You *totally* ambushed her. No wonder she didn't reply. I'd have blocked your ass too.'

'No! I said I was open to that discussion.'

Lainey shakes her head. 'There are ways and then there are ways.'

'Well, look, my point still stands; she'd have been in touch if it was anything to do with me. She was never afraid to speak her mind.'

'That's true,' Lainey concedes. 'What a mess.'

We sit on my bed for a few minutes. Neither of us says anything. Then Lainey slides her arm around my shoulders and pulls me towards her. 'Oh, honey,' she coos. 'When Travis called the other day… He said you seemed really happy. He actually said you both did.'

'I was. We were.'

'What did she mean about building a life?'

'Oh, right, that. Yeah, two days ago we decided to make a proper go of it. We were watching a movie in here, and she just said, yeah, okay, let's do this. And I was going to do it. Anything it took. Anything at all, for her to be here.'

'I'm so sorry,' she says. Her eyes are sad. She chews her lip.

'Yup, thanks,' I say, but suddenly I'm exhausted.

'For what it's worth, we really liked her.'

'Yeah,' I say, kicking off my shoes, 'I knew you would.'

'Brandon and I thought we might stick around a while. Just for a couple of days.'

'You don't have to do that. I'll be okay.'

She looks at me. She doesn't believe me. I don't believe me either. 'Well, we are. Do you need anything? You didn't eat. There's lasagna.'

'No. Thank you, though. Look, I'm pretty tired. Think I'm going to just turn in.'

'Alright,' she says. She pulls her arm from around my shoulder and swings her legs over the side of the bed. She clicks the door shut on the way out and I roll onto my side. There's a black tank top sticking out from under a pillow. Cassie wore it to sleep in most nights she was here. What is it about women leaving clothes they slept in here? Now she's at LAX, possibly already in the air. And wherever she is, it isn't here, and already things feel different.

Chapter Thirty-Six

Cassie

I'm standing outside LAX, case in hand, hand luggage thrown over my shoulder, watching as the taxi drives away. I had arrived here less than two weeks ago so excited, so happy, so *smitten*. I hadn't given any thought to leaving but if I had, this would categorically not have been how I'd have imagined it. I wonder what he's doing now. I wonder what he said when he went back inside. How Travis and Holly reacted to my leaving. I hope they all rallied around. Despite the fact he's broken me with the potential paternity he absolutely knew about and made the conscious decision to keep from me, I hope they are kind to him. I think back to how shocked he looked when he saw my luggage and clocked that I was off and momentarily, I feel awful.

Then I remember the reason I left, and the feeling of awfulness intensifies until I think my chest might collapse. It's a different kind of awful, though; it's a lonely, stupid, self-loathing kind of awful. Of course it was too good to be true. Of course he was never really mine. He's Jesse Franklin, my teenage crush, and I'm just Cassie from Amersham. No one gets that sort of fairytale unless their name is Kate Middleton.

I push through the door and make my way over to Virgin Atlantic.

'I need to change my flight,' I mumble at the lady. I hand my flight documents over to her and she looks them over.

'I'm sorry, this ticket is non-transferable,' she says. I stare at her.

'Are you having me on?' My voice is louder and more aggressive than I mean it to be. Her colleague glances over at me, and double-takes when he sees my puffy face and smudged eye make-up. *What of it?* I think.

'I'm sorry, ma'am.'

'What can I do then? I need a flight out of here. To London. As soon as possible, because I've just found out my boyfriend has probably fathered some other woman's baby and I need to leave. It's really important that I leave.'

'Oh, honey, no!' Ticket Lady says. She looks outraged on my behalf. 'Kick him to the kerb.'

'Yeah. Sucks to be me, huh?' I mutter.

'You'll still need to purchase a new ticket,' her colleague says. I wipe my eyes again and bite my lip to stop it from quivering.

'Fine,' I sigh. 'I'd like a ticket to London, on the next flight out of here I can get on.'

Ticket Lady taps away at her computer and looks uncomfortable, and I know she can't help me.

'The next available flight is tomorrow.'

'Well, that's just shit,' I sigh. She slides my travel documents back across the desk. 'Who else can I fly with? Delta? Lufthansa? That nice Dutch one? BA?' I reel off names of other airlines, 'Where is British Airways?'

BA will help me, I am sure of it. They are an airline you can trust. Their motto is *To Fly, To Serve.* They will fly me home and serve me alcohol on the way. They won't leave a heartbroken woman stranded in America in her time of need. Virgin Atlantic lady tells me they are based at a different terminal and says something about a shuttle bus, and my heart sinks even lower. She's trying to be kind but this is not an easy process, and right now I need this to be easy. I pick up my useless ticket and head back towards the exit, dragging my bag behind me.

British Airways do help me, and relieve me of over a thousand pounds for the privilege. I have less than an hour before I fly and I head through security in a daze, then wander aimlessly around the departure lounge, not knowing quite what to do with myself. I can't eat anything because I don't think my stomach could handle it. I don't want to buy anything. I've finished my book, not that I could have concentrated on it even if I hadn't. I text Rachel, and I can't quite believe the words my fingers are tapping out. I have to read them over and over to convince myself of what has happened.

> It's all gone so terribly wrong. I'm coming home right now. Please please meet me at Heathrow, I can't face going home alone. 4pm (Sunday), BA268, T5 xx

My seat on the plane is on the aisle and I've never been more grateful. The last thing I need to see are the bright lights of LA at night. We were going to go out tomorrow night. We were going to go to Malibu for dinner. I was going to see it all from the ground. I can't bear to see it from the air.

Once the seatbelt signs have been switched off, the flight attendant comes round with drinks and snacks. I ask for a vodka and drink it neat. It's rough and it burns my throat but I don't care. I just want it to numb everything so I don't have to face up to what has happened. On her way back, I get a gin and tonic, and slam that, too. The man sitting next to me shifts. I glare at him. I recline my seat as much as possible, not giving a shit that I've blocked in the person behind me, and put on an eye mask to encourage people to leave me alone. I don't want the chicken, or the beef.

Eventually, I fall asleep and I dream about Jesse. We are hanging out at his house. We are sitting outside on the deck with drinks and nachos, in the sunshine. We are eating big slices of cheesy pizza in the living room. We are walking on the beach, hand in hand. We are doing all the things we did. The scenes flick through my mind like old grainy home videos, and it's all so realistic, except that I can't touch him. Whenever I try, he

253

moves out of the way. I open my eyes and push the eye mask up on to my forehead. In front of me is a small screen mounted onto a rim of grey plastic. Next to me is a man who is not Jesse. I'm no longer in his house on the beach. I'm tens of thousands of feet up in the air, somewhere over Canada. The plane rattles with turbulence and for a few seconds I hope we fall out of the sky. My heart breaks all over again.

–

It's a real howler of a day when we land in England. Rain falls in sheets across the tarmac and drips down the windows.

The queue at customs is long and I haven't switched my phone back on, so I don't know if Rachel is going to be there to meet me. Perhaps I should have asked Dad instead, but she was the first person I thought of. And maybe ruining one of the last Sundays before her wedding wasn't the most considerate thing I could have done, but I'm scared to check my phone in case Jesse has messaged me, or tried to call.

At baggage reclaim, the man I was sitting next to on the plane is staring at me across the carousel, probably wondering why I am such a mess. I catch his eye and he looks away. Cases trundle rhythmically around the belt. I grab mine and head off.

I shuffle through to arrivals and finally I'm free. Officially back in the UK. California feels like a surreal dream.

It's busy. Stacks of people are waiting to pick up friends and loved ones. There are smiling faces everywhere and that just makes this whole thing even worse. A small child ducks under the barrier and runs to his father, his mother waiting patiently behind. The child is scooped up and Dad is showered with toddler kisses. He makes his way over to his wife and they kiss. She rubs his back and they walk off. It's Jesse and Nicole and their kid, a couple of years from now. An older couple are greeted by grown up children.

'How was the flight, Ma?' their daughter asks. I don't hear the response.

Rachel is standing there, her lovely face contorted with worry and concern. Her hair is scraped back in a ponytail and strands fall around her face. She's carrying a cardboard coffee cup. Like the little boy, she ducks under the barrier and walks up to me. I drop my case. She envelopes me in a hug. Neither of us say anything. She strokes my hair. I crumple. My sobs echo around the arrivals hall.

Chapter Thirty-Seven

Cassie

'George is in the car,' Rachel says gently, 'I hope you don't mind that he's here. I didn't think you'd fancy the tube.' Rachel can't drive, so of course George is here. I sniff. She hands me the coffee.

'Got anything stronger?' I ask.

'Fraid not, babe.' She links her arm through mine and takes my case. We walk to the car park.

'Can I stay with you tonight?' I ask. 'I can't go home and be alone, I just can't. You won't even know I'm there. I'll kip on the sofa.'

'You'll kip in the spare room and you'll stay as long as you need,' Rachel says, opening the car door. I get into the back. George looks over from the driver's seat. His left arm is gripping the headrest of the passenger seat.

'Hi, mate,' he says, sympathetically. He knows. Of course he knows. Rachel wouldn't have said they were driving to Heathrow for a fun afternoon out. Nobody drives to Heathrow for a fun afternoon out.

'Hi, George,' I say, glumly.

'She's had a shock,' Rachel explains and I nod. A shock isn't even the half of it. George gets on the motorway and everything is grey. Rain beats a tinny rhythm on the roof of the car. The clouds are grey, George's car is grey. Almost black, actually. Everything in my life is grey when just yesterday it had been in vibrant technicolor. I lean my head on the window and soon we are back in Crouch End. Rachel makes up the spare bed, and I crash.

'I'll just stay tonight,' I tell her, 'I'm sure you've got wedding stuff to do, and, no offence, but I can't help you with that right now.'

'It's fine,' she soothes, stroking my forehead. 'Shall we get a takeaway tonight?'

'Yes, but not a Chinese,' I tell her, remembering the first dinner Jesse and I ate together in California. I don't think I'll ever be able to look at a spring roll again.

'Okay. I'll put away the bottle of Californian red I was going to open, shall I?'

I roll over and bury my face in the pillow. 'Too soon,' I wail. It sounds muffled.

'Cassie, you haven't told me what happened out there? I mean, we were just talking online about you running off into the sunset and shacking up with this guy, and the next thing I know I look at my phone and there is this text asking me to come and get you. I get it if you're not ready to talk about it, but when you are, what happened?'

I sit up and take a deep breath. Despite having what felt like endless hours on the plane to process everything, I'd tried to numb it all with sleep and booze whilst hiding under an eye mask.

'There's a baby,' I say. 'His ex girlfriend's about to drop a sprog and apparently they only broke up in January. It's probably his, given the time frame.'

Rachel's eyes widen. 'Holy plot twist, Batman,' she says. 'Is this the ex who moved to New York?'

'Yeah,' I say, grimly. 'So that happened.'

'When did he tell you this?'

'Ha!' I say. '*He* didn't. He didn't think it was important. Holly did.'

'Who's Holly?'

'Travis' wife.'

257

'How does *she* know?'

'Rachel. They *all* knew. Apart from Lainey, I think.'

'And Lainey is?'

'Brandon's wife. We saw her on Jesse's Facebook that time. Nice woman, actually. I liked her.'

'Gotcha. I have to say I'm very disappointed. Especially in Travis. I thought better of him.' She tuts and shakes her head. 'I mean, obviously that's unforgivable of Jesse too. Lay it out for me, how did all this go down?'

All of a sudden, my eyes feel leaky again. I think back to what happened and I know I'm not going to get through the next bit without crying. My mouth twists into an ugly grimace. My chest heaves. Rachel pats my hand.

'So we're all outside, about to have lunch, but then Holly turns to Lainey and asks how far along she is, and then makes a huge deal of the fact that... the fact that Nicole is... is further along.'

I'm off again. Wailing. Splashy tears fall on Rachel's mauve satin bedspread. Why has she put a mauve satin bedspread on the bed of a heartbroken woman who is definitely going to weep all over it? Those tears are going to leave stains.

'And I was desperate for an explanation that would make it all okay, but he didn't have one. You could see the fear in his eyes. He was absolutely shitting himself, Rach. He couldn't tell me either way.'

'Bastard!' she says, and her eyes are mad. 'Prick!'

'After that, I obviously couldn't stay. So I packed up my stuff and I left. When I sent that text I was waiting to get on the plane.'

'Had everyone gone?'

'No. It all unfolded so fast and I had to get out. Didn't really think about it.'

'You just left? In the middle of everything? Dramatic!'

'Yep. How could I stay after that? I could hardly even look at him.'

'And what did he have to say for himself?'

'He asked me not to go. He actually got really upset, and I think he was crying a bit.' I remember how he looked just before I got in the car and before that, even, by the front door and I shudder.

'Oscar-worthy,' she says, clapping her hands, 'I think you belong in LA. The pair of you.'

'Well apparently I don't,' I sniff.

'Cass,' she says, taking my hand. 'Do you want me to contact him? I will absolutely tear him to shreds on your say so.'

I consider what she's said. Replay everything that's happened in the last two days in my head. From when everything was perfect, sitting on the pier with Jesse as the sun went down, curled into him, telling him I love him; to later that night, agreeing to give up everything for him, and knowing in the very core of me that I've never meant anything so much in my life. And then the horror that unfolded over drinks and olives and the best almonds I've ever eaten in my life, and the look on Holly's face, almost gleeful in the destruction she engineered. And finally, the look on Jesse's face when he couldn't categorically tell me for certain that Nicole's baby isn't his, because at the end of the day, he didn't know himself. And that's a bit of a deal-breaker isn't it? What kind of masochist would I have been to stay when he could at any point decide to give things another go with the mother of his child? That and the blatant withholding of the truth would have marred the whole thing. Cast a shadow on the rest of the trip, and that shadow would have followed me everywhere, and if the kid is his, he'd never really be mine.

'No,' I say firmly. 'But thank you.'

'I'm so angry with him.'

'I'm just empty,' I say. 'Still can't believe it.'

'I can't believe it's happened again. I'm so sorry.'

'Rach, let's not go there,' I say, sadly. 'I want to believe it's different. I can't let myself think he's like Jack.'

'Alright.' She pats my knee.

'Think I'm just going to lie here for a bit.'

'That's cool,' she says. 'Whatever you need.' She stands up and turns to leave.

'Hey, Rach?' I say. She stops at the door. 'Tell me something about your wedding that I don't know?'

She smiles at me. It's the first time I've asked about her for weeks. I'm a terrible friend. I'm selfish as well as stupid and heartbroken.

'We're having a ukulele group,' she says. 'They are called The Highly Strung.'

'That's adorable,' I tell her.

–

I am exhausted and I sleep until after Rachel and George have both left for work the next day. I miss dinner but the oil-stained paper bag and the faint whiff of jalfrezi tells me they got a curry. Rachel has scrawled a note letting me know they have saved some for me and it's in the fridge. I pick at the turmeric-yellow rice and the leathery naan bread, staring out of the window at everyone going about their business. I shouldn't be in Crouch End. I should be in California. I take a shower, the first since before I left America, and catch the bus home, lugging my suitcase behind me. It's overcrowded and smelly and I don't get a seat. Someone is drinking an energy drink and eating a McDonald's breakfast and the vaguely sweet smell makes me feel nauseous. An old lady tuts at me because my case is ever so slightly in her way. *Oh piss off*, I think, *you intolerant old hag*. The lady on the beach wouldn't have tutted.

There is no one at home when I let myself in. Someone has piled my post up on the radiator cover in the hallway. It was undoubtedly Jon. It's all in order of envelope size. I ignore it. There's a rip in the wallpaper I haven't seen before, exposing a crack in the plaster underneath. Sara's washing hangs on an airer in the living room. There's a lot of tie dye. The house is eerily quiet and floorboards creak under my feet. I haul my case upstairs and into my room at the front of the house. No one has been in here for days and it's stale. I heave open the sash window and my curtains billow in the breeze. I don't want to unpack because once I've done that my trip really is over. But I don't want to think about Jesse either, and putting on a wash seems like a welcome distraction. I unzip my case and crammed-in clothes and shoes burst out over the sides; balled up t-shirts, creased sundresses, underwear that's wrapped itself around the heels of shoes. I've probably left things there but that's just too bad. I methodically put away my shoes and I notice my sandals still have sand in the seams. Two of my t-shirts have a slight Jesse smell from where we'd slept pressed up against each other. I put them under my pillow. I'm not ready to lose that yet. Even after everything, I still want a reminder that most of the time we were brilliant. The day passes glacially, with coffee I make but don't drink, a knock on the door that I don't answer, my laundry, sitting wet in the machine, and shadows that creep across the room.

Sara and Jon are surprised when they get home and find me moping in the lounge. Jon can see something is up, but he doesn't know what to say. Sara cooks us all a rice dish for dinner, leaving the components separate for Jon. She grates cheese and chops up salami for us to sprinkle on top, *and* does the washing up without saying anything about fair distribution of the household chores. They both offer me the TV remote but I don't want to watch anything. I slope off to bed early.

–

How was your flight? Can we talk? I miss you.

Nope. And later:

261

> I'm sorry about everything Cass. I understand that you might need some time but can you at least let me know you got home safely. I didn't know which flight you got on so I couldn't track it.

Not today, Satan.

> Cassie, can you let me know that you're okay. It's been a couple of days now. I tried calling you but I think your phone is off?

It isn't. I couldn't deal with the phone calls or the texts so I took a leaf out of Nicole's book. Amazed he didn't guess, to be honest.

> Please, Cass. I know you're reading these. It says you've read them.

Ugh. Damn you, Zuckerberg.

Chapter Thirty-Eight

Cassie

I go back to work the next day. There's no point in wasting my holiday allowance wallowing in my bed, crying my eyes out on my own. Actually, I'm not sure I have any tears left to cry in my bed, or anywhere else, in fact. The rims of my eyes are swollen and sore and the whites are bloodshot and pink. I don't see Sara before I leave, but I encounter Jon in the kitchen and he finds it all so painfully awkward and difficult that he can't get away from me fast enough. He thinks I can't see, but our kettle is stainless steel and I watch his reflection back out of the room as I lean against the corner unit. On the tube, I lean against the door and stare out of the window at the soot and grime and miles of thick cables as the train rumbles and rattles through the tunnels. At Oxford Circus I go straight to Starbucks and order my usual skinny latte. Everything is like it always has been. The same baristas make my coffee. The same homeless man sits outside, staring into his lap with his paper cup and his black fingernails. It's like I've never been away. It's like the last ten days haven't really happened at all. Except they have, and nothing will ever be the same again.

Our receptionist, Jenna, beams at me as I walk past.

'Oooh, not seen your face for a bit,' she says, cheerfully. Her hair is pinned up on the top of her head in tiny little clips shaped like butterflies. I think they are glittery.

'I've been on my hols,' I tell her.

'Somewhere hot, judging by your tan,' she says. She's observant, that Jenna.

'California.'

'You don't seem happy to be back.'

Funny that, I want to say. *Neither would you if you'd had your heart broken by someone you've been a bit in love with for half your life.* 'Oh, just post holiday blues,' I reply. The phone rings. She picks it up.

'Beauchamp and Taylor, good morning,' she trills into her headset. I punch the button to call the lift.

Mimi stops when she sees me at my desk.

'You're not due back in until the end of the week,' she says. 'It's Tuesday today.'

'I had to come home early,' I say, my voice monotone, my eyes staring blankly at my screen.

'Everything all right?'

'Not really.'

Mimi shifts. 'Well, since you're back, we need to run through a couple of the new lines for winter next year. Shall we nip to a break-out room at ten for a catch up?'

'Sure.'

In our meeting, Mimi reminds me sign-off is approaching, and that Sam and I will be presenting next year's kitchenware lines to senior management. The chief exec will be there, the finance will be scrutinised. I have to go through all our profit margins and report on what kind of sales we'll be looking at. She hands over a stack of reports and tells me to pretty them up into graphs and tables. I try to get enthused about it all, really, I do. But all I can do is nod along, and all I can think about is that today should have been my last day with Jesse.

'Wait here a minute,' she says. I do as I'm told and cradle my head in my hand. After a minute or two I cross my arms and lay on them. I am annoyed with myself for wallowing at work. If I'd wanted to sit and mope I could have done it at home. The very reason I came back to work early was to provide me with a distraction. The door opens again, and Mimi puts two coffees and a bar of Dairy Milk on the table. She pulls a travel pack of tissues from her back pocket and drops it next to my coffee.

'Spill,' she says.

'What?'

'You're home from your holiday early, and you've come back to work instead of just taking the days. You look, frankly, terrible and your eyes are pink. Talk to me.'

I look up at her and sigh.

'Back in July,' I start, 'I had a sort of date with someone. Do you remember? You let me leave early that day.' She nods. I don't know if she remembers or not. It doesn't really matter either way. We didn't talk about it again. 'Well, I didn't think it would be anything more than a quick drink, because he was in a band I absolutely adored when I was a teenager.'

'What?' Mimi laughs. 'Who *is* this guy?'

'Jesse Franklin. He was the bass player in Franko.'

'Oh. I thought you were going to tell me you'd shagged a Backstreet Boy or something.'

'Fraid not,' I say. 'They were really big in Germany. Smaller fan base here. Anyway, I found him on the internet, said hi. Didn't expect a response but got one and we started chatting, and then he came here for a gig and we met up. And it went well. Unexpectedly so. He took me out for dinner and we had a romantic walk and a snog by the river and then I stayed over, and… well you know. But the thing is, he lives in California.'

'You mentalist. I love it.'

'It was brilliant. So brilliant in fact, that we talked about visas and stuff.' I rip open the chocolate bar and dunk a square into my coffee. 'We were ridiculously in love. Absolute fairytale stuff.'

'I mean, hasty, but stranger things have happened. Be a shame to lose you though.'

'Right, well I don't think there's much danger of that. Because it turns out it's very likely he is about to become a father, and he hadn't thought to mention it.'

Mimi spits her mouthful of coffee back into her mug. It's possibly the least refined I've ever seen her, and Mimi's charade on the away day was *Deep Throat*.

'Fuck off,' she gasps.

'Yeah,' I shrug forlornly.

'So, baby mama crawled out of the woodwork whilst you were there? Absolute bastard!' she says, and even after all this, I feel protective of him.

'He isn't sure,' I say, quickly. 'The mother of the child is his ex. But as far as I can tell the dates are very questionable.'

'How questionable?'

'As in, she's due imminently and they broke up in January but only because she got a job in New York.'

'Hmm, admittedly, not looking good. But maybe it's not his and she's just saying this to get at his pop star megabucks? Did he ask her? Isn't that the first thing blokes do when responsibility knocks?'

'Hmm, I don't think there are any pop star megabucks, to be honest.'

'Spent it on coke and women? Snorted it through rolled up hundreds off their tits and bleached arseholes?'

'Mimi!' I say.

'What? It's possible! That's rock 'n' roll, baby.'

'I think you'd find him entirely too salubrious. As far as I could tell his best things are music and tacos. Definitely no Colombian nose candy. Anyway, he says he did ask her but she blocked him. He also tried to call her in front of me but didn't get through. But I was so upset that I left.'

She looks at me as if she thinks I've jumped the gun. Why does she think I've jumped the gun? I haven't jumped the bloody gun.

'Well, if you know you did the right thing then it sounds like it's for the best,' she says, diplomatically. 'Seems like a waste of a nice holiday though.'

—

During the afternoon lull, I sign into Facebook.

Cass, I know you're home, I can see you've been online, so I'm not sure how fair it is to cut me off over something neither of us know for sure, especially when you know I've been trying to contact you. I wish you hadn't just left. We should have been able to deal with this like adults.

I'm sorry, what? Did he just tell me I haven't dealt with news of his probable fatherhood like an adult, when he had a classic ostrich moment and didn't seem to want to deal with it at all? When he knowingly kept it from me and was absolutely hoping it would all just go away? All things considered, I think that's really quite rich.

I hadn't cut you off, I was taking some time to think about everything after a giant comedown and frankly, a hideous shock. Did you manage to speak to her?

No. I'm still blocked.

And there's no email or parents to call?

Let's be real, there's no way I could contact her parents about this even if I did have their number (I don't, for the record. Met them once. They live in Michigan.) As for her email, I don't know it.

You don't know your ex girlfriend's email address? Convenient…

WTF, Cassie? Literally none of this is convenient. What do you want me to do?

Go back in time and make the (correct) decision to tell me, so I wasn't massively humiliated in front of your entire family.

And I told you why I didn't: 1) I didn't want you to react in exactly the way you have. 2) If we're really being honest, it's not exactly your business. I have to go now but this isn't over.

Not my business? What is the matter with you? You broke up because she got a new job across the country. Then you find out she's pregnant and are concerned enough about the timing to ask if there could have been an oops moment. And what if it turns out to be yours?

You seem to expect me to roll with this like it's no big deal but I can't do that. I don't want to have to share you and right now you can't be sure I wouldn't have to. My head's all over the place and I can't do this.

I'm sorry but it IS over. I love you but I can't put myself through this. Not with you.

By now there are tears spilling down my cheeks and I'm grateful that Sam and Mimi are both in meetings. I hadn't woken up this morning with the intention of ending it, but after the way it spiralled and the things he said? I'm not sure you can come back from that.

I close down my browser and head out for a walk. I eat overpriced and not very nice sushi for lunch. The claggy rice sticks to the roof of my mouth. The specks of tuna distributed through the middle of the roll are the only hint that it's ever even seen a piece of fish, and the wasabi is pasty and mild. I stay late at work because I don't want to go home and face up to the realisation that my life has taken a turn for the shit. That I still live with Jon and Sara in grotty Shepherd's Bush, when less than a week ago I had the first spark of a plan to move to California and live out my days by the beach with the love of my life and I'm not even remotely close to that anymore. And I'm not sure, all things considered, that I ever was.

In an attempt to avoid Jesse, I steer clear of Facebook and instead shift my focus to Rachel's hen night. Turns out I'm not the only one.

From: Marie Michaels
To: Cassie Banks
Subject: Hen do

Hi Cassie,

I spoke to Rachel. She told me what happened. I'm sorry. I feel bad for ribbing you when we went out for tapas before you went away :(Can't imagine how shit that must have been for you.

I know this is probably a bit insensitive given the circumstances, but I was wondering if you'd managed to book the roller disco? It's just that it's not all that long until the hen, and we do really need to give her a send off she'll remember. Let me know if you need any help.

Marie

From: Cassie Banks
To: Marie Michaels

Subject: Re: Hen do

Yes Marie, it's all booked. I'll forward you the confirmation. I got us on some kind of list so we don't have to queue. Oh, and we have a reserved table and some fizz, too. I had to pay upfront, so I'm going to send round another email so I can recoup costs. Obviously Rachel isn't paying.

Don't worry about me. I am fine. It was fun whilst it lasted, but you know how these things go. I will be fine. Can't wait for the hen night, it will be just what I need to take my mind off everything. Anyway, I'm sure I will be fine.

See you soon,

C x

From: Marie Michaels
To: Cassie Banks
Subject: Re: Re: Hen do

You DEFINITELY sound fine :-/
Marie

–

In the morning, the red notification symbol of doom is there again, glaring at me, angrily, from the corner of my Facebook profile. I used to love seeing it, but now it troubles me. I have a message and I am scared to look at it.

> Is that how it's going to be?

> That's how it HAS to be.

As things stand it is. Because the thought of waiting for her to give birth and then him calling me to break the news, or, worse, waking up one day to some kind of announcement would be more than I can handle.

He doesn't reply. Not then. Not later on. Not the next day, or the one after. He doesn't fight for me. Doesn't try and stop the end of us. Doesn't promise to make everything okay again. Doesn't even try to. So I hover over a button I never dreamed I'd ever press, and click, and I'm sure, if you opened me up right at this point in time, you'd find my heart torn from the safety of my chest and tangled up with all my other organs. Away from where it should be, mashed up and squeezed to nothing more than a misshapen, bloody lump.

> You are no longer friends with Jesse Franklin

Chapter Thirty-Nine

Jesse

'Okay, I'm sorry, can we go again?' I say into the mic. It's a little over a week since my final, dreadful conversation with Cassie and I'm still just trying to blot everything out and get on with stuff. The days sort of merged after Brandon and Lainey went back to San Francisco, and today is the first day I've left the house at all. I'm in a studio in Hollywood, and it's fair to say things are not going well.

'Yep, not a problem.'

The guide track starts again. I count along in my head and start playing. It's a simple bassline to begin with, repeating over and over throughout the verses, with nice little fills in the chorus that change slightly each time, and then finally, a fast, relatively tricky solo in the middle eight, before the chorus repeats until the end of the song. I haven't even got as far as the solo yet. I'm messing up the second chorus fill every single time. It's infuriating. It's *my* fill. I made it up, and it's all played on one specific part of the neck, so it's not even a stretch to reach the frets. But the fast string skipping, and the hammer on, and the octave I have to hit are all throwing me today. I get to that point in the song again and I know what's about to happen. The string skipping is fine. So is the hammer on, but my finger slips and I miss the octave on G. A bum note rings out and I stop playing.

'Shit, man, I'm sorry.'

'No big deal.'

'One more time?'

'As many as you need.'

The relaxed approach is definitely appreciated but I'm not used to needing this many do overs. It's been more than a handful. Usually I get in, run through a couple of times, record, and am out of there. I'm efficient, everyone knows it, and that's how I like it. Now everyone is watching me from behind the glass, and it's putting me off. I turn away from them all slightly as the track starts again in my headphones, in the hope that I won't get distracted. I'm going to nail it this time. But I hit the wrong string during the hammer on and it sounds awful. A jarring twang that absolutely does not work in the key. Eddie, the sound engineer, stops the track before I even have time to ask. I am frustrated.

'Fuck!' I snap. 'Fuck this. Fuck it all.'

'You okay?' he says into the mic. 'Do you need to take a minute?'

'I'm fine,' I insist.

But I'm very much not fine. I can't concentrate. My mind is elsewhere. My mind is, as it has been since September eighth, on Cassie and the way she left, and the dimness of her eyes as she sat in that car. And still I can't completely believe it. It's almost as if wherever we went, little parts of her broke off and dispersed, and they hang in the air like a spritz of that perfume she wears. She's everywhere I look in my house. She's on the beach, sitting on the pier, staring out to sea. She's curled up on the couch or switching TV channels whilst I get a drink from the fridge. She'll be in Venice, too, leaning against the bridge, and at Griffith Observatory, gazing back at the hazy view of DTLA and holding my hand.

And it all feels surreal, and certain details are becoming hazy and fuzzy around the edges. Like it was nothing more a dream, and what happened the day she left was just my waking up from it.

'You sure? You seem a little... not yourself today.'

'Really, it's okay. I'm just...'

Eddie waits for me to say more, but I don't.

'You want to go again?' he asks.

But before I can reply an assistant enters the control room and starts whispering to him, and then they're both looking at me.

'Uh, Jesse,' he says. 'There's someone here to see you.'

For a second I think Cassie's come back, and there's a flicker of excitement, but then reality caves in on me again. She ended it and unfriended me, and even if she hadn't done those things, she doesn't know where I am today.

Eddie continues. 'A Holly?'

'Oh, Jesus. I am *so* sorry. Can you get rid of her?'

The assistant approaches the mixing desk. 'I tried,' she says. 'I told her you were recording. But she said it's, like, super important.'

'Uuugghhhh,' I tip my head back and groan.

'You can't bring your girlfriend to the studio, man,' Eddie says, but he's smirking.

'She's so *not* my girlfriend,' I say. 'She's my sister-in-law. Look, do you mind if I take five to get rid of her?'

'Nah, it's cool,' he says. 'We could probably use a break anyway. We might get some pizza delivered.'

I yank off the headphones and shove my bass, roughly, back in the stand.

'Sounds awesome,' I say.

Holly's in the reception area, perched on the edge of a couch. She stands up as I approach.

'Jesse. I—'

'You can't just ambush me at work,' I snap. 'And you know this.'

'I'm sorry but you didn't answer your phone. Or your texts. I've been trying to get hold of you.'

'And it didn't occur to you that there might be a reason for that?'

'I even stopped by your place.'

274

'I was probably out running errands.'

I was not out running errands. I knew she'd been by. I'd heard the music in her car even before she pulled up, and then she'd knocked on the door. And then, a few minutes later, she walked around to the beach and tapped on the back doors. I'd sat on the upstairs landing, out of view, hiding in my own house, until I heard her drive away again.

The assistant is back behind the desk now, and she's definitely listening. 'Come on,' I say, nodding towards the door. 'Not in here.'

Out on the street, Holly fiddles with her purse and I crouch down against the wall and close my eyes. 'How did you even know I was here today?' I say. 'Do you realize how inappropriate this is?'

'Trav had it in his cell and we have a shared calendar. This was a last resort, Jesse. I messed up, okay. Is that what you want me to say?'

'Not really, no, because it means shit coming from you.'

'He yelled at me. On the beach, that day. He never yells at me. Said I shouldn't have gotten involved.'

'He's right. You shouldn't have. And look what you did, Holly. She left because of what you stirred up. And she's not coming back.'

I'm expecting her to argue, to give me shit about how I should have been more honest, and she'd be right to, but she kicks the sidewalk with her shoe and squints up at the sky.

'I'm sorry,' she says, eventually.

'When did Nicole tell you she was pregnant?'

'She didn't. I found out via the medium of Instagram,' she shrugs.

'Wait, what? She hates social media. I have to tell you, Holly, I have questions about this now.'

'She started an account after she moved. I don't know, new life, new Nicole, or something. She showed up in a list of people I should follow. Anyway, she posted a cutesy scan picture. I thought you'd have seen it.'

'Why would I have seen it? I don't use Instagram.'

'Well I didn't know that. You're so locked down on everything.'

'Yeah. It's this thing called privacy. It's called keeping yourself to yourself, Holly. It's called minding your own damn business. You should try it some day.'

'Alright, I get it, you're mad at me,' she mutters. 'You don't have to keep on. I said I'm sorry.'

'What else do you know?' I say.

'Nothing,' she says. 'Just what I've already said.'

'Show me this picture.'

We sit down and lean against the wall and she opens up the app. We look like a couple of bums with an iPhone. She leans in and we scroll through the pictures. There aren't many, and mostly they're just shots of skyscrapers, and her apartment, and the occasional selfie. And then, posted on the fourth of July, a photo of her with quite a pronounced bump, holding a grainy sonogram image. I can't tell what I'm looking at. A black and white image of a face in profile. *Surprise!* reads the caption. *Late to the party, but I wanted to wait for a special day to share the news! Happy #fourthofjuly #babymeijer #pregnant #momtobe #mommyinthemaking*

There's another picture, too. Of Nicole's bump with a giant blue bow tied around it. And another, of her surrounded by cake and gifts.

'Cute babyshower, no?' Holly says, but I'm not focusing on that. I'm looking for anything at all that pulls me out of the running. But there's nothing, and we're back to pictures of the Chrysler building and stacks of pancakes.

'Holly,' I say, 'none of this tells me anything.'

'It tells you she is pregnant,' she replies. 'Duh.'

'What about if you contact her?'

'Uh, no can do,' she says, shaking her head.

'Uh, yes can do, I think it's the very least you can do.'

'No. I don't follow her.'

'Huh? But you said—'

'Look. Nic and I didn't part on amazingly good terms,' she says, shiftily. 'Just because she showed up on a list of people to follow, doesn't mean I actually did, you know?'

'What do you mean?' I ask.

'Let's just say she was not intending to stay in touch with *anyone* out here. And I might have called her out on it.'

'Oh. I thought you guys were friends? Why have you been mad at me for months?'

'Yeah,' she snaps. 'So did I. But I guess she felt like she wanted a clean break, which I didn't think was entirely fair. *I* never did anything to upset her. Anyway, the point is, if she knows I look at her photos, she might lock this shit down and that doesn't help *you* right now, does it?'

'But you took her to the airport?'

'Ugh, it was the shortest drop off ever. She couldn't get out of the car fast enough.'

'Holly, you've never mentioned this.'

'Can you stop fixating on shit that isn't important right now. The fact is, if you'd tried harder with her, I'd still have my friend.'

And this is Holly to a tee. No understanding at all that her actions have consequences of their own.

'Do you realize how stupid you sound when you say that? For the last time, *she* broke up with *me*. Your friendship with Nicole was yours to keep. And maybe she didn't want to stay in touch with you because you're an asshole who doesn't know when to keep her mouth shut?'

She gapes at me and snatches her phone back.

'Fuck you,' she says, standing up. 'I was trying to help you.'

'You've done more than enough,' I say. 'Really.' She narrows her eyes at me and then stares around her, but for once, she doesn't say anything. 'I have to go, they're waiting for me. Don't come to my work again.' And I push the mirrored doors open and leave her there, standing on Sunset Boulevard, clutching her purse, and her phone, with her mouth hanging slightly open.

Chapter Forty

Cassie

It's two weeks since I left California now and the day of the sign-off meeting. There's no hiding behind my computer screen today. Mimi hovers over me as I make final amendments to the spreadsheets and graphs I'll be presenting. We all feel a little on edge.

All except Sam, who isn't as flustered as I'd expect him to be. He has all his samples ready to show, and if he's worried, he's hiding it. I really think he needn't be; he's taken the brief and run with it. There are melamine pieces in bright vibrant mix-and-match colours; a mustard yellow, jade green, bright, pillar-box red and a rich brown, and Picardie-style Pyrex bowls and vintage-looking serving dishes, some with patterns, some with serving suggestions printed on them. There are tins and jars and plates, both branded and own label. He's sourced some cast iron dishes in a gorgeous mid blue, that the creative team got entirely too excited over. Together, we load everything onto a trolley and take it up to the meeting room.

'You're looking sharp today,' he says, checking out my outfit whilst we wait for the lift. A knee-length electric blue pencil skirt, a cream blouse with a Peter Pan collar, and high heel brogues. I feel like I've been appraised. He's right though; I do, indeed, look sharp.

'Thanks,' I tell him. 'I wish I felt sharp.'

'You'll be fine,' he says. 'You know it all. We've got this. Dream team!'

The meeting room is already set up. There's a hot water urn heating up in the corner and neatly stacked coffee cups, sugar lumps and packets of sweeteners. Platters of mini croissants and Danish pastries sit under tightly pulled cling film. Sunlight floods in through the windows, unobstructed, as the meeting rooms are on the top floor of the building. The only thing above us up here is the sky. At one end of the room is an interactive white board with a laptop connected to it. In less than an hour I'll be presenting the figures from it, and just looking at it makes my stomach flip. Carefully, we unpack the trolley and place the samples in the middle of the table.

When we're done, he pulls out a chair and sits down.

'Might as well wait up here now,' he shrugs, looking at his watch. 'They'll all be coming up in a minute.'

I pace over to the window and look out over Oxford Street. It's busy. People move down the pavement, in and out of shops. Rushing along. Taking their time. There's a busker playing an accordion with a few coins in his hat. He's there a lot, always in the same place. Always playing the same tunes. A crowd of teenagers monopolise a bench close to a bus stop, laughing loudly and smoking cigarettes whilst sitting on the back rest, their feet on the seat. An elderly gentleman hovers nearby. People run across the road, ignoring crossings and dodging cabs and buses.

'You nervous, babes?' Sam asks. I turn and look at him.

'A little,' I say. 'Actually, a lot. Got stuff on my mind and I'm worried I'll forget something important.'

'What's up?'

'Oh, it's not work stuff.'

'I gathered that. You haven't been yourself since you got back from your hols.'

'You wouldn't be either, I imagine.'

'I don't follow,' he says.

'You mean you don't know why I unceremoniously came back from Los Angeles early?' I ask, shaking my head. Sam sits next to me on our desk of four. He was there on my first day back in the office. And I was sure he'd seen some of my angry message to Jesse on Facebook, but he shakes his head. 'I went to California to visit someone I thought I had a shot of being with. Turns out I probably don't. Things got messy. I came home.'

'Long distance almost never works out well,' he says. 'Too tricky.'

'It wasn't intended to be long distance forever. I might have gone there, one day.'

'And leave me here on my own? You can't do that. They'd give Pol your job, and I can't stand her. I'd have snuck out of here in your suitcase.'

'You'd have tried to nick him off me,' I tease.

'Oooh, reckon I could have done?'

'Not a chance. You're not his type.'

'There's always a chance,' he says, winking at me. I look back out of the window. The teens on the bench have moved on. The elderly chap has his seat. *Victory*, I think.

'So have you got a picture then?' Sam asks, and it pulls my attention back.

'Of Jesse?'

'If that's his name,' he says, nonchalantly. As if he doesn't know.

I do have a photo. In fact I have lots. I have photos of us on the beach, taken on my phone with my arm outstretched in front of us, and we're kissing in some of them. There are a couple of him that I took just before sunset. He's catching the sun like it's a ball. It took heaps of tries to get right. He looked ridiculous, with his arms in the air catching nothing and I felt like a knob, yelling across the sand to move a little, this way and that, just a fraction, until it was perfect.

I have sneaky photos he didn't know I took, and now he never will. Of him driving the car. Of him sitting on the deck. Of him walking slightly ahead of me in Venice. They're all there on my phone. I didn't delete them after I got back because that meant looking at them, and I couldn't bear to do that. So there they have stayed.

'On my phone,' I say. 'Knock yourself out.' Sam blinks at me, and then pulls my phone out of my handbag. I watch his fingers brush over the screen as he finds the photo album and flicks through. I watch his face for a reaction, but he has a good poker face.

'Pretty,' he says, eventually. 'What does he do?'

'He's a musician,' I tell him. 'Bassist.'

'I knew it,' he says. 'He looks like he should be in a band or something.'

I laugh. Sam looks up. 'What?'

'He was, once upon a time. That's how this all started.'

'So why didn't it work out? With you and him.'

I don't feel like going over it. Not before the meeting.

'Oh, it's too long to explain now,' I say.

'Lunchtime then,' he says.

Our conversation is cut short by the door opening. Sam throws my phone back in my bag and stands up. I leave my spot by the window and move over to the chair next to him. In walks the creative director Hattie, Mimi's boss Paula, the buying and brand director Simon, and Robert, the head of business development.

Drinks are made, the platter of pastries is brought over to the meeting table, and everyone sits down. When all is quiet, and I've distributed my booklets of figures, Sam begins.

'So, we're here to discuss the Autumn-Winter lines for twenty thirteen-fourteen,' he says. Everyone nods. He refers back to the colour palette we've been given by Hattie's team, and briefly goes through his samples. He's enthusiastic and engaging, talking about the products he's picked, answering every question he's asked, about the materials, their durability, the supplier. Sam is really good at his job.

'Now,' he says, 'Cassie's going to present the numbers.' This is it. I flip up the laptop and it buzzes into life. I wish Mimi was here for extra support. With shaky fingers, I click open my spreadsheets and watch them open up on screen.

'If I can ask you all to look at the whiteboard,' I say. My mouth is dry. I reach for my water and take a sip. Four heads swivel to the back of the room. I glance over at Sam and he smiles at me. He thinks I've got this. Like he said, dream team. Columns of numbers fill the screen.

'I'll go in the same order as Sam, starting with the melamine range,' I say. 'This column represents the sales figures for last year.' I hover over a column and highlight it. 'As you can see, it matched up to the forecast pretty accurately. We didn't have too much to mark down at the end of the season.' I leave the figures on screen for a few more seconds and no one speaks. 'And so, running with that, if you look at page two of your handouts, you'll see the stock required for each store.' Everyone opens the booklets I have prepared and turns to the table. Next to it is a photo of the melamine bowls.

'Does this include the Christmas stock uplift?' asks Paula. She taps her pen against the tip of her nose.

'No, uplift figures are in the next column along. Based on last year, there will need to be a six point nine percent uplift to cover Christmas sales. And that brings the figures to this many units across the board.' I highlight a row of numbers at the bottom of the first spreadsheet and all eyes are on the whiteboard again. Robert nods. I look once more at Sam and behind his handout he gives me a discreet thumbs-up. I take another a sip of my water and continue.

'Moving on to the Picardie bowls.' I click through to the next spreadsheet.

–

It's a long meeting. We break for lunch at twelve thirty but have more to go through. The senior management team seem to like the vast majority of what Sam has put together. Simon isn't convinced about the dishes with the printed serving suggestions, but Sam isn't fazed.

'They were my wildcard line,' he tells me as we head out of the office towards Pret. 'I always throw something in there I am not sure the powers that be will like. If they don't go for it, then fine. If they do, I'll feel like I've helped to push the brand, creatively.'

I pick up a crayfish sandwich. Put it down. Pick up chicken and avocado. Eventually decide on soup and a roll.

'Someone is indecisive today,' Sam says. We walk back towards the offices but veer off to the square and sit on a bench. 'So, if you don't mind me asking, how did you meet that pretty fella?'

'In a bar,' I say. 'He was who I had that platonic date with, that wasn't at all platonic, back in July.'

Sam looks incredulous. 'You had one date and then nipped off to America to see if you could shack up with him?' He shakes his head, 'I don't buy it. Something isn't adding up. Knowing you and how much of a planner you are. Sorry Cass, but I just don't buy it.'

He's right not to buy it. I'd never normally behave the way I did this summer. Going to California like that was crazy. I stir my soup and let my eyes unfocus. A big sigh escapes from my mouth and I feel my shoulders slump.

'Alright, so I told you he was in a band. Well, I used to love that band years ago. My friend Rachel came over one evening back in April and we got a bit drunk and ended up looking them all up on the internet. Don't ask me why we did it... just curiosity I suppose. So then...' I trail off.

'So then?' Sam asks. I rip a bit of my roll apart and dunk it in the soup.

'I added him on Facebook, and quite randomly he added me back, and we started talking, and it was good, you know? Then, he had a couple of gigs over here and we did actually end up meeting in a bar, and... things happened.'

'Naughty things?'

I look at him and smirk.

'Ooh, you filthy little groupie! I love it. And that, I take it, wasn't the end of that?'

'Perceptive,' I say, and Sam laughs. 'And then I went over to LA to visit, where it was all going superbly, hence those mushy pics and talks about visas and whatnot, until his family came over and his sister-in-law dropped a nuclear bombshell about how his quite recent ex is up the duff.'

'So?'

I give him a long, hard stare. 'His *quite recent* ex.'

'Oh,' he says. 'Balls.'

'Balls indeed. So that happened in January and apparently she's now ready to pop.'

'Ouch.'

'Tell me about it. Not really what I signed up for. So I came home.'

'Are you sure it is what you think it is? Like, one hundred percent sure? As in, paternity definitely confirmed?'

'No,' I admit, hesitantly, 'and she seems to have gone completely off the radar.'

'Cassie. Maybe she's gone off the radar because she's moved on with her life. How many of your exes are you in contact with?'

'That's different. I wasn't knocked up by any of mine.'

He looks exasperated. 'Okay, let's try this another way. Why has everyone jumped to the conclusion that he's the daddy? There *are* other guys, you know. He's not the only virile man in the United States.'

'Then why did the sister-in-law say anything at all?'

''Cause she's a shit-stirrer?'

'And apparently her mate.'

Sam throws his hands up in the air. 'There you have it then. A tenner says she was messing for drama, and it went too far.'

He finishes his sandwich and throws the packaging in the bin next to our bench. 'Anyway, how are you feeling about it all?'

'Shit, if I am honest,' I say. 'Just really sad. I miss him so much. Every minute. All the time. I realised when I was out there that there was nothing I wanted more in the world than for it to work out with us.'

Sam leans back on the bench and doesn't say anything for a while. I watch a pigeon waddle over to us and peck at crumbs on the ground. He kicks up his foot and it flies away. Finally, he speaks.

'Well it still could, no?'

'I don't know,' I shrug. 'Maybe the whole thing was just a ridiculous pipe dream and this is the universe's way of telling me to be happy with my lot. I mean, LA with my teenage boyband crush? I am such a twat.'

'Oh, my darling,' he says. 'You're not. This is your comedown talking. But don't let it rule you. Park this one for a bit. And if it isn't what you suspect and you still don't want it, then get back in the sea. There are, apparently, plenty of fish out there.'

'I guess.'

'Chalk it up to a nice holiday and a summer romance. You'll be telling this to your kids one day, all about that time you went and had a mad Hollywood love affair with a rock star. Focus on the stuff that made you giddy and swelled your heart. Not on the thing that broke it.'

I close my eyes and allow myself to think back to everything good that happened in California. Mainly the little things. Possibly tiny, incidental things that Jesse might not have even known he was doing. I felt looked after out there in a way I realise I have never felt here. I was a bit scared of all the really intense feelings I was having, too. But I never didn't want it. Leaving the way I did hadn't felt like much of a choice at the time. I was protecting myself.

Sam looks at his watch. 'Sorry to cut this short, but we have to get back. On to round two.'

The meeting goes on for the rest of the day. We are questioned about suppliers and costings and profit margins and Sam writes down a load of action points that involve trips out of the office. On the whole, everyone is happy. Management trickle out just before four fifteen and Sam and I stay back to pack up the samples.

'That went okay, right?' I ask, stacking up the melamine.

'Absolutely,' he says. 'If they hated it, we wouldn't be going to negotiate prices with suppliers. It would be back to the drawing board.'

'Did I sound like I knew what I was on about?'

'You did. And you do. Don't doubt yourself.'

It's nice, hearing him say that. It gives me a much needed boost. I might be a bit rubbish at picking men. I may be living with people who have no idea how to deal with such epic heartbreak and misery except to back slowly away from it, but at least I'm doing okay at work. At least I'm not a complete screw-up somewhere.

'Shall we see if we can sneak off early and go to the pub?'

'Err yes,' he says. 'Shall we see if we can get Mimi to buy the first round?'

Chapter Forty-One

Jesse

The Monday after my run-in at the studio, Brandon calls whilst I'm at the grocery store. I suspect, if the conversation is anything to go by, that he and Travis have been talking about me, and I get the feeling they do this a lot. I'm not sure how keen on that I am, but I can't even begin to unpack that right now.

'I feel like you were a bit harsh to Holly, perhaps,' he says, evenly.

I'm pushing my cart through the dairy section and I'm so astonished by what I've just heard that I stop, abruptly, by the half and half and the woman behind me crashes into me. She's all apologies but I wave them away and move to the side.

'Really? Is that so?'

'Yeah, I think she was just trying to patch things up. Apparently she was pretty upset.'

'She interrupted my session to show me some bullshit photos that didn't prove or disprove anything. Could that not have waited? Her timing was pretty shitty.'

'Yeah, well, *that* wasn't cool, but apparently she'd been trying to get hold of you. She probably just worked herself up.'

'No, it really wasn't cool. None of it was *cool.*'

'I think maybe you should go easy on her. She's not the only one who made a mistake here.'

'I know,' I admit.

'And it shouldn't be down to her to prove or disprove anything. Have you talked to Nicole?'

I sigh down the phone and it gives him his answer.

'Jesse,' he says, exasperated. 'You can't keep running from things that scare you.'

'I don't—'

'You *do*. You invest yourself to a point, and then when things get tricky or don't pan out the way you want, you run. You are a path of least resistance kinda guy, but it's not always the way, you know?'

Always nice to be reminded of just how much Brandon has his shit together better than I do. I feel like I'm being told off, and I think maybe he should pipe down.

But I don't call him out. All I say is okay. I'm not getting into an argument by the milk. Travis has been uncharacteristically quiet since *that day*, and I really don't want to fall out with *all* of my brothers. By taking the path of least resistance I'm avoiding an argument. This time it really is the best way.

'You doing alright?' he asks, tentatively.

'Peachy, yeah. Just peachy. Getting on with shit, you know?'

'So, we were thinking, you need to get away from LA,' he says. 'You're not going to feel better by trying to pretend none of this ever happened.'

'I'm not trying to pretend none of this ever happened—'

'Sounds like you've been trying to pretend this thing with Nicole didn't happen for a few months now.'

Alright, that's enough.

'Brandon, can you just not? I really don't need this. No one knows anything for sure, and I'm actually right in the middle of—'

'You're a mess, Jesse.'

'Yep. Thank you. I know, but—'

'Lainey has not stopped worrying since it all happened. You need to get it together. Come and visit. I'll buy your flight. We'll head to Marin for a few days. Get away from everything. Hike up Mount Tam. Or drive out to Tahoe? Your call. I think it will give you some clarity and perspective and help you decide what you want.'

'I'm good for my flight,' I say, ungraciously.

'I know you are. But we want to. No arguments. You need this.'

I don't have the energy for this battle. Plus, he's right. I do need to get out of here for a while. At the moment I'm just spiraling.

'Alright. Give me some time, though. I have some loose ends to tie up. In fact, I'll come the weekend of October thirteenth if that's cool? Tam sounds good.'

Something tells me it would be better for me to be around people the weekend I was supposed to be going to that wedding with Cassie.

'Sure… why specifically that date? That's three weeks away yet. I was thinking maybe sooner.'

'I was meant to be in England then.'

'Oh.'

'Yeah. Oh.'

I'm almost done shopping, and I don't want to stay here any longer than necessary. 'Can I talk to you later. I'm actually in Ralphs right now.'

'Sure, why didn't you say?'

'I don't know… path of least resistance?'

–

Trav's phone rings eleven times before he answers, and when he does, he's wary.

'Things have been weird,' I say. 'And I don't want them to be. So I'm wondering if you felt like getting a drink. Putting the world to rights. Clearing the air, that kind of thing.'

We meet at the same bar in Los Alamitos we went to with Seth all those months ago. It's mid afternoon and the place is empty and echoey. I buy him a beer and we play a few games of shuffleboard whilst we wait for our food.

'I owe you an apology,' I say, when we're back in our booth. The table's slightly sticky. He waves his hand and shakes his head. Picks up a tortilla chip and dips it into salsa.

'Don't sweat it,' he shrugs. 'I shouldn't have said anything about Nicole to Cassie, but in my defence I didn't know you hadn't had that conversation.'

'She brought it up, you know? The day after. We talked about it. The stuff you'd said. She said your intentions were good.'

'They were, man. I wasn't trying to cause trouble.'

'Not like...' I say, and stop myself when Travis flinches. 'Sorry. I'm not going to say any more about that.'

'What's going on with you two anyway?'

'Trav, you don't have to pretend like you don't know. Brandon called me on Monday, I know you guys have talked. He gave me some home truths. Do you think I run away from shit?'

'Well, I mean... you know... I know you don't like to talk about it, but Franko... every relationship you've ever had. Now this.'

'So that's a yes?'

He wrinkles up his nose and nods.

'I mean, it's just *you*, you know? We're all sort of used to it.'

'I was trying to be more open with people.'

'And yet...' he trails off. He doesn't need to say it.

'I know. Isn't it ironic?'

'Alanis Morissette eat your goddamn heart out. Look, all I'm going to say is this: my dude, you gotta learn how to play the long game. Delayed gratification, that sort of thing. And you need to remember that when something gets tough it doesn't always mean it's gone to shit. You have to figure out what you want with this one, and to hell with anything else.' He tears off all the meat from a chicken wing and drops the bones on a plate. 'I saw what you guys had. That shit doesn't happen every day, man. That shit was magical.'

'Hmmm, my brother the hopeless romantic,' I say, but he's right. 'When did you get so wise?'

I pick up a stick of celery and Travis knocks it out of my hands and shakes the basket of wings at me.

'Have a proper fucking bar snack,' he laughs.

Chapter Forty-Two

To: CassieB83
From: FredTed49

Hi Cassie, are you there?
Fred

To: FredTed49
From: CassieB83

Hi Fred, yes, I'm here.
How are you? Things going well with Tyler's sister?
Cass

To: CassieB83
From: FredTed49

Ah that didn't come to anything. She sided with Tyler. And now he's moved out. Tried to take Martin. What an absolute bastard.
Anyway, how are you?
Fred

To: FredTed49
From: CassieB83

No! The brass neck of it. You can't take someone else's cat! I've been better, Fred, to be honest.
Cass

To: CassieB83
From: FredTed49

What happened? You can tell me to piss off. But… *dons Frasier Crane hat* … Go ahead, Seattle, I'm listening.
Fred

To: FredTed49
From: CassieB83

Ah, it's complicated. That's all there is to say really.
Cass

To: CassieB83
From: FredTed49

I'm sorry. *Removes Frasier Crane hat*
Fred

To: FredTed49
From: CassieB83

It's not your fault.
Cass

To: CassieB83
From: FredTed49

I could listen over a pint if you felt like it? Saturday? No expectations or pressure.
Fred

To: FredTed49
From: CassieB83

Thank you. But I can't on Saturday. I'm going to the roller disco in Vauxhall for my friend's hen night. Maybe another time. When I'm not so miserable. I'd be shocking company at the moment.
Cass

Chapter Forty-Three

Cassie

The season turns as October rolls around and it's properly autumnal the day of Rachel's hen do. There's damp in the air and leaves underfoot. I'm the first to arrive at Rachel's flat – which is unsurprising, since it's well before the designated four p.m. arrival time. She opens the door and looks me over before squeezing me and inviting me inside.

'How are things?' she asks, relieving me of the fizz I've brought. I shake out my plastic-bag-strangled fingers and they throb as blood returns to the fingertips.

'Things are okay,' I lie.

'Heard anything?' she probes. I should have guessed this would happen. I swallow.

'No. And I'm not expecting to.'

She shakes her head. 'Still can't believe it. What an arse.'

He's not an arse, though, I want to say. *He's actually very lovely, and if you knew him, you'd know that.* I still can't reconcile everything, even a month on.

'Look, can we not do this now, it's all still really quite raw,' I say. It's the understatement of the year. She nods and opens the fridge, shifting the contents around to make way for the booze. She opens a tub of cream and sniffs it, before throwing it in the bin.

One by one her friends arrive. Bottles are popped, glasses are chinked.

'You're looking well, Cass,' Lauren says.

'How are you holding up?' Mandy asks. They both have the same look about them. Sad eyes and sympathetic eyebrows. They both press their lips together in a way that suggests they know exactly how I am feeling. But how could they possibly know how I'm feeling?

'I'm great,' I tell them through ever so slightly gritted teeth. 'More than great. Totally on the pull tonight.'

Rachel and Marie exchange glances and Mandy beams and claps her hands. I instantly wish I'd never said anything. I am so not on the pull.

'Brilliant!' she exclaims. 'I love it. We'll find you a nice rebound shag.' How depressing.

The party kicks off in earnest once everyone arrives. Lauren brings out the willy straws, and she wasn't lying; they are obscenely detailed, what with the veins and the wrinkles. Mandy makes Rachel perform oral on the chocolate penis with the minty fondant inside and Marie looks like she might be unwell.

'What's in there?' Rachel asks, nodding to the box on the side Marie tipped up with.

'It ties in with what we're doing tonight,' Marie says. 'Open it.'

Inside are a pair of skates from the summer Rachel and I spent pretending we were in *Starlight Express*. White leather lace-ups with pink and purple lightning bolts up the sides. 'Sadly they're not showing *Starlight* anymore,' she continues. 'So instead we're going for a nice dinner, and then on to a roller disco.'

'Aw, you guys!' Rachel says. She pulls everyone together for a group hug. 'I hope you're not expecting me to wear those skates, though. There's no way they'll fit now. I got them when I was eleven.'

'To be honest, I think Mum just wanted to get rid of them,' Marie says, shrugging.

The restaurant is in Holborn, tucked away around a corner off Kingsway. You'd overlook it if you didn't know it was there, but the food's delicious and we have a good time, even if a group of twenty-something women with crimped hair and heavy eye make-up do stand out like a sore thumb. The maître d' is worried. We are not his preferred clientele. He's not keen on the party poppers Lauren distributes from her bag of hen night tricks or the confetti we sprinkle on the table; pink and silver metallic hearts and teal-coloured stars and horseshoes. He thinks we are going to cause a scene. We don't, but we are louder than he'd like, yet not crass enough for him to say anything. Except maybe for Mandy. She talks loudly about how much of the honeymoon destination Rachel and George *won't* be seeing. She ends almost every sentence with 'am I right, gals?' and holds her hand up for high fives. Sometimes she gets them, mostly she has to style them out. We leave a fairly hefty tip because some of the other, classier diners don't seem massively impressed.

On the way out we stop in the toilets to get changed. My coral shift dress is replaced with a My Little Pony t-shirt and black skirt. I put on another pair of shiny flesh coloured tights for that shimmery skater look, and shake out my crimped hair. Mandy gets to work, her brushes flying over our faces until we are transformed. There is no denying it; I look like the lovechild of Crystal Tipps and Ziggy Stardust, in the clothes of a seven-year-old girl. Lauren distributes sashes and pins a plastic tiara into Rachel's hair, complete with pink jewels and a veil made from cheap netting.

In the street Marie enlists a bewildered tourist to snap a photo. We huddle together, all pouts and peace signs. We hold in our stomachs and push out our bottoms.

'This is *so* going on Facebook,' Rachel says and for the briefest of moments I remember making the booking for tonight, sitting on Jesse's navy sofa with my legs crossed on his lap. *I'm going to want to see pictures*, he'd said, and I wonder what he'd have thought when he saw them and the things he'd have asked about the evening, all in that drawly accent. I'd have told him everything, in minute detail. But then the reality of it all closes in on me again and I remember that none of that will happen at all. He won't see the photos, and we won't have that conversation, and I won't get to tell him how much I miss him.

Because I really do, and my heart thumps heavily in my chest, as it does, every time thoughts of him catch me off guard. I push it all out of my head and help Lauren hail taxis instead and it's forgotten by the time we arrive at the roller disco. We saunter past the line to the doors. Our names are down and we are definitely coming in. There's a reserved booth and bottles of champagne waiting in a bucket of melting ice. Brightly coloured lights beam down on to the rink, flashing in time with the beat of the music. People zoom around the room. Some cautiously grip on to friends, or the wall, others glide around effortlessly, spinning without falling, changing direction as if it's as easy as walking.

Mandy cracks open the wine and it fizzes half-heartedly, and dribbles down the bottleneck. We all drink.

'We're on a mission, ladies,' she shouts. 'Cassie's pop star boyfriend turned out to be a bit of a prick so we're finding her a new man.'

No, I think, *this is not what I want*. Even if I did say it earlier.

'What happened?' Becky, George's sister, asks. 'You seemed quite into him in your emails.'

'Err, there was an issue. His ex is pregnant… actually it's likely she's had it by now. It's probably his.'

'No!' Mandy howls, her big eyes wide and shocked. 'He *never*?'

'Well,' Rachel cuts in. 'We don't know for sure. No one's really had a chance to speak to the pregnant woman in question.'

I don't like her tone of voice. The incredulity of it stings. And it's come out of left field. She was quite ready to tear him a new one when I got home.

'Well, what would you have done, hmm?' I say, feeling a little put upon.

'I'd have at least waited until we knew for certain before making any decisions. Especially if you were thinking of moving out there.'

'What?' Lauren gasps.

'It was briefly mentioned,' I say, but now it seems childish and like it was little more than my teenage fantasy and I want to change the subject.

'How were you planning on moving out there?' she asks.

'I could have got a job.'

'Babe, they want people with exceptional skills. Like, doctors who can cure diseases and scientists and engineers. They're probably not looking for kitchenware merchandisers.'

'Be an actor,' Mandy suggests. 'You can live there easy-peasy if you're a film star.' And I guess she'd know, what with her inside connections. 'Ooooh you could be like Gwyneth Paltrow and what's his chops from Coldplay. Or Nicole Kidman and that Keith fella.'

'Why didn't you wait to speak to him?' Lauren asks.

'How could I have that hanging over me? If we'd carried on and it turns out to be his, he might want to get back with her and I can't get in the way of that.'

'But, Cass,' Marie says, 'what if the baby's not his? How will you know?'

'Look, you don't understand. It was *so* awful,' I say, but I'm feeling prickly behind the eyes again. 'Everyone knew. And he hadn't said anything. It was secretive and shifty. Why wouldn't he tell me if he knew it wasn't his? Why would he put me through that?'

'Cass, we're only saying this because we are your friends,' Lauren says. She touches my cheek. 'We just want you to be happy. You seemed so happy.'

I nod but I don't say anything. I can't because there's a lump in my throat again. Why is no one else concerned by the dates? I wonder again what would have happened if I'd done things differently. What would we have talked about if I'd stayed?

Would we have found a way to get hold of her? Would we have had some proof?

'It doesn't matter now,' I say. 'It's over. Shouldn't we be giving Rachel a send-off rather than talking about this?'

The song changes and the opening bars knock me for six. I can't believe I haven't heard it since that day in Jesse's car but I suppose that'll happen when you shut yourself off from everything. Carly Rae Jepsen's breathy vocals fill the club and all I can think about is how carefree and happy we were, singing along that day. I grab hold of Mandy's hand to steady myself but she takes it to mean I'm back to being Fun Cassie.

'Atta girl!' she shrieks, but I notice a look between Rachel and Marie. A roll of Marie's eyes and the tiniest shake of Rachel's head.

We all get up and throw shapes and mostly we are clumsy and inelegant. None of us know how to dance on roller skates. We bash into other revellers. Everyone falls over. Rachel is bought a lot of drinks. There is a direct correlation between alcohol consumption and how funny the night is. We have jugs of fruity, sweet cocktails and bottles of Mexican beer with dry wedges of lime shoved roughly into the necks. After countless rounds, we've all morphed into amazingly talented skaters. There is no one in the club who is cooler than us. Or sexier. Mandy buys everyone a shot of something bright blue that tastes of syrupy mouthwash and everything spins.

'That guy at the bar is going to ask you to dance in a bit,' she says, pointing at a tall chap with dark blond hair. 'I saw him looking your way when I was buying our shots and I thought he was a perfect rebound candidate. So, you are welcome.'

I squint through the purple lighting towards the bar and do a double-take. Because I recognise my rebound suitor. It's Fred, 31, Clapham Common, from Date My Mate. FredTed49. For a second I'm astounded at what an enormous coincidence this is, before I remember I told him I'd be here when he asked me out tonight, and it hits me that Fred is a giant creep.

'Oh… god,' I mutter. He looks like his photo. Good teeth and a nice tan. He's smiling sheepishly at me now, and those teeth glow a little under the black lights. He knows he's been rumbled.

'Well, I think he's quite nice,' Mandy says, haughtily.

'What did you say to him?'

'I said, excuse me, I just wanted to tell you that you are perfect for my mate.'

'Great line,' I tell her.

'I know, right?'

I am not convinced she has much more than a rudimentary grasp on sarcasm. He clutches the safety barrier and gingerly skates over.

'Oh, his name is Fred,' she hisses over the music.

'I know,' I say.

'What?'

'Nothing.'

He's reached us now. Mandy and I stand there, staring at him. 'Hello,' he says, nervously.

'What a surprise,' I say, raising an eyebrow. 'What are you doing here?'

'Cassie!' Mandy squeals. 'Your flirting is *terrible*.'

'Feel like a turn of the room?' he says, holding a hand out.

'Go on Cassie,' Mandy urges, guiding me forward by my elbow.

'Fine,' I say. He grabs my arm for support and we glide out into the middle of the floor. 'So, Fred, why are you here?'

'I'll be honest,' he says, and I'm immediately sceptical, which I don't think is unreasonable given my sketchy track record with 'honest' men. 'You said you were coming here and I wanted to meet you.'

'Do you know how creepy that is?' I hiss. 'Did you actually just listen to what came out of your mouth?'

'I know,' he says, deflated. 'Look, can we sit down? I'm shit at this. The skating mainly, but also, the not coming off as a twat in front of women.'

I lead us over to a booth and he follows me, gingerly, hobbling on the toe-stops of his skates like some graceless ballerina. What a weapon. No wonder Tyler's sister wasn't interested in the end.

'I wasn't lying, you know,' I say, pointing at my Maid of Honour sash. 'I really am here for my friend's hen night.'

'I didn't think you were,' he shrugs, and I think, this is a man with nothing to lose, least of all his self-respect. 'But you seemed really sad, and not like how you'd been before, and I wanted to make sure you were okay. Seemed a bit creepy to just say it online.'

'The irony of that is outstanding,' I tell him.

'I know,' he says, and laughs. He has a dimple in his left cheek, and to my utter disgust, I find myself thinking it's quite nice.

'Look, Fred, I'm in a shit place for this,' I tell him, gently. He means well. He's so earnest. I can't be unkind to him.

'You said that, too.'

'And I can't reiterate how weird this is. Like, this is borderline stalker behaviour. Sting's got nothing on you, mate. If you want to get dates off that stupid website, you're going to have to rethink your tactics.'

'Why are you in a shit place?' he says, suddenly.

'That's absolutely none of your business,' I say, affronted.

'I know,' he shrugs. 'But you've alluded to it a few times, so you obviously want to tell me.'

'I obviously do not,' I say.

'Things didn't work out with you and the American guy.'

'How do you know that?' I ask, coldly.

'Your profile on DMM is linked to your Facebook account. You were about to go for a drink when we started talking, and then you mentioned a holiday, and then all these photos of you kissing a man with long hair started cropping up.'

Oh yeah.

'And then they were all gone. Seemed weird.'

'Well, yeah, if you must know, it has everything to do with that.'

'I'm sorry,' he says. 'You looked really happy in those photos. Really bloody authentically happy.'

'I was,' I say. And then I hear myself telling FredTed49 all about Franko, and all about Jesse, and how being with him was everything I'd ever wanted, and then about Nicole and how devastating that Saturday was, my fight or flight response and my running away to LAX and home before I could be hurt any more. I tell him how I'd wanted to shake the member of cabin crew who welcomed me aboard the plane and scream at her that I shouldn't have been on it at all, and that I should have been eating almonds and sipping cold beers by the beach. How flying away and cutting him off had felt so unutterably wrong, but what else could I do given the circumstances?

'Do you want to know what I think?' he says, and I shrug.

'Why not? Everyone else has thrown in their two pennies. What's another opinion?'

'I think you idolised him,' he says, slowly. 'And that stopped you remembering that he's human, and he's flawed. Just like the rest of us. And I also think him liking you back scared the shit out of you.'

'Riiiight.'

'No, I'm serious. When you were a teenager you fancied him because of what he did and who he was, and I daresay how he looks. And that's the reason you found him again all these years later. And it's always been there in your head. And that's why it felt too good to be true and maybe also why you didn't afford him the same allowances you might have with someone else.'

'Fred, no, you're wrong. I'd have given him anything. I'd have stopped the world for him.'

'But you didn't. And no judgement, because if Drew Barrymore came knocking, I'd be scared shitless, too. But you didn't give him *time*, and I think it's because he's still this untouchable

302

teen heart-throb to you. This perfect being. And he displayed a pretty big flaw by not telling you something you felt he should have, and you couldn't handle it.'

I take a really deep breath and wish I had a drink to neck. How has this person, who has sent me the occasional message on that dreadful website, and who stalked me at my friend's hen night, got me so undeniably spot on? How is that fair?

'In those photos you posted, he looked really bloody authentically happy, too. It was sickening and lovely all at once. I bet you can find a way to open that door again.'

'No,' I say, quickly. 'The baby's probably been born now. He's probably in New York, getting back with *her*. Falling in love with someone who isn't me.'

'And if not? Don't forget there's a possibility none of that is happening. Isn't it better to take a chance and to know, rather than to always wonder?'

Marie skates over.

'Are you coming back to the hen do or not?' she asks, and side-eyes Fred. 'Be nice to spend a bit of time with Rachel tonight.'

'She is,' Fred says. 'And I'm going to go.' He stands up and wobbles on his skates. 'I know I went about this the wrong way and I'm sorry for that, and for my unsolicited opinions.'

'Better than an unsolicited dick pic,' I say.

'Okay.' He smiles at me again, cute dimple and all, and I think, in another world, if things had been different, we'd have gone for a pint and talked nonsense in Shoreditch.

'Well, how did it go?' Mandy asks, excitedly, when I rejoin the hen party.

'Yeah, alright. But probably not. Thanks, though.'

'There's always Marcus,' Rachel snaps. She purses her lips at me across the table and it makes me bristle. For a few seconds, no one speaks.

'More drinks?' Lauren says, finally.

I go with her to the bar and as we're queuing it occurs to me that even though Rachel and Sam have said some of the same things that Fred did, it was different, more altruistic maybe, coming from him. Because he'd come here with an agenda, and that agenda was not to talk me into what I know I need to do when I get home tonight.

Chapter Forty-Four

From: Cassie Banks
To: Jesse Franklin
Subject: <no subject>

Hey,

So it's been a little while.

And I wanted to see how you are. And I wanted to tell you that whatever happens, I miss you. And I love you.

And that I'm sorry for running in the way that I did.

I don't know if you know if you have a baby yet or not, and I wouldn't blame you if you felt that I didn't deserve to know after the shitty way I just cut you off.

But if it turns out you don't have a kid, I'd really like to hear from you again. And I'd really like to see you again. So you could call me, maybe.

Because, a friend told me it would be better to take a chance and know than to always wonder, and after careful consideration I think they are right.

And besides, I love you. Let's not forget that.

Cassie

Message sent

Chapter Forty-Five

Cassie

Unsurprisingly, Sunday is a write-off, and I barely leave my room. I check my emails a few times throughout the day but hope fades with every inbox refresh that brings me nothing. Sara knocks on my door at dusk, offering me sweet tea and chocolate digestives.

'Good night?' she says. 'I was half expecting to find a man in here with you.'

'Not a sniff of one I'm afraid,' I mutter. I don't get too close to her; my mouth feels furry and I could really do with a mint. She sits on my bed whilst I drink my tea, drumming her fingers on the edge of the mattress and occasionally fiddling with her nose ring.

'Are you feeling a bit happier about life these days?' she asks.

'Not really. I was hoping getting out for the evening would help, but I'm still gutted.'

'Well, I won't tell you to forget about him because I know it's not that easy... although, I will say with confidence that the best way to get over one man is to get under another one, and if you ever want to talk about it, I'll listen.'

'Thanks Sara,' I say, and it occurs to me that I may have been a little dismissive of her. Worried, perhaps, about what Jesse would have thought of her, as if her being my housemate would have had any bearing on my relationship with him, and anyway she's only ever been kind and supportive of me and would have been welcoming and friendly when he visited. It doesn't feel good. 'That means a lot.'

She stands up. 'I'll just leave you to it then,' she says. 'My washing's done, and you know how funny Jon gets about leaving wet laundry in the machine.' She takes another biscuit as she leaves, and I text Rachel to find out if she's as hungover as I am.

By the time Monday morning rolls around the hangover has faded, but the hollow ache in my chest hasn't. Mimi is already at her desk when I arrive at work. She's nibbling on a cheese twist from the staff canteen. A mug of black coffee sits, steaming, beside her, with the rest of the cafetière next to her phone. There's a little brown splash of coffee between the mug and the cafetière and she has a crumb of pastry clinging to her jumper. She beams as I sit down opposite her.

'How was the hen do?' she asks. She's chirpy in that I-got-shagged-to-within-an-inch-of-my-life-last-night kind of way. Lucky Mimi.

'Very, very messy,' I say, cringing at the memory of my bird's nest hair and the pink and silver star Mandy drew in eyeliner across half my face. 'There's a photo on Facebook.'

'Any final snogs for the bride?'

'Nah, she's not like that.'

Mimi eyes me over the top of her monitor and raises one eyebrow, 'Any snogs for you?'

I don't meet her gaze. My computer boots into life with a white glow and a chimey chord. 'No. Although someone I chatted to on a dating website showed up and gave me a pep talk. It was all very odd.'

'What about?' she says. She sips her coffee. She looks intrigued.

'What happened with Jesse,' I say. 'He told me I still see him as a boyband heart-throb and not flawed like the rest of us.'

'Good grief,' she says. 'Sounds like some sort of deeply awkward therapy. Did you go home with him? Best way to get over someone is to get under someone else.'

'My housemate said the exact same thing,' I say, slightly mystified. 'But no, I didn't.'

'She's not wrong,' Mimi says, dusting off her hands and sipping her drink. 'Can't you try and talk to him? Jesse, I mean, if you want to. Otherwise, cut your losses. Life's too short to carry this around with you forever. You'll have to let it go eventually.'

She trots off to a meeting with Paula shortly after, and she's excited when she returns. She's almost skipping through the office.

'I've had feedback about sign-off,' she says. 'They were very impressed. Said you were professional, engaging and know-ledgeable about the products and about the "Beauchamp's Direction."' She makes air quotes with her fingers as she says it. 'On a similar note,' she continues, 'all your extra effort lately hasn't gone unnoticed here, as well.'

I'm a little taken aback, but pleased nonetheless. I'd stayed late a few times to keep me distracted and stop me wallowing in bottles of wine and boxes of chocolates, but I didn't think for a minute anyone had noticed.

I briefly feel hopeful, like I have something good and tangible to hold onto, then I want to tell Jesse about it, and immediately the hollow feeling returns.

'Thank you, Mimi, that's really good to hear,' I say. My phone buzzes. A reply from Rachel.

> Can you meet for lunch in the square today? 1pm
> x

She's quiet and not her usual bubbly self. We buy our lunch; tubs of chicken pie with squares of puff pastry, like little flakey edible mortarboards, on top, and find a seat on a bench.

'How did you enjoy Saturday?' I ask, blowing on a forkful of my lunch.

'Loved it,' she says. She bites into a mouthful of pie. 'Jesus, this is nuclear.'

'Mandy was on form.'

Rachel looks at me for a few seconds. 'Hmm yes. She's a funny one.'

There's no more talking as we both attempt to eat lunch without burning a hole through our soft palates, but it's not our usual easy silence. Something isn't right. She wrinkles up her nose. 'You did kind of make it all about you, though.'

Oh here we go. I stab my fork into a piece of chicken and put the pot down on the bench beside me.

'How did I do that?'

She shrugs. 'Come on, Cass. Everyone just rallied around you. It was The Cassie Show. When you all turned up at my flat it was all, *aww poor Cassie, how are you coping?* And at the club after you looked like you might pass out and Mandy was all over finding your rebound guy. Where was my last-fling guy?'

'I didn't ask her to. I didn't ask for any of it, and the reason I looked unwell was because that "Call Me Maybe" song came on a lot in Jesse's car and we sang along and, hearing it again—'

'You're missing the point,' she interrupts.

'Am I really?'

'Yes. You only get one hen do. And you made mine all about you. You can't stand not being in the limelight, can you?'

'Not true and not fair,' I snap. 'And by the way, you don't get a last-fling guy because you have a *for-life* guy.'

I shove another mouthful of the hottest pie in the world into my mouth and chew furiously, whilst simultaneously trying to stop it searing off the roof of my mouth.

'For fuck's sake, Cassie. This is crap. You're being crap! I knew this would happen.'

'What's that supposed to mean?'

'You promised you'd help me with the wedding, and I knew the minute you swanned off to America it wouldn't happen.'

'I've helped you loads, Rach. That's not fair.' I count everything off on my fingers, but she interrupts.

'You haven't *been* there. You haven't been there since all this first started. You've turned into this selfish, *distant* person and I don't even recognise you lately. You've kept stuff from me—'

'What have I kept from you?'

'Oh, bloody all of it. All the Jesse stuff. When you arranged to meet up. You didn't tell me any of it until the last minute. Franko was *our* thing but you kept it all from me.'

'Because Jesse was *my* thing. And you have other things. And this is fucking ridiculous, Rachel.'

'No, Cassie, it's not. I've needed to talk to you but you've always harped on about him. Every single time.'

'Well, what do you want me to say? Sorry the shit hit the fan at such an inconvenient time for you. It's not my fault George is being crap,' I snap, and immediately regret it.

'Unbe*lievable*,' she hisses, and shuffles down the bench a little. Half of me wants to flip her off, pick up my bag and my lunch and stamp off back to work. But the other, more rational side of me knows that doing that could unleash a bridezilla-shaped beast mere days before the wedding.

Anyway, she has a point. I have been wrapped up in my life, and Jesse, and me and Jesse, and what happened in California, and I could have made more of an effort to help after I got back. I can see that now. It's my job as her bridesmaid to smooth everything over. I am like a palette knife on a dollop of icing. I am like a screaming hot iron on crinkled sheets. I am like a finishing trowel on freshly applied plaster. I'm going to have to eat some pie, all right, but it's definitely more humble-flavoured than chicken.

'That guy at the roller disco,' I say. 'He wasn't just some random. We'd been messaging on Date My Mate for a while.'

'And you thought it was okay to invite him along to my hen night? Because it was very much not okay. A gross lapse in judgement on your part, Cassie. So much for being heartbroken—'

'Hang on,' I say. 'I most certainly did not invite him to the roller disco. It wasn't some sort of BOGOF night out, you know. I was fully committed to your night. I turned down a date with him because of it. How was I supposed to know he'd show up?'

'He just showed up? How did he know?'

'I stupidly told him why I couldn't go out with him that night. He must have researched it.'

'Bit weird.'

'I know. But this is what I've been dealing with on that website. And believe me, he was the best of a very bad bunch. You have no idea how lucky you are not to have to wade through the pool of single men in London these days, because it's a fetid cesspit.'

'But you spent a lot of time with him. Can you see how I thought it was planned? What did you talk about?'

'I told him all about Jesse, and what happened. Harped on about him, in fact. He knew a lot of it anyway. Saw the photos I put on Facebook, and noticed when I deleted them.'

'What did he make of it all?'

'He had a theory. Said I still idolised him the way I used to. Said it probably clouded my judgement.'

Rachel looks thoughtful. 'He's probably right,' she says.

'When I got home, I sent him an email. Hugely awkward as there hasn't been even a sniff of a reply.'

'Why?'

'How should I know? He's probably off being dad of the year or something. I feel stupid. It was too much, wasn't it?'

'How can I know without seeing it?'

I hand her my phone. 'It'll be in the sent folder.' She reads through it slowly.

'Aw, babe,' she says. 'Not at all too much. Maybe he hasn't seen it?'

'Yeah,' I say. 'Let's go with that.'

But not a single atom of me believes her. His phone pinged every single time he got an email, and he almost always looked at it straight away. She takes my hand and squeezes my fingers. She doesn't believe her, either.

'I'm sorry I messed up your hen night and brought all this drama just before your wedding. That was not classy of me. I wouldn't blame you if demoted me from maid of honour. Marie probably deserves it more than I do.'

'I wouldn't give her the satisfaction,' she says. 'But, look, promise me you won't mope at my wedding. I know it probably won't be the easiest weekend for you, but please try and be happy. For me.'

'I won't mope,' I say, and as soon as the words pass my lips I know I have to hold myself to it. 'I want to help you. What do you need me to do?'

'Well, since you ask,' she says, and pulls a folder out of her bag. She's typed out and printed pages and pages of instructions and notes, titled *Rachel and George's Perfect Wedding*, in a scripty, flowery font. It's very unlike Rachel. My name is next to a lot of the tasks: collecting the dresses, confirming the delivery time with the florist, delivering the order of service to the church. She goes through it all with me, item by item. On Friday morning we have a breakfast meeting with Eloise the wedding coordinator. Rachel's gone so far as to type up an agenda, and on it are words like 'wedding favours' and 'receiving line' and 'toastmaster' and a lot of it goes over my head, but I'm so relieved to be back in her good books that I'm happy to be involved. It'll give me something else to think about anyway. At least for the time being.

Chapter Forty-Six

Jesse

Hi, Rachel.

Jesse Franklin as I live and breathe. This is… bizarre.

Yeah. I know. I found you via Cassie's profile. I know it's a little weird for me to reach out to you, but on Saturday afternoon I got an email from Cassie and I don't know what to do with it.

Yeah, I know you did. I've seen it. Thought it was pretty self-explanatory personally.

OK…

She loves you. She misses you. She wanted you to know that. What part of that don't you know what to do with?

Wow. She's a little frosty. Still, what am I to expect, all things considered?

> Guess it's more to do with the situation. Pretty sure you know.

> Of course I know. I'm her Person. And now she's panicking because you haven't replied. Are you even into this? What's the deal, heart-breaker? You didn't seem all that fussed when it all ended between you two.

> Definitely into it. Definitely fussed. I didn't want things to be like this. But what am I meant to do? She said it was over. I didn't want to accept it but at the same time it was her choice, you know?

> I haven't replied because I don't know what the deal is. The email clearly says 'if'. I don't want to bug her.

> Jesus Christ, Jesse! What's the matter with you? BUG HER. She's opened up the channel of communication again. She wants to hear from you. Are you always like this? Handle this better! Baby's been born, right?

> I don't actually know.

You have to get in touch with Nicole and find out.
Can you see why I asked if you were into this? I
sort of feel like if you were, you'd be more on it.

I get it, but Nic made it very clear she doesn't
want to talk to me. Or any of us. Seems like she
just wants to start over.

But if it turns out you did knock her up, then it
isn't just about her. You need to think about what
YOU want, if that's the case, and how you can
step up. You cannot have this hanging over you!

I'm going to level with you, if we were having this
chat face to face, I'd be shaking the shit out of
you right now. Cassie is devastated. You should
have been honest from the start.

I know that. On reflection it was not a good
choice. But I still really think that if it was anything
to do with me, Nicole would have been in touch.
Which is why I didn't say anything.

OK well I'm not particularly interested in excuses,
but I do want to know if there's a chance this can be
salvaged. Because she's miserable and I can't bear
it. Not sure if you've realised this, but she lives in her
head, and you are her fairytale. And she's adored
you since she was 15. She probably won't admit it
now, but trust me, I was there, and it's all true. So
when it all blew up, it completely broke her. She
wouldn't have coped with being rejected by you.

315

She was protecting herself by running.

She did admit it, and of course there's a chance. I didn't want any of this. I wanted to be getting on a plane this week. I wanted her to stay so that we could figure it all out. I wouldn't have asked her about any of the visa stuff if I didn't think we were going somewhere. And I haven't exactly been walking on sunshine either.

OK. Well, you know what you need to do, then, don't you?

Yeah. Holly showed up where I was working and showed me an Instagram feed. It was vague though. Nothing substantial to go on.

Well then. WTF are you waiting for? I have to go. Interesting chat. May the odds be ever in your favour etc etc.

Right...

Uhhh, I feel like I'm going to regret getting involved but get back in touch once you know. We'll take it from there.

OK. Thank you.

And then she signs off. And the foggy cloud of dread and panic is back, because I really have to face this now. There's no putting it off any longer. It's time to rip off the Band-Aid.

Chapter Forty-Seven

Jesse

The first thing I do is download Instagram.

Actually, that's not even a little bit true. The first thing I do is chug a beer. And then I pace the house a while. And then I restring my Jazz bass and polish between all the frets. And then I throw some laundry into the spare room. I sleep on it, *and then* I download Instagram when I wake up in the morning. But I still haven't looked.

It's a terrifying predicament. I sort of don't want to know, but at the same time, I don't have a choice, and besides, I can't change the outcome. Before he passed, Grandpa Nev used to tell us that worrying solves nothing and changes even less, and he was right. I held on to that when things were going to shit with Franko; when I could see us crashing and burning, and Dad was an asshole about it. And again, when *Now or Never* tanked. But it hasn't brought me any comfort this time, and all my stress and worry has manifested as procrastination disguised as productivity. Apparently there's nothing like the fear you might be about to find out you're a reluctant parent with someone you don't want to be with to make you super interested in getting shit done around the house.

Because I *am* reluctant, and it sucks to admit that, and it doesn't feel good. But I don't want this with her, and I'm absolutely certain the feeling is mutual. And it was while I was trying and failing to get to sleep whilst mulling everything over that hindsight truly became twenty-twenty and I could see things for how they really were. Nicole and I bounced along, but it wasn't hard for her to leave, and if I had been truly cut up, things would feel different. I just didn't care enough. There would be no sickening sense of dread at what may or may not be waiting for me on Instagram, and all the things that felt unworkable, and like they mattered, wouldn't have done. When she'd told me, that night, in her apartment, whilst the fireworks were starting to explode over the *Queen Mary*, that she was leaving, I'd have pushed to go too. When she said visiting would delay the inevitable, I'd have proved to her that it wouldn't. When she'd said she wasn't planning on coming back, my immediate thought would have been to figure out how to make it work, not to get up and walk out. I wouldn't have accepted that we were done. I wouldn't have been okay with her radio silence or felt the tinge of relief that was there when she blocked my number in July. I wouldn't have taken that silence as my answer, and been happy not to press it any further. And I would have told Nicole that I'd be there. Anything she needed, I was good for it. Anything at all.

But the truth is, it wasn't long after she left that I stopped thinking about her at all. And if Holly and I had never had that conversation, she'd only have come up fleetingly, in those conversations you have with your new partner about your old ones. The kind of conversations that cement it for you that you're better off, that you've moved on. I don't want to be linked to Nicole, and I don't want her baby to be mine.

I don't know how to use Instagram, and I'm not planning on keeping it long enough to really find out, but I've made an account and logged in and fumbled around until I found the search function, all before I realize I don't know what Nicole's handle is. And I'm not asking Holly. Fuck that, I absolutely do not require her help with this, and besides, how many Nicole Meijers can there possibly be?

But after an hour sifting through account after account I have to concede that actually there are quite a few. Many I can discount immediately based on the profile photo alone. A lot of the Nicole Meijers are Dutch or German. They appear to be stylists. Or nutritionists. These Nicole Meijers live in white apartments with expensive-looking furniture and lots of plants. They post photos of smoothies with goji berries and pomegranate seeds scattered artfully around the bottom of the glass. They stare wistfully out of big windows at European cityscapes and their photo feeds are littered with bullshit inspirational quotes. '*When you love what you have, you have everything you need*', '*You attract the energy you give off*', '*Use your smile to change the world*'. Seriously?

Just as I'm beginning to think this is going to lead precisely nowhere, and that I might have to call Travis and ask him to snoop through Holly's phone, another Nicole Meijer catches my eye. NicoleInNY, and I jab at the screen.

And there she is. Glossy-haired, dimpled Nicole. Looking tired, but happy, sitting on a gray couch in front of a big window overlooking a New York street – brownstones in the background, leaves on the sidewalk – surrounded by plants. Some things, I guess, are the same the world over. And she's smiling into the camera and cradling a baby. A tiny little person with dark hair and staring eyes.

For a few seconds I stare at the picture, not feeling much of anything, whilst I absorb it all, and then I'm flooded by a spectrum of emotions. I read the caption, and reach for my laptop again.

–

> I've just tapped a photo on Instagram and a red heart appeared. What does that mean? I was trying to zoom in.

It means you liked the picture. Also, are you serious?

Yeah, I don't really do social media. Like to keep myself pretty low key, you know.

Well, you definitely need to rethink your Facebook privacy settings. You weren't hard to find.

Anyway, did you find what you were looking for?

I did.

And...?

Do you have it? She is NicoleInNY

Nothing for a while, and then,

You need to speak to Cassie.

–

She's right, I do need to speak to Cassie but it's crippling, and I don't know how to approach it. I think back to the message about meeting in London and how hard that felt at the time, but it's nothing compared to this. Not even remotely the same, and yet one is synonymous with the other. So I re-read her email. Hit reply. Type a bit, and delete it all, over and over. Nothing sounds right. Nothing comes across the way I want it to. Eventually I give up and go out for a walk instead.

Ask Holly to show you Nicole's Instagram.

Oh wow. What are you going to do?

I'm still figuring it all out.

I think you already have.

Chapter Forty-Eight

Cassie

At five minutes to six on Wednesday evening I am running through Marylebone station. I need to catch the five fifty-nine train, because Mum has made a very specific point about what time dinner will be served, and if I'm late, she won't be happy. And if Mum isn't happy, I'll have to sit through an evening of churlish comments from her and baleful looks from Dad. So I don't feel guilty about shoving someone out of my way, or when the wheel of my mini suitcase catches on the corner of a briefcase and sends it skidding across the concourse.

I only just make my train, and it's crowded. The doors beep and close just seconds after I get on and there's that awkward moment when you just manage to jump on a train everyone else managed to catch in good time, and you pant by the door whilst everyone pretends they haven't seen you. We rumble through north London and out towards Aylesbury. People jostle and bump, apologise and read copies of the free newspapers distributed at stations. A girl in her early twenties chatters on her phone. A man chews gum loudly, his jaw clicking disgustingly as he masticates. I'm pleased when the doors open at Amersham.

Dad is waiting in the car, and he hugs me tightly and takes my case, despite my protests that I can put it in the boot myself.

'It's nice to have you home, darling,' he says, as we pull into the driveway. Mum is watching from the window, the way she always does when she's waiting for company, and she greets us at the door, smoothing her hands over her pinny.

'Come on in,' she says. She kisses my cheek and rubs my upper arms briskly. Then she frowns. 'You've lost weight.'

'Not intentionally,' I say, 'I've just not been very hungry.'

'Pining and heartbreak will do that to you, love.' Suddenly a tsunami of grief knocks me for six all over again. I was doing so well today, too. I've only thought about Jesse seven or eight times. Maybe nine. Now ten.

'Yup,' I choke.

'I've got a pasta bake in the oven,' she says. 'That'll see you right.'

'And garlic bread,' Dad adds. Carbs are Mum's cure for everything.

'Right. Well, I'll just put this in my room,' I say. They watch as I scurry up the stairs.

My bedroom hasn't changed since I lived here. The pine bed with its knobbly bedposts and too soft mattress is still behind the door. The matching nightstand sits under the window with my light and ancient clock radio. The time flashes at twelve o'clock where it hasn't been reset properly after being switched off and on again from the plug socket. Pushed up into the frame of the mirror is a strip of photo booth photographs of Rachel and I, aged about thirteen. We're posing like Charlie's Angels, blowing on our hands shaped into guns. We are pouting our lips in exaggerated kisses. In the bottom photo we are laughing. My hair is pulled into a high ponytail, with a sweeping fringe across my forehead, hers is cut in a short, dark bob. Mum's put a blue floral duvet set on the bed and it smells of fabric softener. The pillowcase has neat, ironed-in creases. I sit down on my bed and look around my room. It's so familiar with all my stuff, and yet it doesn't feel like any of it belongs to me anymore. Mum calls me down for dinner and I click my door closed on the way out.

'We got a call from Rachel,' she says as we're eating. 'Not long after you got back from your holiday.'

'About the wedding?' I say. But I know it wasn't about the wedding.

Mum shakes her head. Her wavy hair bounces around her face, set with too much hairspray. I feel a fondness towards her. 'No, love. She was worried about you. Said you were in a bit of a state when she picked you up from the airport.'

'This is true,' I say, glumly, and it occurs to me she's known I've been sad for four weeks and she hasn't called other than to ask what train I was getting.

'What happened?' she presses.

'Ahh, just… something with… someone. Anyway it didn't work out. These things happen. I'll get over it.'

She doesn't respond for a while. Then she exhales out of her mouth, puffing out her cheeks.

'Musicians are fickle creatures,' she says, finally, and I look between them both. Dad smiles kindly at me. They absolutely know exactly who I was with in America. 'You know,' Mum continues, 'we'd rather thought you'd grown out of all that business.'

'Apparently not,' I say.

Dad presses his lips together and Mum pats my hand over the table.

'Latimer Abbey is just wonderful this time of year,' she says, changing the subject. 'The trees will just be turning. The photos are going to be stunning.'

'I didn't realise you'd ever been,' I say.

'Yes, darling,' she says, looking at me as if I really ought to know this. 'Afternoon tea for Tinie's birthday.'

'Who's Tinie? That can't possibly be her real name.'

'Oh, it definitely is,' Mum says. 'She's the wife of one of Daddy's friends from the golf club. Chair of the committee.'

Of course she is. I eat my pasta and pick at a slice of garlic baguette.

Afterwards, we retire to the lounge and Dad pours us all an after dinner sherry which we drink from tiny crystal glasses. Whenever Mum leaves the room, he tops us both up. I hold my glass up to the light and study the patterns etched into it, rolling the glass between my fingers. When we were children, Rachel would come over to play and we'd have a picnic in here with all my soft toys. We used to get all the sherry glasses out of the cabinet and pretend to pour wine for my teddies. We were always so careful not to break any of them for fear of getting caught. It's a fond memory.

'That's the first time I've seen you smile today,' Dad says. I flinch, unaware he was watching me.

'I'm sure I'll be right as rain in no time,' I tell him. Not because I believe it, but because I think that's what he'll want to hear.

—

Mum wakes me up on Thursday morning with a cup of tea.

'Breakfast is on the table,' she tells me. I know what it will be; half a grapefruit, cereal, toast, more tea. Orange juice, too perhaps. Smooth, no juicy bits. My old dressing gown hangs on the back of my door, pink and frilly and slightly moth-eaten, and I put it on as I follow my mum downstairs and into the dining room. Dad's already seated, mulling over the paper, and he waits until I sit before he starts on his fruit. I sprinkle sugar on mine and cut between the segments with a knife. Radio Two plays out from the kitchen. No one speaks except to ask for the butter or the milk. Dad's teaspoon chinks against the inside of his teacup as he stirs in sugar.

'I need to drive to Chiswick today,' I say, 'to pick up our dresses. Can I take your car, Mum?'

'What time?' she asks, putting her grapefruit bowl to one side and taking a sip of tea.

'I said I'd collect Rachel at ten-thirty. I should think I'll be back by one.'

'Have you thought about which way you'll go?' Dad asks.

'Can't say I have,' I tell him. I reach for a slice of toast. It's cold. The butter sticks to it in hard, unyielding lumps.

'Your best bet,' he continues, 'is to take the M25 to Heathrow and then switch to the A40 and drive in that way.'

'Or she could go via Northolt,' Mum offers.

'But if she goes by Heathrow, she'll shave a good few minutes off her time.'

'David, it's a longer journey,' Mum says.

'Christine,' Dad says.

I put my knife down on my plate more heavily than I mean to and the sound stops their debate. There is no way I can drive past Heathrow. Remembering the last time I was there makes me feel hot and sick. I can't finish my toast.

'I'll go the Northolt way,' I say firmly. Mum looks triumphant, but she wouldn't if she knew why. 'I'm absolutely *not* driving past Heathrow airport today.'

Dad makes an 'o' shape with his mouth and I think he's realised. I slurp the remains of my tea. The clock on the wall ticks, loud and constant. It's almost nine. 'Do you mind if I leave the table now? I need to get a move on.'

Within twenty minutes I'm ready. It's a personal record. I reach for my ring on the bedside table but it slips from my fingers and falls on to the floor, bouncing off the carpet and rolling under the bed just out of reach. *How annoying*, I think, as I kneel down on my knees and peer under it. The ring has been stopped in its tracks by a cardboard box which has my writing on the side in thick black marker pen. It stops me in mine, too. *FRANKO STUFF*, it says in thick, bold letters, *DO NOT THROW OUT*. I've drawn little hearts and stars all over the side. I've written 'CB 4 JF' inside a big heart with an arrow through it. Oh fucking hell, I know what this is. I shove the ring roughly on my finger and pull the box out from under the bed. Now I'm running on autopilot. Like I'm witnessing something terrible. I don't want to look, but I can't help myself. I drag the box into the middle of the room and fold back the flaps. Inside are rolls of posters, torn from magazines, carefully secured with rubber bands. I pull out the nearest one and tug the elastic until it flicks off the end. The pieces of paper unroll in my hands, still curled from years of being packed so tightly together. I spread them out. Picture after picture of Franko stares up at me from the floor. They are holding their guitars, looking moody and serious. They are on a beach, windswept and wistful. They are in a lift, crammed in and looking up at the camera. It's meant to look like a still from grainy CCTV footage. They are lying down on a huge coloured floor, four shaggy dark heads together. They are wearing leather jackets, or slogan t-shirts, or vests. Baggy jeans or oversize denim shorts. Skater shoes with fat laces threaded through and pushed down inside.

I pull out another roll of papers. These ones are articles and interviews. I sift through them and stack them up, one by one on the floor beside me. Write-ups and reviews. Adverts for albums and singles, back when people carried Discmans and wound cassettes on with pencils, before everyone just downloaded their music. I come across an article from *Smash Hits* magazine; '50 Things You Need To Know About... Franko'. One of the first articles there was written about them. There's some blurb at the top and then fifty bullet points about the band, spanning three pages; ten facts about each member, then ten about the band as a whole. I put it down, reach for another. Another *Smash Hits* interview. This time tricky questions just for Adam. He looks stricken in the adjoining photo and he's holding his hands up as if shielding himself from a biscuit tin. 'Does the path of excess lead to the palace of wisdom?' is the first question. It joins the pile.

I poke around in the bottom of the box. There's a plastic envelope full of autographs, a few CDs, and a form to send off for information (Franko, 3 Alveston Place, Leamington Spa). There's a paper beer mat and I wonder where that could possibly be from, before remembering the night Rachel and I got backstage. In the bottom corner is a plastic plectrum with remnants of Blu Tack on the back. Adam had tossed a bunch of them into the audience at a gig and I'd caught one, and shoved it inside my bra for safe keeping. I reach for the last roll of posters and pull off the elastic band. It perishes in my hand, crumbles into nothing. As soon as the papers unroll I wish I had just left it well alone. It's all Jesse. More posters and more interviews. I feel overwhelmingly sad as I look at the pile of paper on my lap. I pick one at random and hold it up; it's a double page spread. He must be seventeen or eighteen at the very most.

The poster that accompanies the article is split into three images; photos from the same shoot, black and white, taken in a long corridor. He's standing against whitewashed breeze blocks. In one, his mouth is open, as if he's talking and in mid sentence. In another he's looking down, and in the last photo he's smiling away from the camera with his arm reaching back behind his head and his right hand resting on the back of his neck. I've seen him do that so many times. The familiar dull ache in my chest expands and throbs. The title screams up at me, stark on the page. Black letters on a white background.

> Jesse Talks Love; We caught up with Jesse Franklin, Franko's swoon-worthy bassist to find out exactly what he looks for in a girl: '*She should be funny, adventurous, with a cute smile.*'

I skim over the article, reading snippets here and there.

> What star sign are you? Do you believe compatibility is ruled by the zodiac?
>
> My birthday is March 19th, but I have no idea what star sign I am (Editor's note – he's a Pisces). And no, I don't believe in any of that stuff. How can compatibility be as rigid as that? How can you meet someone and write them off because someone said your signs don't match? That's crazy to me.

What qualities do you look for in a girlfriend? Do you have a type?

Not a specific type. It's generally not what's on the outside that attracts me, but more about her personality. She should be fun to be around. Adventurous for sure. Up for chilling out one day and then doing something totally crazy the next. And a cute smile. She should definitely have a cute smile.

I heave a huge sigh, and the ache feels bigger and emptier than ever. I skim down the page and the last question catches my eye.

Finally, have you ever dated a fan? Would you?

(laughs) I haven't ever dated a fan, no. We're never in the same place long enough. As for whether I would? Well, never say never, I guess.

–

Fuck! I can't read any more. What was I thinking, sifting through all this stuff? It's not making me feel any better about any of it. I put the pile of paper down and look at the box again. *CB 4 JF*. My eyes well up and I don't even try and stop it. A tear rolls down my cheek and splashes on to the interview, then another and another. My shoulders tremble. Choking sobs heave out of me. There is a soft tap at the door, and when I don't say anything, another knock, a little louder this time. I look towards the door and see my dad. He looks back at me for a few seconds, his face a picture of parental concern. He is holding their satnav. I just want him to make everything better but we both know he can't. He comes into the room, throws the satnav on the bed and kneels down beside me. He looks down at the tear-splashed pictures of Jesse in my lap and my spread out collection of posters, then he puts an arm around my shoulders.

'Oh, Cassie,' he sighs.

'He was meant to come to the wedding with me, Dad.' I sob, 'I don't know how I am meant to deal with any of this. I can't see how I am *ever* going to get over this.' He rubs my back as it heaves up and down.

'There, there, lovely girl. Give yourself a bit of time.' He pulls a hanky out of his shirt pocket and holds it out for me. 'It's clean,' he says.

–

I pull up outside Rachel's parents' house soon after eleven. She takes one look at me and decides it's probably best not to ask why I am late. We pick up the dresses and stop for a coffee in a café close to the shop.

'Are you going to tell me what's up?' she asks.

I stir my cappuccino before I talk and I look down at the table, unable to meet her eye.

'I found a box of Franko stuff this morning. All my posters, everything, basically, that was on my wall. Then I looked at it all and got upset.' She nods over her coffee cup. 'Dad found me weeping over a *Smash Hits* interview.'

'Oh God.'

'He didn't know what to say.'

'No, I'm sure he didn't.'

'No one knows what to say, do they? Mum said I've lost weight.'

'You have.'

'People screw up relationships all the time.'

'They do.'

'And they get over it. Why am I no closer to being over this?'

'Because you guys were *crazy*. Most people don't cram an entire relationship into a holiday. And then it all came crashing down unexpectedly. No wonder it's all caught up with you. It was bound to eventually.'

'I read somewhere that a relationship takes half of its length to get over.'

'Yes, but Cassie, this is something that you've been harbouring since you were a teenager, whether you admit it or not. Don't you see? If you had really and truly got over it when Franko broke up, then you wouldn't have added him on Facebook. You'd have just thought, meh, he's on Facebook, big deal, so are millions of other people. So you're not just trying to get over your two weeks in California, and whatever you had going on before that, you're actually trying to get over the last thirteen years of your life and all these dormant feelings you had for him.'

'Bloody hell,' I say. 'You missed your calling. You should have been a shrink.'

'Maybe,' she continues, 'you did actually have a love at first sight moment all those years ago. Maybe that's why it's never worked out with anyone else, because subconsciously you've compared every single boyfriend you've ever had to Jesse, and none of them ever matched up. None of them *could ever* match up.'

'You sound like you've given this a lot of thought,' I tell her.

'Well, as it happens I have. And I have to tell you that I feel partly responsible for this.'

'Don't be daft.'

'No, it's true. It was my idea to look them up that night. If I hadn't done that, you wouldn't have been crying over your posters this morning.'

I take her hand across the table.

'Rachel. You mustn't feel guilty. Because up until… all that, I was having the best time of my life. It was so intense. He told me things that he hasn't told anyone else. When it was good, it was magnificent. It was tremendous. There are people who go through their entire lives not even coming close to feeling the way I did in America. So don't feel like this is your fault, because all this shit... well it's just really shitty and unfortunate. And I should have handled it better.'

'I think you handled it the same way a lot of people would have done.' She looks me straight in the eye. 'Look, Cassie, you should know...' She stops midway through the sentence. Chews her bottom lip and looks contemplative. 'I really think it's going to get easier.'

'So people tell me,' I sigh.

'Yeah, but it will,' she says.

I look down into the dregs of my coffee. There is chocolate smudged around the inside of the cup. Foamy bubbles pop.

'Let's talk about your wedding,' I say, squeezing her fingers again. 'How excited are you?'

When I get home, there is no sign of my Franko box. Nothing is mentioned.

Chapter Forty-Nine

Cassie

Friday morning starts in much the same way as Thursday. Mum's made bacon sandwiches for breakfast and Dad snaffles his up in a way that suggests it's not their normal fare. I wonder if it's Mum's way of trying to cheer me up, so I eat what she serves me, despite the breakfast meeting Rachel and I have with Eloise the wedding coordinator at Latimer Abbey.

Rachel is bristling with excitement as I pull into the gated entrance.

'You're going to love it, Cass,' she says.

'I've always been kind of curious about it,' I say, driving slowly up a long, gravel road, lined with spherical outdoor lamps. If I get a chip in the windscreen from a rogue stone, Mum will not be impressed. 'I used to think it was one of the Queen's houses when I was a kid,' I admit. Rachel smirks.

'It's basically a hotel with a spa, mate,' she says. 'I bet the Queen hasn't even heard of it.'

The road twists and turns and eventually opens out into a huge driveway with a flower bed in the middle of it. There are immaculate lawns stretching all around the grounds with enormous trees dotted across the land. A woman in a trouser suit with very neat hair is waiting just outside the main entrance and Rachel waves at her and tells me it's Eloise. I park in the car park and we traipse back around to where she is still waiting.

'I'm afraid George couldn't get the day off work for this,' Rachel explains. 'So I've brought Cassie. She's my maid of honour.'

'Fantastic,' Eloise beams. We shake hands. She turns to Rachel, 'So, tomorrow is the big day.' She bounces on her sensible heels as she speaks. 'I wanted to make sure we have everything you need here at Latimer to make it spectacular.'

The car is loaded with Rachel's fishbowls and bag after bag of glass pebbles and floating candles, as well as tiny drawstring bags of bonbons and colouring books for the kids. The seating plan, too, although I've made a point of not looking at that in case I get upset about not seeing Jesse's name on there.

Eloise leads us past a long mahogany reception desk and through grand wooden doors. There's an imposing staircase with swirly banisters and brass stair rods. We end up in a large, bright room with French doors that open out onto a patio, a rose garden, and a croquet lawn. Beyond all that, Eloise explains, flicking her wrist down a gently sloping hill, is a lake with reeds and wildlife. It's a great location for photos.

Light streams into the room. Twelve circular tables, each with ten chairs around it, are laid out and one of them has been made up with pressed white linen and formal place settings.

'So these will obviously all be made up tomorrow,' Eloise says. 'But this was just really to give you a feel of how it'll look.'

'Fantastic,' Rachel beams, stroking the table cloth, and I don't think I've ever seen anyone so enthused by white linen and multiple forks in my life.

'Shall we discuss the final details over a coffee?' Eloise asks, gesturing back towards the door. We follow her into a tearoom where she makes a signal to a waiter who takes our drink orders and brings a tray of miniature pastries. We discuss where the receiving line will be, the order of the speeches and where The Highly Strung will be playing. Eloise finds the idea of a ukulele band being called The Highly Strung hysterical.

'I've been at Latimer for eight and a half years,' she muses, 'and in all that time, I've never had a couple have a ukulele band as their entertainment. We get a lot of tribute acts, especially Robbie Williams and Michael Bublé, but never, ever, a ukulele band.'

'Well, George and I got engaged in Hawaii,' Rachel says. Eloise sits forward in her seat; she knows there will be a story here, and she's right, and it's a lovely one. Maybe she'll relay it to other prospective couples when they come to look around. She laps up the details as Rachel continues. 'The evening he proposed, we were in an amazing restaurant, eating the freshest seafood I think possibly in the world, and these four ukulele players come over and start playing at our table. They performed a cover of "Somewhere Over the Rainbow", in the style of some really famous Hawaiian ukulele player and singer, and it was just gorgeous. I was enthralled by them and when I looked back at George, he was on one knee with this,' she rubs her fingers over her ring. 'So ukuleles are pretty special to us. He'd planned the entire thing.' She shakes her head and looks wistful. Eloise looks like she might well up.

'That's just such a wonderful story,' she says. Her hand is resting on her chest. Her eyebrows are slanted downwards, and I think hearing all these stories must be one of the best parts of her job.

'It really is,' I agree.

When we are finished, Eloise comes back out to the car and helps us to unload everything. It takes multiple trips. I do not carry the seating plan.

'So we'll be welcoming you tonight,' Eloise smiles as our meeting ends. 'And I believe you have dinner reservations with us this evening?' Rachel nods and turns to me.

'You're sharing with Lauren,' she says, and honestly, I'm pleased to get out of my old bedroom, if only for one night.

—

Dad drops me back at Latimer Abbey soon after five, and I check into Lauren's room and sit down on the bed. There's a big window that looks out over the land we could see from the dining room; a pretty view of lawns and gardens and woodland and that lake. A sweet wooden bridge arches over one section of it and briefly, it reminds me of the bridge Jesse and I walked over in Venice, but I push that memory aside and turn away from the window.

I hang our dresses, in their bags, in the wardrobe and wonder what to do before dinner. There isn't really time to visit the spa, and sitting in a steam room isn't much fun when you're on your own. Neither is going to the bar. Rachel still hasn't arrived, and Lauren and Marie won't be turning up for another hour. I could have a nap, but that feels like a waste of time, and besides, I'm not tired. Eventually, I decide on a walk.

Mum was right. It *is* beautiful here in October. The leaves on the trees rustle, yellowing and curled up at their edges, drying out ready to fall off the branches. Soon, the trees will be bare. It's not just how it all looks though; the silence of the place is beautiful, too. And the clean, grassy-smelling air. I bet the stars are mesmerising out here, twinkly and abundant, hanging in the sky. It won't be tomorrow, but for now the place is tranquil. I pull my cardigan around me to ward off the breeze as I walk across the lawn to one of the gardens. There is no one else here and I sit down on a bench and look back at the abbey. The problem with being alone is that it gives me time to think, and I don't want to do that. Not really. I don't want to feel maudlin and sad anymore. I want to get on with things. I want to celebrate my best friend's wedding. I don't want to wake up in my old bedroom on Sunday morning, nursing a hangover and knowing I have nothing to look forward to besides going back to work on Monday. I don't want to be thinking that I should have been at Heathrow this morning, waiting at arrivals, jittery and excited. And yet that's precisely what is stuck in my head, like a roadblock that I can't get around, or a CD that skips, jarringly.

I need to know, one way or another, what the outcome is. Fred was right, the insightful bastard; I'm never going to truly be able to put myself back together if I'm still clinging to those what ifs. I pull my phone out of my pocket and tap the Facebook icon. Type his name into the search box. *Jesse Franklin, Freelance Musician.* The results load and he's halfway down the page. The photo's the same, but now I recognise that it was taken in the living room. The shelves in the background are the ones behind the sofa. The plant is the one on a console table near the back doors. It's like I've passed through his life and nothing has changed for him. It's like I was never there. I tap his name, and the profile loads. I can't see much. It's exactly as it was that evening back in April. My heart's racing now, my fingers are trembling. I click to send a message, but I don't know where to start. The lack of response to my email spoke volumes and no words come. Instead, I stare at the screen until it times out and fades to black.

Calmly, I close the app and put my phone down next to me on the bench. This needs more time and consideration than I can devote to it now. I force it all out of my head and amble back towards the hotel.

Dinner is civilised. Far more so than the last time we all ate together – what with there not being any phallic straws or obscene confectionery. Rachel thanks us all for being great bridesmaids even though I feel like I've been anything but, and we call it a night just after ten. Marie is flagging and Rachel wants to cram in as much sleep as she can before tomorrow. After they have disappeared I make eyes at the lumbering, unfortunate looking barman for something to put in my hip flask and Lauren buys another bottle of wine which we take up to our room. She conks out the minute her head hits the pillow, so I drink it by myself whilst watching repeats of American sitcoms, and I allow myself just a few minutes to wallow and pine. Niles loves Daphne. Frasier is hapless. I am not with Jesse.

Chapter Fifty

Cassie

The alarm on my phone jolts me awake, and I slowly look around the room, pushing hair out of my face and rubbing the sleep from my eyes. It's dark in here, only cracks of light creep around the edge of the curtains. There are scatter cushions all over the floor and the TV is still on mute. The almost empty wine bottle is on the bedside table with my glass next to it and beside me, Lauren is still sleeping like the dead, her leg hanging out of the bed. There's a sharp rap at the door and I get up and pad over. Marie is on the other side of the peephole, and the fish-eye lens distorts her, making her head look enormous whilst the rest of her is tiny. She raises her hand to knock again but I pull open the door before she can.

'Good,' she says. 'You're up.'

'Well, one of us is,' I say. Marie peers around the door at the lump in the bed that is Lauren. She sighs and pushes past me into the room and over to the window, yanking open the curtains. Light streams in. Lauren groans and pulls a pillow over her head.

'They are bringing breakfast up in ten,' Marie announces. 'The hairdresser has already put Rachel's hair in rollers, and Mandy should be here in a bit. You can shower in my room if you like.'

'Righty-ho,' I say, as cheerfully as I can manage through my foggy head. Marie touches my arm.

'Cass, she's very on edge,' she whispers. 'Can you come now?'

339

'Of course,' I say. 'Give me two minutes.'

The phone rings. The florist is here. I greet her in my pyjamas and we carry the boxes of flowers up to Marie's room. I flip one open and inside are three identical miniature bouquets of dark purple freesias, interspersed with flawless cream roses and a few sprigs of gypsophila and dark green leaves, all tied together with cream satin ribbon. They are true works of art. Inside the other box is Rachel's bouquet, a larger version of ours, round and blousy.

Marie wasn't kidding; Rachel is agitated and fraught, decidedly different to the poised and composed bride she's pretended to be in front of everyone but me. She paces around Marie's room in her fluffy robe and slippers and I perch on the bed.

'Lauren is showering in her room,' I say, 'but she'll be here in a while, and she's bringing a bottle of champagne.' Marie nods and disappears into the bathroom. I turn to Rachel, 'Shall I get you a hot drink?'

'Yes but not coffee,' she says, shaking her head. 'I'm already jittery enough as it is.'

'I have some Rescue Remedy,' I say, 'in my Bag of Brilliance,' and she stops pacing and smiles.

'Your what?'

'My Bag of Brilliance,' I repeat. 'It's that little clutch jobby that came with our dresses. I packed it full of everything you might possibly need today. Even one of those mini sewing kits you get in Christmas crackers. Oh, and a full hip flask, obviously.'

'Let's hope you don't need the sewing kit,' she says. 'You can barely even do a running stitch.'

'I know. So don't rip your dress!' I go to the breakfast trolley and pick up a pain au raisin. 'Have a nibble on that,' I say. She does as she's told.

'We really ought to start on your hair,' the hairdresser says, and Rachel flops onto a chair. The rollers are removed. Sections of hair are backcombed and volumised and held in place with pearly pins. Finally, two front sections are curled into ringlets, and with a final spritz of hairspray, Rachel's hair is finished.

We are helping her into her dress when there's a knock on the door. Marie runs to open it and Mandy bustles in, all business, in platform Louboutins, with a big metal make-up case in each hand. Her hair is piled high on the top of her head and she's done flicky wings of eyeliner on herself.

'So sorry,' she breezes, 'I got a bit lost. Forgot my satnav.'

'You're here now,' Rachel says, and I hurry to do up the last few hook and eye clasps on the back of the dress. Then she's back in her chair and Mandy whips around her with primer and powder, mascara and lipstick, a look of sheer concentration on her face. She doesn't let Rachel look in the mirror until she's finished and Rachel concedes, which I consider pretty brave and trusting of her, given the hen night make-up. When she's finished, she steps backs and spins the chair around to the mirror.

'Tah dah!' she says, pleased with herself. Rachel gasps. The rest of us coo, and I feel a little mean for ever doubting Mandy's abilities. She might be loud and a little unrefined, but she certainly knows her way around a make-up bag. Rachel has perfect dramatic Disney eyes and almost nude lips, with just the subtlest hint of pink. Almost as if she's just bitten them rather than had any make-up applied at all. It's flawless. She's beautiful.

'It's so George doesn't end up with smudged lipstick all over his mush,' she says. 'If you want to go brighter at the reception, I'll sort you out.'

When we're all dolled up and ready to go, Mandy claps her hands together and takes her camera out of her handbag.

'You bunch of stunners!' she exclaims. 'I want to take the first picture.' We gather together and pose with our flowers.

Just before we head downstairs, Rachel takes a final look in the mirror. We've been best friends for life, inseparable throughout school, and even university, and I've seen her dressed up to the nines plenty of times. She's always gorgeous to me, but she's never looked as beautiful as she does today. She smoothes her immaculate manicure over her dress – a mermaid-style gown in ivory satin with a delicate lace overlay. The skirt skims her hips and flares out just above her knees, and the fabric crosses under a sash at the bodice into a sweetheart neckline. She has pearl earrings and a matching necklace and pinned into her hair is a pretty lace veil with tiny pearly beads sewn in.

'You look properly amazing,' I say, and behind me, Mandy, Marie and Lauren nod in agreement.

'Thank you,' she says, but I can tell by her eyes she's nervous. I take her hand and squeeze it.

'Today is going to be epic,' I tell her. She takes a deep breath that reaches all the way up to her shoulders and nods.

'I'm bricking it,' she admits.

'I know you are, but I have something for that,' I say.

'In your Bag of Brilliance?' she asks and I nod.

'Exactly.'

Jeff and Diana Michaels are waiting for us at the bottom of the stairs. We can hear them chatting loudly all the way down the corridor, but they stop short as they see us. Diana's bottom lip trembles as Rachel treads carefully on the plush maroon carpet. It's the kind of carpet that's so thick and spongy you feel like you could probably sleep on it. Every now and then her stiletto heel pings against the brass stair rods.

'Oooh our biggest little girl!' she gushes, grabbing on to the sleeve of Jeff's morning suit. 'Getting married! I can't believe today is finally here.' She reaches into her handbag for a tissue and daintily dabs at her eyes. Jeff doesn't say anything. I think he's been rendered speechless, and even though I've known him almost all my life, I don't think I've ever seen Jeff Michaels, speechless, before.

'It's not too late to change your mind, petal,' he finally says, gruffly, and I think it's an attempt at a joke so he can hide the fact that he's feeling weepy, too. Jokes in place of heartfelt words is a tactic I know inside out.

'Dad!' Marie scolds.

'That's enough of that, Jeffrey,' Diana says.

'Calm down, Di. I'm only having her on.'

Rachel rolls her eyes. 'Can we just go, please?' she says. 'Mum, you're in the car with Marie and Lauren, Dad, you're coming with me and Cass.'

We step outside into the sunlight. A crisp, autumnal breeze blows through the trees, making the leaves rustle and the branches sway. The cars are waiting, sleek navy vintage Jags, each with white ribbons tied onto their bonnets and secured to the front grills with a bow. Diana, Marie and Lauren leave first, and they start off down the gravel driveway whilst I am still helping Rachel into the car. Jeff shifts from one foot to the other and his shoes crunch against the stones. He wants to help but he's not sure how so I hand him our bouquets until we are both safely strapped in. Rachel grabs my hand and doesn't let go as we follow the other car towards the church. She doesn't say anything, just stares out of the window at the hedgerow. A few passing cars honk their horns at us and each time she squeezes my fingers a little tighter.

'Are you okay, Rach?' I ask. I appreciate she's nervous but I am not convinced abject fear is a reaction a bride is supposed to have. This isn't something she's been forced into, after all. She looks over at me and opens her mouth to say something, and finally, after months of this odd fractiousness, she starts talking.

'Cassie, what if he doesn't turn up? What if we get there and the vicar comes out and tells me he's not coming and I'm left loitering outside the church? I won't be able to go in.'

So this is what has been bothering her. She's scared she'll be jilted. But she'll never be jilted. I've seen the way he looks at her. 'I mean, he hasn't been bothered with the planning, what if he's not into this? What if he and Marcus have done a bunk?'

'He and Marcus have not *done a bunk*,' I say. 'Where would they go? Your dad would track them down. It wouldn't be pretty.'

343

'I don't know. Prague? That's where Marcus wanted to go for the stag do.'

Of course he did. Marcus is a walking cliché. We stop walking and I take her hand.

'Is this what's been bothering you all this time?'

She nods.

'He probably hasn't helped much because he knows he'd likely get stuff wrong. Like the beer pong thing. Remember that? Or when he suggested the three peaks challenge as your honeymoon. Or that his parents' dog should be the ring-bearer.'

Rachel laughs. 'He wasn't even joking about that one,' she says.

'And I bet you let him know none of those things were ever going to happen?'

'Too right.'

'Well then. He knew it wouldn't be how you wanted it and he'd rather not have that grief. I bet this is him just being a bloke.'

'I'm not convinced, Cass.'

'Well *be* convinced. He will be there, and he's going to look back as you walk towards him and there will be delight and amazement written all over his face because he won't be able to believe just how far above his weight he's punched.' Rachel seems a little reassured. 'I'd give anything to have what you have with G-Man. I thought I might have it with Jesse but obviously not even close.' She opens her mouth to say something but I shake my head and don't let her speak. 'I'm not moping. I promise. I'm just trying to tell you, he'll be there.'

'Thanks, Cassie,' she says. We hug and I rub little circles on her back.

'And if he isn't, well I'll go in and tell everyone that it's all off, and then we'll stick two fingers up to the lot of them and you and I will go on your honeymoon and spend the entire time getting pissed on Bahama Mamas on the beach.'

She laughs. 'It wouldn't be right not to go on holiday,' she says.

'Here, have a nip of this,' I say, taking my hip flask from my bag.

'What's in it?'

'Peach schnapps,' I tell her, 'and I had to flirt outrageously with Igor the bartender to get it. So you'll drink it and you'll like it.'

She takes a sip and giggles. 'Ah, it's like being back in Greece.'

I sing the chorus from 'Girls and Boys' by Blur and make my hands into box shapes. 'I wish you'd told me this was what you were worried about,' I say.

'You had your own problems,' she shrugs, and even though it's true, I get a pang of guilt that she hasn't felt able to confide in me about it.

We pass through the church gate and pull up outside the front door and the car crunches over the gravel, momentarily drowning out the sound of the bells. Diana, Marie and Lauren are waiting outside the door. We help Rachel out and shake her dress for her, smoothing out wrinkles with our hands. I grab her bouquet from the car seat and Marie comes back with the vicar, an elderly, mole-like man, slightly doddery but very sweet, and he encourages us into the church vestibule.

Then it's just about time to start. All three of us rally around, giving Rachel a final once-over like ladies-in-waiting to a queen. We dust her dress down one last time. We pull her veil over her face. She looks terrified again as she takes Jeff's arm. He pats her on the hand affectionately and Lauren holds the door open for them as the Wedding March begins, time-honoured and familiar. Every single eye in the church is on Rachel as she walks down the aisle. Except mine. I'm looking at George, and I'm pleased to note that I was right. The look of love is very definitely in his eyes.

After the first hymn, during which Rachel's uncle steals the show with his baritone voice, and my dad makes no attempt whatsoever to sing, the vicar starts talking. He says some inspirational things that I think are probably from the Bible and then starts the ceremony.

Rachel's dad puts her hand in George's and we're asked if anyone knows any reason why they can't get hitched and there're those tense few seconds where everyone looks around the church, but exactly no eye contact is held with anyone. Rachel and George make their vows and slide rings on each other's fingers. She speaks quietly and her voice is shaking a little. He gazes into her eyes the entire time and he's looking at her like she's an angel. My vision starts to blur, and I rummage around in my bag for a tissue.

'Can I get one of those?' Marie whispers. I hand her the packet.

And then they're pronounced man and wife and George lifts the veil and plants a juicy smacker of a kiss on her. The register is signed, Rachel's mum and George's dad do a reading each, and finally The Highly Strung begin to play. The chords of 'Somewhere Over The Rainbow' ring out through the church.

The wedding party follows Rachel and George back up the aisle and handsy Marcus guides me towards the entrance.

'I'm expecting a dance with you later,' he leans in and whispers. His breath tickles my ear lobe, and his hand is slightly too low on my back.

'Sure thing, Marcus,' I say, tightly.

Outside, the photographer snaps away at Rachel and George as they leave the church, and the sunlight hits me square in the eyes. Bells ring and pastel-coloured confetti is thrown. It flutters to the ground like paper snow, and Rachel, calmer since it became apparent George definitely did want to marry her, is back to her usual, confident self. Guests crowd around them, kissing their cheeks and shaking his hand and admiring her dress. Marie, Lauren and I hang back together in our little gang of three, posing for photos and chatting, and as Rachel and George make their way towards their car she reaches up, brushes a petal of confetti from his hair, and leans in for a kiss. I feel a pang of longing that I immediately push straight back down to where it came from.

'Aww,' Lauren says. She saw it, too.

'This is lovely. They're lovely,' I say, linking our arms. 'Did you see the way he looked at her?'

'He was all lit up,' she coos.

'I'm glad they found each other,' I say.

'Feeling wistful?' Lauren asks, tentatively.

'No. Yes. Not about Jesse,' I say. 'She's my person, and now he's her person. And he's a good person. So if I have to lose her to anyone, I'm glad it's him. It's a new chapter for them. It's exciting. That's all.'

The wedding car pulls away from the church and everybody waves. I blow Rachel a kiss as they drive past, and she catches it in her hand through the window.

Chapter Fifty-One

Cassie

'All right, big smiles,' the photographer commands. *Click.* 'And again, that's lovely.' *Click.* He studies the screen on the back of his camera. 'Just the bridesmaids now.' We shuffle around, getting into position. *Click, click, click.* 'And now with the best man.' I inwardly groan. Marcus has been giving me the eye relentlessly since we walked out of the church together. He's really trying hard but I'm not feeling it. I've promised him one dance at the reception, and then I'm going to discreetly avoid him for the rest of the evening.

Because even if I was ready to think about meeting someone, that someone would not be Marcus Lewis. He's not even remotely my type. And despite the fact that he likes to think he's a lad, to me he always comes across a bit desperate. I do have to concede, however, that he does have a nice smile, and he's a good height. When I stand next to him, we fit snugly against each other. But it doesn't really matter; he's hit on me loads of times before, most notably at George's thirtieth birthday, and on New Year's Eve, and I have never once taken the bait. It's almost getting embarrassing now. If I was going to pull Marcus, I'd have done it a long time ago. He edges his way in between Marie and I, and slides his arm around my waist. I can feel the heat of his hand through the fabric of my dress. I smile for the camera but I know it doesn't make it to my eyes. It will be one for the album, not for display. Finally, I am released and I scarper back to the car and slide onto the leather seats. Marie and Lauren are close behind and we are off back to Latimer Abbey.

—

A waiter hands me a glass of Pimm's on the croquet lawn. Chunks of cucumber and strawberries bob around in the glass and a mint leaf sticks to the side. People chat and laugh. Another waiter weaves through the crowd holding a tray of canapés; little goats' cheese and red onion tartlets, squares of fried potato with a neat strip of rare steak on top and choux buns filled with cream cheese and chives. Rachel and George are off with the photographer, probably down at the lake, kissing on the bridge whilst her veil billows around them. Mum totters over in her early nineties stilettos with Dad in tow.

'You looked wonderful up there, button,' he says, raising his glass. I briefly wonder if he'll always call me button, or poppet. I bet he will. Old habits die hard.

'Thanks,' I tell him. 'Are you enjoying yourselves?'

'It's lovely,' Mum says. 'Isn't it lovely, David?'

'Lovely,' he agrees.

'I just knew, as soon as Diana told me it was going to be here, that it would be wonderful.'

'Well, you weren't wrong,' I say. Another tray passes. I take a tartlet and pop it in my mouth.

'How was your evening last night?' Mum asks.

'Fine, thanks. I took a walk around the grounds, then we had dinner. And then I watched episodes of *Frasier* until gone midnight.'

'Oh, *Cassie*,' Mum says. She looks disappointed. I don't understand. What was I supposed to have done?

'What, Ma?'

'You're moping.'

'I'm not moping. I just think *Frasier* is funny. What's mopey about that? If anything I was trying to cheer myself up. I was trying to do the opposite of moping.'

The waiter comes by with a full jug of punch. I stick my glass out and Mum watches as the glass fills up with amber liquid. A piece of apple plops in with a hollow sounding splash. She scrutinises me, her eyes slightly narrowed.

'Were you drinking?'

'I beg your pardon?'

'Wine. Did you drink any? Last night? Whilst you were watching your *Frasier*?'

'What's that got to do with anything?'

'You're not eating, and you're drinking a lot.'

'I *am* eating. I have eaten everything you've put in front of me.' Another tray of canapés materialises. I grab two little choux buns and shove one in my mouth. 'See? Eating!' I say with my mouth still full. Dad looks like he wants to back away slowly into the crowd. Mum tuts.

'Cassandra!' she snaps. 'Manners!' Cassandra? No one has called me Cassandra since I was in school. I swallow my choux bun and take a big gulp of drink. Mum and I stare each other down the entire time. She breaks the eye contact first, and looks to Dad for help.

'We're just worried about you,' he mutters.

'Well, you needn't be,' I say. 'Really.'

'You're coming up thirty,' Mum says.

'A fact of which I am well aware.'

'We'd like to see you meet someone.'

I roll my eyes. I should have known this would happen. I had hoped she'd be less crass than to do it at Rachel's wedding reception, though. As if today isn't hard enough.

'I *did* meet someone,' I hiss, 'and look how that turned out. People do actually like me, you know. Men do actually *like* me.' I stop myself from descending into a rant about Date My Mate, and look around. I am relieved to find no one is paying any attention. I lower my voice to little more than a whisper. 'Look, I don't need this. From you. Right now. Or ever, in fact.'

She backs off. She looks a bit stung. I feel guilty. She has an uncanny ability to get under my skin, even after she's goaded me into snapping at her.

'I'm sorry, Ma,' I say.

'It's fine,' she says in an odd, clipped voice. We stand together for a little while longer, but no one says anything. I look at the ground and tap the grass under my feet down with the toe of my shoe. Mum looks at her watch. We are all glad when it's time to go inside.

During the wedding breakfast I am seated next to Marcus at the top table. We are slap bang in the middle of the room and Rachel says this is so she and George can see everyone. Our glasses are filled and bread rolls are distributed. Little curls of butter lay in a silver dish and they sort of remind me of Marcus' hair. We reach for it at the same time and his hand brushes against mine. I pull it back.

'I'm sorry,' I murmur.

'Ladies first,' he says, at exactly the same time. I look up at him and his eyes dart over me in the same, almost leering way they had in the church. I butter my roll and nibble a dainty bite.

The starters arrive: feta and roasted red pepper tart with a few leaves plonked haphazardly on the plate next to it. It's drizzled with balsamic glaze. George's father talks to me about how glamorous we all look today. He tells me he remembers his mother having a dress not dissimilar to mine back in the fifties. She used to wear it to dinner parties and she had a furry muff to go with it. Rachel's eyes widen and I choke on my drink, and beside me, Marcus bursts out laughing. George's dad looks momentarily confused, and George gently explains, with a hilarious series of hand gestures and eye movements, that 'furry muff' might be somewhat of a double entendre. For a moment I am worried George's dad might be horrified by how juvenile Marcus and I apparently are, but then he laughs, too. Wine glasses are topped up, but now Mum has mentioned it, I am hyper aware of my alcohol consumption and I pour myself some water from the jug on the table instead.

Tables are cleared and Marcus tells me I look tanned. He hasn't seen me since the beginning of the year so I am surprised that he is so well versed in my skin tone.

'I've been on holiday,' I tell him, and then, because the obvious next question is to ask where, I say, 'LA.' Marcus lets out a low whistle.

'Nice,' he says. 'Do anything fun?'

'Plenty,' I say. 'Loads of touristy things, went to see the Hollywood sign, spent a lot of time at various beaches, went to a really cool music shop, ate at lots of nice restaurants. You know, the usual.' *Fell ridiculously in love, had it all snatched away from me in one terrible exchange of words, came home heartbroken*, I say in my head.

'Go with friends?' he says. I shake my head.

'No, my… I was seeing someone who lives out there.'

'You *were* seeing someone, or you *are* seeing someone?'

'Um, were.' I am not going into details. Not today. Not with him. Not when I think he'll see it as another way to hit on me. He will try and be the shoulder for me to cry on if he thinks I'm broken.

'That's a shame,' he says. *Yeah, right*, I think.

'Yep.' I've gone all stiff and awkward. I want desperately to change the subject.

'Maybe I can buy you a drink later,' he says. *Jesus, Marcus*, I think, *I know God loves a trier, but give it a rest*. I look at Rachel. She's talking to her new mother-in-law. But she's got one eye on us, too. As soon as she sees my head turn towards her, she catches my eye, and then immediately looks away again.

'Maybe,' I tell him. It's casual, noncommittal.

I pick my way through my main course. Talking about Jesse has given me a queasy feeling in the pit of my stomach, and the slice of roast lamb lies, barely touched, on my plate. Marcus has had no such reaction.

'Good grub, mate,' he says to George, waving his knife across the fish bowl centrepiece. 'Lovely spuds.' A globule of gravy flies off and lands on the white tablecloth next to my glass and I stare at it. 'Are you going to finish that?' he waves his knife at my plate. I shake my head and slide it towards him.

After dessert, waiters come around with flutes of champagne for the speeches and toasts. Jeff stands up, shifts on his feet a little awkwardly, and chinks a teaspoon on the side of his glass. The room falls silent. One hundred and twenty pairs of eyes are upon him.

'Good afternoon everyone,' he says. 'For those of you who don't know me, my name is Jeff, and I'm the very proud father of beautiful Rachel here.'

I sit back in my seat and cross my legs as he talks. He starts with a quip about living in a house with three women and never being able to get a word in edgeways, which is funny because as far back as I can remember he's had something to say, and definitely can get a word in any which way he fancies. He moves on to thanking everyone for coming, cracks another joke about embarrassing his daughter, and then starts on the anecdotes. He talks about the day she was born and it's heartfelt and sentimental. He talks about when she started school, and how she caused him a lot of sleepless nights and anxiety in her teenage years. I get a mention here, and there are rumbles of laughter throughout the room. Then he moves on to meeting George, and welcomes him into their family. 'To be honest,' he says, 'I began to see him as the son I never had when he drank all my beer and asked to borrow the car – not on the same day, I hasten to add.' More laughter. Finally, he rounds off with a toast to Rachel and George, and we all stand up and raise our glasses.

When everyone else sits down, George remains standing. He puts his hand on Rachel's shoulder and she gazes up at him.

'Ladies and gentlemen,' he says. 'On behalf of my new wife, and myself, thank you all for being here. Doesn't she look stunning today?' There are nods and murmurs around the room. Rachel blushes. 'I want to start off by saying that every so often, every once in a while, two people meet, and it's like the world tips on its axis. It's as if the stars align.'

Oh no, I know that feeling so well. I've felt the earth shift on its axis. I've seen the stars align. My heart pounds inside my chest and the back of my neck suddenly feels hot. I close my eyes and try desperately not to think about Jesse, because I know I will cry if I do. George talks about their first meeting and it's a story I know well, because I was there. They met at a gig in Camden. Just a small one, down in the basement of a pub. Rachel and I had bought our drinks and were hurrying to a table and she'd turned around, bumped into George, and accidentally thrown her pint down his jacket. She insisted on paying his dry cleaning bill and they swapped numbers and snuck glances at each other the entire evening. The rest, as they say, is history. If you ask them now, neither of them can remember who the band were. He finishes his speech with a toast to Marie, Lauren and me, and everyone drinks.

Marcus' speech is last, and he stands up next to me and begins by agreeing with George that we bridesmaids did do a wonderful job, and carries on to say he's known all three of us for a few years and we've never looked so lovely. He glances down at me as he says it and I concentrate hard on my glass. Then come the jokes about George, the banter and the full on character assassination, and I have to hand it to him, it's a good speech. He's engaging and he's funny. 'Finally, George,' he says, 'I want to thank you, for eventually conceding, after years of friendship, that I am indeed the best man.' George guffaws and Rachel looks lovingly at him. 'So, please be upstanding for the bride and groom. The new Mr and Mrs Smith: George and Rachel.'

We all stand for the third time. There is wild applause. Marcus sits back in his chair and smiles, pleased with himself.

'Great speech,' I tell him. He grins at me, and he's all white teeth and crinkly eyes.

'I meant what I said earlier, you know?' he says. He leans back and spreads his legs before reaching across and resting his arm on the back of my seat. Good grief, he's the very definition of gauche. 'I'd like to have a drink with you, and I really am sorry about what happened with your chap. It's his loss, though. The man's crazy, Cass.'

I don't believe he's sorry for a second, but it's nice to be complimented and I could do with the ego boost.

'Thanks, Marcus,' I say, and then I hear myself agreeing to that drink. After all, I'm definitely going home with my parents, so what harm can one drink do, right?

Chapter Fifty-Two

Cassie

After coffee over petits fours, people trickle through the double doors to the bar. There's a tab, and a crowd getting their drinks in before it runs out. Mandy is right at the front shouting her order at the barman.

'I'll just take the bottle, yeah?' she's saying. 'Four glasses. Thanks, mate.'

She totters in her platforms over to a table and puts the tray with the wine and the glasses down. She scans the room and waves Lauren and me over.

'Where is Maz? I got this for us,' she shouts across the room.

After a little while, the lights in the room dim and everybody shuffles towards the dance floor. The ukulele band huddle together on a small stage in the corner of the room and it's the first time I get to properly look at them. Two girls and two guys. Well turned out, in a hipster sort of way. The girls are wearing flower crowns and floaty dresses. The boys are in undone waistcoats and rolled up sleeves. One of them is sitting on a cajon. Rachel and George move into the centre of the circle and the music starts. One of the girls begins to sing into the microphone. A cover of 'You've Got The Love'. Her voice doesn't really match up to the way she looks. She's a delicate, ethereal, pixieish little thing with big, frightened eyes, but her voice is confident and loud and beautifully controlled.

Lauren is next to me and she links her arm through mine as we watch the dancing. We sway a little, in time to the music.

'This is nice,' she says. 'They've made it all really personal, haven't they? With the band and the Florence and the Machine cover.'

'Yeah, it's a good wedding. The wedding coordinator couldn't get over the uke band.'

'I don't suppose it's all that common.'

'Probably not.'

'What were you all laughing about at dinner?'

'Huh? Oh yeah. George's Dad was talking about furry muffs.' I waggle my eyebrows at her.

Lauren giggles. 'He seems a bit strait-laced for that kind of chit-chat.'

'He was talking about hand muffs. You know, the ones you put your hands in to keep them warm. Not fannies. Apparently George's granny had one back in the fifties. She had a dress like these that she used to wear to parties. And she paired it with a furry muff.'

'I'll bet she did,' Lauren says, still giggling.

'She's here somewhere,' I say, looking around the room. 'She might be right behind us this very second, listening to us talking about her furry muff.'

We look back at the dance floor. George is twirling Rachel around. Her dress fans out at the bottom. She reaches her arms around his neck and they do the hug-and-sway slow dance that you see at weddings and proms and nightclubs just before they turn the lights back on and kick everyone out. He whispers something in her ear and she throws her head back and laughs and I think it's funny that something as personal as the first dance as man and wife is watched by so many people. Especially when they whisper to each other in the way they do. It's like we're all watching a private moment between them. Surely they must know that everyone watching wants to know what's been said. If I ever get married and have the kind of reception that calls for a first dance, I'm going to whisper something obscene into my new husband's ear, just so I can watch his reaction. They look into each other's eyes and rub their noses together as if they are the only two people in the room. I ignore the pang in my chest.

Pixie Chick sings the last line of the song and her voice rings out across the room and then fades to a breathy whisper. Rachel and George stop dancing and everyone claps. 'Thank you,' she says into her microphone. The band take a little bow and regroup. Fairy lights twinkle around the room.

'I'm getting another drink,' Lauren says. 'More champagne before the tab runs out?'

'Yes please,' I tell her. There's a pause before the band start playing again, and I look down at the carpet and stare at the pattern. And then they start, staccato plucking, and I know exactly what song it is, it's been following me around all summer. 'Call Me Maybe', for goodness' sake. I heave a sigh and try not to think about how often I heard it on the radio in California. The cajon comes in with upbeat, steady little thumps over and over, but I just feel deflated. I briefly consider slipping off to find Lauren but if we somehow miss each other she'll have both glasses of champagne, and I wouldn't put it past her to drink both, so I stay put. And then the singing starts and I'm momentarily confused by the familiarity of it all, and not because the singer is Carly Rae Jepsen, because obviously Carly Rae Jepsen is not moonlighting as the wedding singer at Rachel and George's wedding. But because I've heard that voice before, singing this song, in a silver Honda in California, and before then, too, on CDs I still have at home.

Mandy sidles up to me, and I'm pleased I have someone's arm to grip.

'Cassie, babes, I think the singer has the hots for you,' she says, excitedly. 'It's really funny, he just rocked up. Snuck in and shuffled down the side of the stage. Fancy being late to your own gig. Don't you think that's funny? You might be in there though because he's definitely looking at you. Probably wondering why you're looking so miserable. You could work that to your advantage, rebound take two.'

Oh my god, it can't be.

Now the girls are doing harmonies and they are pitch perfect, and underneath all the lovely singing I can hear my heartbeat in my ears because it's all clicking into place. Mandy carries on, completely oblivious.

'Not sure the song's entirely right though, I mean, for a wedding. I mean, surely if you're getting married, you've called them, *definitely*.'

'The song's perfect, Mandy,' I mumble, but she's not really listening.

'God, Cassie, will you *look*? You're definitely in there. One hundred percent. He's really trying to get your attention. I have to tell you, your flirting still needs a lot of work. Put the poor bastard out of his misery.'

But I can't look because in my heart I know exactly who it is, and I want it to be him so much, but after everything, I just can't believe it could be, and if I look up and it's just someone trying to pick up a sad girl at a wedding I don't think I'll be able to cope. So I shake my head instead, and look at my shoes. She grabs my wrist. 'Cassie, people are staring! And moving out of the way. It's like the parting of the red sea. Or was it the dead sea? I can't remember.'

Lauren comes back with glasses of champagne.

'What's going on?' she says, holding mine out for me. I can't take it. I can't move. I am rooted to the spot. Mandy gasps as the penny drops, and she grabs my glass of champagne from Lauren.

'Oh my *Christ*! I know who that is. You sent us a photo when you were in California,' she hisses.

'Shit the bed,' Lauren whispers. She clamps her hand over her mouth.

'Lauren, you look like you've been spooked, mate,' Mandy giggles. 'Don't tell my cousin, but this is my favourite bit of today.'

Suddenly I'm all hot and a bit sweaty behind the knees. The room is spinning and I can barely hear the music. It's drowned out by my pounding heartbeat. Does Rachel know about this? She must do. But how?

Finally, I work up the courage to tear my eyes from the floor. They dart around the room, at Rachel and George's guests watching this all unfold, and finally settle on Jesse, strumming away on a baby blue ukulele, as real and as present as anyone else in this room. And he's scrubbed up really, *really* well. Wedding Jesse is the *best*. Charcoal-grey trousers, a white shirt with the sleeves rolled up to his elbows, a skinny black tie, a fraction too loose. He's had his hair cut, and it's shorter now, but still nicely dishevelled. And Converse. Always Converse. He looks like he just rolled out of bed this morning, threw on a suit, and decided to come to a wedding, and I love it, more than I thought possible. I let him catch my eye, and now that I have, I can't look away.

'I take it back about the song. This is the most romantic thing ever,' Mandy squeaks. 'People are going to be talking about this for *years*.' She knocks back the champagne, leaving less than an inch in the bottom of the glass just as Pixie Chick taps his arm and nods towards me, and he takes his cue, jumping off the stage.

'Okay, you're up, Cass, go to him,' Lauren whispers, nudging me sharply with her elbow, propelling me forward, off the carpet and onto the dance floor, and as the band carry on with the song, Jesse and I stand in front of each other, still not breaking our nervous eye contact. I don't know what I think or what to say. My mind is blank and overloaded all at once. I just can't wrap my head around any of it.

Suddenly I'm really shy, and that feels new because I've never really felt shy around him before, not even at the beginning. *Not even* when I told him I was, the day I landed in California. He tucks the ukulele under his arm and takes hold of my hands and it's familiar and comforting.

'I thought you were a bass player?' I say, and nod towards the tiny instrument. 'Bit trebly for you, no?'

He rolls his eyes and his whole posture changes, relaxes. 'Right, but Dad started us all off on ukes. It was all part of his master plan for Billboard Chart domination.' He drops one of my hands and passes the ukulele to Lauren.

'Why didn't you reply to my email?'

'Some things are better said in person,' he says, and looks around the room. 'But probably not right here.'

I reach my arms around him and cling on tight, squeeze my eyes shut and bury my nose into the crook of his neck. He smells just the same as he did when we first met in London and I'm there again. In that bar. By the river. Up in his room. The song finishes. Around us people clap. Someone even wolf-whistles.

'I've missed you,' he says into my hair. 'And I'm sorry I fucked everything up.'

'I've missed you too,' I whisper. 'And I'm sorry I ran.'

'Let's get out of here, people are looking. Oh, and someone's filming.'

We leave with the half full bottle of wine that Mandy bought, and head out into the sprawling grounds. The light's faded and trees loom in stark black silhouette, barely lit by the thin strip of a crescent moon hanging in the sky. A fallen tree juts out on to the lawn and we make for it. My dress catches on a shard of bark as I perch against it, and a breeze whispers through the trees. Neither of us speak and aside from the music inside, it's silent. I swig the wine.

'So…' I say, when I can't stand it any longer.

'So,' Jesse repeats.

'That was unexpected,' I say, nodding towards the abbey. 'In there. With the ukulele. Did you pick the song?'

'No. Rachel forced me into it,' he says. 'She said it would mean something to you. She also said when I arrived that I had to perform with the ukulele group or I wasn't allowed to see you. Didn't want to argue. Everyone knows you don't cross a bride on her wedding day.'

'Wait, what? I don't understand.'

'So, I got in touch with her after your email. She told me to get my shit together.'

'Ha! Yeah, that sounds about right.'

'Yeah. Anyway, I stopped acting like an asshole, and I found this… hang on.'

The light from his phone illuminates his face. He's concentrating. He taps the screen, swipes through something and then hands it over. 'Take a look.'

I swap the wine for the phone and look down at the device in my hand. Instagram. A woman and a baby, and a screen name. NicoleInNY.

'Oh my god,' I gasp. 'This is her. Nicole.'

She's a babe: gorgeous wavy auburn hair, clear skin, bright eyes, dimples. Made up and styled nicely and holding her tiny little baby in her arms. Looking incredible for someone who probably still couldn't even feel her own vagina at that point. And sitting with her is her rather dashing boyfriend. He's tagged. Kevin Ito. its_kevin_ito. He looks well turned out and rich, and she looks like she's hit the jackpot and knows it. One thing's for sure, I'll be creeping on this couple later on.

'Uh huh,' he says, swigging from the bottle and looking down at his shoes. 'Read the caption.'

'*Introducing Aiden Ito-Meijer, born on October 4th (4 days sooner than scheduled). 6lbs8oz. Mom and baby are doing great #blessed #love #family.* So this means—'

'Exactly,' he nods, and the relief is almost palpable. It's radiating off him. 'And now read this.'

He takes the phone back and opens up his text messages. Hands it back.

> Nic. Please can you reply. I've met someone. I don't want to fuck that up. So I just really need to know.

Guess my Instagram photo gave you your answer. You don't have a baby, Mazel tov!

Congratulations Nicole. I hope it's all going well.

Thank you Jesse. It is, and I appreciate that you asked. I guess you might have questions about how fast it all happened with me and Kevin, but you have to know that I didn't know him before I left California.

It's fine. I'm happy for you. Genuinely.

So... did you fuck it up? Can I ask that?

I did. Spectacularly actually. But I'm going to try and fix it.

Well, good luck. Be happy.

–

'I know I should have said something,' he says. 'But I was just so wrapped up in every minute of being with you, and I didn't know how to. I guess I wanted to know for sure one way or the other, you know? And I really wasn't lying when I said she was hard to get hold of.'

'It's okay,' I say. 'Everything's going to be okay,' and we grin at each other like loons. Then he slides his arm across my shoulders and pulls me close and I shiver as his hand moves across my skin. And he kisses the top of my head the way he did all the time in California, and for the first time since I left him there, I feel light.

'Hey,' I say, into his chest. 'You never told me you were on Instagram.'

'I'm not really. I'll probably delete it later.'

'Or you could keep it,' I say.

'Yeah? Why?'

'Well, you liked her photo. So now she'll be checking up on you.'

'You think?'

'God, Jesse,' I say, rolling my eyes. 'Yes. There'll be a part of her that's a little bit curious to see if we did patch it up.'

He looks like he's weighing up this thought in his head.

'Perhaps,' he says.

'Or don't. Delete it. Tell me to fuck off if you like.'

'I don't think I'll ever tell you to fuck off, Cass,' he shrugs.

'Where are you staying tonight?'

He nods towards the abbey and suddenly it's clear that when Rachel told me over coffee she knew things would get easier, it's because she really did know.

'Oh, thank God. Is there room for a little one? I am meant to be staying with my parents, but they'll both be wrecked, and if Dad starts getting amorous with Mum in the taxi, I swear I'll throw myself out of it.'

Jesse laughs. 'We can't have that,' he says. 'Not after I've flown five thousand miles to get you back.' We finish what's left in the bottle and I link my hands together around him and lean my head against his shoulder.

'I'm so happy you're here,' I say. 'I've listened to a lot of sad music in the last few weeks. Mostly Coldplay.'

'God. You must have been pretty miserable.'

'You have no idea.'

'I think I probably do,' he says. 'Do you want to go back inside? I have some drunk parents to meet, no?' He takes my hand and we walk back towards the party. Inside, the band has finished their set and 'Here In Your Arms' by Hellogoodbye is playing, and it's all autotuney with a happy pop rhythm.

'Just a heads up,' I say, stopping. 'My parents know exactly who you are. And so do all my friends.' He stops and sighs and looks up at the sky.

'I'm gonna need more wine,' he says. I laugh. We kiss.

And up in space, the sliver of moon shines. The stars are aligned.

Epilogue

January 2014

(Fifteen months later)

The departure lounge at Heathrow is bustling and I can't really get comfy on my chair. Why don't they have better chairs? People wait around for ages in these places, the chairs should be comfier. I've done some shopping and I'm in possession of a giant Toblerone and new mascara that promises to make my lashes look like falsies. I reckon it will be a killer to get off. Outside is the plane I am about to board, and it's being loaded up with luggage by men in fluorescent yellow vests and thick gloves. If you really look you can see their breath in the freezing air as they toss each case on board. I think I saw mine get chucked on but I can't be sure.

It's the last time I'll be seeing this airport in a while. This time I'm not coming back. It took long enough, what with all the paperwork and the processes and the interview at the US embassy about how we met. But I have a beautiful sparkly ring on my finger, and a visa stuck in my passport. I'm off to live in California, under the condition that Jesse has ninety days to make an honest woman of me after we land. He tells me it's a lot warmer there than it is here. I'm wearing shearling-lined boots all the same.

A tap on my arm pulls my attention from the frigid tarmac.

'I got you a latte.'

'Ooh my hero,' I say, taking the cup. I pull off the lid and blow on the foamy top and it separates, revealing hot milky coffee underneath. Jesse sits down next to me and looks at his watch.

'Not long now,' he says. 'How are you feeling?'

'A little nervous. Mainly excited. It's going to be weird not having to leave this time.'

'Weird, but… excellent?'

–

Cabin crew walk past and they stop at the gate. Shiny red shoes and sensible skirts. Purple neck scarves and immaculate hair. Our flight is called. He takes my hand, the one with the ring on it, and squeezes it. We are off.

A Letter from Stephie

Recently, one of my best friends reminded me that when we were sixteen I swore that one day I'd get a book published. It took another eighteen years, but here I am. This has been the dreamiest of dreams come true, and I'm thrilled to be able to call Hera my book home.

And I wanted to say a big thank you to you, the reader, for choosing *Call Me, Maybe*. I hope you have enjoyed reading it as much as I enjoyed writing it. What started out as a fleeting daydream after I found my own 90's teen crush on Instagram quickly bedded down and grew roots and turned into one of the best things I've ever done.

It's been a blast creating Cassie and Jesse's story, from ambling around London, looking out for the tiny little details that would bring this story to life, to learning how to play the bass for book research, and sitting on the pier at Seal Beach, California, drinking iced tea and watching the way the sun sparkles off the Pacific. I've tried to recapture the intense magic of a teenage crush, and all the feelings, relatable, I think, to us all, that that brings.

I'd love to hear from you, so if you have any comments or just wanted to say hi, you can find me on my social media channels:

twitter.com/imcountingufoz
instagram.com/imcountingufoz
facebook.com/stephiechapmanauthor

And if you felt like leaving a review, that'd be wonderful too.

Thanks again for reading my book and being so wonderfully supportive – it really does mean the world!

Big love,

Stephie

Acknowledgments

First of all, to Keshini and Lindsey – Thank you millions for the support and encouragement. For believing in Cassie and Jesse, and for the dream come true. I'm so ecstatic to be able to call Hera my book home. Thanks to super editor Jennie – yes, nine times out of ten it was 'fragment for style'!

To all my family, but especially to my mum, thanks for letting me sound off story ideas on the way to work. You were usually right, proving yet again that Mother really does know best. Thanks to Ross for living and breathing this book with me for the last four years. For taking over when I needed the time to write, for providing me with wine and dinner and telling me when Jesse wasn't blokey enough. To Ruby and Elliot for not bickering *too* much and for understanding when Mummy had a deadline. I love you all.

To my writing babes, Becky Williams, Lia Louis, Laura Pearson and Lynsey James for being the best cheer squad a girl could wish for. Thanks for the support, the unwavering belief and all the Ben Barnes gifs (and insta messages!). Thanks to Aimee Horton, who probably doesn't know I did a weep when she said she knew this book was my heart, but who does now. It's true. I felt seen.

And to my soul sisters Katherine and Ve. Thank you for being such queens. Female friendship is precious and little fragments of ours have worked themselves into this book. Thanks to Rich for all the slap bass vids, near constant validation of all my life choices ('YOLO') and music recs, but especially for Call Me Maybe. Bet you didn't realise when you chucked that suggestion my way just how far I'd run with it, eh?! Thank you as well to my work fam-jam, for the often hilarious office chat and the walks-with-a-fag around campus and, quite honestly, for the bags of inspiration for a future book!

To Adam for bestowing upon me the bass. My dude, where to even start with this one? You've helped me more than I think you could ever imagine. Without you I'd still be listening to songs without trying to figure out what key they're in, and if that really *was* a pentatonic scale I thought I just heard. And I'd definitely assume that 'playing in the pocket' meant something smutty.

And finally, to four brothers from Canada, not Nebraska, who still to this day hold a little piece of my heart. Thanks for the music and the memories.